Until the World Falls Down

Jordan Lynde

Book cover design by: https://www.brosedesignz-bookcovers.com/

Illustration design by: @nikespera

Proofread by: Erica Ball https://bio.site/ericamartaball

First paperback edition October 16th, 2024.

ISBN: 979-8-9915861-0-8 (paperback)

AUTHOR'S NOTE

Please be aware this fantasy romance contains darker themes and includes sexually explicit scenes. All intimacy between the main couple is consensual and with enthusiasm, but the overall setting has elements of kidnapping, coercion, and kink. This story contains a power imbalance, profanity, violence, and explores themes such as love and loss, including mild mentions of the loss of loved ones.

P.S.

I did the calculations and this book is 22% smut. Do with that information what you will ;)

DEDICATION

To those who know the devastation of a broken heart.

To those who have fought to heal from one.

And to those who have always wanted to be swept away by a goblin king.

PROLOGUE

Unbidden, a melancholic whisper caressed Enver's mind—*love me,* it implored. The sound was a lovely yearning, a desperate plea as enticing as the promise of a new mouse for his labyrinth.

He closed his eyes, focusing until the faint sound grew into the morose wail of a wounded soul. They were close by. His eyes snapped back open, scanning the room, gaze sweeping from sweaty body to sweaty body, searching for the source of such sweet sorrow. He found himself drawn to an unusual place this time—one he did not have time to question. Not that he questioned much anymore.

It did not take long for him to find his prize, and something inside him burgeoned when his gaze finally fell upon the one calling out so desperately—something he did not recognize, settling into the core of his being. Something powerful and intimate.

The hollow ache that ceaselessly haunted him faded, replaced by a wholeness he could not quite understand. He paused, waiting for the moment to pass. When it did not, his hand drifted to his chest, brushing against the constricting fabric of his shirt as though attempting to touch what now dwelled inside him.

Her desperation was suffocating and overwhelming, pressing in on him. It was no wonder he had been led here.

Love. She yearned for. *Love.* She would do anything for.

That same love she was so desperate for would entice and entrap her.

His eyes narrowed, and his fingers tightened, digging into the fabric of his shirt before he forced himself to release it. He started toward her with a slow, predatory grace. The pulsating crowd parted for him, unconsciously giving way to his target, as though they were aware of the danger that stalked toward them.

She stood still amidst the swarm of people, her pitiful form trembling, her eyes closed, unaware of his approach. Unaware of what her desperation would bring her.

Long, white hair spilled in wavy curls down her back, and a tight black dress clung to her curves, accentuating the flare of her hips and the dip of her waist. Yet, what drew him to her the most were her lips—parted in a delicate, pleading way. Soft and enticing.

Desire stirred in his blood, and he clenched his jaw to stifle the unfamiliar hunger that surged through him.

He came to a stop in front of her and simply watched for a moment. Watched her chest heave in an uneven rhythm. Watched her tears stain her flushed cheeks. Watched her tongue dart out to moisten her lips, still oblivious to his presence.

His restraint slipped, and he lifted his hand, his fingers brushing along the nape of her neck. He cupped his hand around it, causing her eyes to snap open. There was a momentary look of surprise and a flicker of fear in her gaze, but as he turned his smile into something warm and inviting, she relaxed again. He put pressure on her neck, urging her closer to him, and her breathing hitched as she stepped forward. Her chest pressed against his, and he gazed down at her, relishing in the heartbreak in her eyes. The way they seemed to echo her desperate plea.

Love me.

Her beautiful, heartbreaking face revealed it all.

He could not have found someone better. This would be too simple. She was so desperate. So, *so* desperate.

Once he set the trap, he would have her.

His hand moved up to tangle in the soft hair at the base of her neck, his fingers curling into the silky strands, tugging them down, so that her chin lifted toward him. He could hear her heart beating faster in her chest, feel how her body yearned for his touch, see the tears gathering in her dark lashes...

He leaned in, his lips ghosting across hers, and he felt her take a shuddering breath before her eyes fluttered shut again. Waiting. Anticipating.

Yes.

She would be his.

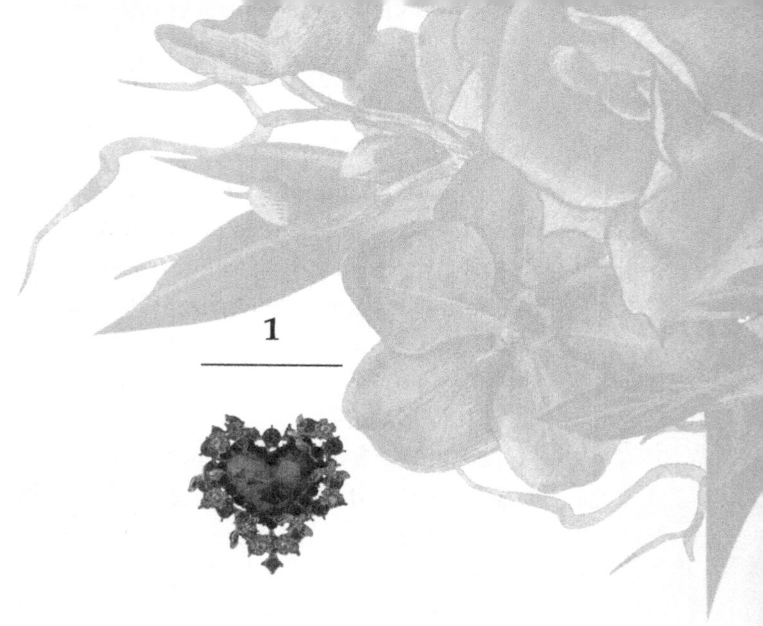

1

Nestled in my trembling arms, a pile of books spanned from my hands to my chin, precariously balanced against my torso as I maneuvered my way up to the library's checkout desk. With every unsteady step, my heels clicked on the old wooden floor, and a few people threw curious glances at me as I struggled. I figured it wasn't the number of books I carried that drew their attention, but rather the tight, short black dress and three-inch heels I wore—not the usual attire for a visit to the public library.

Liana, the middle-aged librarian with greying hair and kind eyes, raised an eyebrow as I approached. I nearly collapsed against the counter, causing some of my books to slip off the top of the pile and fall to the floor.

"I see you're at it again, Nell," she commented.

I bent down to pick up the fallen books, blushing faintly. "Sorry. I even came with a list this time and still found more. I think I went a little overboard."

"A little?"

"I'm on vacation from work this week," I explained with a sigh. "Finally. I plan to spend the entire time reading."

"Not going anywhere?"

I shook my head. "Being away from that place is enough of a vacation for me. They fired a lead designer and then made me take over their work. If they didn't pay so well, I'd be gone. I've been pulling near twelve-hour days, and I'm over it."

"And now you're going to read for ten hours straight instead," she said jokingly.

"I am," I replied seriously.

"What type of book has you in a chokehold this time?"

"Marriage of convenience," I admitted sheepishly. "Maybe an arranged marriage thrown in there, too."

She checked out my books, glancing at my outfit of choice. "Dressed for the occasion?"

A bubble of excitement rose in my chest, and I leaned closer to her, lowering my voice. "Actually, I'm getting engaged after this."

Her eyes widened, and she nearly dropped the book in her hand. "You are?"

"Yes!" I said, unable to contain my excitement, and the smile on my face grew to a size that made my cheeks ache. Saying it out loud to someone sent a thrill through me. "I can't even believe it! I had no idea Julian was even thinking of proposing!"

Her eyes crinkled as she smiled warmly at me. "Congratulations, Nell. Be sure to show me the ring when you come back to return these. How long will it take you to read them all? Two days?"

I laughed. "Let's say three. I might be busy celebrating with Julian."

"Now I understand why you picked out these books this time. How romantic."

"It's even better than in the plot in these books, though, because he chose me," I said, warmth spreading throughout me. "Not because it would benefit his company or because his parents forced him to."

He chose me.

The thought alone was enough to make my head spin. No one ever chose me.

But Julian had—and he'd chosen me forever. Instead of reading about happily ever after, I would have one. I would no longer be left behind or tossed to the side. Someone wanted, loved, and chose me.

I rocked on the balls of my feet, resisting the urge to hum, and scanned the area behind Liana, seeing her ever-growing collection of owl figurines.

"Oh, right," I said, digging around in my purse for a moment before retrieving a small ceramic owl reading a book. I held it out to her. "I saw this at the store the other day and thought you'd like it."

"You didn't have to do that, Nell," she said, taking the owl from me and smiling down at it. "It's absolutely adorable. Thank you."

"No problem," I answered, thrilled by her response and pleased by the satisfaction that settled over me. It felt good to see her happy. "Thanks for always dealing with me."

"It's my job," she told me.

My smile faltered. Right. She only talked to me because I was a patron of the library. She didn't really have any other choice *but* to deal with me. I was just—

"But it's always a pleasure," she continued, winking.

I managed a breathy laugh, trying to let the tension go, but it clung to me. "Right."

She finished checking out my books and pushed them closer to me. "Alright, you're all set. Congratulations again, Nell. I hope you have a great engagement! Let me know how it goes."

And that was all I needed to hear to send me soaring again.

I stacked the books in my arms again, refusing her offer to help me bring them out. Somehow, they didn't feel as heavy anymore. My body was weightless as I returned to my car, spilling the books into my back seat, the sight of engagement rings on the cover sending a shiver of excitement through me.

I held out my jewelry-free hand and imagined the ring I'd found in Julian's sock drawer adorning my finger. Imagined the diamond resting there that I would look at every day, reminding myself that Julian loved me—that someone loved me enough to spend their entire life with me.

I grinned to myself, turning on my car. I still couldn't believe it. It didn't feel real. But here I was, driving to the five-star restaurant Julian asked me to meet him at. I was going to say yes to a proposal. To my happily ever after.

My phone lit up with a text message as I went to type in the restaurant's address, showing a text message from my mom: *Eleanora, send me $300. I need to get my hair done.*

My smile almost faded. *Money? Again?*

I hesitated. I'd just sent her a few hundred the other week. Where was it all going? I wanted to ask, but I also didn't want to threaten the fragile relationship we were rebuilding. It was only recently that we'd started talking again after years of silence. If I questioned her now, what if she shut me out again? I didn't want to risk that.

I opened the money transfer app and sent her what she wanted before pulling up the directions to the restaurant, trying to keep her from my mind. I wouldn't let this ruin my good mood. Nothing could.

As I drove, my heart raced a mile a minute, thoughts of my mom completely forgotten and replaced by what kind of wedding dress I wanted to wear. Something with long sleeves? Lace? A ball gown type? My hands shook as I parallel parked on the street. The shops were always too crowded at this time of day to find a spot in the free parking lot. I dug around for change, trying to calm my nerves, but they only grew worse as I stepped out of my car, the cool October air nipping at my exposed skin. I'd forgotten to bring a jacket, too preoccupied with thoughts of Julian and our future together.

I slipped a few quarters into the parking meter, catching my reflection on the rusted metal. My roots were coming in. I regretted not getting them touched up first, having opted to save money instead. I wanted this to be perfect. I wanted to *look* perfect.

My hands smoothed over my hair, careful not to mess up the curls I'd added to my natural waves, and then glided over my dress, adjusting it lower on my thighs.

Then, I took a deep breath and headed for the restaurant.

Julian caught my gaze immediately as I turned the corner, my heart leaping into my throat at the sight of his blond hair. He wore a button-down shirt and jeans, attire that seemed too casual for such a fancy restaurant, but he still looked as handsome as ever. I opened my mouth to call out to him when someone else caught my attention.

My sister.

I halted, staring at the pair of them. They stood close to each other, talking quietly.

Suddenly, my nerves were for a different reason. Why was Veronica here? Had Julian asked her to be a part of our proposal? Why? Had he assumed I wanted her to be here?

I didn't dwell on it, forcing my feet forward. Veronica and Julian had always gotten along, even if Veronica and I hadn't. Their conversation dropped when they saw me approaching. Veronica gave me a strange look, one that caused a wave of insecurity to wash over me.

"What are you wearing?" she asked.

"What do you mean?" I replied, hating how small my voice sounded.

"Don't you think that dress is a little bold for a coffee shop?"

"Coffee shop?" I asked, looking at Julian. "I thought we were getting dinner."

Julian nodded toward the cafe we were standing in front of, his expression unreadable. "No, we're getting coffee. I have something to tell you."

They walked inside before I could respond, and I followed, my stomach churning. The coffee shop didn't seem as romantic as the restaurant, but then again, Julian was never one to care about things like that. He was the practical type, which could explain why he wanted Veronica here. It was a celebratory moment. She was probably the only person he could think of with whom I would want to share it.

But I would have rather had Liana here over Veronica.

We ordered drinks, and they went to sit down while I paid. As each second passed, I grew more and more confused and uneasy. The earlier excitement I felt was replaced with an odd, sick feeling.

I carefully carried our drinks over to the table, and I hesitated, noticing that Veronica had chosen the seat right next to Julian, leaving me to sit across from them. Veronica reached for her macchiato and a flash caught my eye. Something glittered on her finger and she yanked her hand back.

"Is that a ring?" I asked, her fingers now hidden behind her drink.

"Sit down, Eleanora," Julian said.

The use of my full name made me freeze, but when my eyes met his, I obeyed, sitting in the wooden chair. "What's going on?"

Veronica and Julian shared a look and then she placed her left hand on the table for me to see. "We're engaged."

"We?" I studied the ring on her finger. It looked exactly like the engagement ring I'd found weeks ago. The one I was sure was meant for me. "Who are you engaged to, Veronica? I didn't know you were even dating anyone."

"Me," Julian said, placing his hand on top of Veronica's. "We got engaged last night."

His words knocked the breath out of me, my heart stuttering. "What…?"

"Come on, Nell, let's not make a big deal out of this," Julian muttered.

"You and Veronica?" I said, my mind grasping for any explanation that didn't lead to my boyfriend admitting he was cheating on me with my sister. There was no way. They wouldn't do that to me. This had to be some kind of prank. "You're not proposing to me?"

Julian scoffed. Actually scoffed. "Why would you think that?"

I swallowed, the sound so loud it startled me. My entire body was stiff, aside from my shaking hands that were cupped around the iced latte I'd ordered. Across from my latte was Veronica's caramel macchiato, and next to it was Julian's black coffee. Their entwined hands rested between the drinks that I'd paid for. I didn't know why my mind caught on that fact—that I'd paid for their drinks. They knew they were coming here to do this, and they'd still let me pay for their orders.

They're engaged.

He's breaking up with me.

The world seemed to fall from under my feet, leaving me dangling in the air, and I struggled to hold on to anything that would keep me from plummeting. My hands tightened around my latte, trying to anchor myself, my knuckles shining bone-white through my pale skin. What had I done wrong? Why was this happening?

"You should have seen this coming," Veronica said, her voice loud and sharp. Defensive. The accusation in her voice threw me—like it was my fault for being blindsided by this. She flipped her chestnut hair over her shoulder. "You can't ever make a relationship last, Nell."

I hadn't even said anything for her to justify herself over yet. My eyes finally lifted from my hands to her face, so similar to my own, but I could barely recognize the resemblance now. Her blue, almond-shaped eyes narrowed as if daring me to speak back to her. Her lips formed a flat line, and the burgundy color of her lipstick served as a brutal reminder that I had gifted it to her for Christmas last year after Julian had said it would suit her.

Had it started all the way back then? December of last year? That couldn't be. That would mean it'd almost been a year. How would I have not noticed?

I couldn't even bring myself to look at Julian. My gaze went back to my latte, focusing on the way condensation slid down the side of the plastic cup in tiny droplets.

A to-go cup. Because they thought this would be a brief conversation.

"Don't you have anything to say?" Veronica asked after another moment of silence.

"No," I managed to get out, trying not to hunch in on myself, trying not to fold into nothingness.

"I told you she wouldn't care," Julian said, and I tensed again, the warm voice that once set my blood alight now sending ice through my veins. "Why doesn't *anything* affect you? Am I nothing to you, Nell?"

My chest tightened, but I refused to look at him. "You're seriously asking me that right now?"

"This wouldn't have happened if you were capable of showing even an ounce of love toward anyone or anything," he said, his words as accusing as my sister's. "You can only go through the motions. Did those stupid romance books you always read really never teach you anything?"

His question stung, and I found I didn't have a response. "They're not stupid—"

"You never learned from your past failed relationships how to be a better partner, did you? But Veronica was there for me through all your selfishness."

"Selfishness?" I repeated, my grip tightening on my cup further, the plastic starting to cave in. "You've lived off me for the past two years. I did everything for you. I forgave *so* much—"

"I knew you'd throw that in my face one day," Julian snapped, and I finally looked up to find him glaring at me.

"I'm not throwing it in your face, I—"

"You let me do whatever I want," he said. "You willingly forgave me every time. If you hated providing for me so much, why didn't you say so? Why didn't you tell me to leave? You were the one who always said you'd rather me stay home with you than go to work."

My mouth opened, but my words died in my throat as I caught sight of the ring again. Julian didn't have a job. He had my credit card.

He'd bought that ring with my money.

My boyfriend bought an engagement ring for my sister with *my* money. And I'd thought it was for me. I'd thought he'd asked me out today to propose to *me*. I'd worn the dress he always begged me to wear—too short, too tight, too black, but his favorite—only to be made a fool of.

My cup finally collapsed as I squeezed it even tighter in a jerk reaction. The liquid sloshed out as the top popped off, splashing over all our hands, coating that stupid ring, and spilling across the table. I stood then, ignoring Veronica as she cried out and jumped up from the table, my latte gushing over the edge and dripping onto her white dress.

I froze as I finally recognized that dress. It was mine. One she'd complimented me on before. One that I hadn't been able to find in months.

Anger surged within me. "How could you—" I started, but cut myself off, the anger fading as quickly as it overcame me. Why had I expected anything else? Why had I let myself believe Julian truly loved me? What was so wrong with me that he felt the need to do this? Was it really all my fault?

"Don't be overdramatic, Nell," Veronica snapped. "It's just a breakup. Aren't you used to them by now?"

Did anyone get used to having their heart broken over and over again? Did anyone ever get used to not mattering enough for anyone to stay? To being the last priority? The one always left behind?

I turned to Julian, hating the question I needed to ask. The one I already knew the answer to. "Did you ever even love me? At all?"

"No," he responded, not even hesitating a second. "I never loved you. I tried Nell, but I couldn't. You can't blame me for this. But you also don't really care, do you? It won't be hard to replace me. You'll just throw yourself at the next person who offers you the smallest amount of affection. That's how it went with me, wasn't it? Because it was never *me* you actually wanted. Anyone would have done. At least Veronica chose me for me."

And he chose her.

I stared at him for a moment, feeling like I was looking at a stranger. "Why didn't you just tell me when it first started?"

"We couldn't do that," Veronica said, sounding exasperated.

"Why not?"

"You had that big design project due," she told me. "The one you did for the healthcare company."

"The healthcare company? But that was..." I couldn't finish my sentence. That was *over* a year ago.

She jutted out her chin. "We didn't want to mess it up. Then too much time passed, and there was never a good time to tell you."

My mind couldn't comprehend it. Julian had been cheating on me for over a year, and this was their excuse for it? I hated my job. Veronica *knew* I hated my job. I would have rather been fired than cheated on.

I opened my mouth to ask *why*, but my voice caught as the answer hit me. I paid Julian's bills. And if my project had gone south, so would have my income. They didn't tell me because they didn't want to lose my money.

"Mom agreed," Veronica added, and I thought I might choke.

Mom? Our mom knew about this, too? Knew that Julian was cheating on me with Veronica? Was *okay* with it?

I tried to remember when she'd first reached out to me saying she wanted me back in her life again. It was nearly a year and a half ago. When I'd bought Veronica a stupidly expensive purse after finishing that healthcare company project. Had they all been in on it even then?

I didn't want to know the answer.

"Is that all?" I eventually got out, my voice hollow.

A muscle in Julian's jaw feathered. "You're not even going to attempt to fight for me?"

"Even I'm not that pathetic," I said, and although I intended the words for him, it sounded like I was trying to convince myself.

"Even if I promised I would go back to you?" he asked.

My traitorous heart leaped at the thought.

Julian huffed out a breath. "Not that pathetic, huh?"

Shame flooded me. "I don't understand. I love you—"

"No, you don't," he said, cutting me off, sounding so sure, so cold. So final.

"I do," I whispered, my eyes beginning to burn, and although I didn't want to say them, the next words slipped out of me. "I did everything for you. How could you do this to me?"

"It was never love between us, Nell. Why can't you understand that?" he snapped, and his words sliced right through my heart. "You're desperate for something you don't even understand. You can blame me for this, but it isn't the first time it's happened to you. Ask yourself why this keeps happening—*why* you can't find someone to love you. You'll find you're the common denominator."

I fell back a step, my gaze falling to Veronica. Her brows knitted together, her lips pinched. "I told you," she started quietly. "I told you when Dad left us. I told you when Mom cut ties with you. When Emmy left you. It's *you*, Nell. You're the reason you can't be loved."

"No, I—" the words choked out of me, and I couldn't finish them because, deep down, a cruel part of me whispered that what she said was true. That I wasn't good enough. Not for Julian. Not for my mom or dad. Not my ex. Not for anyone. I should have fought against their accusations. I should have demanded they tell me why they would do this to me. Why my sister would betray me this way. But I didn't.

I could only do what I was best at.

I ran.

A tear escaped down my cheek as I twisted on my heel, hurrying out of the cafe. My body was on autopilot as I returned to my car, started it, and began the drive back to my house. I clung to the steering wheel, trying to concentrate on the road, trying not to let my thoughts wander. A lump appeared in the back of my throat, but I swallowed it back.

I wouldn't cry. I knew this would happen one day. It always did. This was nothing new. I had nothing to be upset about. I'd already accepted it.

I entered my house, immediately struck by the scent of Julian's cologne. It clung to me as I kicked off my heels. I used to love the woody scent, but now it made me sick. I wanted it off me. I didn't feel like I was in control of my body as I stripped off my too-tight dress and threw it onto my bed before going into the bathroom and stepping under burning hot water. It scalded me, but I stood there, letting the steam suffocate me.

I couldn't be upset. I couldn't.

Sinking down to the shower floor, I brought my knees to my chest, wrapped my arms around them, and let the water pelt down on me.

I stayed in that position until the water turned cold and my skin wrinkled. Shivering, I finally climbed out, swathing myself in a towel and exiting the bathroom. The house was silent around me. Julian hadn't come back. He probably wouldn't. I approached my bed—*our* bed—

wanting nothing more than to crawl in and sleep, but I froze at the sight of the messy sheets. They were exactly how we'd left them after we woke up together this morning.

A sob lodged itself in my throat. I forced it back. *No.*

I couldn't sleep in our bed. It would smell like him. Like us. Everywhere in my house did. I couldn't do this. I couldn't stay here.

I threw on the first pair of underwear and bra I found in my drawer, then slid back into the black dress, not wanting to stick around and find something new to wear. I grabbed my keys and headed back out. My car was chilly as I climbed back into it, making me wonder exactly how long I'd zoned out in the shower.

Out of habit, I checked my right, ensuring that my second car—the one Julian usually drove—wasn't parked too close to mine. The empty spot stung, but the sight of my books scattered across my backseat hit me like a physical blow to the chest as my gaze swept over them. The diamond rings on the covers were a brutal reminder that this was real while the stories I read were fake. That the promise of happily ever after was now out of my grasp. The tears I'd held back spilled then, my throat tightening, and I gripped my steering wheel, sucking in sharp breaths. A cold settled over me, deep in my bones, and it made me shake, rattling me to my core.

Why? The question kept repeating in my head. *Why me? Why always me? What do I do so wrong?*

Why did everyone always leave me? Why did I always have to be alone? Why couldn't anyone love me?

"I just want to be loved," I sobbed, curling in on myself. "Why? Why...?"

The fact that Julian cheated on me with Veronica hurt less than him revealing he'd never loved me. I shivered, biting my lip hard, whimpering as I tried to hold back my sobs. I'd fooled myself into thinking someone wanted me for the past two years.

No. I'd fooled myself into thinking I could *ever* find someone who wanted me.

No one did.

No one ever would, no matter what I offered them.

I turned the car on, tears still streaming down my face. There had to be someone out there that wanted me. Even just a small part. There *had* to be. I backed out of my garage, heading downtown. If Julian didn't want me, I would find someone who did. I didn't care who.

I parked at the busiest club I found, shucking off my jacket and heading to the doors. The bouncer checked my I.D. briefly before allowing me inside. When I stepped inside, the scent of sweat and alcohol blasted across my face, and a moist warmth enveloped me, fending off the cold from outside. The bass from the music rattled my ribcage as I walked toward the bar.

Julian always said he didn't like women who drank, so I hadn't touched alcohol during the two years we'd been together. A lump formed in my throat again, and I forced it down as I waved the bartender over. "Can I have..." I trailed off, realizing I didn't even know what to order. "Um, your strongest drink?"

She gave me a pitying look before nodding, procuring a clean glass, and filling it up with alcohol before sliding it over to me. I took it gratefully, paying for it with a twenty and telling her to keep the rest. The scent of the alcohol met my nose as I raised the glass to my lips, making my eyes water, but I pressed ahead, swallowing down a large gulp—only to choke on it as it slid down my throat. I coughed loudly, my eyes watering even more than before. This earned another look from the bartender, and I turned away, the heat in my cheeks having nothing to do with the alcohol.

My eyes scanned the dark club, zeroing in on the multiple couples making out on the dance floor. The sight had my chest tightening, and I second-guessed my decision to come here. But maybe these people were here for the same reason I was—to find someone who wanted them, even if only for a night.

I steeled myself, marching myself onto the dance floor, joining the others. My limbs were tense and unfamiliar with the rhythm of the music pounding through the speakers. I attempted to replicate the movements of everyone around me, but only managed to crash into someone, causing my drink to spill all over the floor.

My cheeks flaming, I moved further into the crowd, being jostled along as I did so. Self-consciousness crept in as the other club goers danced effortlessly around me while I stood still. Some gyrated on their partners, sharing kisses under the dim lights, hands exploring each other. For a moment, an image of Julian and I flashed through my mind, his breath on my skin, the way he always seemed to hesitate before he kissed me. I hadn't thought much about it before, but now...

I turned away, my chest constricting, but it was too late. More and more memories flooded my mind. How I'd forgiven him for cheating on me not once, but twice before. How my girlfriend before him had told me how she hated how pathetic and desperate I became when she was upset with me. How my first boyfriend would try his best to hurt me, to try to get me to become angry with him because he hated how I never reacted to anything.

I placed my drink down on a nearby table, balling my shaking hands into fists. Was *I* the problem, after all? Because I just wanted a partner who cared for me? Because I would put up with anything just to believe someone actually loved me? Was I so desperate in their eyes? Was that why everyone left me in the end? Why, no matter how much I gave in a relationship, no matter how hard I *tried*, no one loved me in the end?

My eyes burned as tears crested again, making the club and dancers blur into a watery and distorted haze.

"Why?"

I couldn't take it anymore.

"I'll do anything," I pleaded into the dark, my words lost in the music, my eyes closing as a tear rolled down my cheek. "I'll give anything."

I just wanted to be loved.

"*Please...*"

A cool touch on my throat had my muscles tensing. Long fingers curled around my neck, and a rough palm grazed my skin, sending a shiver down my spine. I opened my eyes again, my breath snagging in my throat as I caught sight of the stranger towering over me. Although the darkness of the club cast shadows over him, it did little to blanket the sharp angles of his jawline and the way his broad shoulders tapered down to a slender waist. Inky black hair curled around his ears, starkly contrasting his pale skin. A few errant strands fell into his eyes as he leaned down, his dark gaze pinning me in place as much as his grip on my neck.

There was something strange about the way he looked at me. Piercing, as if he saw right through me. Knowing, as if he understood my pain and yearning. And predatory, as if I were prey for him to exploit.

A trickle of fear spread through my veins, but then his lips curved up, revealing a languid, enticing half-smile. Pressure on my neck urged me closer to him, and I inhaled his scent—amber, vanilla, something heady and warm. Our gazes never lost connection, even as his chest pressed against mine, our proximity sending my pulse racing. His hand slid from my neck into my hair, fingers tangling in the strands, pulling gently, forcing my chin to tilt up toward him as he moved his face closer, his warm breath fanning across my lips.

My lips parted, but no sound came out, my mind clouded by his intoxicating presence.

"Have I left you speechless? How sweet," he murmured, his voice low and sultry.

He closed the distance between us with a soft kiss to the highest point of my cheekbone, making me jolt at the intimacy of the action. He repeated the action on the other side, and when he pulled away, he moved his hand to cradle my cheek, wiping away my drying tears with his thumb.

Blood rushed to my cheeks, and warmth bloomed throughout my body, pooling in my stomach.

His head tilted, a glint of amusement dancing in his charcoal-colored eyes. "Are you not just perfect?" he asked, his thumb swiping over my lips now, applying enough pressure to part them, sending another thrill through me. "What is your name?"

"Eleanora," I responded, my tongue brushing against the tip of his thumb, which still rested between my lips.

His gaze darkened before he pulled his thumb away and released my neck, taking a step back. I immediately felt cold at the loss of contact and took an unwitting step forward, my hand reaching for his waist, trying to get close again.

A smirk graced his features as his hand caught my wrist. "Patience, Eleanora," he said, my name on his lips making my heart skip a beat. "We have all night. And you have certainly caught my attention."

My eyes roamed over his body. He wore a black button-up shirt tucked into black slacks. The first two buttons of his shirt were left undone, hinting at the expanse of skin underneath, and his sleeves were rolled up to his elbows, showcasing his lean muscle and prominent veins. A silver belt buckle gleamed under a passing strobe light, drawing my attention to it for a moment too long.

"And I have apparently caught yours," he whispered into my ear teasingly.

My head snapped back up, flushing again, our faces so close together I would barely have to move to kiss him. "Sorry—" I began, but my words died as his lips ghosted across mine.

"No need to apologize for anything," he told me, his hands going to my waist. "You are exactly what I have been looking for."

I caught his gaze again, sensing a deeper meaning to his words but not understanding it. I didn't care to understand it, either, when he released my wrist and pulled my hips flush against his. A soft gasp escaped my lips as his belt buckle pressed into my stomach, sending a wave of desire through me.

"And am I? What you have been looking for?" he asked in a low voice, his hand rising to my jaw again, grasping it gently.

My mouth went dry, and I had to swallow before I could answer. "I..." I didn't know. I could barely think straight. His presence seemed to muddle my thoughts. It overwhelmed me with attraction but also raised the hair on the back of my neck, making my muscles tense as if I needed to be ready to escape at any moment.

And then self-reproach hit me. How could I be doing this when Julian was—

When Julian was out there fucking my sister.

"Fuck it," I said, my hands curling into the front of the stranger's shirt, drawing him closer as I stood on my tiptoes to crash my lips against his.

His breath came out in a sharp exhale, and his fingers dug further into my skin, making my lips part in another gasp. He wasted no time in slipping his tongue into my mouth, the hand on my face now moving back into my hair to angle my head in a way he preferred as he deepened the kiss. His other hand moved from my hip to my lower back, guiding me impossibly close to him as his tongue tangled with mine, causing another ripple of desire to course through my body.

I forced myself to release the grip I had on his shirt, flattening my palms against his chest. His muscles rippled under my touch, and my hands moved lower, feeling the firm expanse of his abdomen as his hand on my back slid lower to rest lightly on my ass. I made a noise of contentment as his lips moved from my mouth to my chin, then down to my neck, kissing and nipping at my skin along the way. I tilted my head to the side to give him better access, and he placed hot, open-mouthed kisses on me that made my skin erupt into goosebumps.

"You are precious," he breathed into my neck, punctuating his words with another kiss. "So beautiful."

"I'm not," I said, my voice shaky as my hands moved from his hair to his shoulders, clinging to him as my knees grew weak. "Otherwise, my boyfriend wouldn't have cheated on me."

"You are," he murmured. "Your face." He kissed my cheek. "Your body." His hand trailed along the line of my spine, leaving behind a wake of fire. "Every inch of you."

I hid my face in the crook of his neck, unable to face him, the praise making my heart beat faster and faster. No one had ever said things like that to me.

"So perfect for me," he said, leaning in to kiss my neck again, this time softer, more sensually.

My eyes closed, and my nails dug into his shoulder as I let myself be swept away in the moment. The bass of the music reverberated through my chest, matching the tempo of my heartbeat. I moved in closer, pressing our bodies flush together again. I froze as something hard pressed against my thigh. The stranger noticed my hesitance and moved away, planting a small kiss on the corner of my lips.

"I apologize," he said, his voice low and raspy. "I cannot control that. You are quite tempting."

For a second, I couldn't comprehend his words. Julian could barely ever get it up and blamed it on me. It always took a blow job to get him decently hard enough. But this man was saying just a kiss was enough?

He stepped back again, and I realized he misunderstood my silence. I gathered my courage, dragged him to me once more, and purposefully ground myself against his erection. A low moan sounded in his throat, and our mouths melded together again.

"Were you looking for something more tonight?" he asked, his breath hot against my lips. "I was not, myself, but now..." His touch grew more demanding, more commanding as his hands skimmed down my sides, gripping my hips again, securing me against him. "Now I am."

Arousal shot straight to my core, his every word filled with allure, but I went still again, my mind spinning with conflicting thoughts. Could I do this? Sleep with a stranger? The same day I broke up with my boyfriend?

Were we even broken up?

Would I willingly take Julian back if he apologized and said it was all a mistake? If he had a change of heart? If I could be a better girlfriend, if I could convince him to stay—

I never loved you.

My lungs constricted as Julian's voice echoed through my head.

You're the common denominator.

"Can we get out of here?" I breathed.

The stranger's lips curved up into a smile. "I would *love* nothing more."

2

The emphasis on *love* set off that unnerving feeling in me again, but before I could say anything, the stranger took my hand in his. I attempted to reach for my forgotten drink, abruptly deciding I wanted the liquid courage, but he stopped me, shaking his head.

"How much have you had tonight?" he asked, pulling me away from my drink.

"Barely anything," I responded.

"Good. I want you sober for this. And I believe you will, too."

His words caused a new blush to spread across my cheeks as he led me away from the dance floor and toward the exit. I couldn't believe I was doing this. I wasn't the type to go home with a stranger. To have a one-night stand with someone I had just met. Even with Julian, I hadn't slept with him until after we'd been dating for a few weeks.

The thought made me pause, my feet coming to a halt. The stranger stopped, his gaze shifting back to me, releasing my hand. "Are you having second thoughts?"

"No! I just, um," I started, grabbing his hand again, anxiety seeming to creep up my throat as I struggled through my words. "I want to be safe. I get tested when I get my yearly checkups, and I'm on birth control. Are you...?"

For a moment he tilted his head to the side, as if confused, then realization dawned. "Yes," he responded. "There is nothing to worry about there. You have my word."

"Okay," I said, deciding to believe him, if he believed me. "Let's go."

Fresh, cold air filled my lungs as I took a few deep breaths —trying to both calm myself and cycle out the stale air from the club. The stranger led me toward an alleyway beside the club, his steps quick and purposeful. My ears rang as they tried to adjust to the quiet night, and I tried to calm my racing heart.

As we stepped into the alleyway, the stranger pressed me up against the frigid brick, his lips finding mine, kissing me hungrily. I shivered as the cold seeped through the fabric of my dress, but his hands helped stave off the chill as he caressed my back.

He shifted, and I tumbled backward, the hard brick behind me disappearing.

The stranger held me tight as I lost my balance, pulling me to his chest as I tried to find my footing. The only light came from the moon outside, and it did little to illuminate where we stood. I tried looking around, only finding inky blackness. I could barely make out the stranger's face as he urged me further into the darkness. The opening we came through—a door?—closed behind him, leaving us in pitch blackness. He dragged me further into the dark, seemingly unbothered by the lack of visibility.

I suddenly became nauseous. It felt like the dark room was bearing down on me, making it difficult to breathe and causing my limbs to feel heavy. Anxiety clawed up my throat as the sensation grew, but when I blinked, it all went away, leaving me with only a lingering feeling of alarm.

My heart pounded, and I reached for the stranger's arm, trying to ground myself, wanting him to stop moving for one moment. Before I could open my mouth, though, a silver glow filtered through a crack that then widened into a doorway in front of us. We stepped through, and my gaze went straight up and up, the soaring ceiling above us filling me with awe. A skylight revealed the source of the soft light cascading down onto us, broken up by a glass chandelier hanging below it.

My eyes followed a beam of moonlight down to the sight of a luxurious four-poster bed sitting in the center of the room. It was draped in cascading see-through curtains that took on an otherworldly sheen. I tried to look around, noting other various pieces of furniture scattered around, but the blanket of darkness kept me from seeing anything in too much detail. Two plush armchairs stood near a floor-to-ceiling window, the shades of it drawn, hiding the view outside. A wardrobe towered next to them, and on the opposite side, a bookcase took up the entire wall, each shelf filled with books, the night obscuring all their titles.

I furrowed my eyebrows, disconcerted. Had there always been a house like this next to the club? I'd thought there were only businesses nearby. I didn't remember seeing a door in the alleyway before, either.

"You are not afraid of the dark, are you?" the stranger asked, turning to face me.

My pulse quickened as our bodies brushed against each other, pulling my attention away from the decor and my thoughts. "No."

His hands ran down my sides, gaze meeting mine in the low light. "And do you still want this?"

His question made my confusion dissolve, replaced by a nervous want. I'd been worried my feelings would change after leaving the club, but no. They hadn't.

I still wanted him.

This.

"Yes," I said.

"My favorite word," he breathed before leaning in, capturing my lips in a kiss.

It differed from our earlier ones. This was a slow, passionate caress. The lust from earlier returned in full force as he backed me up toward the bed in the center of the room. His hands moved to my back, finding the zipper of my dress and toying with it as if waiting for permission. I broke apart from him to nod, and he grabbed my waist, forcibly turning me around so my back was to him.

Goosebumps broke out across my skin as he swept my hair away from my neck so he could unzip me. I had to resist trying to catch my dress as it fell to the floor, leaving me only in the black lace bra and underwear I'd thrown on before leaving my house. He hummed in approval, kissing the back of my neck, then the space between my shoulders.

He turned me back toward him before pushing on my collarbone with his palms, forcing me into a sitting position on the edge of the bed. My breathing hitched as he knelt down in front of me, taking my foot in his hand and sliding off my heel. He massaged my bare foot for a moment, surprising me. His thumb dug into my arch with the perfect pressure before moving up to the pad of my foot, making me sigh. I couldn't remember the last time someone had rubbed my feet. I'd forgotten how intimate it could be. He repeated the same actions to my other foot before standing again, gazing down at me with a look I could only describe as hunger.

"You are beautiful," he said, beginning to unbutton his own shirt.

I watched with rapt attention as his shirt fell open, revealing the muscles underneath. A gasp caught in my throat as my gaze trailed across his bare skin, catching sight of a brutal scar marring his otherwise flawless skin. It covered the entirety of his left pectoral, and the pale, jagged edges stretched out in all directions—toward his collarbone, his sternum, his stomach. It didn't resemble the uniform scars left by surgeries performed by medical professionals. Instead, it looked like someone had savagely torn his chest apart with their hands.

He paused, tilting my chin up with a finger so my gaze met his again. "I would prefer your eyes on me. Do not concern yourself about the scar. I do not."

Although curiosity rose in me, I pushed it back, nodding instead.

He let me go, now sliding his arms out of the sleeves of his shirt, tossing the fabric aside. My eyes followed his hands down to the shiny metal of his belt again, and he smirked, pausing for a moment. "Take it off for me," he said.

I didn't want to admit how much the command turned me on. My fingers were shaking again as I brought my hands up to his belt, undoing the metal buckle, then sliding the leather away, letting it fall to the ground with a soft thump. I didn't stop there, swallowing as I unbuttoned his slacks, pulling the zipper down slowly, my fingertips brushing against him in the process.

Hot. Hard. Ready.

We'd barely even kissed this time.

He seemed to sense my thoughts as he slid his slacks over his hips, letting them drop to the floor and revealing his boxers and noticeable bulge. "You look surprised again. It is quite flattering."

I hoped the dark could hide the redness of my face.

He suddenly paused, and a crease appeared between his eyes. "You are not a virgin, are you?"

"No," I answered, reaching a hand out to press my palm against his abdomen, then moving down to curl my fingers into the waistband of his boxers. "I just..."

His hand covered mine, then adjusted it lower, pressing it

against his clothed erection. "This is because of you. Because I want you."

I swallowed, looking up at him. He used our conjoined hands to push down his boxers, revealing his straining arousal. The air was thick with tension as he brought my fingers to the hot, silky length of him. I automatically curled my fingers around him, feeling him throb in response. He released a soft breath that turned into a contented hum as I stroked him. He was thicker and longer than Julian, and my heart beat faster at the thought of him being inside me. My thumb traced the veins along his shaft, then circled his head, smearing the wetness there.

Out of habit, I slid off the bed to my knees, ready to take him in my mouth. He tensed in anticipation for a moment before releasing my hand to stop me. "No, Eleanora. Come up."

Confused, I let him help me back to my feet. He scooped me up and all but threw me back onto the bed. I bounced as I landed on my back, pushing myself up on my elbows. He climbed on after me, settling on the mattress between my legs. "You don't want me to?" I asked, my heart sinking as self-consciousness ate at me. "Is something wrong? Am I—"

"Hush," he said, moving his body over mine to kiss me. "Nothing like that. I simply do not want this to be over so soon."

My cheeks warmed. "Oh. Then." I rolled out from underneath him, pushing myself up to my hands and knees.

"What are you doing?" he asked, resting a hand on my ass, absentmindedly stroking it.

"I'm ready," I told him.

His hand stopped moving. "What?"

I glanced over my shoulder back at him, taking in the way his lips set into a frown. "I thought you wanted to..." I started.

"I do," he responded swiftly, "but why do you want to skip the best part?"

"What?" My embarrassment grew the longer I stayed in this

position, so I faced him again, sitting back on my calves. "I thought you didn't want me to go down on you?"

He considered me for a moment before tutting softly. "I see. You have had a selfish lover."

I watched his face for a moment, confused again. Julian had told me I was the selfish one.

"Enver," the stranger said, his voice dropping to a seductive murmur.

"What?"

"My name. So you know what to cry out."

I gasped as he pushed me, making me lie flat on my back. His hands skimmed my waist before he gripped my thighs, pulling my legs up and placing them on either side of his hips. I instinctively tightened around him, and he hummed in response, moving up my body, letting his erection drag against me.

He hovered over me, staring down at me, curly wisps of his black hair falling across his forehead. My mouth went dry as I looked back up at him. The moonlight haloed him, making him seem celestial. His dark grey eyes glimmered with promise.

"Enver," I said, testing his name and reaching out to touch the curve of his jaw.

"That sounds nice," he said softly, "but I believe I can make it sound even sweeter."

He took my hand in his, kissing it, before pushing it back to the bed. When his hands slid between the mattress and my back, I lifted myself, giving him access to unhook my bra. He made easy work of it, and I once again thought of Julian. It would sometimes take him minutes to unhook my bra, and he would complain the entire time and ruin the mood. What little he ever set of it.

Annoyed I was thinking of Julian again, I surged up, slotting my lips against Enver's as he pulled my bra off me. He abandoned it immediately, opting to tangle his hand in my hair, tongue gliding along my bottom lip before pushing into my mouth. A moment later, he broke off to trail kisses down my neck to my collarbone, letting his teeth catch on the skin there.

I moaned in encouragement as he bit a little harder, making me shudder. He placed a soft kiss on the spot after, and then continued his descent, lips leaving a trail of heat in their wake as he moved between my breasts. My breath hitched in my throat as he brought his hand up to cup my right breast, and I let my head fall back as his mouth moved to my left breast, tongue teasing my nipple before sucking it into his mouth. I stilled, not usually very sensitive there, but the pressure he exerted on me as he bit down had my back arching, a pleasure bordering on pain shooting through me, but in a way that made me want more.

As if reading my thoughts, his other hand moved up to pinch my other nipple, applying the same pressure. I gasped, and a rush of pleasure shot straight to my core. When he swapped sides, I whimpered a little at the loss of contact, surprising myself, but any embarrassment dissipated when he reapplied the pressure, making me suck in a long breath.

I could feel him smile against me before he pulled away to kiss down my stomach, one hand still on my breast, continuing to tease me. My abdominal muscles tensed the lower he went, my hands fisting at my sides as his lips found the edge of my underwear.

I nearly jumped as he pressed a kiss against my mound, the thin fabric doing little to dampen the heat of his breath.

His hand left my breast as he sat back on his heels, gazing down at me, fingers teasing at the waistband of my underwear now. "Would you like me to continue?"

I nodded.

"I want to hear you say it."

"Yes," I whispered.

A satisfied look crossed his face as he hooked his thumbs in the lace and pulled my underwear off, purposefully dragging the tips of his fingers down my thighs and calves.

I automatically tried to press my knees together and hide myself, but my attempt was short-lived as his hands returned to my legs, spreading me open before him again. My breathing sped up in anticipation as he adjusted himself so that he lay between my parted thighs now, his mouth inches away from my center.

A wave of self-consciousness rocked into me, and I let my head drop back, closing my eyes, trying to relax. Enver must have sensed this because he leaned forward, leaving gentle, calming kisses on the sensitive skin of my inner thighs.

I took a deep breath, and it came out as a gasp as his lips pressed a light kiss straight to my clit. It only lasted a split second, but then he pressed another in the same spot, barely touching me, yet causing my entire body to quiver. When he did it a third time, he let his tongue brush against me, and I moaned.

My fingers clenched into the sheets as he kissed lower, keeping the same delicate pressure, each sensation pulling a soft noise from me. I bit my lip to hold them back. I'd never been vocal with Julian, so why—

I sucked in a harsh breath as he licked a long stripe up me, and then repeated the process again, and again, before finally closing his lips around my clit and sucking. My head fell back, and I closed my eyes as he once again found the perfect amount of pressure to make me tremble. His hands dug deeper into my thighs as he leaned forward, my calves coming to rest on his shoulders, giving himself better access. His tongue circled my clit before sweeping down to my entrance.

My hands shot to his head as he dipped his tongue inside me, my fingers grasping his hair, another breathless moan leaving my lips. He murmured his approval as my body writhed under his ministrations before plunging his tongue in again. I clenched around him, wanting something deeper, bigger.

After a few more strokes, he pulled back, adjusting us once more, his hands leaving my thighs, letting them rest on the bed again. I took the time to catch my breath, but it was short-lived as his finger circled my clit once before sliding lower to sink into me. I would have been embarrassed about how wet I was if I wasn't so desperate to feel more of him inside me.

"Another," I breathed.

"So eager," he responded, pulling his finger out and rubbing along my entrance with two. But he only pushed one back in.

I brought my hand down toward him, wanting more, but he quickly intercepted it, once again withdrawing his finger. He straightened out, taking my other hand, bringing both above my head so they stretched out above me.

"Keep them there," he ordered before releasing them.

I started to nod and then stopped. "Yes," I said instead.

His eyes darkened, and he bent down to kiss me. I could taste myself on his lips as he sucked my bottom lip into his mouth, sinking his teeth into it. He didn't let go as he pulled back, causing my lip to pull tight. I groaned when it became too much, and he finally let it slip from between his teeth.

I fell back to the bed as he moved back between my legs, lips and tongue immediately going back to work, no longer teasing, but with purpose. Pleasure made me feel like I was floating, and it took everything I had to keep my hands above my head instead of carding them through his dark hair again. His fingers brushed against my entrance, and I cried out as he suddenly thrust two fingers into me, giving me what I'd asked for. His long fingers reached deep inside me, and combined with his attention on my clit, I could feel an orgasm approaching quickly.

I tried to fight it off, not wanting this to end too soon,

trying to focus on anything but the feeling of his fingers thrusting into me. He hit a spot that made my toes curl—a spot I didn't even know I had inside me. I began to lift my hands, wanting to slow him down, but I found them immobile. As if stuck to the bed by an unseen force. I glanced above me, only seeing shadows so thick they could have been physical.

Enver crooked his fingers inside me, and I forgot about the force on my wrists, my hips bucking as he repeated the action. A warm, tingling sensation spread through my body, and my breaths turned ragged as my muscles tensed.

"Wait," I gasped. "I'm close, I—"

He hit that spot inside me again, and my vision blurred as my orgasm hit me with such force I forgot to breathe. He didn't stop, working me through it, prolonging it until I was a sopping, trembling mess under him. And even then, he didn't remove his fingers from me, only slowed them so I could feel every drag against my inner walls.

I opened my eyes, finding Enver watching me, having straightened out again. I flushed under his heated gaze, letting out a small moan as his thumb swept over my sensitive clit. "This could become my new favorite sight."

"W-what?" I asked, trying to focus on his words, but finding it hard as he idly stroked me.

"The sight of you coming undone like that."

I moaned in response, my fingers twitching from where they still rested above my head.

"I believe I would like to see it again."

He was between my legs again before I had the chance to respond, his lips replacing his thumb, his fingers resuming their previous pace. He slid his free hand under my lower back, effortlessly lifting me to give himself more room to work with. Everything felt ten times more sensitive now. My head tossed back and forth as I fought with clashing sensations—the pulsating pleasure of his touch and the sweet soreness of overstimulation.

Another orgasm approached swiftly, leaving me disoriented. I barely ever came once with Julian, let alone twice. I could feel the telltale signs starting again, and I fell silent, concentrating on the feeling, my eyes squeezed shut.

"No," Enver said, commanding and sharp. "Eyes open. Look at me this time."

I obeyed, opening my eyes again, and the sight of him between my thighs sent me over the edge. My entire body shuddered, and I clenched around his fingers. "Enver," I managed to get out, my throat tight, his name only a small, choked sound.

Overstimulation turned to discomfort quickly this time, but he removed his fingers before I could voice it.

"Lovely," he commented, bringing his hand to my cheek, his fingers still wet with my arousal. "But not nearly enough."

I tried to move my hands again. This time I had full control, and I dismissed my earlier confusion of them being stuck as being too overwhelmed and making things up. As I sat up, I caught sight of Enver's erection, still hard and leaking, and my core clenched in desire.

Enver caught me staring, and that knowing smirk graced his features. "Do you need a moment?"

"No," I answered, heat searing through me in anticipation, turning over, and pushing myself onto all fours again on shaking limbs.

"Ah," he said, his voice deep. "This again? Is this how you like it?"

I started shaking my head, then caught myself. "No. I mean, it's fine. This is just how we usually—" I cut myself off, revealing too much, bringing up Julian *again*.

"A shame," Enver responded softly. "Then he does not know how beautiful you look when you come apart."

Something started nagging at the back of my head. Julian never looked me in the eye when we fucked. I hadn't really thought about it until now. Why didn't he?

Enver's fingers traced along my spine, and then his hands slipped around my hips, guiding me up, so I knelt on the bed. He moved in closer behind me, his chest pressing against my back. "I do not want you like this. I want to watch your face as you come apart because of me."

I stilled as the realization hit me. Why Julian always put me in this position. Why he always wanted to take me with my face away from him.

"I want to see you, Eleanora," Enver murmured, his hot breath caressing my ear, his hands splayed across my stomach possessively as he held me close to him.

It all made sense. And I knew who he was imagining every time.

A memory slammed into me. Julian whispering a name I'd convinced myself he hadn't said as he released inside me, holding my head so I wouldn't turn back and look at him.

I trembled. It was never me. He never cared for me. He'd only used me. And I let him. I let him because I wanted him to love me. But he didn't. He never would.

Just like everyone else.

No one would ever love—

Enver's lips grazed against the nape of my neck, nipping at my skin, pulling me from my thoughts. "Not yet," he whispered. "I want you here, with me, completely."

I didn't protest as he turned me around, pushing me onto my back once more and crawling over me again. My legs parted, and he lowered himself until he was completely on top of me, forcing the air out of my lungs as I bore his weight, his erection gliding against me. His weight was comforting in a way, forcing me to focus on my breathing rather than any negative thoughts.

I wrapped my arms around his back as he kissed my neck, then a sensitive spot below my ear. "Do you want to continue?" he asked.

"Yes. Can you kiss me again?"

"Needy, are we?" he teased, but desire burned in his eyes.

I couldn't voice my answer before his lips crashed into mine. I closed my eyes, throwing myself into the kiss, forgetting everything else. His tongue stroked mine, easily riling me up again. I melted into the mattress, letting him take the lead, warmth spreading from my chest to my toes.

He brought up his knee to shift even closer to me, my leg hooking around his, creating more space for him to grind against me. I moaned softly as he reached a hand between us to dip two fingers into me. A low groan left his lips as he felt how wet I'd become again, and he rubbed my clit for a moment, making me shake. He pulled his hand back, using it instead to line himself up with my entrance. He rubbed himself against me teasingly, the pressure causing me to squirm. I'd never been fucked by someone with his... proportions.

"What is it?" he asked, pausing.

"Nothing."

"Tell me," he said. "Would you like to stop?"

I immediately shook my head. "No! I want this. You're just... bigger than what I'm used to." My words ended in a mumble, and I couldn't meet his eyes.

Enver smirked, rolling his hips slowly, not pressing in yet. "You flatter me, but you can take me. I will make sure of it."

3

I bit my lip at the promise in Enver's words. My legs wrapped around his waist, and I used them as leverage to buck my hips toward him, trying to penetrate myself on him.

His hand immediately came down on my pelvis, holding me down. "No. I am going to take my time with you."

"Please," I said breathlessly.

His hand slid up to my belly button. "Here, then?"

"W-what?"

"I will bury myself this deep inside you," he told me. "That is what you are begging for, is it not?"

My stomach fluttered. "Enver—"

His hand moved to my face, grasping my jaw, keeping me looking up at him. The intensity of his stare only made me want him that much more. "Keep your eyes on me."

"Yes."

His other hand gripped my waist, holding me steady, and my breath hitched as he began to press into me, then came out in a low moan as he unhurriedly sank in, making me feel every throbbing inch of him. My eyes fluttered shut, but then his fingers dug into my jaw, a silent reminder to keep my eyes open. I forced them open, trying to breathe as he pushed further in, deeper than his fingers had reached before. Deeper than anyone had been before. My body stretched to accommodate him, the initial burn giving away to sweet friction as I made myself relax, giving in to him. He continued to move maddeningly slow, his gaze never leaving mine, making my pulse pick up in a way that had nothing to do with his languid movement. Everything felt so much more intimate like this—our eyes locked together, bodies flush, his weight pressing down on me.

He let out a soft exhale as he finally stilled, his entire length sheathed inside me. My inner walls quivered around him as I adjusted to his size, and he pulled back slightly, only to push back in with more force, drawing another moan out of me.

"See? You take me so well," he murmured. "Are you ready for more?"

"Yes," I responded, my hands gripping his biceps, feeling the power in his muscles as he held himself over me. "You can move faster."

He drew back until only his tip remained inside me, and I held my breath, anticipating a hard thrust. However, he slipped back in at the same steady pace as before. Wanting more, I lifted myself to meet him, but his hand pushed against my hip, pinning me back to the bed. I let out an impatient groan, and he chuckled, his elbow dropping to the mattress as he came closer to kiss me.

As our mouths came together again, I moaned anew, the intimacy of it both irresistible and almost devastating. I felt more connected to this stranger in that moment than I had with Julian over the course of our entire relationship. I felt more attraction, more arousal. Each idle stroke had me trembling under him in pleasure, wanting more and more. He released my hip to take my hand in his, pinning it next to my head, entwining our fingers.

I panted as we broke apart, and I stared up at Enver with half-lidded eyes as he continued his rhythmic rocking. With my free hand, I reached up to cup his firm jaw before sliding my fingers into his silky black hair, dragging my fingernails through the strands and then down his neck. He closed his eyes, savoring the sensation, and his hold on my hand tightened.

Then, out of nowhere, a memory of Julian struck me. Hovering over me, complaining about how he always had to do the work during sex.

I didn't know I had a physical reaction to the memory, that I'd gone still, until Enver stopped, his hand leaving mine to touch my cheek. "All right?"

"I, um," I started, hating how my heart hammered for the wrong reason now. "Are you tired? Should I get on top?"

"No," Enver said, beginning to move inside me again. "Why would I ever want to give up this view? Your cheeks flushed with pleasure because of me." He pulled back and then drove back into me with the force I asked for earlier, punching a gasp out of me. "Your eyes clouded with pleasure because of me." Another hard thrust had my head lolling back, my eyes closing, and I moaned shamelessly. "Your lips producing such sweet sounds because of me."

"Enver—"

"I could come just from this," he said huskily, lips dipping down to my ear, his breath tickling me as he slowed. "Just from the sight of you writhing under me."

His words had me clenching down on him, and this time, it was him moaning—a deep rumble in my ear, encouraging me to repeat the action, needing him to move faster, harder. I jerked my hips up toward him, my legs sliding higher on his waist, trying to draw him closer and deeper. The hand not in his hair flattened against his chest, exploring until I found his nipple. I pinched it hard, trying to goad him into action.

He groaned, jaw clenching. "Gods, you are so desperate."

Desperate?

"So perfect."

I twisted his nipple again and he grasped my greedy hand in his, forcing it to join my other above my head. I didn't resist as he adjusted them, so only one of his hands held down both my wrists. His now free hand went to my thigh, gripping it firmly as he nearly pulled out of me again.

"Enver, please," I pleaded, my hands curling into fists where he held them down. "I need—"

"Desperation suits you," he murmured before driving into me.

The air left my lungs with the force of his thrust, and I didn't have a chance to catch my breath before he repeated the action again and again and again. He fucked into me with abandon now, his fingers digging into my thigh possessively as my body jolted with the force of his thrusts. I arched against him, meeting him stroke for stroke, panting as pleasure began to coil within me.

"I love the sound of you begging, but the breathless silence you surrender to when I give you what you need is just as sweet," he said, voice rough and low.

I moaned in response. It'd never been like this. Sex with Julian hadn't even come *close* to this. I didn't think anything ever would. Each movement Enver made drove me closer to losing my mind to pleasure. Like he knew exactly what made me feel best. Exactly *where* made me feel best.

Enver's hand on my thigh moved under me, pressing against my lower back to hold me closer to him, angling his hips so he could hit the spot inside me that made me toss my head from side to side, whimpers escaping my lips as he slammed into me with precision and purpose. He nearly folded me in half, my calves above my head, the muscles in my legs causing me to shake from the strain.

But any thoughts of discomfort left my head as Enver thrust into me so deeply my mouth fell open in a silent cry. My toes curled, my hands fisting at nothing. My gaze met his again, and the lust burning in it had me squeezing around him. A rough sound came from deep in his throat, and he slammed his lips against mine with bruising force. His tongue thrust into my mouth as his hips crashed against mine, and I moaned, the sound swallowed by his mouth.

A familiar tightening bloomed within me, and I kissed him more urgently. His teeth caught my bottom lip, sinking into it with just enough pressure to make me jerk against him, groaning as my head fell back. His mouth moved to my neck, teeth scraping across the tender skin there before biting down.

That, matched with his relentless pace, was too much. I could feel my orgasm building.

"I will give you this one," he told me, lifting his lips from my skin, "but the next one you have to earn."

I wanted to ask what he meant, but all thoughts left my head as he slipped a hand between us, his thumb swiping across my clit. Another whimper escaped me as he skillfully stroked it, my legs shaking from both the strain of my muscles and the effect of his touch.

My orgasm approached me swiftly and strongly. I cried out sharply, my body convulsing beneath his as it swept over me. He kept moving through it, and I struggled, overwhelmed, clenching around him as a second wave hit. For a second, I actually thought I was going to pass out, unable to get air into my lungs from the overpowering sensations. I had never come with someone inside me before. It was so different from how I usually got myself off after Julian and I were done. More intense. Like I was losing control.

"Breathe," Enver said, slowing his movements but not pulling out of me.

I hadn't realized I'd stopped breathing. I took a deep breath, letting it out shakily.

"There you go," he praised. Sweat beaded on his forehead, sliding down his perfect skin. "So good for me."

As the aftershocks faded, Enver repositioned himself so my shaking legs could rest on the bed. It took me a moment to realize that both his hands were now in sight again, trailing across my stomach, but my hands remained pinned. When I raised my chin to look above me, Enver grasped it, pulling it back down so I met his gaze again.

"I want to touch you," I said, my voice sounding absolutely wrecked.

Enver's length throbbed inside me at my words. "How could I say no?"

I tested my hands again and found I could now move them. My brows furrowed, but before I could think more about it, Enver ground himself into me before retreating off the bed, leaving me empty and yearning. He grabbed my calves, dragged me to the edge of the bed, and raised my legs up so my ankles rested on his shoulders. The new position had me tensing, but he slipped back into me easily, his hands moving to my feet, massaging them soothingly for a moment, giving me time to adjust.

The minute I relaxed, he picked up the pace again, pounding into me, and my hands flew to his thighs, his muscles flexing under my touch as I clung to him for support. The sensitivity from my orgasm and the position made everything feel new again. Every thrust punched a moan out of me, and I held onto him tightly.

"You went to the club searching for something tonight."

It took me a moment to realize he spoke. I tried to find enough breath to speak. "W-what?"

"I could feel it," he said, fingers curling around my ankles, spreading my legs open. "Your pain. Your despair."

"What?" I said again, distracted by the way his heavy gaze dipped down to where our bodies joined. A blush burned on my cheeks, but instead of trying to close my legs again, I let my head flop back, eyes closing, giving in to the pleasure.

"I can give you what you so desperately crave," he continued.

What I crave?

"But you need to do something for me first, my little lover."

I choked on a gasp as he released one of my ankles to circle my clit lightly with his pointer finger. Not enough pressure to give me what I wanted, only enough to leave me wanting. "Enver!"

"Eleanora," he murmured, applying a little more pressure, but still not enough.

"Ah," I whimpered, trying to grind against his finger.

"The pleasure is not consuming you fully, is it? You can still understand me?"

I nodded, but I barely registered his words. "Yes. Please, Enver, I need—"

"I will give you what you want." His thumb replaced his pointer finger, rubbing my clit in small, slow circles, making me squirm. His thrusts slowed again, adding to my frustration as he stopped completely. "I will give you so much more than that if you let me."

"Please," I said, my fingernails digging into his flesh.

A ghost of a smirk crossed his face before disappearing. He leaned in closer to me, eyes dark and piercing. "I need you to say it."

"Say *what*?" I asked, exasperated and desperate. "God, will you just fuck—" I couldn't finish my sentence as he drove into me while moving his thumb against my clit with the friction I was coming to love.

"Come with me," he urged roughly.

I clung to him, moaning loudly, unable to do anything else as he fucked me.

"You will have what you desire," he promised, his voice growing more and more strained. "And I will have you."

He'll have me?

"I can be everything you need—everything you want. I will love you. That is what you crave, is it not? To be loved?"

Love? I clenched around him, wetness beading at the corner of my eyes from the intensity of his pace. I could feel something nagging at the back of my mind. How did he know? How—

"Enver!" I inhaled sharply as something circled and pinched my nipples, sending jolts of electricity straight between my legs, adding to the pleasure building inside me. But I could still see his hands holding my ankles, so what...?

When I tried to look down, I found myself unable to move my head, only able to stare up at Enver as he continued to pound into me. His angle changed, and every thought left my head but the feeling of my impending orgasm. My body shook uncontrollably and my hands slid from Enver's arms, falling limply at my sides.

"Gods," he groaned. "*Gods*. Come with me. It could be like this forever, my little lover. *Forever*. Until the world falls down."

"I..." I tried to speak, my body tensing, eyes rolling back as pleasure threatened to overwhelm me. The world dulled around me, nothing mattering but the need to come.

A pressure on my throat pulled me back to the present, making me aware of the way Enver watched me, his eyes dark and his face shadowed.

"Say yes," he commanded. "Say yes, and I will allow you to come."

"Yes!" I cried immediately, and something shifted between us. Something intangible and powerful that had me trembling in the wake of its arrival. "Yes, please, *yes*!"

His pace stuttered, a choked groan escaping him. "Good," he rasped. "Now come."

It was all it took to bring me over the edge. "Enver!" I whimpered, my nails tearing into the bedsheets, my vision darkening.

Enver didn't make a sound as he climaxed, kissing me roughly instead, his warmth flooding me as he lurched into me one last time. My hands went to his back, crushing him on top of me as we both rode out our orgasms. When he finally broke the kiss, he panted against my neck, his breath ragged.

My heart beat frantically between us, but I couldn't feel his, making me wonder how I was so much more exhausted than he was, when he'd done most of the work. But my thoughts were disrupted as he pulled out of me. I gritted my teeth, sore now, and Enver moved next to me, throwing his arm over my waist. I curled toward him, chasing his warmth, my face pressed against his chest.

"Can I stay the night?" I whispered into his skin, weariness washing over me.

His hand slid into my hair, and he idly played with it. "You will stay forever."

The finality of his words sounded like a promise. One I smiled at initially, believing it to be a hint of his desire to repeat the night. Yet, the word stuck in my mind, repeating over and over as sleep weighed down on me.

Forever.

Forever.

"Rest now," Enver murmured, and the exhaustion grew heavier, my eyes drifting closed. "You will need it."

4

Lost in a cocoon of warmth from the comforters piled over me, I woke up feeling more well-rested than I had in a long time. I rolled onto my side, snuggling into the pillow under my head, not ready to fully wake yet. As I pulled up my leg to bring it closer to my chest, an ache between my thighs had me jolting up, remembering everything that had happened. I scanned the once pitch-black room, taking in every detail anew as bright sunlight streamed through a partially drawn set of curtains.

The room was more expansive than it'd seemed in the dark, with multiple floor-to-ceiling windows stretching along the furthest wall, all draped in heavy silk fabrics. And the décor was odd. Like something I'd see in a fantasy movie. Black sconces lined the wall, and antique rugs adorned the dark hardwood floor. A fireplace with a carved mantlepiece rested on the wall to my left, unused and collecting dust. And the furniture I'd barely been able to make out before now caught the daylight, revealing intricate wood carvings—ones mirrored in the ebony wood of the walls. Everything appeared luxurious and well-crafted.

I had to give the hotel props. They'd really pulled out all the stops.

I pushed the blanket off of me, blushing as I realized I was still naked. The floor was cold under my bare feet as I hurriedly searched for my clothing, dragging the sheets off the bed with me to keep me covered. But not even my underwear was in sight. The lack of light hindered my search, and I went over to the window, noticing a wooden door on the wall adjacent to it.

As I reached out to pull the curtain open further, the door swung open, and Enver entered the room, a rush of warm air following him. My mouth went dry as I realized he only wore a towel around his waist. His black, curly hair lay flat against his head, wet and dripping. I watched as a water droplet fell to his collarbone and slid down to the scar over his heart.

"Good morning," he greeted in a deep, rumbly tone.

I couldn't stop my cheeks from flooding with heat, and I forced my eyes away from his scar. "Sorry. I didn't mean to fall asleep so quickly last night."

"You could not help it," he responded, stepping closer to me, the scent of amber and vanilla permeating the air. His scent. "You look lovely wrapped up in my sheets, by the way. Almost as lovely as you looked writhing on top of them."

My face grew hotter, and I turned to reach for the curtain again, but his hand intercepted mine, and he pulled me to him. I stumbled a bit as I stepped on the sheet, my foot slipping, sending me careening against his hard chest. His arms wrapped around my waist, holding me against him.

"Careful, Eleanora," he murmured.

"Nell," I told him, finally thinking clearly enough to cringe at the use of my full name. "I usually go by Nell."

"Nell," he uttered softly. The way he spoke my name made it sound like the most precious thing in the world.

His lips brushed my forehead, the intimacy making me lean toward him, but I stopped myself. It was only a one-night stand.

"I should probably go," I said, pushing away from him, trying not to think about how good it felt to be in his arms.

"Go?" he repeated, his hold tightening around me, not releasing me.

I chewed on my bottom lip, meeting his gaze now, seeing a hint of amusement in his eyes. "Do you know where my clothing went? I can't find it. It's a little dark in here."

As soon as I finished speaking, the black chandelier and metal sconces along the walls lit up, flooding the room with golden light. A little startled, I tried to back away from him again. I must have missed him flipping on the switch... but his hands were still on me. Was I going crazy?

"I do not want you to be on your way quite yet," he said, his lips curving into a frown, as if surprised by his admittance. "On the off chance you succeed."

I stared at him, not understanding what he meant. *Succeed in what?*

His hands palmed my sides, and his fingers dug into my soft skin. "Stay."

A swooping sensation appeared in my stomach, and the ache between my legs turned from soreness to pure want. How did he have such an effect on me? I didn't think I could say no to him. I didn't want to say no.

Enver peeled the sheet off me, leaving it to pool between my feet. I let out a stuttered breath as he backed me against the wall. I could feel the patterns carved in the wood against my back as his intoxicating gaze trailed over my naked body, his hand coming up to my collarbone, pressing on it, keeping me still.

"It has been a long time since I have given in to these desires," he said, his thumb pressing into the hollow point of my throat. "And I have no reason to now, so why..." His pupils darkened as I swallowed under his touch. "Why do you entice me so?"

I wanted to ask him the same—why just a look from him made my body thrum with desire and need. But as he shifted closer to me, towel falling, his arousal hard against my lower hip, I lost all sense of thought again. We hadn't even kissed yet this time. I bucked against him, needing to confirm his desire, gasping when I did.

"You want it, too," he said, tilting his head to the side, lips only inches from mine. "Am I wrong?"

I didn't bother to lie. "Yes."

God, my voice already sounded desperate. Needy.

"Show me," he ordered, stepping back as he rested a hand on my shoulder, applying pressure to it.

My last bit of resistance melted. I sunk to my knees in front of him, looking up, watching the muscles in his abdomen tense as my cheek brushed against his hardness. One of his hands cupped my neck, and I thought he'd stop me again like before. "Let me," I said quickly.

He didn't pull me away. He simply stared down at me, muscles tensed, standing unnaturally still.

He remained that way even as I pressed a kiss to the head of his erection, then another, and another. I let my tongue flit out, tasting him briefly, before mouthing along his shaft, my saliva coating his hot flesh, tracing every vein with my tongue. His fingers twitched against my neck, but that was the only movement from him.

Until I took him into my mouth, swallowing him down as far as I could in one go.

A quiet hiss escaped his clenched teeth, and his hips jerked forward, pushing in further, making me choke. I didn't let it hinder me, though, grasping his thighs, and running my tongue against the underside of his erection, tasting every inch of smooth skin. I hallowed my cheeks as I sucked. I bobbed my head, swirling my tongue around him, taking him deeper and deeper until his tip hit the back of my throat. I gagged, causing him to thrust more shallowly.

It didn't take long for my jaw to ache, his size stretching me to my limit, but I pushed through it, encouraged by the way his breathing picked up. His fingers slid into my hair, holding me, but not forcing me to move faster or deeper, allowing me go at my own pace. I rewarded him for his self-restraint by cupping his balls and massaging them.

"Gods," he groaned above me, his other hand now propped against the wall, his head resting on his biceps as he watched me.

I met his gaze, dragging my lips slowly back up his length, then sucking hard on his head.

He rolled his hips against my face, pushing himself further into my mouth, his control slipping again. I redoubled my efforts, bringing my other hand into the mix, curling my fingers around what I couldn't easily fit into my mouth, twisting and pumping him, moving in time with my tongue, my saliva acting as a lubricant.

After a moment, he exhaled sharply, moving back, and sliding himself out of my mouth. I looked at him, confused, my hands falling off him and into my lap.

His fingers trailed across my cheek, his thumb swiping across my lip. "Open," he ordered.

Again, the authority in his voice had me squeezing my thighs together, arousal shooting through me. I obeyed, parting my lips, and as a split-second decision, I stuck out my tongue as well.

Enver groaned, his thumb moving to press down on my tongue before replacing it with the weight of his erection, dragging his head against my tongue, then easing deeper into my mouth again. I kept my mouth as wide open as I could as he continued on, flinching as he hit the back of my throat again. He paused for a moment before pushing further, making my hands clench, and my lungs fight for air on instinct as he blocked my airway. I gagged a bit but managed to recover.

"Easy," Enver said, stroking the side of my neck. "Relax. You are doing well."

I took a breath through my nose, loosening my shoulders, easing the tension there.

"Good," he praised, gathering my hair up into his hand. "You can take it, my little lover."

I didn't know if I could, but I wanted to. I inhaled again, focusing on relaxing my throat, but it still took everything in me to keep from gagging.

"Just like that. Use your tongue," he instructed.

My tongue lolled against him, and the lack of air made me feel lightheaded. He held my head steady, the heat of his thick tip moving further down my throat. My chest heaved, my body instinctively fighting for air, and I could feel my throat begin to lock up. Tears blurred my vision, a reflex of my body fighting not to choke.

"Yes, let me in," Enver breathed, ragged, strained. "Take all of me."

Just as I thought I couldn't take any more, my nose brushed against his pelvis, and a surge of accomplishment went through me. My gag reflex kicked in only a second later, and I choked, pulling my head back quickly. Enver assisted by giving me space, letting me breathe for a moment as saliva slid down my chin. I sucked in deep breaths of air, trying to blink away the wetness.

"My, how you continue to flatter me," Enver murmured, his wet length brushing against my cheek. "Keep going."

I turned my face to him, leaving butterfly kisses wherever I could, then took him back into my mouth when I'd caught my breath. He hit the back of my throat again but didn't push in further, inhaling sharply as he rolled his hips. His grip on my hair became firmer as he guided me in a rhythm he set. I sucked gently on his downstroke, then flattened my tongue against him on the upstroke, moaning at the prickles of pain on my scalp as he pulled my hair taut.

"Your mouth was made for me," he said, voice raspy and breathless. "You were made for me."

I stared up at him again, and the sight of him had searing desire pooling in my stomach. Eyes closed, dark lashes resting on his cheeks. His head tilted down, his jaw clenched. The muscles in his biceps were rigid with tension as he braced himself against the wall, using it as leverage to thrust into my mouth. His momentum quickened, chasing his own pleasure.

I cupped his balls again, wanting to bring him over the edge, to taste his release in my mouth. A heavy groan came from above me as I did so, his hips jerking against me, erratic, urgent. I worked him harder, applying as much suction as I could, my tongue dancing around the underside of his head, then pressing into the slit at the top, his scent and taste all around me.

Without warning, he yanked my head back, pulling free of my mouth with a wet popping sound. I winced in pain, looking up at him as he backed away. He released my hair, only to enclose his hand around my wrist, tugging me up and off the floor. I barely had time to catch my breath before he gripped the back of my thighs, lifting me up, and shoving my back against the wall again. My legs hooked around the crooks of his elbows as he bracketed me with his arms, and I clung to his shoulders for support.

His erection rubbed against me, and I shuddered as he positioned himself against my wet entrance. "Tell me you want this."

"Yes," I groaned, the need to have him inside me almost painful. "Fuck me, please—"

He thrust into me, and I sunk my teeth hard into my bottom lip to keep myself from crying out. Still sore from last night, the friction burned, but in a tantalizing way. The pain was both sweet and addicting as he drew out of me, then plunged back in, not giving me a moment to adjust.

All I could do was take it as he took me against the wall, my feet dangling in the air, bouncing with every thrust, heels colliding with his ribcage. I wrapped my arms around his neck, bracing myself. This wasn't like the slow, teasing love-making he'd shown last night. It was rough, fast. He'd *given* before—now he *took*. It had me gasping, his mouth swallowing the sounds as he kissed me fiercely. I clung to him the best I could, fingers digging into his shoulders for better purchase.

His hands moved to just below my armpits, taking my weight off the wall and into his control. Gravity helped him reach further inside me, and I trembled, moaning out loud as he manhandled me effortlessly, fucking me on him, relentless in his pursuit.

"I have half a mind to keep you here." He lifted me higher, then seated himself inside me again, a low groan coming from deep in his throat. "I would not even have to force you to stay. You would choose to stay. Willingly. Am I wrong?"

I whimpered as his thrusts turned brutal, the pleasure and torment almost too much to handle.

"You want me to take you. Again and again. Until you cannot walk straight." His breathing quickened, the breathlessness of his voice almost as sexy as his dirty talk. "You want me to make you come. With my fingers. With my tongue. With me deep inside you."

Heat spread through my body, beginning at my toes and working its way up until I felt as if I were on fire. I didn't think I could be so affected by words. I didn't think I could orgasm just with penetration either, but I could feel one building, being wrested from me by his voice and savage thrusts.

"You want me to make you mine."

My body arched into his, my breath coming so fast I became lightheaded. "Enver, I—"

"You want me to love you."

He murmured the words so sweetly, so *sincerely,* my heart lurched.

"You need nothing but me," he continued, brushing his lips against mine. "Is that not right, my little lover?"

The strange, nagging feeling returned. I tried to fight through the haze of my lust, attempting to grasp the feeling and hang onto it, but his presence was too potent. The way he moved, the way he made me feel. My mind tried to battle against the onslaught. There had to be something. What could it be? What—

Something velvety and cool brushed between my legs and every thought left my head. The sensation furled around my wanting clit, stroking and caressing it, soft but demanding. That, combined with Enver's unfaltering tempo, had me stiffening, needy noises I didn't know I could make slipping from my lips.

"Come for me," Enver demanded.

My orgasm struck me harder than ever before. Sudden and intense, sending me spiraling. I convulsed around Enver, every nerve in me flaring to life, flooding me with overpowering pleasure. My eyes rolled back, and I felt like I wasn't in control of my body. My mouth opened, but no sound came out as I came apart.

Everything became too sensitive, too quickly. "Enver," I gasped, unable to take much more.

He shoved me back against the wall in response, sliding into me to the hilt with a ragged exhale, and shuddered against me, finishing with one last thrust.

My head fell limply against his chest as I panted, a puppet in his arms. He remained inside me for a moment more before pulling out, but he didn't put me down, readjusting me so my legs wrapped around his waist, his hands gripping my backside. I rested against him as he re-entered the room he'd come from, letting him bear all my weight.

Humid air encompassed us, and I cracked an eye open, then lifted my head. My eyes widened at the sight of an enormous bathtub, steam rising from the water in the porcelain basin. Hanging from the ceiling above it was another expensive-looking chandelier, lights on and dim. I turned to look at the other side of the room, my gaze meeting my reflection in a lengthy mirror above a marble counter. I was a messy-haired, flushed mess in Enver's arms.

The sight made me shy—as if we hadn't fucked twice already. I lowered my head, studying the patterned tile making up the floor, then looked at the thick frame around the tub as we approached it. Scattered flowers and lit candles adorned the frame, creating a romantic atmosphere. There were no shampoo or conditioner bottles and no bars of soap. Only glass jars filled with various liquids.

"Did you bring me to some sort of sixth century-themed hotel?" I asked.

He sat me down on the frame of the tub, and I squirmed at the feeling of the cold porcelain. "Care to bathe?" he asked, ignoring me, dipping a hand into the water to test the temperature. "I drew you clean water earlier."

Before I could answer, he stepped into the tub, holding his hand out to me. I hesitated, the idea of bathing with him intimidatingly intimate. But I could still feel the sweat on my skin, so I took his hand. He helped me into the tub, the warm water enveloping my body as I sank into it. Enver settled in behind me, his legs on either side of me, his chest against my back. His body felt warmer than the water.

I tried to relax, settling back into him, but my body felt stiff.

"What is wrong?" he asked.

"Nothing," I responded. "I've never done this with anyone,

so I feel a little shy," I admitted, not embarrassed to be honest with him. Not after what we just did.

He chuckled, his breath against my neck. "This is what makes you shy? Not when I was between your legs, tasting your—"

I twisted around to press my hand to his lips, blushing. "Don't."

His eyes revealed his mirth, and he nodded. I turned back around and saw him reach for one of the jars sitting on the tub's ledge. He squirted a small amount of the liquid into his hand, then brought his hands to my shoulders, the subtle scent of flowers meeting my nose. I made a small sound of contentment as he massaged my shoulders, his hands moving easily against my skin, made slippery by what I assumed was soap.

It was strange to be treated like this. I didn't know what to do with myself. No one had ever washed me. I'd read about it in books but thought it was just something left to fiction. I became lethargic as he cleaned me, both the water and his fingers soothing my tired muscles. He washed my hair, pushing it all to the side to ring it out and kissing my newly exposed neck. I could feel him getting hard against my back again as I murmured softly at his attention.

"Enver," I said, sitting up to look back over my shoulder at him. "I don't think I can, um..." I let my eyes drop to his erection.

He cupped my chin with his hand. "I am not asking anything more of you. I told you before—I cannot help this."

"I don't understand."

"Understand what?" he asked, brushing his thumb over my cheek. "Why I am so aroused by you?"

The way he put it made me blush. "I'm just—"

"Just what? Perfect for me?" His eyes flashed with something that had me freezing despite the innocuousness of his words. "Have I not told you that already?"

I didn't respond, and my heart skipped a beat as he turned me around, crowding me back to the other side of the tub.

"I knew from the moment I heard you last night," he continued, placing his hands against the tub's edge on either side of me. "You were meant for me."

Heard me? What did he mean by that? I knew I needed to ask, but he was leaning in, and I automatically closed my eyes, melting into him as he kissed me. His tongue traced the seam of my lips before sneaking between them, and I sighed, allowing him entrance. It was easy to get lost in his kiss and the warmth of the water surrounding us.

"Let me taste you once more," he said as we parted, his hands moving to my thighs. "I will be gentle."

I breathed out shakily as I nodded.

He wasted no time in hoisting me onto the frame of the tub, spreading my legs, and kneeling between them. I leaned back, surprised to find something soft under my elbows, protecting me from the hard marble. Towels, I realized. When had they appeared there? I swore I hadn't seen them before.

Enver kissed the skin of my inner thigh, and I stopped caring about the towels. I rested against them and let my eyes fall shut as he spread me open, licking a torturously slow path up my seam. His tongue swirled around my clit, but didn't touch it before he moved back down. I swallowed, the feeling of him on my sore entrance leaving my mouth dry, but true to his promise, he was gentle, not pressing inside.

I squirmed as he lavished attention everywhere but where I really wanted it. "Enver—"

"Patience," he replied.

My hips jerked as his tongue flicked out, just barely brushing against my clit. His eyes were on me, watching my reaction. I wondered if he thought I was as sexy as I thought he was. The sight of him between my legs was almost doing more for me than his teasing. I moved one of my hands to his hair, tugging on it, and bringing his mouth to where I wanted it. "Stop teasing me. Just make me come."

His gaze grew heavy with desire, and he ducked his head down, sealing his lips around my clit. My back bowed as his tongue applied that perfect pressure. I yanked on his hair, earning myself a low rumble in response, and his teeth suddenly enclosed around my clit, making me jerk and cry out. He pressed a soothing kiss against me before returning to licking and sucking me in a way that had my legs quaking within moments.

The water rippled, gaining my attention, and I realized he was touching himself beneath the surface, his hand stroking in sync with the rhythm of his tongue on me. I moaned, lifting my hips, almost there. The tension was building in my body, a tingling sensation spreading all over. I just needed...

Enver slipped a finger in me, and I came hard, going still. His own moan met my ears moments later, his head falling against my thigh.

I didn't move for a moment, catching my breath, but then Enver pulled me back into the water again, holding me against him.

"I will find you some clothing," he said after a moment, rising from the water. "Come."

I let him help me out of the tub, and he wrapped a towel around me before wrapping one around himself. We exited the bathroom, and he led me over to the luxurious wardrobe in his bedroom.

My head was beginning to clear again, and I looked around for my dress. "I can wear my own clothes. I really should get going."

As I said the words, disappointment flooded through me. I focused my gaze on the floor, biting my lip. I almost didn't want to leave. I knew this was only a one-night stand, but Enver had taken care of me so well. In more ways than one. In ways I wouldn't even dream of Julian doing.

The thought of Julian had my heart plummeting. What would today bring? What would Julian think if I told him I'd slept with a stranger? Would he feel the same hurt I had when he'd shown up with my sister last night?

I would have to face him. Soon. Either to kick him out of my house, or...

If he apologized, would I take him back? Did I want to take him back? After everything?

"Your despair is calling out to me again."

I nearly jumped, not realizing Enver had moved closer to me again. Our gazes met, and once again, I felt unsettled. His eyes were piercing and hard, and I couldn't make out a single emotion within them. I fell back a step, and Enver's hand shot out to grab my wrist and stop me. He stepped even closer, looming over me, making my heart rate spike. "Enver, what are you—"

"You will not be leaving," he told me, his tone steady and commanding. "You are mine now."

5

What...?

"What are you talking about?" I asked, trying to pull my arm away, but Enver's fingers tightened around it.

"You have been so compliant, Nell. I hope you continue to be," he said, and I noticed his voice sounded different. Cold and distant. No longer coaxing. As if he was no longer trying to lure me in. As if he already had me. "Although, either way, you have already consented."

"Consented?" I repeated, the air in the room chilly against my bare skin. "Consented to what?"

"That depends on your choice," he told me, releasing my wrist and stepping away to circle me slowly, like a predator stalking its prey.

I took a shallow breath, unmoving and unnerved as he positioned himself behind me. "My choice?"

"You could remain here. With me." His lips brushed my ear, making my skin prickle. "I told you I would give you everything you ever wanted. I did not lie. Anything you wish for will be yours."

His words hung the air, and his presence behind me became suffocating as the uneasiness settled deeper. Something wasn't right.

I needed to leave.

"And my other choice?" I asked, my voice shaking as my eyes darted to the only other door in the room.

It had to be the exit. If I could make it out of the room, I could flag down the hotel staff if I had to. I didn't want to believe Enver would hurt me, but anxiety crept through my veins. I didn't really *know* this man. I'd followed him here without any regard for my safety—an oversight I regretted now.

"You take on my labyrinth," he said, moving in front of me again, hand skimming across my waist. "Make your way through it. Conquer it. You could still get what you want from it, too... just at more of a cost."

Labyrinth?

I studied his face for a moment, the seriousness of his tone sinking in when I found no trace of humor in his expression. A nervous laugh escaped me. "A labyrinth? I don't think there's anything like that around here."

Enver tilted his head, his gaze cool and detached. Nothing like the man I'd just spent the night with. "You are already in it," he told me. "You are in my castle."

Castle?

Oh, God. That settled it. I'd slept with a maniac.

My weight shifted on my feet, my muscles tensing, ready to spring into action. I just had to make it to the door. I glanced at it again, preparing myself.

But I'd barely lifted my foot before Enver's rough voice cut through the air, halting my movements. "I advise against running from me. You will not get very far."

I complied at first, my foot returning to the floor. His expression relaxed.

Then I twisted on my heel and bolted for the door.

He didn't move to stop me, and my heart pounded from adrenaline as I raced across the room, my bare feet slapping against the polished wood. I reached for the handle, wrenching it open as I looked behind me, seeing Enver still standing by the wardrobe. My chest tightened in triumph. I could escape and never have to see him again—

My foot met nothing as I stepped outside the room and into pure darkness, not the hotel hallway that I thought would be on the other side of the door. Unable to stop my momentum, I pitched forward, completely losing my footing. I shrieked in fear, and my hands flew out in an attempt to grasp anything that could keep me from plummeting into the nothingness. But I only met the air as it rushed by me, sinking me further into the dark.

Panic clawed at my chest, but before I could cry out again, my fall came to an abrupt halt as silky tendrils wrapped around my body, enclosing my waist, wrists, and ankles in their hold, suspending me in the dark void.

"I warned you," Enver tutted softly, appearing at the threshold of the door I'd just fallen through. The dim light behind him framed his silhouette, casting shadows that danced across his features. "Do not attempt to run from me again."

Frozen in fear, I could only stare up at him, my chest heaving. Whatever held on to me *moved*. It snaked, curling around my arms and legs, featherlight but substantial at the same time. The tendrils tightened their grip and lifted me up toward Enver.

He stepped out of the way, and the light from the room washed over me, allowing me to see the tendrils that held me. *Shadows*. Physical masses. Swirling around me and cold to the touch. I recognized the feeling. I'd felt them before—on my body, holding my wrists down, sliding between my legs. I started struggling again, frantic to get out of their grip.

The shadows placed me on my feet again, and I nearly

collapsed when they released me, my body quaking so severely I could barely stand. Enver reached for my towel, pulling it up where it'd slipped down. I jerked back, nearly falling out of the room again, but the shadows braced me, keeping me upright. I stumbled away from them, but it only brought me closer to Enver again, and I forced myself to stay still. "Who are you?" I asked him shakily. "*What* are you?"

"My name is Enver," he replied, lifting his hand to trail his fingers along my jaw. "And I will be whoever you want me to be. Whatever you want me to be. Your lover, your master, your thrall. Even your god."

"Stop," I said, even though my body yearned to lean into his touch. It was a strange feeling. I wanted to run away from him, but there was another part of me that wanted him closer, wanted his hands on my body again. "Don't," I added, unsure if I was talking to him or myself.

His hand fell back to the side, but his gaze hardened.

"Where am I?" I demanded.

"My home," he answered simply.

"And where is that?"

"I will answer all your questions," he said, eyes raking down my body before meeting mine again, "after we dress."

I wanted to argue that he would answer them now, but I also didn't want to remain in only a towel. I felt too exposed. And the shadows surrounding me had put a chill in me I couldn't shake. "Where's my dress?"

"That attire will not suit you here, I assure you."

"I want my dress," I said, my voice strained.

Not even a second later, my dress hung before my face, dangling from a twisting shadow.

I flinched, and I swore one shadow stroked my hand in a soothing manner as I snatched my dress from it. I shuddered, my mind reeling. What was happening? Was I dreaming? This couldn't be real, could it? But everything had felt real.

Enver's touch, the shadows, the way my heart raced in my chest.

I took a careful step away from the shadows, eyeing them warily. "What are these things?"

"They will not harm you. Not unless I will them to."

My head snapped back to Enver. "Are you trying to tell me you control *shadows* right now?"

Enver tilted his head. "I said I would answer questions after we dress."

Gritting my teeth, I turned my back to him as I dropped my towel and slipped my dress over my head. I didn't want to believe anything I was seeing, but it was hard to fight against the proof right in front of my eyes. "This is insane," I whispered to myself, reaching around my back to zip my dress up.

Enver's hand brushed mine aside as he took the zipper from me, his knuckles grazing my bare back. "For what it is worth, you are coming to terms with this far more easily than others in your situation have."

I tensed as he swept my hair away from my neck to zip me up. "You've done this to others?"

"Yes," he replied, not moving his hand away, his fingers curling around my neck. Not tight enough to feel threatening, but enough that I could feel the weight of his palm against my skin. "There have been hundreds before you and there will be hundreds more."

My stomach rolled, nausea creeping through me.

"But I have let none of them touch me as you have touched me," he continued, his voice lowering, breath caressing my skin as he leaned forward to place a chaste kiss on the shell of my ear. "And I have tasted none as I have tasted you."

Once more, conflicting reactions shot through me. I hated this, but I also couldn't deny the goosebumps that broke out across my skin at his touch and words. I slowly turned toward him again, his hand sliding from the back of my neck around to my throat. His fingers pressed in just a little as he watched me, his face unreadable.

"Are you going to hurt me?" I asked.

"No, my little lover. I will not hurt you."

"What do you want from me?"

He released me but said nothing else. He crossed the room back to his wardrobe, opened it, and pulled out a fresh set of clothing. I watched as he put his arms through a black silk shirt, leaving it open as he pulled on a pair of black slacks, forgoing any underwear.

"Let us discuss the rest over a meal," Enver said, striding back to me.

"No, I—"

"I will not poison it. But if you are concerned, I will taste everything first."

That wasn't what I cared about, but I could already tell there was no way out of this. Not without Enver's permission. Not when he or his shadows could force me to do what he wanted, anyway. If I wanted to have any chance at escaping, I needed to be compliant for now. "Fine. I need to use the restroom first, though."

He gestured back toward the bathroom. "Of course."

After using the bathroom, and searching and failing for an escape there, I reluctantly went back out through the door. But it wasn't Enver's bedroom I stepped back into. Instead, it was a grand dining hall. I looked around wildly, taking in the elegant tapestries decorating the walls, the tall, arched windows made of stained glass, and the sprawling dining table made of polished mahogany that stretched almost the entire room length.

A wide assortment of food lined the table, from seared meats to flaky pastries, ripe fruits, assorted cheeses. The sheer amount of food was staggering. Yet, no one sat at the table. Empty seat after empty seat lined each side. Stepping closer, I noticed a layer of dust on the back of each elegantly carved chair.

"Have a seat." A voice came from behind me, and I whirled to see Enver merely a foot away.

"How..." I started, finding myself unsure of how to word my question. "Why isn't this your bedroom anymore?"

He raised an eyebrow. "Did you want to return to it?"

"No," I blurted.

A ghost of a smirk flitted across his lips. "The entire castle is under my control. From its shadows to its arrangement. Now sit."

This time I obeyed him, sitting in the chair closest to the head of the table, where I assumed his normal seat was. It was the only chair without any dust.

The scent of the food wafted around me, mouthwatering and tempting, but I didn't make any move to eat it. "What are you?" I asked again.

He didn't answer right away, a flicker of a frown on his face. "The same as you."

I stared at him.

"Well, presumably older."

My lips pressed into a tight line. "Humans can't *control* shadows."

He shrugged, reaching for a bowl of fruit, picking up a peach, and examining it. "Nor can they live hundreds of years, yet here I am."

Hundreds of years? He didn't look a day over thirty.

"You're not human," I protested as he picked up a knife.

He paused, the knife's point against the flesh of the peach. "Then what am I?"

"I don't know, but—"

"No," he interrupted, slicing the knife into it, eyes still on me. "Tell me. Since you are so certain I am not human, what am I in your eyes?"

I shook my head. "I... I don't know."

He handed me a slice of the peach. Juice dripped down his fingers, and I swallowed reflexively, an image of me taking his fingers into my mouth to clean them entering my mind unbidden. *What is wrong with me*?

Forcing the thought away, I reached for the peach but didn't eat it right away, waiting for him to eat his piece first. "See? Not poisoned," he said after he swallowed.

"If I eat this, it won't keep me trapped here, right?"

"No," he answered, and I ate it, its sweet and tangy taste coating my tongue. He carved another piece out as he spoke again. "You will allow yourself to be trapped here instead."

I nearly choked. "No, I won't," I said as I collected myself. "I'm going to go home. You're going to let me go home."

"I cannot," he said, holding the other piece out to me. "You have already consented."

I refused it this time. "When did I?"

"Last night. I know you remember. I asked you if you could still think straight."

The memory finally hit me. "That shouldn't count! You waited until I was about to..." I couldn't even bring myself to say the words, my cheeks heating.

"You would have agreed even if I had not done that," he replied confidently. "You would have agreed the moment I first approached you, had I asked then."

I wanted to say I wouldn't have, but deep down, I knew I would have. I would have agreed to anything last night, even if he wasn't edging me. He'd preyed on my emotional state and taken advantage of it. "What's stopping you from just letting me go, even if I did consent?" I asked.

"We have something of a contract between us now." He held up his left hand. "Hold out your left hand."

I debated about resisting him for exactly two seconds before lifting my hand, holding it out in front of me. Something told me he would have forced me to obey, anyway. As I did, though, I suddenly became aware of a gossamer shadow encircling my ring finger. It sparkled with an ethereal darkness, seeming to pulse with energy as delicate strands wove together, taking the shape of a ring.

I yanked my hand back, startled, and doing so drew my attention to a slender, string-like tendril attached to the ring on my finger, having grown taut with my action. My gaze followed the shimmering string all the way to Enver's hand, to the shadow that wrapped around his left ring finger in a perfect imitation of the one around mine.

"I cannot just let you go," he murmured. "You and I are bound until the demands of the labyrinth are fulfilled."

"I didn't sign anything, though," I objected, but my voice lacked any kind of confidence.

The tether between us felt weightless, but I could sense a pull toward him. Were all the contradicting feelings I had because of whatever connection he had created between us? I tried to touch the ring, but my fingers went through the shadowy wisps.

"Not all contracts are created by physical means. Here, they are engraved in shadows. Sealed by whispered consent." Enver reached out to brush his fingers against mine, and our rings seemed to react to each other, tendrils reaching out for each other. "Or cried out consent, in your case."

I tried to pull my hand away, but he seized it. "Why a ring?"

"I wonder," he responded, studying our hands, eyes narrowing briefly before he let go.

Silence stretched between us as my mind raced. I couldn't doubt this was real. Not with proof right before my eyes. I either remained here forever or took on his labyrinth. I grimaced a bit, my mind still trying to battle with the idea that this wasn't a twisted dream. But no matter how desperate I'd been last night, I couldn't abandon my life like this. "These demands of your labyrinth," I started, settling my hand back into my lap. "What are they? Challenges? All I have to do is complete them, right?"

Enver didn't respond for a moment, his focus still on the murky ring on his own hand. Then he snapped out of it, looking back at me. "What the demands look like depends on the participant. I cannot tell you what yours will be. The labyrinth will bring you to what you desire most, and after that, you must figure out the rest yourself. But yes, all you have to do is complete it."

"How many people have completed your labyrinth before?"

"Two."

"Two? Like, two hundred?" I pressed. "Thousand?"

"Two," he said again, unequivocally, leaving no room for misinterpretation this time.

It felt like a rock had settled on my chest, crushing the air out of my lungs. *Two*? Only two out of the hundreds who'd attempted his labyrinth had completed it? How was that possible? What did his labyrinth entail?

"What about the ones who fail? What happens to them?" I asked.

"They become mine. Forever."

His words echoed in my ears, sending a shudder through my body. The possessiveness in his voice was unmistakable. "Yours?" I repeated. "As in?"

"As in, they serve me in any way I see fit. They are mine to do with as I please, whatever that may be."

I abruptly stood up from the table, my heart hammering in my chest. The way he spoke, like those who failed his labyrinth were his possessions, made me feel sick. He sounded proud of it, even. Preying on the hopeless, forcing them into his messed-up, twisted world. It was despicable. "I know what you are now."

His gaze lifted, following my movements. "And what's that?"

"A monster," I said, louder than I'd meant to, the word echoing around the empty dining room.

He went still for a moment, and then his eyes narrowed. Neither of us moved. The silence grew, thickening between us, and my skin prickled at the darkening of Enver's expression, the intensity of his gaze as it burned into mine. "A monster?" he finally spoke, his tone deceptively soft.

I swallowed. "What you're doing is wrong."

Enver rose to his feet as well now, the muscles in his jaw tensed. "Is it? They all agreed to it. They knew the risks. The rewards."

"They agreed to become your—your possessions?" I said in disbelief, backing away from the table, my body screaming at me to run.

"Yes," he responded, his voice low and hard as he approached me. "Some did not even bother with the labyrinth. Some came crawling to me, begging me to take them. Begging to become mine. To forget everything else and exist only for me."

I shook my head, my back bumping against the wall as I continued a steady path backward, wanting as much space between Enver and me as possible. "No. No, I don't believe that. You must have forced them—"

"I do not force anyone into doing anything," Enver snapped.

"What do you call this?" I cried.

"An *agreement*," he all but growled, pressing a hand against the wall next to my head, trapping me in.

"You tricked me!"

"You consented. And I have been generous with you. I have given you a choice. One I have never offered anyone else."

My breath caught in my throat as I realized what he meant. "To become yours? How is that any different from those who failed to beat your labyrinth?"

"Because I would also be yours," he said, bringing his free

hand up to my jaw, grasping it gently. "Entirely. Every breath I take would be for you. Every inch of my being would belong to you. I could be your sanctuary and your undoing. I would give you everything you ever wished for. Follow your every word. Obey your every command. There is nothing I would deny you. Nothing, my little lover—as long as you are mine."

I found myself unable to breathe as Enver leaned in, closing the distance between us, his cheek brushing against mine as he inclined his head, his lips now ghosting over the skin of my ear. My eyes fluttered shut, his sweet promises weaving into my mind, ensnaring me in their grasp. Wasn't that what I always wanted? Someone to cherish me? To want me? Entirely and wholly? Enver offered that to me. An eternity of everything I ever dreamed was right here. All I had to do was let go.

"I would unravel the constellations and lay them at your feet," he promised softly. "I would tear the stars from the sky and build you a throne of stardust and worship you upon it until the end of time. All you have to do is say yes."

Despite everything, I once again yearned to lean into his touch, to feel his lips on mine.

It would be easy to give in to his promises. To him.

"I would love you," he breathed into my neck, his arms coming around my waist to drag me against him, his lips now pressing against my throat.

The tension snapped as ice rushed through my veins. His words might have been filled with promise and allure, but I knew his intentions were deceitful and self-serving. I couldn't fall for it. I pushed against his chest, turning my head away. "Stop it!"

When he stepped back, arms falling away from me, I knew he'd done it by his own will rather than my strength. Like how everything that had happened between us had been done by his design. "Why do you refuse what you are so desperate for?" he asked, his expression cold and distant once more.

Why...

You'll just go throw yourself at the next person who offers you the slightest bit of affection. You're desperate for something you don't even understand.

My hands curled into fists. I wouldn't prove Julian right. I wouldn't let Enver take advantage of me.

Enver watched me with a calculating look. "I assume you have made your decision."

"I'm not yours," I said, straightening my back, as if appearing taller would add some force to my words. "I won't *ever* be yours. I'm going to challenge your labyrinth, and I'm going to overcome it."

"Your despair is strong, but it seems your will is stronger," he remarked. "You are welcome to challenge my labyrinth. I will not beg you to become mine. Though, the result will be the same as all the others, my little lover. You will be mine in the end."

"I won't," I responded, my hands clenching into fists. The shadow ring on my finger settled coolly against my palm, a stark reminder of what I had to lose if I failed. "Tell me how to begin the labyrinth."

His gaze flicked to the door behind me. "Exit this room, and you will find yourself at the entrance. Make your way back up to me. Do that, and you succeed."

I waited for more information, but he stayed silent. "That's it?" I prompted.

He tilted his head in mock consideration. "I suppose, for someone as committed as you, I can do something more. You may have forty-eight hours to complete it."

Forty-eight hours? Was that supposed to be a lot of time? "How much time do you usually give people?" I asked, nervous now.

"I do not give anyone else time limits."

My eyes widened. "What? That's not fair—"

"You claim I am a monster for what I have done," he said, cutting me off as he pressed closer again, his voice dropping dangerously. "I would rather be a monster on my own terms."

My heart hammered frantically as he reached for the door handle behind me, my nose brushing against the silk of his shirt. "I didn't—"

He swung the door open. "Your time begins now."

6

Harsh wind whipped around me as I spun and stepped through the door into a flower garden—or what I assumed used to be a flower garden. The dense scent of decay filled the air. Wilted petals clung futilely to the skeletal remains of perhaps once vibrant flowers, now brown and melancholy. Vines twisted around crumbled pillars. Weeds claimed every inch of the ground, brushing against my calves. Hedges towered over me, sickly brown and wiry, stretching the length of the garden, their dead limbs stretching up high into the night sky.

Night sky?

My head tilted up toward the bright glow of the moon. It had just been morning. I'd seen daylight peeking through Enver's curtains. How was it nighttime now? I turned back, but the door I'd come out of was gone, as well as any hint of the enigmatic man himself. I shivered, wrapping my arms around myself, regretting now that I hadn't taken up his offer on warmer clothing.

But no sooner had the thought entered my mind than I

forced it away. *No*. I would not take him up on anything anymore.

"I just need to find my way back to him," I told myself, looking beyond the abandoned garden to the castle silhouetted in the distance.

It loomed across the sky, daunting and beautiful. Spires crowned towers, their steep points piercing the night, threatening to cut the clouds. My gaze followed the skyline to its midpoint, where a monumental clock tower jutted out, the moon casting beams of light across its ornate face. The second hand ticked down as I watched, reminding me my time was dwindling. It struck the hour, and the resounding, heavy toll of its bell reverberated through me.

I forced myself to look away, turning my attention to the ground, noticing my heels resting amongst the sagging crabgrass. I didn't know how they got there and didn't want to. I slipped into them, glad I didn't have to go about this barefoot, then faced the hedges again, noticing an opening in the shrubbery. An entrance to the labyrinth.

I braced myself before crossing the overgrowth to the entry. I nearly tripped on the uneven dirt, my heels sinking into the soft soil. What little light the moon provided all but disappeared as I entered the hedges, immediately met by a wall of dead bramble and a sense of claustrophobia. The tall hedges blocked all sight, leaving me unsettled. I looked left, then right, only seeing muddled darkness waiting each way down the narrow path.

"I can do this," I assured myself. "I'm good at corn mazes. This won't be any different."

I turned to the right, placing my hand against the thicket to keep myself grounded, and started making my way down the path. I'd approach this like a corn maze—follow along the wall and turn in the same direction whenever I came to a fork. Then I'd be able to make my way out of it easily.

Or so I told myself.

The longer I walked along the path, the more unsettled I became. Silence enveloped me, my footsteps and heartbeat the only source of noise. Errant branches stretched into the path, catching my skin and dress, making me jump at every unexpected touch. Shadows cloaked the edges of the path, and I eyed them warily, wondering if they were sentient or harmless.

At each fork I came to, I turned right, and then right again. On my tenth turn right, I saw a break in the hedges. A satisfied smile crossed my face as I hurried to the gap, slipping out of the maze.

Only to find myself in the same place I started.

I stood still for a second, trying to process it. The crumbled pillars seemed to taunt me as my gaze fell upon them, annoyingly familiar.

"How is that possible?" I asked out loud, facing the labyrinth again, my brows furrowing. "Did it just lead me in a circle?"

Maybe I'd turned left when I thought I'd turned right? I frowned, annoyed with myself, and then plunged back into the labyrinth, attempting the same strategy as before. Only to be spit out at the beginning again, and again, and again.

My frustration mounted. I shoved my way through the hedges, not caring if the branches scratched me. I picked up my pace, jogging, then nearly sprinting, following the same path I took before again and again.

"Oh, come on!" I cried out, irritated, as I appeared back in the flower garden again, the castle even further away now. As if I'd been walking in the opposite direction the entire time. And for all I knew, I *had* been walking in the wrong direction, judging by the fact that this time, I'd ended up in a part of the garden I hadn't seen yet.

But it was still the garden. Not the castle.

The whole thing had to be a trick. Some messed up scheme

by Enver. For all I knew, he was watching me, getting a sick satisfaction from my struggles.

I whirled around, ready to storm back into the maze, when a flicker of light in the distance caught my eye. Slowly turning back toward it, I realized the glow came from a fountain. Moonlight danced off water flowing down its indistinct form.

That was strange. The entire garden seemed forsaken, yet the fountain still held water? I began moving closer to it, my footsteps crunching against the dried leaves and weeds. The babbling sound of water splashing gently into the basin filled the air, breaking the otherwise eerie silence of the place.

As I drew nearer to it, its shape became more distinguishable. I halted involuntarily, a disquieting feeling coming over me. Like I was somewhere I shouldn't be, seeing something I shouldn't see.

Carved out of statuary white marble stood one of the most beautiful women I'd ever seen. Bathed by the lunar glow, a soft halo shone down from her delicately sculpted hair, her long and straight tresses cascading down to her waist. Every inch of her voluptuous body seemed sculpted with careful attention to detail, from her flowing gown that seemed to ruffle in the wind to her soft smile.

The water cascading down her alluring visage was crystal clear, as was the marble creating her. No sign of algae or any kind of overgrowth, unlike the rest of the neglected garden.

One of her hands was outstretched as if reaching for me, welcoming me closer, and I obeyed the silent command. I approached the basin, kicked off my heels, and climbed over the wall into the freezing cold water. The frigidness of it had me sucking in a quick breath. Up close, she looked even more lifelike. Almost alive, if not for her unnatural stillness.

I reached out to touch her cheek, wondering if it would feel warm under my palm.

"What are you doing?"

The sharp cry of a feminine voice made me jump, whipping around to face the source of the sound, losing my footing in the process. Before I could catch my balance, a blurred movement caught my eye, and I cried out as hands gripped my shoulders, shoving me down. I plunged into the water, but I didn't hit the bottom. My eyes flew open in shock as I sunk down, down much further than the shallowness of the basin should have allowed. I opened my mouth unconsciously, allowing water to rush in, choking me as I descended further down.

Everything turned black, and I panicked, trying to swim against the hands pushing me down. My lungs burned, screaming for air I couldn't find, and I reached out, frantic, grasping for anything, anyone.

My fingers grazed something small and solid, and I automatically closed my fist around it. As I did so, a momentary sereneness came over me. I closed my eyes, and warmth spread from my palm up my arm, fending off the biting cold.

I felt... safe.

Then, a pair of hands grabbed my shoulders—a different pair. Smaller, warmer. I barely had time to react before they hauled me out of the water and onto the basin's wall. I gasped, then choked on the sudden intake of air, rolling onto my side, water dribbling from my lips as I coughed.

"How in the hells were you drowning in there? It's like two feet of water!"

I blinked, trying to clear my vision. Looking up, I saw a young woman standing over me, her hands on her hips. Her black hair dripped at the ends, dampening the front of her white off-shoulder top.

"Are you okay?" she asked, her voice lowering, concern creeping in.

"Yes," I managed to say, pushing myself into a sitting position and looking up at the statue. Unmoved. Inanimate. Decidedly not trying to drown me.

A faint pulsing sensation came from my hand, and I glanced down, unraveling my fist to reveal a heart-shaped pendant resting against the center of my palm. Black filigree resembling wispy shadows encased a slim, fractured ruby shard. The rest of the stone missing, leaving the setting empty. A thin chain curled around it, delicate and untarnished, despite me having found it in the water.

The woman's attention turned to it. "Oh, did you drop something?"

I immediately closed my fist around it again, feeling overwhelmingly protective of it. "It's nothing." I slipped it into the pocket of my dress, more grateful than ever to have found a skintight dress with pockets.

The woman cocked her head to the side but said nothing else.

"Thank you," I said, my hand hovering over my pocket, hoping to direct her attention away from it. "For pulling me out."

"I really don't understand how you couldn't yourself, but you're welcome, all the same," she responded, flinging her dark hair over her shoulder. "But you really shouldn't be here."

Ah, she'd been the one to call out to me. "Why?"

"The lordling doesn't let anyone back here."

I tilted my head, confused. "Lordling?"

"You know. The one who kidnapped you."

I sat up, more alert. "Wait, are you doing his labyrinth too?"

She nodded. "Yes. How did you even end up back here?"

"I keep getting lost in the labyrinth."

"You mean the garden maze?" she questioned, glancing back at the hedges, confused.

I frowned. "Yeah. Isn't that his labyrinth?"

She laughed, loud and razor-edged, tinged with bitterness. "Gods, no. You haven't even started it yet."

A sour taste formed in the back of my mouth. "What?"

"The labyrinth is in his castle. *Is* his castle," she told me, folding her arms over her chest and pursing her lips. "The maze is just, I don't know. A test? Something to persuade people to give up before they even start the labyrinth? Although I'm not sure why he would want that. He benefits from someone succeeding as much as we do."

I rose to my feet, my mind reeling. "Wait, what? How does he benefit if we succeed?"

She let her arms fall against her sides again as she sighed. "I see he's still as cryptic as ever with his new participants. I'll tell you what I know, but we should leave this place for now."

"Okay," I agreed, starting to shiver. My dress and hair were completely soaked through.

"I'm Isla, by the way."

"I'm Nell," I responded, putting my heels back on, wincing at how sore my feet were from walking through the maze.

Isla's gaze swept over me, eyes softening as she took in my disheveled state. "When you enter the castle, you should find something dry to wear."

"If I make it into the castle," I muttered, walking alongside her as we made our way back to the maze.

"I can get you there," she told me as we entered the hedges again.

I glanced at her, cautious. "You can? Is that allowed?"

"The lordling has never said we can't help each other, so I take that as a yes."

"By lordling do you mean Enver?"

"Enver?" she repeated, glancing at me.

"That's what he said his name was."

Isla's brows furrowed. "He introduced himself to you by that name?"

I flushed because he'd done way, *way* more than that. "Yeah."

Isla remained quiet for a moment before shaking her head. "Well, I wouldn't call him by his name, even if he told you that. He doesn't let anyone call him by his name."

"He doesn't?"

"The last time someone did, he ensured they wouldn't ever speak again."

I didn't want to know what he did to ensure that. A shudder went through me. "How long have you been here, Isla?"

"A while. I don't really keep track of the time anymore," she responded, trekking down the path with purpose.

"So, it's true no one else has time limits," I muttered, doing my best to keep up with her.

She stopped now, turning to face me, her mouth falling open in surprise. "Wait, you have a time limit?"

"Yes. Forty-eight hours. And I think I've already wasted four getting lost in this stupid maze."

"What in the world did you do to him to make him do that?"

"Nothing!" I said immediately, but the image of me on my knees before him, taking him into my mouth, flitted into my mind. I shoved it away. "I mean. I might have insulted him."

Isla started moving again, her mouth twisted into a frown. "I didn't think he could feel offended."

"He does seem... composed."

"No, I mean, he *shouldn't* be able to feel offended," she said, and then abruptly stepped into the dead bramble. "This way."

I watched in shock as she disappeared through it with no resistance. No branches tore at her clothing or skin. "What the hell?"

"Illusions," she called from the other side. "Did you expect anything less?"

I stepped up to it cautiously, putting my hand out first, and drew in a breath as my hand went right through. My body followed as I moved forward, not feeling the slightest scratch of the dead hedge. "No wonder I couldn't find my way through," I said dryly.

She gave me a half-smile before starting off at a brisk pace again. "You need to rely on more than just what your eyes can see. The lordling can manipulate more than just me and you."

"What did you mean Enver shouldn't be able to feel offended?" I asked, curious.

"The way you call him by name so easily is unsettling," she said, giving a dramatic shudder. "But to answer that—he doesn't have emotions."

My body froze and my feet suddenly felt heavy. "What do you mean by that?"

"I mean exactly that. A long time ago, his emotions were taken from him. And that's why I said when someone succeeds, it benefits him. Every time someone completes their labyrinth, he gets an emotion back."

"But that's..." I trailed off, my chest feeling tight.

That couldn't be right. Enver had promised me love—*vowed* he'd love me if I stayed with him. He'd sounded so convincing that I was almost tempted to stay. To not even bother with the labyrinth. To become his.

"This is all a means to an end for him," Isla said, now a few yards ahead of me, not realizing I'd stopped. "A way to regain what he's lost. And he doesn't care what cost it comes at for anyone."

I forced myself to catch up to her again, lost in my thoughts now, mindlessly following her through another fake hedge.

If what she said was accurate, it meant that nothing Enver had promised was true. Nothing he *said* was true. Everything was just to manipulate me. Even sleeping with me. My jaw clenched, anger and shame surging through me. And I'd just let him do it. Not just once, either. I'd fallen for his tricks twice and then some. I'd been in my most vulnerable state, and he'd exploited that.

"How do you know all this?" I asked, my voice sounding scratchy as I tried to dislodge the lump in my throat.

"I told you." She glanced over her shoulder at me with a hard look. "I've been here for a long time."

Without another word, she held out her arm, gesturing toward an opening, and this time, when I stepped through, the monstrous castle I'd only seen from a distance now loomed before us. We stood in front of the grand clock tower, which meant we were at the center of the castle. Its wings stretched out on either side of us, enclosing us in a sweeping courtyard.

Up close, I found the castle as menacing as it was beautiful. Weathered by time, various stones made up its walls, creating a faded mosaic. Vines crawled up as high as I could see, stretching across the glass panes that made up the arched windows. Not one source of light shone through the dozens of windows I could make out, keeping everything in a bleak murkiness.

The steady ticking of the clock tower's hands met my ears, echoing over the grounds. The sound alone enough to make me nervous.

"The castle will allow you inside," Isla said. "Go through the courtyard up to the giant metal gate. You won't miss it."

I tore my attention away from the castle and back to her. "What will you do?"

"I'm trying to find something," she responded distractedly, shifting on her feet. "Good luck. I hope you make it out of here."

"Thank you for your help. All of it," I said sincerely.

Isla waved me off, smiling. "Don't mention it. Keep your wits about you, Nell. Don't fall for his traps."

My hands curled into fists. "I won't."

Isla disappeared back into the maze, and I watched after

her for a moment before turning to face the courtyard. Wiry and overgrown shrubs decorated the grassy area, surrounded by a brick pathway. I started across the lawn, my damp clothing clinging to me uncomfortably, my hair limp and still dripping.

The center of the courtyard housed a gazebo made of marble. I walked up to it, trailing my hand along one of its thick pillars as I climbed the three steps to its platform. A dome made up its roof, not entirely covered, a latticework of elegant filigree allowing slim beams of moonlight to shine through.

Suddenly, a slight tug came from my ring finger, and I looked down to see the thin strand of shadow reaching out behind me.

"I see your lover is not the only cheater in your relationship."

I didn't jump, but my pulse quickened at the sound of Enver's low register. "What are you doing here?"

"I am considering sending you back to the entrance of the maze to teach you a lesson."

I spun toward him, my pulse jumping as I took in his appearance. He had changed his outfit from the last time I'd seen him. He now wore a short, sheer kimono-like top left undone so his built chest and brutal scar were on display. His trousers sat low on his hips, revealing the tempting V of his abdominal muscles.

My fingers longed to touch him, but I kept them at my side.

I had to force my gaze back to his face, afraid of what I'd do if I kept staring. "I'm not a cheater," I said, his words catching up to me.

"No? Then what would you call this?"

"I got help. From a friend."

Enver watched me for a long moment, his gaze so intent I found it difficult to maintain eye contact. "Help from a friend," he repeated slowly, testing the words as if they were foreign.

"My, are you ever the trusting one. You just met that nuisance, yet you already refer to her as a friend?"

"She helped me."

"Is that all it takes? I shall keep that in mind if I want you to believe my words blindly."

I glared at him. "At least she didn't sleep with me to deceive me."

His eyes hardened. "I did not sleep with you to deceive you."

"No? Then why did you?"

"You *wanted* me," he said, stepping closer to me. "Do not lie," he added sharply as I opened my mouth to disagree.

I pressed my lips together as I backed up, trying to keep the distance between us. "You just wanted to trick me."

"Did you forget? You kissed me first."

"You should have stopped it there, then," I said as my back hit one of the pillars. "If you were so sure I'd agree back in the club, you should have just stolen me away then."

"I would have if you had not offered me so much more. A mere kiss or an irresistible night of pleasure? Why deny myself when you desired me as deeply as I desired you?"

My mouth went dry as he lifted his hand, fingertips grazing my throat, sending static electricity through me. Again, I wanted to lean into his touch. I wanted more of it. "You did something to me," I accused weakly. "You made me want you—"

"No," he interjected roughly, the low and gravelly sound of his voice making desire pool within me. "You wanted me of your own volition. You still want me, even now."

"I don't—"

"Do not lie to me," he warned again, his fingers trailing down to my collarbone, where he traced its length before following the curve down my sternum.

The air caught in my throat, and my voice came out breathy. "I'm not."

"Then, if I touched you right now, I would not find you as soaked as your pitiable appearance?"

My face flushed as I met his intense and provocative gaze. The hand on my sternum splayed out, keeping me pressed to the pillar as his other hand touched the bare skin of my thigh, just under the hem of my dress, causing me to jolt. My legs parted unconsciously, and Enver's fingers skated up higher toward where he would find the affirming answer to his question.

I needed to tell him to stop. To move away.

His fingers halted just shy of where my body yearned for him to touch. "Tell me to stop. Tell me you do not want this."

The words refused to form. His fingers teased closer. Their heat burned against my cool skin, but once again, he stopped before they reached their mark.

"My little lover," he murmured. "Still so eager for me. Even now, after you claim that I have used and deceived you. Tell me to touch you, and I will give you everything you crave."

It took a mortifying amount of resolve for me to pull myself together and push his hand away. "Stop."

"You are not denying that you desire me," he said, but his hands returned to his sides as he fell back a step. "My offer still stands. Come with me, and I will be everything you need. Give yourself to me, and I will fulfill your every wish and desire. I will love you and adore you—"

"Will you?" I said, cutting him off, willing my legs to stop quivering. "*Can* you? Are you even capable of being anything other than cruel?"

He stilled, his features turning sharp, and I knew Isla had told me the truth.

"How can you promise to love me when you can't even feel love?" I demanded, advancing into the space he'd created, the heat of his body warming my cold skin again. "Can you even feel anything?"

"That mouse never knows when to hold her tongue," Enver said, a muscle in his jaw jumping.

"What was your plan?" I asked. "I would have found out you couldn't love me, eventually."

"Would you have?" he challenged, his gaze boring into mine. "You? Who would do anything for love? I would have easily continued to manipulate you. I would have given you all the pretty promises you wanted, empty as they may have been. I would have had to do nothing other than praise and please you to make you fall for me. And you would be none the wiser, simply content with my attention. Content with me keeping you as mine."

I flinched, his words stinging me. It scared me to realize how much of what he said was true. How much he could have gotten away with had I let it happen. I couldn't deny what he said, even if I wanted to.

"What does love mean to you?" he asked.

I didn't answer. I'd turned down his offer of what I'd thought love was—to offer myself entirely to someone. To sacrifice everything for them. To take validation in their choosing to be by my side. But if it wasn't that, then what was love?

"I will answer for you," he said. "Your notion of love is one where the actual emotion is not required to provide you with what you desire. You would have been satisfied with my presence. My touch. My validation of you. You would have misled yourself into believing I was in love with you, and I would have never told you otherwise. You would have let me take advantage of you and your heart without complaint."

"No," I said, lowering my gaze, trying to hide that his words had hit their mark. If Isla hadn't told me the truth, if I had let myself be swept away by Enver, then...

"Do not be upset," he murmured, tenderly cupping my face

in his hands, angling my jaw up so I looked at him. "I can be so terribly tempting."

"I understand now," I whispered, my throat tight.

"Understand what, my little lover?"

"You're not only a monster. You're *heartless*."

Enver's expression iced over, his dark eyes narrowing, pupils constricting. His grip tightened on my jaw, and I knew I needed to run. I twisted on my heel, but he didn't attempt to stop me as I ran for the exit. Instead, shadows rose swiftly from the ground, growing taller and taller until they encased the entire gazebo, blocking off the exit and the moonlight, shrouding us in darkness. I came to a stop, tentatively reaching out, only to feel how solid and impenetrable the shadows were.

"You are right," Enver breathed against my ear. "I am."

I gasped, unable to see anything. "Enver—"

"Heartless. Cruel. A monster."

His fingers circled around my wrist, forcing me to spin around. The pitch black disoriented me as he flattened my hand against his bare chest, just over his heart. I reached for him with my other hand, gripping the silky fabric of his top to steady myself.

"What are you doing?" I asked, my voice rising. He didn't respond, and I tried to pull my hand back, but he kept it against him. "Enver, let me..."

The rest of my sentence died on my tongue. I fell silent, focusing on the lack of... *anything* coming from his chest. No thud of a heartbeat, no reassuring pulse under his skin. Nothing. I pushed my hand harder against him, searching for any kind of movement, but only an unsettling stillness met my efforts.

No heartbeat.

No heart.

"You're heartless?" I repeated, this time in horrified disbelief. "How? Why?"

The clock tower overhead sounded off, filling the courtyard with deep, dissonant chimes. All at once, the shadows dissipated, suffusing us in the moonlight once more. Enver had stepped away from me in the dark, his back now toward me as he glanced up at the clock tower. "Your time is wasted here. Enter the labyrinth."

"Wait," I started, but shadows swirled up from the ground again, obscuring him, and when they vanished, he was gone.

7

Enver didn't have a heart.

I stared down at my hand as I made my way across the rest of the courtyard, the phantom sense of *nothingness* under my palm making goosebumps break out across my skin. How was it possible for Enver to be alive with no heart? How had he lost it? Had it happened at the same time he'd lost his emotions? Was his loss of emotions a direct consequence of losing his heart? Had it been his choice, or...?

The shadow ring on my left finger eddied, capturing my attention. I couldn't see the string that connected me to him anymore. Did it only appear when he was near?

At least that could serve as a warning.

Anxiety settled in my gut as I approached the front gate of the castle. Intricately wrought with scrollwork, I couldn't help but admire it, reaching my hand out to brush against the cool metal. Behind it, a giant solid oak door marked the entrance to the labyrinth. However, as I stepped back and scanned the gate, I could see no way past it. No lever on either side of it. No button of any sort. I couldn't even tell if it opened by sliding diagonally or vertically.

"Isla said it would open for me," I said to myself, placing a hand on my chin, and studying the metal again. I didn't see any sort of machinery that would allow the gate to move on its own, though.

I hesitantly reached out, pressing my hand against the cool metal. A subtle vibration met my touch as if the castle itself acknowledged my presence. The feeling resembled a purring cat under my hand. I gasped and jerked my hand back as the intricate designs melted away, disappearing before my eyes until only the oak door remained in front of me.

Cautiously, I touched the weathered door, feeling deep grooves under my palm, revealing scars of time the gate hadn't shown. The ancient wood yielded to my hand. A hushed creak echoed across the courtyard as the door swung open, revealing the yawning darkness of the labyrinth beyond.

My hand fell back to my side.

Darkness.

What else had I expected?

A chill I'd come to associate with Enver's shadows swept over me, sending goosebumps across my skin. I took a steadying breath and then stepped inside, blanketing myself in the blackness. I didn't look over my shoulder as the door closed behind me again with a muted thud, trapping me inside. Although anxiety had already started to weigh my limbs down, I forced myself to move forward slowly, hands stretched out in front of me to feel through the dark.

Something suddenly wrapped around my wrist.

I nearly screamed. Another joined the first, snaking around my forearm, and another, now on my ankle. "Get off me!" I cried, trying to shake them off, kicking out my foot, spinning around, trying to find the source of the tendrils, my heart in my throat. Was it Enver? "Let go!"

More converged on me, encircling my arms, legs, waist, and hair. I shouted now, being shoved forward off my feet. I squeezed my eyes shut, fighting against the shadows, but they were too strong, too many. They pulled me further into the darkness, my cries breaking the surrounding silence. The cold tendrils dragging me overloaded my senses, making me panic and writhe within them.

And then suddenly, they released me. I fell to all fours, eyes opening to see a plush burgundy carpet under me. The quiet was deafening now, my ears still ringing from my own cries as I looked up, finding myself in a haunting corridor. It stretched endlessly in front of me, lined with faded tapestries and dimly lit sconces chipped and worn with age.

"What the hell was that?" I said out loud, unable to move, my skin still prickling from the residual shock of the encounter.

"Mistress."

I threw myself sideways, scrambling backward as a voice spoke from above me, but this time, to my relief, it wasn't any kind of shadow. A young man stood above me, gazing down at me with a kind smile. He wore black trousers and a tailored waistcoat woven with gold stitching over a black button-up, with a black bowtie adorning his neck.

"Do you need a hand, my lady?" he asked, offering a gloved hand out to me.

I hesitated before taking it, allowing him to help me back to my feet. "My lady?" I repeated.

"My lord has instructed us to refer to you as such."

"Your lord?" I took in his outfit again, and my eyes widened. "You're one of his servants?"

He bowed his head. "My lord wanted me to bring this to you."

I looked down as he held out a bundle of white fabric. I took it, letting it unravel to reveal an elegant satin dress decorated with light blue embroidery, the shade startlingly similar to the color of my eyes.

"And this," the servant said, handing me a silky white cape. "Will you require help in dressing?"

I inspected the cape, confused. "Why did he want me to have this?"

"He hoped you would be warmer with it on."

My heart skipped a beat despite myself. I couldn't be grateful to Enver for simply offering me dry clothing. And if my damp dress hadn't been so uncomfortable, I would have refused this, but I couldn't imagine continuing the labyrinth like this. An incessant chill was in the air, and I doubted it would go away. "Thank you," I said.

"I'm sorry the castle's appearance isn't at its best," he responded, glancing down the corridor. "The lord returned in a mood earlier."

I frowned. What did that have to do with what the castle looked like? "Where are all the other servants?" I asked.

"We're everywhere. Call on us whenever you need to," he told me, bowing again.

It made me uncomfortable. "Uh, no need for that. I'm just a participant in the labyrinth like you are. Were." I grimaced inwardly, hoping that didn't insult him.

Instead, the servant glanced up at me again, confusion clouding his eyes. "Labyrinth?"

"Is that not where we are?" I asked.

"We're in the castle," he informed me.

"Yes, but aren't you his servant because you failed the labyrinth?"

"No, my lady, I serve my lord willingly," he responded. "My lord selected us to become his loyal servants. I'm grateful to have the chance to serve him. I don't recognize this labyrinth you speak of. Perhaps you refer to the castle garden?"

My grip on the dress in my hands became tighter. Something wasn't right here. Enver said those who failed the labyrinth had become his servants. So why was this man saying he was serving him willingly? How did he not know about the labyrinth? Did they lose their memories when they failed?

"How did you come to be here?" I asked. "When did you come here?"

He hesitated. "I..."

"What's your name?" I continued. "Were you promised something if you came here?"

The servant's eyes darted around nervously. "How *did* I come to be here? I can't remember. I think I wanted something. How long has it been?" His gaze met mine again, eyes round with distress. "The labyrinth—" His mouth suddenly closed, his gaze turning vacant.

"What about it?" I prompted.

"My lady, you should change before you catch an illness," he said, a smile returning to his lips, his expression serene once more.

Dread caused the hair on my neck to rise. Enver didn't just rule over the labyrinth—his control had to extend to the people inside his castle. He had some kind of influence over those who failed. They weren't servants of their own free will, even if Enver claimed they were. Something was preventing this servant's memory from returning. Keeping him under Enver's control.

It was so *wrong*.

And if I failed the labyrinth, I would end up just like them.

"Thank you for your help," I said tersely. "I'll be on my way."

"Of course, my lady," he responded, bowing his head and disappearing through a door that suddenly appeared in the corridor wall as he approached it.

Alone again, I clutched the dress in my hands, trying to keep my approaching panic at bay. There was more at stake than I'd thought. Enver said his servants served him willingly but failed to mention that he *mind-controlled* them into it. He enticed and entrapped them. And he planned to do the same to me.

I stared down at the dress, wanting to throw it away, but rationality won over the urge to refuse anything Enver offered me. This dress was longer and less restrictive than my current one. Not to mention less wet.

I moved into the dimmest corner of the corridor before peeling my dress off and sliding the new one on. The satin clung to me with welcoming warmth, although the neckline plunged deep between my breasts, showing more cleavage than I would have liked. I struggled to clasp the cape over my shoulders, unused to the garment but wanting the extra layer to fend off the cold of the labyrinth.

A strange feeling came over me, and I paused. The dress felt... off. Not in texture, but in a way that made a tightness form in my chest. It felt wrong. But I couldn't explain why. It formed to me perfectly, as if tailored to my exact measurements. Was that why it felt off? Had Enver somehow made this for me in such a short amount of time?

I hesitated another moment, then brushed off the feeling. It was clean and warm. I'd take it.

My old dress pooled on the ground, and I decided to leave it there. It didn't mean anything to me, especially now. I would never dress to impress Julian again. I started to walk away when an almost physical tug pulled at my heart. Turning, my attention returned to my dress, and I knelt beside it, following the phantom pull.

The pendant.

I reached into the pocket that held it, retrieving it. It pulsed faintly in my hand—in the way Enver's heart should have under my touch—warm and alive. Like it'd been resting against my skin the entire time, soaking in its heat.

It made me pause for a moment. If Enver's heart was missing, then...

No, I told myself. That couldn't be. A heart wouldn't fit into a pedant like this, to begin with.

I touched the thin piece of ruby that remained in the setting. Where was the rest of it? What happened to it?

Why did I even care?

Still, I refused to part with the pendant, standing back up. I moved my long hair over my shoulder, clasped it around my neck, and let it settle against my chest. I didn't understand why, but it felt essential to keep with me.

As I faced back down the corridor, I shouted in surprise as a shadow appeared before me, dangling something from its misty form. Shoes, I realized. Some sort of style of ballet flats. To replace my heels, I was sure.

"I'm not going to say thank you," I said, taking the new shoes from the shadow and kicking off my heels.

After putting on the flats, which somehow also fit me perfectly, my feet immediately felt better. I abandoned my heels with my old dress, then moved down the corridor again. The shadow followed alongside me, twisting and undulating, phasing through me every time it got too close.

I stopped. "Do you need something?" I asked, feeling absolutely insane for talking to a shadow. But I'd seen even more unbelievable things here already, so I didn't know why I felt like that.

It shimmied over to the corridor's wall and raised a tendril as if beckoning me.

I hung back for a moment before sighing and walking over to it. It morphed into the wall, creating the silhouette of a doorway. When I reached out to touch it, it manifested into a physical door. I hesitated, and the pendant on my chest pulsed softly as if encouraging me. I reached for the door handle and pushed it open.

When I stepped through, I found myself in a sunny garden. It took a moment to adjust to the sunlight, and I blinked rapidly, bringing up a hand to shield my eyes. The sweet scent of flora wafted over me alongside a gentle breeze, but it did little to soothe my irritation.

The damn shadow had tricked me into going back out to the garden.

"Oh, my. What do we have here?"

I turned quickly, squinting against the sun, my gaze landing on a beautiful woman dressed in a gown fit for a queen. Dark green, cinched at the waist, and opening to a wide skirt, every inch stitched with gold embroidery. She had brown skin and chestnut hair twisted elegantly into a cascading braid that rested over her right shoulder. Her hazel eyes shone in the sun as she walked toward me. And not only her eyes sparkled—scales did, too. On her cheeks and neck, shimmering iridescently in a kaleidoscope of colors.

Startled a bit, I moved back, noting her webbed ears. "Oh!"

She laughed, melodic and alluring. "Is this your first time meeting merfolk?"

"Merfolk?" I repeated, my mouth dry.

"Don't worry. I won't lure you out into the sea," she teased. "But my younger sister might. She's had a hard time adjusting to the new laws, and I think you're just her type."

I took another step back.

Another musical laugh left her lips. "I'm just teasing. I suppose I should start with hello."

"Um. Hi," I replied awkwardly, realizing now that this wasn't Enver's castle garden, and unable to tear my gaze away from her scales.

She smiled at me. "How did you get here?"

I didn't know if telling her a shadow turned into a door and led me here was a good idea. "Where is here, exactly?" I questioned.

"It seems like a place from my memories." She stretched

her hand, glancing down at it curiously. "Although it also seems I've returned to my past self, too."

I stared at her. Because that was a normal sentence that people said. Although, I wasn't sure what normal was anymore. Not since that night in the club. I couldn't even confidently say it had only been last night with the odd way time seemed to work in the labyrinth. "What exactly is that supposed to mean?" I asked, keeping my tone light so the question didn't sound rude.

"I'm trying to figure that out myself," she responded, a crease appearing on her forehead, but then her lips curved up again when she looked back at me. "If I may be so forward, are you challenging the labyrinth too?"

"I—yes," I said, taken aback at the fact she'd mentioned the labyrinth so casually. I was still coming to terms with it. "I am. How did you know?"

"Aside from the fact you appeared out of thin air?"

"Ah. Right."

She laughed, hiding her mouth with her hand. "This is strange, though. I haven't met anyone else during my journey so far."

"I just started it," I told her. "Is it not normal to run into other participants?"

"In my experience, it seems that would be the case."

I frowned. Then why had I run into Isla before? And now this woman? Enver had said Isla helping me was cheating, so maybe I wasn't supposed to be meeting anyone at all?

The woman held out her hand. "I'm Neima."

"Nell," I responded, shaking her proffered hand. Her grip was delicate and slack, so I loosened my grip as well. "I don't really know what I'm doing, though."

"That's something you need to figure out yourself," she told me, her expression falling a bit as she gazed out at the garden behind me. "Although I believe I now know why I've appeared here during this moment."

A shout came from behind me before I could ask her what she meant. The sound of heavy movement on dirt approached, and I turned just in time to see multiple swords being swung upward and pointed at my heart. I stumbled back, bumping into Neima, a startled squawk leaving my lips as I caught sight of five different men wearing shining steel armor.

"Halt, intruders," the man in the middle demanded, his voice full of authority.

Neima put a hand on my shoulder reassuringly. "Steady your hand, guards. I'm Neima of Veldaria. I suggest lowering your swords before I take offense to them."

The guards didn't budge, their weapons still poised and ready. "Quiet, monster," one of them snapped.

Neima moved to stand in front of me, the rich fabric of her dress brushing against the sword tip of the man in the middle as her chest came dangerously close to it. "Do not make me repeat myself."

"Lower your weapons," a different voice commanded, and the soldiers immediately lowered their swords, dropping to one knee.

Neima inhaled softly as another woman came into view. She was dressed in similar armor to the men, but her armor was black, tailored to her form. The only part of her not covered by armor was her head, her ebony skin smooth and her face angular. Braids of black hair encircled the crown of her head, and her brown eyes narrowed as she took in the sight of me and Neima. "Princess Neima," she greeted.

"Queen Paloma," Neima responded, curtseying.

I blinked. Had I heard that right? Why were they referring to themselves as a princess and a queen?

"I did not receive any word you would be visiting," Paloma said. "Where are your guards?"

Neima's grip on my shoulder tightened. "I've only brought this one along."

Paloma scanned my body, pursing her lips, a disappointed expression crossing her face. "Surely, she offers little to no protection. I've seen more muscle on a worm."

I tried not to feel offended. Working full time from home hadn't done any favors for my health. I kept meaning to sign up for the gym, but Julian always said he didn't like muscular women and deterred me from going. I turned my head down, biting the inside of my cheek. Had Julian even realized I was missing yet? Would he even care if he had?

"I have full trust in my lady-in-waiting," Neima said, nudging me with her elbow and breaking me from my thoughts.

I nodded along immediately, unsure of what lady-in-waiting even meant. However, staying by Neima's side seemed like the smart move until I figured out what exactly I was supposed to do in the labyrinth.

"And also, I saw no need for protection since you're here," Neima added.

Paloma folded her arms over her chest, the sun glinting off her dark armor. "She looks rather human. I wasn't aware you hired humans in your service."

"She's just still maturing," Neima said, patting my cheek. "Her scales will come with time."

A slightly harder tap on my cheek had me nodding. "Right. I'm still... maturing."

Paloma didn't seem to believe me but let it drop. "Very well. Let's return to the castle before you're seen. I've been meaning to discuss something with you."

"It would be my pleasure," Neima responded, guiding me forward.

I swallowed nervously as we approached Paloma. She loomed over both Neima and me, her posture ramrod straight, eyeing me suspiciously. A slight sneer crossed her face as our eyes met, causing me to freeze before her gaze softened as she looked upon Neima.

"This is going to be hard," Neima muttered under her breath, unable to keep her eyes off Paloma.

She stepped forward and promptly tripped on her dress, falling straight into the taller woman. Paloma caught her swiftly and easily, holding her to her chest tightly. "Princess, please be careful."

I didn't miss Neima's blush as she clung to Paloma. "My apologies."

"Hold on to me. The dirt is uneven here," Paloma said, offering Neima her hand.

Neima started reaching for it but then drew back, her expression falling as she clasped her hands in front of herself. "I think it's best I don't."

Paloma frowned for a moment but then gave a brief nod. "As you wish, Princess."

Paloma's gaze lingered on Neima for a moment longer before she turned and started down a dirt path leading out of the gardens. There'd been a fondness in her eyes that made me wonder what the history between them was as I followed along, taking in the scenery. The air was summery. Not a cloud hovered in the sky, and birds chirped all around us. Mountains stretched in a long range in the distance, creating a breathtaking backdrop for the concentric castle we headed toward.

My attention caught on formidable-looking turrets perched on the outer walls of the castle. Each spire held an air of intimidation, increased by the presence of stoic guards who stood by them at the ready. They stood so still I could have mistaken them for statues displaying armor had one of them not shifted subtly.

I felt like someone had transplanted me into the Middle Ages. And for all I knew, I had been. I probably wasn't even on the same continent. Or in the same world. Was that even possible? Had Enver transported me into another world? Was his labyrinth some kind of multidimensional maze? The thought gave me anxiety. What else existed that I didn't know about? Bigfoot? The Jersey Devil? Multiple timelines?

I ran into Neima's back, not realizing she'd come to a stop, and nearly knocked both of us over. She gasped in surprise, and I wrapped my arm around her waist to keep her steady. Paloma turned back toward her, her sharp eyes immediately zeroing in on my arm holding Neima. I steadied Neima before giving Paloma a pacifying smile.

Her jaw ticked, and she scowled at me in response.

I took a step back from Neima experimentally.

Paloma's expression relaxed marginally.

Aha. So that was it.

Paloma held out her arm to Neima. "Perhaps it's best you hold on to me after all, Princess."

Neima bit her lip and nodded, placing a hand on Paloma's forearm. "Thank you."

I watched the pair curiously as we entered two giant oak doors that were not too different from the doors to Enver's palace. Inside, though, was starkly different. Instead of doom and gloom the halls were lit with luxurious chandeliers hanging from the ceiling. Silk tapestries of various colors hung on the walls, vibrant and without signs of wear. We walked on a deep burgundy rug on top of a black, glossy stone floor. Enver's castle looked absolutely decayed in comparison to this one.

We entered what I assumed to be an audience hall with high ceilings and enough room to fit at least a hundred people. Servants and maids scurried about, bowing their heads and politely greeting Paloma and Neima as they rushed by us. Paloma dismissed her soldiers, leaving the three of us alone. We made our way to a set of Victorian-style couches, and Paloma helped Neima sit on the plush bench. I attempted to sit next to Neima, but the metal of Paloma's armor jabbed me in the side as she bumped me with her hip, not so subtly guiding me to a chair next to the couch.

I sat with a stiff smile. Did she consider me some kind of threat? Wasn't a lady-in-waiting just some sort of maid?

"Ah, Princess, you have something in your hair," Paloma said, bringing her hand to Neima's head.

Neima let her, and I raised an eyebrow, not seeing anything there.

With a flourish of her hand, a small white freesia appeared in Paloma's hand, and she presented it to Neima. "For you."

Neima blushed, and to my surprise, I found myself smiling at Paloma's antics. Seeing the couples together at the club had hurt me so badly, but with Neima and Paloma, I couldn't help but feel light-hearted. The playful way they interacted with each other was refreshing and endearing. It made my heart ache, but more in a bittersweet way than a painful one.

"Careful, Queen Paloma, you continue to pretend to use magic, and my country just might label you an evil sorceress," Neima chided, taking the flower. "They already hate that you're a human."

"It's Paloma when we're alone, Princess," Paloma corrected, smirking, letting her fingertips linger against Neima's. "And let your country call me what they wish. I know you'll protect my honor."

Neima's cheeks colored an even deeper shade. "S-so, what was it you wanted to talk about?"

Paloma finally returned her hand to her side. "Let me change out of my armor. I'll have the servants bring refreshments in the meantime." She looked at me, narrowing her eyes slightly. "Sit tight."

I waited until Paloma walked away to turn toward Neima. "What's the deal between you two?" I asked.

Neima stared after Paloma, not turning away until she was

out of sight. A sigh left her lips, and she stared down at her lap. "We're lovers in the future," Neima told me, her voice holding a tinge of fondness and longing. "Despite the outrage from our families and despite the risk to our kingdoms, we found happiness and love with each other. And we were happy. For years. But it turns out happiness is not that easy to keep."

I stayed silent, waiting for her to continue.

"The responsibilities Paloma and I have in the future are many and consequential. Every day seems to be a trial against us. We want to do what's best for our kingdoms, but what happens when what's best is also what's most painful for us? Every day is harder than the last. We love each other deeply—that much I know is true. But we've reached a point where our crowns feel heavier than our love for each other. The tender moments now are replaced with misery and guilt."

Neima bit her lip, her eyes watering, and my heart fell. "Neima," I said softly.

"Paloma suffers worse than I do. Her family never accepted me. They demand an heir. Merfolk and humans used to be enemies. Times have changed, but both sides remain stubborn. But Paloma defends me. From them. From danger. From anything she can. But I can't do anything for her. She does so much for me, but there's nothing I can do. Except this."

"This?" I prompted.

"The labyrinth," she said, finally looking at me, tears clinging to her lashes. "I can stop this all before it even begins. This day is the day we kissed for the first time. I won't do it. I will reject her and save us both the heartbreak later."

My stomach knotted. Was that possible? Could the labyrinth lead to such an outcome? Could it change the future? Enver had said the labyrinth would give its participants what they wanted if they succeeded. For Neima, was it to forget what pained her?

I didn't know what to say to her. The heartbreak on her face mirrored the heartbreak carved in my chest. If I could go back in time and choose to never meet Julian again, would I? Was that what the labyrinth would eventually offer me? Maybe Neima had the right idea here. Maybe it was better to just forget everything and avoid the pain and suffering. Maybe Neima and I were the same.

"But I can't imagine a life without Paloma," Neima continued quietly. "Without her love. Nor can I imagine not loving her."

My thoughts halted, a weight crushing down on me.

No, Neima and I were not the same. Not really. Neima loved Paloma and Paloma loved Neima. They had what I could only yearn for. Julian didn't and wouldn't love me. Where I wanted to forget everything for selfish reasons, Neima wanted to forget to spare Paloma from pain. She was doing it from a place of love.

My hands clenched. I couldn't let them give up their love. Even if I couldn't have my happily ever after, I could at least try to help Neima and Paloma have theirs.

"So, what, then? You plan to be saddled with that heartbreak all alone right now?" I asked, moving to sit beside Neima on the couch. "Paloma doesn't get a say in it?"

"I don't want her to hurt anymore," Neima protested.

"You said you love each other," I said, taking her hand in mine. "Are you sure about that?"

Neima's lips curved down, and she tried to pull her hands back. "Of course I am," she said, defensive. "We have been together for the past ten years. From this very day onward. There hasn't been a moment when we've stopped loving each other despite our struggles."

"Then why are you so willing to give it up? Some people would die for a love like that," I said, feeling my throat grow tight, holding her hands tighter. "The type of love where you would sacrifice everything for each other. Where you would do anything for each other. Where you can't imagine a life without each other. You have something that some people desperately long for."

"Do they long for the pain as well? For the guilt and heartache?"

"I can't answer that," I said, lowering my gaze. "But what you're planning doesn't seem like love to me. It seems like you're running away. And that's something I know all too well about."

Neima stilled.

"I understand you want to save her from pain, but doesn't Paloma deserve a say in this?" I asked, looking back up at Neima. "What if she was the one here, trying to prevent you from suffering just because you love her? What if you were the one who didn't have a choice in this?"

"I wouldn't want that," Neima whispered, her eyes watering again.

"You two won't be able to protect each other from everything, but you can be there for each other. That's what love is. It's not just about the happy moments—it's everything that comes between them, too. If you're scared or hurting, go to Paloma and tell her. Don't do this. Shielding yourself from pain only means you also miss out on the joy."

Tears rolled down Neima's cheeks. "I want Paloma to be happy, but if I cause her pain, then what good am I to her? I don't want to be the source of her unhappiness."

"That's impossible," I assured her. "I barely know you two, but I can tell how much she cares for you already. I'm sure, even in the future, you're nothing but her happiness. That nothing would ever stop her from loving you."

"Really?" she asked, hiccuping.

I cupped Neima's face in my hands, wiping her tears with my thumbs, her scales smooth under my touch. "Really."

"But our kingdoms. Even if we can take a stand against our families, how can we provide an heir?"

"You can't adopt?" I asked. Maybe that wasn't a thing here. Or maybe there were strict rules for royalty. "What about insemination, then?"

Confusion wrinkled her brow. "Insemination?"

I hesitated. Was I really about to explain this to her? Would it change the trajectory of their future if I did? When was it even invented? But if it led to her happiness, then...

Leaning forward, I whispered in her ear, explaining the process.

"What's going on here?" Paloma's booming voice came from in front of us.

I jumped, not realizing she'd returned, and quickly withdrew my hands from Neima's face, pulling back. "Nothing!"

However, the blush once again staining Neima's cheeks definitely did not help my case, nor the flustered way she spoke. "N-nothing," she stuttered, and Paloma's fingers twitched at her side.

Paloma glanced down, but now she was dressed in more casual attire, her sword, thankfully, not attached to her hip anymore. I still tensed, realizing that was what she was reaching for. Instead of spearing me through, she folded her arms across her chest, the white linen of her top pulling against the muscles in her biceps. Her gaze darted between Neima and I, and I went to move back to my original chair, feeling the distrust radiating from her.

But as I did so, an idea hit me.

Maybe they both could use a little push.

"I may not have muscles, but I have other charms," I told Paloma, giving her the most salacious smile I could muster as I lightly brushed the fabric of Neima's dress just above her thigh, making sure not to touch her skin, just the dress.

Paloma's eye twitched, fingers once again moving to where her sword once rested against her. "Princess."

"Yes?" Neima asked, sniffing as she wiped away the remaining tears.

"I think we need to speak. Privately."

Neima inhaled softly. "You're right. We should. But before we do, I need to ask you something."

Paloma finally dragged her gaze away from me to look at Neima. "Anything."

"Paloma, if I caused you nothing but misery in the future, what would you do?" Neima asked, ducking her head, her voice barely a whisper. "Would you still want me around?"

"What would I do?" Paloma repeated, and then her answer came swiftly, "Nothing."

Neima turned her chin up, her mouth falling open as she stared at Paloma. "Nothing?"

Paloma knelt down in front of Neima, taking Neima's hands into her own. "*Nothing*. You could never cause me misery, Princess. No matter what you did. I can assure you of that."

"But what if our standings caused us distress because of our relationship with each other?"

"It would be worth it," Paloma said confidently. "Anything and everything would be worth it. Even if we were exiled from our lands, nothing would matter as long as I'm with you. I wouldn't trade you for anything, Neima."

Neima's lips trembled. "Paloma..."

"And even if it felt like the weight of the world was on our shoulders, I could bear it. I *would* bear it. As long as you continue to smile at me. If I ever seem upset, just smile at me, Neima, and it will all go away."

"A smile," Neima reiterated slowly, and then she brought one of her hands to her mouth, covering it as her eyes widened. "I see. I see now." Her eyes filled with tears again, her chin dropping toward her chest. "I've been cruel to you, Paloma. I've not smiled enough. I've let the misery get to me for far too long."

Paloma's expression turned to bewilderment as Neima began to sob softly. "Princess? What's wrong? Why are you crying?"

Without warning, Neima flung herself at Paloma, dropping onto the ground on her knees beside Paloma, hugging her fiercely. "I'll smile for you, Paloma. I promise. Forever."

Paloma didn't say anything in response. She just hugged Neima closer before pulling back to place a hand on her jaw. "Neima."

Neima put one of her hands on Paloma's cheek as well. "Paloma."

"Can I kiss you, Princess?"

Neima smiled. "Yes."

A lump formed in my throat, and I forced myself to look away from them, wanting to give them as much privacy as I could. What was it like to have someone love you so deeply? Would I ever get to know? Would I find someone who would choose me over everything else in the world? My hands clenched at the fabric of my dress, and I tried to distract myself, not wanting my jealousy to ruin such a sweet moment.

Movement caught the corner of my eye, and I turned to look out the arched windows of the castle, sitting up straighter as I noticed a door forming along one of the windows. Dark and shadowy—much like the one that had brought me here. The pendant on my chest grew hot as the door fully appeared, and I instantly knew it was for me.

Had I completed the labyrinth? Already? I stood abruptly, afraid the door would disappear.

"Nell?" Neima called from behind me.

I twisted around to face her, still in Paloma's embrace. "I think it's time for me to go," I told her.

"I think it is for me, too," she said, looking at something I couldn't see in the distance. "But I don't think I'll go just yet." She glanced at Paloma pointedly. "I want to spend more time here. You go ahead."

I nodded. "Will you be okay?"

"I will now. Thank you, Nell."

I smiled at her. "I didn't do anything. I'm sure you would have come to the same conclusion."

"I'm not sure. I don't think I was in my right mind," she admitted. "I wished so desperately to change things I lured the lord of the labyrinth to me. I'm not sure what I would have chosen if I hadn't run into you."

"What were you so desperate for?" I asked, my chest tightening at the mention of Enver.

"Happiness," she told me, her gaze turning back to Paloma, soft and affectionate. "And I think I found it again—no, I know I did. But what about you?"

"Love," I said.

"I'm sure you will find it," she responded. "You have a kind soul. I can tell. You will meet the one who makes your heart flutter and your cheeks flush soon enough."

The pendant pulsated, and I got the feeling it was urging me to go. "I'm happy for you two. I hope you live a good life together."

"As long as we're with each other, there wouldn't be any other kind," Paloma answered, and amazingly, she smiled at me.

"Goodbye, Nell," Neima said, rising from her knees and coming over to me to pull me into a hug. "I won't forget what you did for me... and what you told me."

Paloma stared hard at me as I hugged Neima back, her lips flattening further the longer the hug lasted. I purposefully gave an extra squeeze before stepping back and waving one last time. "Good luck," I said before heading to the shadow door. It churned, dark and intimidating, and I braced myself. I reached for the handle, pulled it open, and stepped through.

8

Now back in darkness, I paused, my eyes taking a moment to adjust to the lack of light. From that alone, I figured I was back in Enver's castle, and as I made out deteriorating stone stairs in front of me, it confirmed the fact. The pendant was still warm, and as I climbed the stairs, it grew hotter. The stairs winded up in a half-circle with faded carpet running down the center and stained-glass windows lining the walls. At the top, I reached a gilded door dulled by the dimness of the hall.

A lock clicked as I pushed the door open, appearing in another dark, window-lined hall. Darkness weighed on me as I walked down the hall, and the pendant cooled the further I went into the shadows. I approached a window, looking down at the murky garden. It was still nighttime here. How long had I been away? It felt like less than an hour, but I couldn't see the clock tower anymore to check.

A dead rose bush caught my gaze, and I wondered if Neima had escaped the labyrinth yet. Would she be one of the few who completed it? It seemed like she'd wanted to stay with Paloma a bit more. I couldn't blame her.

A fleeting memory of when I'd first met Julian slipped into my mind. A coworker of mine had introduced us, but as I replayed the events of our first meeting and the times that followed, I couldn't recall any lighthearted moments between us. Not like the ones between Paloma and Neima. Julian had never been playful. I couldn't remember him ever flirting with me. We'd met, started a relationship, and I'd been happy enough just to have him. To have *someone*. I'd swallowed my own desires in favor of being with him.

I'd thought I didn't need anything else. But now...

Now, I wondered if I'd been shielding myself the entire time. Accepting what affection was given to me so I didn't have to be alone. Making myself believe I was happy so I didn't have to acknowledge I wasn't. Convincing myself I was satisfied so I wouldn't risk anything by asking for more.

What would it be like to have someone who would tease me and flirt with me? Who would make me smile and laugh and pull me close when I needed comfort? I wanted the shared glances, the thrill of anticipation, the breathless moment when attraction turned to something more. I wanted someone who would feel happy just by seeing me smile.

Was it possible for me to have a relationship like the one Neima and Paloma shared?

A hand seized my wrist, and I jumped, twirling around.

Isla stood there, her face half-hidden by the shadows of the hall, now wearing a long coat. "Nell."

"Isla, you scared the crap out of me," I said, placing my hand against my heart. "What are you doing here? Did you find what you were looking for before?"

"No," she answered, pursing her lips and releasing my wrist. "It must be in the castle somewhere."

"What is it?"

"Something I need," she responded evasively. "I'm sure I'll

find it eventually, though. How have you been holding up here?"

"I think I might have completed the labyrinth?" I said tentatively. "I was transported somewhere and ran into another person facing their challenge. Then, a door appeared after a while, and I returned here."

Isla shook her head. "Had you completed it, you would be free, not standing here with me right now."

My heart sank. "Then what was that?"

"I'm not sure," she answered, her eyebrows squishing together as she studied me. "It does sound like you faced your challenge, but..."

"But?"

Worry clouded her face. "You're still here. That would mean you failed."

"No, that can't be," I said quickly. "I mean, what I'd seen wasn't even about me. It was about someone else."

"That's strange. It should be about what you desire. It almost sounds like you interfered with someone else's challenge. That shouldn't happen."

"So that might not have been my challenge?"

Isla didn't look convinced. "That, or the lordling is messing with you. Making you think you have a chance of escaping when he actually intends to keep you here no matter what."

That thought hadn't even crossed my mind. And now that it had, dread joined the darkness weighing me down, making it hard to breathe. "Can he do that? Keep me here even if I complete his labyrinth?"

"He can do whatever he wants," she said bitterly. "He's the ruler of this place, remember?" She inclined her head in the opposite direction from where I'd come. "Come here. You should see this."

I followed her to the end of the hall, through a door, and into an expansive room. A sturdy wooden railing lay a couple feet in front of us, marking the edge of what I realized was an indoor balcony. The railing surrounded the entire room, with the floor falling away just past it. Isla and I moved closer, and my feet suddenly halted as I looked down at the floor below us.

"These are all people who've failed his labyrinth," Isla said quietly.

Dozens of servants, if not more, drifted about on the floor below us. Their movements seemed mechanic, soulless. Some were cleaning the floors on their hands and knees, scrubbing the stone, repeating the same motions over and over. Others were dusting the walls, folding linen, or busying themselves with menial tasks. They didn't talk, and the silence between them was almost as unsettling as their mindless actions. The only sounds in the room were footsteps echoing against the stone and the occasional scrape of the metal buckets against the floor.

"All these people. Trapped here by *him*," she continued, her voice sharp. "These poor things don't even realize they're being controlled. They're completely gone."

I took a shaky step back, not wanting to look at them. At what could become of me. It was unnatural. Horrifying. "I met a servant earlier. He didn't seem to know anything about the labyrinth until I started pushing, but then, when it seemed like he was remembering something, it was like a switch flipped. He went back into whatever state *that* is. Automated. As if he only existed to serve Enver."

Isla rested her hands on the railing, observing the servants below with a cool gaze. "I'm sure their minds are still in there somewhere. Simply locked away by him."

"But why? What does Enver get out of this?" I asked, folding my arms over my stomach, feeling sick.

"Who knows?" she responded with a scoff. "Why does he force people into his labyrinth in the first place?"

I didn't know how Isla could stand to watch the servants. It made my skin crawl just knowing we were in the same room. "Enver said he never forced anyone here."

"You're right. He only exploits people at their weakest moments and lures them here instead." She finally glanced back at me, knowing. "Isn't that how he got you?"

I shifted my weight. Memories of the club, and what we did after, flashed through my mind. "Yes."

"What caused him to be drawn to you?" she asked. "You don't have to tell me if you don't want to."

"I had just been betrayed," I said, my skin feeling tight as I thought of Julian and my sister. "Then Enver showed up. And here I am."

"A betrayal," Isla echoed, her voice softening. "I think I can understand how you ended up here."

I glanced at her, seeing her contemplative expression. "Were you betrayed, too?"

"Yes," she said. "And now I'm here to return the favor. Either by having my revenge or taking something equally precious away. The lordling has granted me that chance by bringing me here."

"What kind of power does Enver hold?" I asked. "To be able to bring us here? It defies..." I couldn't even give it a word. It defied everything.

"The lordling seems to have powers a god would hold. Yet, if he was a god, why would he remain here?" she mused, returning her gaze to the area below. "A god wouldn't do this, either. Unless it was a cruel one. Not that there aren't wicked gods out there. But his kind is a mystery."

Enver being a god? Well, he was certainly built like the sculptures of gods I'd seen throughout my life, if not even more chiseled. He also held an air about him that made him seem otherworldly and untouchable. Yet, he'd let me touch him. He'd let me do more than that. I could easily imagine myself worshipping him, his body...

I grimaced, stopping that line of thought right there. What was *wrong* with me? I faced becoming a mindless slave for him, but dirty thoughts about him still popped up in my head?

"I need to figure out how to continue the labyrinth," I said, mainly to get myself back on track, shaking my head. "Or I need to figure out how to escape Enver's grasp if I really did fail already."

Isla finally backed away from the railing, her hands clasped behind her back. "I can't offer much advice on how to proceed from here since your situation is a bit unique. I haven't heard of anyone escaping after failing, but that doesn't mean it can't be done. You are still yourself. It's not over for you yet."

"I appreciate the help you've given me so far," I told her, offering her a small smile. "If not for you, I'd still be in that garden maze."

She grinned back at me. "Oh, I'm always in the business of foiling the lordling's plans, so it's no problem." She slipped off the coat she was wearing and handed it over to me. "And here, take this. It's always so dreadfully cold in here. I know where to find more."

"Are you sure?" I asked, but still slipped into it, finding it warm from her body heat. "Thank you. I wish I could do something for you in return. Can I help you find what you're looking for?"

"I don't think so," she replied, crossing her arms over her chest. "But it's okay. I won't give up until I find it. Don't worry about me. Focus on yourself. Get out of here if you can."

"I don't think it'll be that easy," I said, knowing deep in my heart it was true. I opened my mouth to ask about the pendant but then abruptly closed it again, an uncomfortable sensation coming over me. I didn't want her to know about it. "Good luck in your search, Isla," I said instead.

She nodded, and I turned back to the door we'd entered from. I opened it, and for once, was not surprised when I ended up somewhere other than the castle halls. This time, I'd ended up in the lavish dining room I'd been in before.

Enver sat on the other side of the room, at the head of the expansive table.

"What are you doing here?" I asked, my muscles tensing.

"This is my castle," he responded, his eyes roaming over my form, then narrowing at the coat draped over me. "I may roam and reside wherever I desire. The question is—what are *you* doing here, my little lover? You should be busy trying to complete my labyrinth so you can escape this cruel, heartless monster, should you not?"

I crossed the room to him, passing the dusty seats, still unoccupied and forgotten like before. Yet piles of food sat scattered about the entire table span—far more than any one person, or even a dozen, could eat.

Enver's gaze never left me as I walked toward him. "Are you hungry?" he inquired, gesturing toward one of the empty seats. "Sit. There is more than enough."

"Maybe you should share with the dozens of servants you have trapped in the other room," I said, unable to keep the revulsion out of my voice. "Or are they only allowed to make your food and not actually eat it before returning to do your other bidding?"

Enver returned his hand to the table, picking up a bowl of what looked like some kind of bisque and bringing it closer to him, but not making any move to eat it. "No one is trapped."

"I saw them. Moving around like... like *zombies*. I spoke to one of them earlier, and it was like his memories were wiped, only knowing how to serve you," I said accusingly. "You said these people were willing to become yours, but they had no choice. You're controlling them."

Enver gave me a sharp look. "They knew and agreed to the consequences of failing the labyrinth. I did not force anyone into anything."

"I really don't think they did," I responded tersely. "You're not fooling me. You probably get some sick, twisted pleasure out of tricking innocent people into becoming your captives."

Enver abruptly rose from the table, his chair sliding across the wooden floor with a grating scraping sound. "So, you are determined to see the worst in me."

I held my ground as he moved toward me, swift and intimidating. "Is there any good in you?"

He stopped dead, barely a foot from me, his expression turning deadly.

I dug my fingernails into my palm, willing myself to keep my composure. "You can't answer that, can you? You probably can't even understand why what you're doing is so awful. You don't have the emotional capacity to."

"I should not expend effort to prove myself to someone so intent on demonizing me, but..." He snapped his fingers, the crack echoing through the room. "I refuse to let you wrongfully convince yourself I have forced anyone into coming here."

"Convince myself?" I repeated incredulously. "I *saw* them!"

"Yes," he responded. "You saw and came to your own conclusions, disregarding everything I told you previously."

I couldn't speak for a minute, utterly astounded that he thought I was stupid enough to fall for his lies again after witnessing what I had. "You're actually insane."

He didn't answer, and a moment later, two servants entered the room. One was the young man I'd seen when I first entered the castle, and the other was an older woman, her black hair tied into a tight bun at the top of her head.

"Watch," Enver told me, turning to the man.

"What are you going to do?" I demanded, uneasy. "Leave him alone."

Enver ignored me, taking the young man's jaw into his hand, staring deeply at him while muttering something I couldn't decipher.

Something changed in the young man instantly. Gone was the passive, unexpressive look on his face. It melted into pure terror. His eyes widened, pupils dilating as his gaze darted around the room. The color drained from his skin, and he grabbed onto the fabric of Enver's top. "No," he whimpered. "Please, don't send me back. Please."

"Hush," Enver said soothingly.

"Please," the young man sobbed, dropping to his knees in front of Enver, hanging his head. "I'll do anything. Take me back, my lord. *Please!*"

A knot twisted in my stomach at the man's despair.

Enver glanced at me from the corner of his eye before returning his attention to the young man. "You failed my labyrinth, Oliver. Is that correct?"

"Yes," the young man, Oliver, responded, his entire body shaking.

"And I have taken care of you since, yes?"

He nodded, still grasping at Enver's shirt. "Yes. Yes. Please, I don't know what I did, but don't make me go back to them! Let me stay with you!"

"And who called for me? Who asked to challenge my labyrinth?"

"I did," he said, looking up at Enver now. "I begged you to let me challenge it, to go with you."

"And you knew the consequences of failing? You accepted them?"

Oliver nodded again, furiously. "Yes! Why are you questioning me—"

"One last question, then I will let you return. Have I forced you into anything, ever?"

This time, Oliver shook his head. "No, my lord. Never. So, please, bring me back—"

Enver touched Oliver's forehead, and the pleas fell silent on Oliver's lips, a serene expression crossing his face. My heart pounded. The entire scene displayed before me sent goosebumps scattering across my skin.

"What...?" I began.

Enver turned to the woman next, brushing his fingers against her cheek. "Agatha?"

Agatha's eyes turned alert, her hands shooting up to her face as if to protect herself.

Startled, I stepped forward, wanting to defend her from Enver if I had to.

"Why am I here?" Agatha said, staring at Enver, her hands trembling. "Did I do something wrong?"

"No," Enver said softly. "You have done nothing wrong."

Tears formed in her eyes. "Don't do this to me. I don't want to be here."

"I know."

Her hand went to her hair, fingers digging in. "I can still hear their screams. See their blood. The life fading from their eyes. No, *no!*"

My heart plummeted as her voice rose into a harrowing cry. "Enver," I said shakily, unsure how to help her.

"Ask her," he said.

I stared at him. "What?"

"Ask her if she wants to return home. Now."

Agatha turned toward me, her cheeks blotchy red and her lashes full of tears. I didn't have time to react as she flung herself at me, clinging to my dress, much like the way Oliver had held onto Enver. "No, please. Let me stay. Let me stay!"

I stood frozen, my voice caught in my throat, her distress nearly palpable.

"Ask," Enver repeated, an edge to his voice now.

"Do you want to stay here?" I asked.

Agatha looked at me through her tear-soaked eyes, her face etched with an indescribable pain. "I can't leave. I need to forget."

My heart raced. "He is keeping you here by force—"

"If I leave, I'll die. I can't, I can't!" she cried, yanking me closer to her. "Let me stay. Please, you can't do this to me! I can't take it. I'll even challenge the labyrinth this time, I promise! Just let me stay!"

Helplessness welled in me as she sobbed in my arms, begging and pleading, the heartbreaking sound echoing throughout the room, growing more and more anguished. I didn't know what to do. My hands rose to comfort her but then fell back to my sides, my throat growing tight with anxiety.

"Do you see now?" Enver asked, regarding me coldly.

"This is..." I trailed off, unable to concentrate as Agatha's sobs only grew worse, reverberating wails that felt like nails through my heart.

"This is the desperation that leads people to my labyrinth. Failing is not a punishment for them. It is a reprieve."

I barely heard him, preoccupied with the way Agatha so desperately pleaded to go back. "I beg you," she said, gasping, tears splashing onto the floor below us.

I couldn't take it anymore. "Enver, help her," I said, my voice shaking as her cries seemed to rattle my chest.

"Helping her would just make her my thrall, no?"

Agatha was hyperventilating at this point, sinking to the ground. I dropped to my knees beside her, breathing shakily. "Please," I whispered, wrapping my arms around her, looking up at Enver, and wondering what fate I would doom her to by pleading to him.

Without a word, he stepped forward, kneeling next to us. He swept Agatha's hair away from her forehead with a tenderness that took me off guard. "Agatha. Look at me."

She lifted her head, and as their gazes met, it was like a switch flipped. She fell silent, her tears drying up. She pulled herself out of my arms and climbed to her feet, smoothing out her uniform. "My lord," she said, dipping her head toward him, then me. "My lady."

Enver stood to his full height as well, holding his hand out to me. I let him help me to my feet, my mind still reeling from what I'd witnessed. He then let me go to reach out and wipe away the stray tears left on Agatha's cheeks. "We do not require any further assistance. You and Oliver may leave."

I'd almost forgotten Oliver was still there. He gave both Enver and me a slight bow before retreating out of the room with Agatha. The quietude that settled in the room now felt almost as perturbing as Agatha's weeping.

"Desperation is born from the silent screams of shattered souls. The relentless agony of a tragic loss. The endless yearning for something that remains out of reach. The cruel awareness that what once was can never be again." Enver's voice was soft as he spoke, carrying a somber tone that matched the melancholic atmosphere of the room. "The aching emptiness that consumes you, leading you to the edge of hopelessness."

I wrapped my arms around myself, a chill sweeping through me. He sounded as if he understood the weight of that despair. As if he'd experienced it for himself. But, how could he? He didn't have emotions.

"That feeling sustains the labyrinth," he continued. "It can either guide you through your desperation if you challenge it and prevail or take it all away if you fail. But it is not so cruel as to let you suffer in the case of failure."

"You talk about it as if it's sentient."

"This labyrinth is as much a part of me as I am of it. I, too, can guide you through your despair," he said, turning toward me. He held out his hand again, long fingers outstretched, coaxing me in. "Or take you away from it."

I kept my hands firmly tucked under my arms. "And what happens when you take it away?"

"The solace of oblivion."

"How is that solace—"

"You have just witnessed how," he cut in, letting his hand drop back to his side. "When reality is a nightmare, oblivion is a sweet dream."

I didn't know how to respond to that. I couldn't argue that it wasn't true after seeing Oliver and Agatha's unbearable sorrow, and how they begged for the mercy of remaining here with Enver. Whatever happened to them had made forgetting the easier option. But…

"I'm not that desperate," I said.

"You were," Enver responded evenly. "That night we met. If I had offered you oblivion instead of my body, you would have chosen it."

I shook my head, staring hard at the floor. "No. I wouldn't give up on everything just because no one loves me." I hugged myself tighter, a weight settling in my gut as I thought back to that night, to Julian. To the devastation of betrayal, to the wretched reminder that no one would ever love me. To how I would have done anything for love. To how I still would. My chest tightened. "That's…"

That was why I, too, had considered forgetting my pain like Neima had wanted for Paloma.

"Do not feel ashamed. You are not the only one to have felt that way," he said. "Everyone has their darkest moments. Their deepest despairs. Ones that take root in your veins and burgeon in the shadows of your soul—ones that lead to my labyrinth."

"Isla said I'd know if I completed the labyrinth because I'd be home. Is that true?" I asked, a horrible apprehension looming over me.

"I would suggest not believing everything she says, my little lover," he said, irritation bleeding into his tone.

"Why wouldn't I? She's in the same position I am. What reason would she have to lie about anything?"

"She is not in the same position as you," he responded sharply. "You are far more precious to me."

As always with Enver, he pulled unwanted reactions from me. My heart fluttered, and I bit my tongue hard to keep my composure, refusing to look at him. "Just tell me. How would I know I've completed the labyrinth successfully?"

"You would return to your world."

I went still, anxiety growing in me at the implication of his confirmation. "And if I faced my challenge and didn't return home?"

"Then you would have failed. You would reappear in my castle before me just as you are now and assume your new role here."

My heart plummeted, and I swayed on my feet, my legs going weak. No. That couldn't be. But I was here. In front of him. Not home. "I failed?" I asked, terror seeping into my voice, my body breaking into uncontrollable tremors as I finally looked at Enver. "No... I can't be trapped here! You can't keep me here!"

He didn't answer, only stared at me, his steely gaze betraying nothing.

I stumbled back in a panic, trying to put distance between us as fear clawed at me from all sides. "I don't want this! Don't do this to me, please—"

"Nell," he said, cutting me off and advancing toward me.

I twisted on my heel to run but only managed to take one step before a wall of dark shadows rose from the ground in front of me, blocking my path. I took a shuddering breath, attempting to move around them, but Enver threw his arm out, stopping me. I twirled back around to face him, my breath hitching in my throat. "Stay away from me! Enver, please—"

"You have not failed," he said.

"I—what?"

"You have not failed," he repeated slowly, letting me take in each word. "You still belong to yourself."

I searched his eyes for any hint of dishonesty, but they were clear. The shadows that corralled me dissipated, but I didn't move. "But I swear I faced my challenge. And I'm still here."

"You cannot have possibly finished my labyrinth," he told me, taking my hand in his, and leading me over to the edge of the room to look out one of the arched windows. "I said you had to make your way up to me. Look up there." He lifted his hand, pointing to the castle's elegant clock tower. It stood backdropped by the starry night sky, its golden hands and numbers glinting in the moonlight. "That is where you will find me and your final challenge."

"Final challenge?" I repeated, the sight of the clock tower filling me with renewed dread. "There's more than one?"

"Yes."

My stomach knotted. "Is that how it is for everyone?"

He stayed quiet for a moment before finally admitting, "No."

My head whipped toward him, a sudden anger replacing the fear I'd just felt. "Do you like fucking with me? Is that it? Is that why I'm the only one with a time limit? Why I have to face multiple challenges when everyone else only has one? Are you even going to let me leave if I complete them? Or are you going to force me to stay here with you? So you can keep me as your lover, and we can play pretend on the outside while on the inside, you'll remain as cold and unfeeling as the stones that make up your shitty castle?"

He said nothing, only watched me, his jaw tight.

His refusal to respond only fueled my frustration. I grabbed the front of his shirt, yanking him toward me. "Answer me! You can't even get satisfaction or amusement out of this, so why? Why are you doing this to me? Why me?"

"Because you are desperate," he said, not attempting to remove my hands from him, his face a perfect mask of stoicism. "Because you drew me to you."

"You're saying this is all my fault?" I asked through gritted teeth.

"No," he answered. "It is mine. For being the ruler of this labyrinth and for desiring you."

My grip on him slackened. "But you don't feel guilty about it."

He brought his hand up to cradle the back of my neck, his touch delicate and warm. "I cannot."

I released him. There was no point in getting angry. He would never understand how I felt. I'd have better luck receiving compassion from the shadows or servants he manipulated. "I don't understand. Why did you create this labyrinth?"

Enver smoothed out his shirt, pushing the fabric away from the scar on his chest. "I cannot answer that."

"You can't answer why you created this place?" I snapped, my anger flaring again, his nonchalance feeding it into a blaze. "Is there anything you can do? Or can you only manipulate and kidnap innocent people?"

He narrowed his eyes. "Careful with your words, my little lover. You do not want to make an enemy of me."

"I'm not making an enemy out of you—you're already an enemy to me."

"Is that so? You allow your enemies to touch you in the way I have touched you? To kiss and taste you? To make you writhe in pleasure under them?" he murmured, leaning down so his lips were a breath away from mine. "If that is the case, I am pleased to be your enemy. I will make you hate me even more. Until you cannot think of anyone but me, your irresistible nemesis."

I tried to shove him away, but he quickly grabbed my wrists, pushing me up against the window, the chill of the glass seeping through the thin fabric of my dress and cape as he pinned my hands above my head. "Let me go," I demanded, but my voice came out breathless.

He pressed his body into mine, the hard muscles of his chest brushing against my breasts as he brought his mouth to my ear. "I will be the cruel villain who makes you come so hard you forget you are supposed to hate me. The heartless monster you scream and beg for more from."

Air caught in my lungs. His hips shifted, and I could feel the thick ridge of his erection against my stomach. I shouldn't have felt turned on, shouldn't have felt anything other than hatred for him, but I couldn't stop my body from reacting to his touch, his words.

"No," I said, squeezing my eyes shut.

A second later, Enver's body and warmth were gone. My arms fell back to my side, and I opened my eyes to see him standing a few feet away now. His face was devoid of all expression, his mask back into place.

"I do not consider you an enemy of mine, my little lover," he said. "I only consider you mine."

I swallowed. "I'm not yours."

"Everything will end if you give yourself to me. No more pain. No more sorrow," he promised softly. "No more memories of your past or thoughts of your future. Only here and now. With me. Why do you refuse me?"

"Because you can't offer me what I want," I told him. "What you offer is only an illusion of it."

"I wish..." He stopped there, jaw tightening again, angling his face away from me.

I didn't want to think about the longing I'd glimpsed in his eyes before he turned away. It didn't mean anything. It couldn't mean anything. "Even if it's seven or seven hundred challenges I have to face in your labyrinth, I will overcome them," I said.

"Maybe it's true I was desperate when we first met, but it's not true now."

"No," he agreed in a murmur, moving closer again, his hand coming up to cradle my cheek as if he couldn't resist touching me when he stood so close. "It is not true now. Your will is strong, though desperation still lingers. I have rarely encountered those such as yourself here. And those I have..." he trailed off.

"Were the ones to complete your labyrinth," I finished for him, my eyes widening slightly.

His hand moved to wrap a piece of my hair around his finger. "Yes."

Hope planted its seed in my chest. Only two had ever escaped his labyrinth, but maybe only two ever possessed the will to do so. I needed to stop being weighed down by my doubt and cling to my will. I had the will to get out. I knew I did.

Love had gotten me into this, but spite would get me out.

"I will escape your labyrinth," I told Enver, meeting his gaze head-on. "And when I do, I hope the emotion I give you is compassion. That way, you can finally understand what you're doing to those you lure and trap here."

He took a step back, letting my hair slip through his fingers. "Or perhaps you will fail and come to understand why oblivion is so coveted. I would not even make you suffer despite your accusations and insults. I would grant oblivion to you the moment you crawled back to me, forlorn and defeated."

My scalp prickled with unease. "I thought you said I'd stay by your side if I failed. Not become one of your servants."

"If you choose to be with me instead of facing the labyrinth, then yes, I will keep you by my side as my equal. But if you fail the labyrinth after attempting to leave me, then I promise you nothing," he said. "I told you before. I will not beg you to stay with me."

I stared at him, my chest constricting painfully. "You're..."

"Heartless?" he asked, moving closer to me again, shadows rising behind him, creating a dark and menacing silhouette. "Cruel? A monster? Please, I insist you hurl more accusations my way, my little lover. You only make me want to become what you expect of me."

"Why do you even care? You can't even feel anything," I responded, keeping my feet planted on the ground, even though I desperately wanted to fall back. There was nowhere for me to go, anyway.

"I have my pride," he said icily, the shadows behind him now a solid wall.

"Pride?" I repeated, and just as realization hit me, the shadows lunged forward.

They crashed over Enver and me, swallowing us both in their darkness. I put my hands up defensively, squeezing my eyes shut as vertigo slammed into me. Nausea rose in my stomach, and I stumbled, falling to my knees, onto what felt like cool silk. Pressure increased in my ears, making me grimace. Then, something grabbed me, tugging me forward roughly. No, not just something. Multiple of them—shadows.

I vaguely recognized the feeling from when I first entered the castle, but I focused my thoughts on convincing myself not to vomit as nausea threatened to overtake me. And just before I thought I'd lose the battle, everything stopped. The shadows left me, and the vertigo and queasiness disappeared.

Only to be replaced with a rough coldness against the skin of my palms and knees.

My eyes snapped open to see grey cobblestone lit up by an orange glow, and the reddish shine of polished, black leather boots. Lifting my head higher, my gaze traveled up pristine black slacks to a white poet shirt and finally to the unfamiliar face of a man staring down at me. A lantern hanging from a post behind him revealed the source of the incandescence.

"*Bună seara*," he greeted, and then grinned.

My heart nearly stopped at the sight of his elongated canines, the glimmer of firelight catching on them.

No, not canines.

Fangs.

9

Unable to stop it, I let out a startled scream, scrambling backward on the cobblestone to put distance between me and the man with the wolfish grin and sinister fangs. Reddish-brown hair curled around his ears and the nape of his neck, and his white skin was pallid under the moonlight. He said something else—something I didn't understand and couldn't quite place the language of. When he raised an eyebrow, my gaze caught on the crimson of his irises. I gasped, falling back another step.

"My. I think I should be the one surprised here," he said, a slight accent to his voice as he spoke in English this time. "You're the one who appeared in the street from the midst of a void of shadows, after all."

I took a second to get my bearings. Lanterns lit up a narrow street lined with one-story buildings, some made of wood, some of brick, and all with varying historic architecture that reminded me of quaint European towns. The night was silent and still, with dark clouds shifting to cover the moon completely.

"I can hear your pulse racing," the stranger said. "It's very tempting."

My attention shot back to him, and I froze at his proximity. I hadn't heard or noticed him move closer to me. *He's a vampire*, my mind warned me. I couldn't even fight the thought. If someone like Enver existed, how could I be shocked vampires did?

"You're doing the labyrinth, right?" I blurted.

The stranger tilted his head to the side, an eyebrow lifting. "And how do you know about that?"

"I'm doing it, too," I said quickly, hoping it would keep me safe from ever finding out what those fangs were made for. "We're on the same side."

"Oh, are we now?"

"Yes. I can... help you," I hedged, although I didn't know how true it was. I didn't even know what *I* was supposed to be doing in the labyrinth yet.

His gaze dropped to my neck. "I'm absolutely sure you could."

I slapped my hand over my throat. "Not like that!"

"Not like what?" he asked, a smirk gracing his features, revealing his fangs again. "I'm simply admiring."

Admiring what? I didn't want to know. "I'm trying to escape the labyrinth, too. I—"

His hand suddenly shot out, fisting the front of my jacket, and throwing me to the side, nearly knocking me off my feet. I cried out, startled, and heard the whooshing noise of something slicing through the air near my ear. It hit the house beside us, implanting in the wood with a resounding *thunk*, and my eyes followed the noise, seeing an arrow embedded in the siding.

"Follow me," the stranger barked, his fingers encircling my wrist.

Another arrow whizzed by my head, and I didn't question

him, letting him guide me as we ran through the dimly lit streets. We ducked into tight alleyways, keeping low and quiet until we came to a worn-down shack on the outskirts of the town, hidden in a cluster of overgrown shrubs. The stranger surveyed the area before pulling me inside and barring the door behind us with a wooden plank.

My breaths came out unevenly as he finally released me, and I doubled over, winded. "What the hell was that?" I panted.

"Vampire hunters," the stranger muttered, perfectly composed, not even a bead of sweat on his skin.

I straightened out, alarmed. "Is that allowed?"

"They're not after me because of the labyrinth. They're after me because I'm a monster."

His tone had lost all the teasing playfulness it held earlier, replaced by a raw loathing. I didn't know what to say for a moment as he moved to light the room with oil lamps. My heart continued to hammer in my chest, even as I caught my breath. It hadn't occurred to me that I could be in danger in the labyrinth. What would have happened if one of those arrows had struck me? Could I die here? Had others died during their challenges?

"It might not be wise for you to stay here," the stranger said, leaning against a worn wooden desk. "The hunters are relentless. They haven't found this place yet, though."

I didn't know what would be worse—having to deal with vampire hunters or traversing an unknown world alone. Staying near Neima had worked out last time for me, though. "I'd like to stay with you."

He cocked an eyebrow. "Brave, aren't you?"

"I don't really have a choice," I said. "And at least our goals are the same."

"I don't think they are," he responded evenly but held his hand out to me. "I'm Dio."

I shook it, noticing how cool to the touch his fingers were. "Nell."

"A pleasure," he said with a smile, and I once again found myself distracted by his fangs. "Don't worry. I won't bite. Unless you'd let me?"

I immediately shook my head. "No! I'm, uh, good."

He chuckled. "Figured I'd ask."

As the tension in the room eased, I looked around the dingy shack. Cracked cement made up the floor, caked with loose dirt. Two rotten chairs and a dirty bed were the only furniture, and there were no other rooms, making me wonder where the bathroom was. "You live here?" I asked.

"No. Like I said, the hunters just haven't discovered this place yet."

"How long have you been hunted for?"

Dio's brows furrowed. "Seventy-five years, give or take? They're persistent. I'll give them that."

"You're seventy?" I'd thought he was my age.

"I'm ninety-six, I believe."

I gaped at him, though I really shouldn't have been shocked. Enver was even older than Dio. "What?"

"Vampire," he reminded me, tapping his fangs. "I'm frozen at the age I was killed and haven't changed since."

A shiver went down my spine. "Killed?"

"As I grew up, there were always rumors that vampires existed. That they'd been behind some murders that happened in my town. I never believed it, though," Dio said, lowering his head, and scuffing his foot against the dirt on the floor. "Not until one broke into my house and killed my parents in front of me."

Horror washed through me. "What?"

"He moved alone, but my parents still didn't stand a chance. He was too strong. He went after my sister next." His posture grew rigid as he recounted his past. "She was ten at the time. I grabbed whatever I could to defend us and managed to distract him long enough to let her escape. He wasn't happy about that. He snapped my neck, and the next thing I knew, I was lying in blood-soaked snow, a burning in my throat. A sickening craving taking over me."

"That's awful," I whispered. "I'm so sorry."

I couldn't consider myself close to my family nowadays, but at one point, Veronica and I had been inseparable. We were twins. How could we not be? She'd been my best friend. She stood up for me whenever anyone would bully me in elementary school. If I was in trouble with my parents, she'd take on the blame, too. She'd tell the waitress I'd said no peppers when they served me a meal with them in it. She'd been the best sister I could ask for, until things fell apart between us when our dad left and she blamed me for it. I couldn't imagine seeing her killed in front of me, though. Even after what she'd done to me.

He shrugged. "It was a long time ago. And my hands aren't clean now, either."

"What happened to your sister after everything?"

"From what I know, she was taken in by our neighbors. Grew up with them."

"You never went to see her after everything?"

"How could I?" he said harshly. "I'm a *monster*. I became what killed our parents. I've been doomed to live in darkness, to have an insatiable hunger that puts everyone around me in constant danger if I let my control slip. She would not see her brother if she looked at me. She'd see a disgusting fiend. And she'd be right. I left enough blood for the town to believe I died alongside our parents. I only hope she found peace in that."

His self-loathing was almost palpable, a heaviness hanging in the air. I didn't know what to say, so I stayed silent, watching as he glared off into the distance.

"It's better than her seeing what I've become. Cold. Unfeeling. A true monster," he said. "Not like the fictional ones in the stories I used to tell her before bed."

I wrapped my arms around myself, his words reminding me too much of what I'd said to Enver before. "Unfeeling?" I asked.

He nodded, his lips curving into a wry smile. "I suppose it goes hand in hand with the loss of humanity. I can't remember what it's like to feel anything. No matter how hard I try. No matter how much I want to. Everything always remains out of reach. I try to remember what it's like to feel joy, sadness. *Anything*. But I can't. All I know is this disgust for myself and a void where I know something else should be. I just can't tell you what. I feel empty. Yearning for something I can't remember."

"I can't imagine," I said, not liking how I thought of Enver, about the longing I'd seen in his eyes, about the way he spoke of desperation as if he knew it intimately. Did he feel empty like this, too?

Dio sighed, straightening out again. "Who would be able to? It's a hell I wouldn't wish on anyone. Not even my worst enemies."

I frowned, clasping my hands in front of me. If Dio couldn't feel anything, what awaited him when he finished the labyrinth? Did he yearn for a specific emotion or something else?

"Either way, it'll all end soon enough," Dio said.

"How?"

"I know where the vampire who killed my parents is now. The labyrinth showed me. I'm going to kill him and get my revenge. And then I'll get what I so desperately desire."

His voice filled with determination and a resignation I didn't understand.

Yet...

"Let me help you," I offered.

My words stunned us both. I tensed as Dio's brows furrowed. "No. It's too dangerous."

He was right. I'd nearly been shot by an arrow already. What would happen if I died here? Even so, something inside me urged me to help him. "I'm not letting you go alone. We're both trapped in this labyrinth. We should help each other out."

"What do you get in exchange for helping me?" he responded.

"We can figure that out later."

Dio pressed his lips together but then finally nodded. "Okay. Let's go together. He's close by. I need to finish him before the sun comes up. We're running out of moonlight."

He went to the door, and I followed along, my pulse quickening. I didn't know what danger awaited, but as we stepped back into the night and made our way across the quiet town again, the feeling that this was the right thing to do grew stronger. The sky, although cloudy, was beginning to turn lighter with the impending dawn.

Dio moved with lithe grace, and the wind whipped my hair into my face as I struggled to keep up with him. Rain started to fall from the sky, making the worn cobblestone street slippery and breaking the silence of the night with the pitter-patter of droplets hitting the ground. We cut through a narrow alley, and at the end, Dio came to a sudden stop, staring at a dingy cottage.

"He's there?" I asked in a whisper.

Dio didn't respond but continued forward, approaching a half-boarded-up window. I followed him, standing on my tiptoes to peek inside as he wiped away a layer of dust on the pane.

In the low light of a lamp, I could make out the form of an old woman asleep in a bed, her chest rising and falling slowly. Her hand was outstretched, resting on top of a side table. Her fingers curled around a tarnished photo frame, the photo inside yellow and decayed.

Dio placed his palm on the window, his forehead nearly pressed against the glass. "Luliana."

I knew from the adoration in his voice that this woman was his sister.

But before I could say anything, there was a shift in the air behind me. I barely managed to shove Dio out of the way before a silver stake sank into the wooden windowsill we'd been in front of. Dio recovered quickly, tackling his would-be assailant to the ground. I reached for the embedded stake and pulled it free, holding it up in front of me defensively.

Dio and his attacker thrashed wildly on the rain-soaked grass, grunts mixing with the sound of skin hitting skin. I studied his attacker for a moment—long black hair, tangled and wet, pale white skin, fierce fangs protruding from snarling lips. Dio's muscles strained as he fought to overpower the other vampire, hands going around his throat, keeping him pinned.

"It's you," Dio hissed.

"Thank you for leading me back to your sister. I've been so curious about how she tastes even after all these years," the other vampire responded, smirking at Dio.

"You're going to hell!" Dio shouted as he brought his fist down into the other vampire's face.

I grasped the stake tighter, unsure of how to help or what to do. I'd never used a weapon before. The brutality of the two fighting had my heart in my throat. "Dio!" I called as the other vampire suddenly knocked Dio off him, overtaking Dio.

Dio didn't have time to react before the vampire tore his fangs into Dio's neck, ripping into the soft flesh. Blood spurted out, and Dio faltered for a moment, his body becoming motionless, eyes glazing over with a terror that made my breath catch.

"Get off him!" I cried, bringing the stake down into the other vampire's back.

It barely sunk into him. But it did its job. The vampire looked up from Dio, his eyes narrowing into slits as he glared at me. I tried to pull the stake back, but the vampire was faster. He ripped it out of my grasp, twisting my wrist. I winced, looking around desperately for another means of defense, but my world turned upside down as the vampire lunged at me, taking me to the ground. I cried out as my back hit the dirt hard enough for me to lose my breath.

The vampire's hand went around my throat, squeezing so tight I thought my neck would snap. I brought my hands up, trying to claw at him, but he didn't react, his grip cutting off my air supply. I fought to breathe as my senses dulled around me, gazing up at the fangs descending toward my neck. Panic rose in me. "No—" I choked out.

His sharp fangs raked across my throat, but before they could plunge in, he was knocked off of me, crashing into the side of the house from the force of the blow. Dio went after him again, growling as his fangs ripped into the other vampire's neck. The metallic scent of blood filled the air, and I struggled to push myself back to my feet, my entire body shaking. My eyes caught on the stake, still in the other vampire's hand.

"Dio, careful!" I warned, my voice scratchy, my throat sore.

Dio glanced at me as I spoke, and the other vampire used that moment of distraction to plunge the stake up into Dio's chest. Dio didn't make a sound, but his body seized, his gaze going down to where the stake impaled him. Shock swept through me, and I watched helplessly as the other vampire tore the stake out of Dio before thrusting it back in again. Dio groaned, his body lurching with the force of it.

My eyes darted around wildly until they landed on a broken, rusted garden hoe. I threw myself toward it, yanking it out of the dirt, and swung it toward the vampire with all the strength I could muster up. Its jagged edges caught the side of the other vampire's face, digging in and leaving bleeding streaks against his cheek. I brought it back and swung it again, adrenaline fueling me, this time impaling the broken metal into his injured throat.

That got his attention. He ripped the stake out of Dio again, his burning gaze fixing on me. Blood poured out of Dio, and he fell to the ground in a crumpled heap as the other vampire shoved Dio off him.

I needed to get him away from Dio.

I twisted on my heel, ready to run, and shrieked as the black-haired vampire grabbed the end of the hoe and pulled it toward him, taking me along with it. I finally let go of it, but stumbled, dropping to the ground to avoid the claws that reached for me. The vampire swung his hand out for me again, claws tearing through my dress as he swiped my side, pain searing through me as he cut into my skin.

I didn't know how to win against him. I didn't know if I could. But I couldn't let Dio die here. Not with his sister only a few feet away.

"Come get me, fucker," I taunted and tore off down the alley we'd come through.

To my relief and trepidation, the vampire followed me. My steps echoed around me as I sprinted down the alley, knowing it would only be a matter of seconds before he caught up with me.

But as I saw the light cresting at the mouth of the alley on the other side, I realized that maybe seconds were all I needed.

I pushed myself forward, my heart pounding as I raced toward the light. I threw myself to the side as his claws grazed my shoulder again, leaving behind a scorching trail of pain. Gritting my teeth, I forced myself to ignore the pain, focusing on the mouth of the alley. Only a few more steps and then—

A hand entangled in my hair, yanking me to a stop. I cried out, falling back. My fingers dug into the bricks of the alley, trying to anchor myself, but it felt like my hair would be ripped from my scalp. A rough shove had my back against the brick, and the vampire pulled my hair up and to the side, making me rise onto my toes, trying to ease the tension on my scalp. My chin turned, making me bare my neck to him.

"The way your blood rushes through your veins is delicious," he said, pressing a clawed finger into the base of my neck, causing it to bleed.

My gaze fell to the ground, where the shadows were receding.

"Do it," I said, meeting his hungry gaze.

His lips curled into a smirk. "My pleasure."

He descended toward my neck, and I tensed, closing my eyes. Sharp pressure against my throat had my hands fisting.

And then suddenly, the vampire froze.

My eyes snapped open. Sunlight filtered into the alleyway, falling on his face. His expression morphed into one of agony as he shuddered, his hands releasing me, trying to retreat into the shadow again. Before he could, though, Dio appeared in front of me, crashing into the vampire's side, knocking them both down into the sunlight. They fell to the ground together, Dio landing under the other vampire. The other vampire screamed, writhing over Dio as Dio held him tight, refusing to let him go.

Within seconds, his struggles weakened, and his skin started to wither away. He tried to crawl back toward the alley, but his fingers disintegrated as they met the cobblestone. I watched in horror as his skin melted away, revealing bone. The remnants of the vampire crumbled to the ground, exposing Dio to the sun.

I hurried over to him. "Dio, go back, hurry!"

Dio didn't move. He only gave me a weak smile before rolling onto his back and embracing the sun. "No. This is what I want."

"To die?" I cried shrilly.

"As all monsters should."

"No," I said immediately. "No, I won't let you do this."

"Nell—"

Ignoring his protests, I hooked my hands under his armpits, using all my strength to drag him back to the alley. Blood covered my hands, and I nearly lost my grip on him, but I got him back into the shade, setting him up against the brick wall. I knelt in front of him, taking his hand in mine and pushing up his sleeve to inspect his skin. Still intact but burnt.

"You should have left me there," he said, narrowing his eyes at me. "That was my path. The labyrinth guided me to get my revenge and then die."

"No," I protested. "You don't deserve to die. You didn't ask for this, Dio. You're not a monster."

"I'm dead anyway," Dio muttered, eyelids fluttering closed. "These wounds are deep."

I peeled away his bloodied shirt, seeing the gaping wounds where the stake had struck. "No..."

His head fell back, and he let out a low groan. "This would have been easier if I hadn't seen Luliana. Why did my feet guide me home once last time?"

"Tell me how to help you," I demanded. "There has to be some way to heal you."

"Blood," he said dryly.

I inhaled sharply. "And it would heal you?"

"Yes, but—"

I moved my hair, offering him my neck. "Then here. Take it."

"Nell—"

"I don't think the labyrinth was leading you to get revenge. It was leading you toward your sister," I said. "Go to her. Let her know you're alive. No matter what happened in the past, I'm sure she still loves you. Don't give up like this, Dio. It's not too late. Please. Take my blood. Heal yourself and go to her."

Dio stared at me for a moment, unnaturally still. Then he lifted a hand to my cheek, his touch gentle against my skin. "Thank you."

He leaned forward, his hand now moving to my hair, holding me in place as his fangs pierced my neck. I flinched, biting my lip to hold in my cry of pain. It hurt. More than I thought it would, the ache deep and throbbing. His tongue swept against my neck, lapping up the blood that spilled from me. I reached out to steady myself, my hands on his shoulders, eyes wrenching shut. I wanted to pull away but forced myself to remain still.

Seconds passed, and I began to feel light-headed. I swayed on my knees, my grip on his shoulders loosening.

Noticing my dizziness, Dio drew back. I looked up at him, at his lips covered with my blood, at his skin that was now smooth once again. I returned my gaze to his arm, which was no longer burnt. "That's amazing."

A laugh burst out from Dio. "Most people say it hurts."

"I meant the way you can regenerate like that," I clarified, flushing, my hand going to the wound in my neck, prodding at the tender skin. "Ow."

"Thank you, Nell," Dio said, serious again.

"Let's go to your sister now," I said, attempting to push myself to my feet but nearly falling again, my body feeling weak.

Dio caught me, then helped me to my feet, keeping his arm around my waist to take on my weight. "Careful." He hesitated, glancing down the alleyway. "Nell, I don't know if I should go see her. What if she hates me for what I've become?"

"I won't pretend like that isn't possible," I said, a memory of my mom popping into my mind. Her hatred and anger toward me before she ended up kicking me out, even after I strived to be the best daughter I could be. "Sometimes things change and aren't the same anymore. Sometimes, family turns against us for reasons that aren't our fault. And sometimes, it's for no reason at all. But your sister wasn't the one who walked away from you. She could be missing you, Dio. You just have to be brave and find out."

Brave. Something I had never been. I always just accepted what happened to me—including when my mom turned her back on me and when Veronica betrayed me. I never fought back. Never sought closure. Never had the courage to do anything but let myself get hurt and run.

"And if I'm not brave?" Dio asked.

"I can be your bravery for you," I said, meeting his gaze. It was easier to be brave for someone else. I could do this for Dio. "We're going. Otherwise, I'll find a way to take my blood back from you."

"Fine," he relented, a small smile playing on his lips.

We returned to the cottage where his sister lived, and as we walked up to the front door, a younger woman came out, stopping dead at the sight of us.

It was then I remembered we were both absolutely covered in blood.

Her mouth fell open. "By the gods..."

"Um," I began, trying to think of a believable excuse for our appearance.

"Uncle Dio?" she asked, disbelief coloring her tone. "You're Dio, right?"

Dio froze beside me. "Uncle?"

"I don't understand. You look exactly like the photos. How...?" She shook herself. "No, it doesn't matter how. Come inside. You have to see my mom."

Dio didn't move.

The girl glared at him. "Get inside the house now, *Unchi.* She's dying. Her entire life, she's never stopped looking for you, and you only show up now?"

"She's dying?" Dio repeated, his voice tight.

The girl's features softened, her gaze lowering to the ground. "Yes. I don't know how much longer she has, so please come inside."

His grip on my waist tightened, and then he nodded. I glanced at him, seeing the blood on his face, and tore a piece of my dress off, using it to clean him up to the best of my ability. He offered me a small smile in thanks before guiding us into the house. The girl led us to the room we'd seen through the window, where Luliana still lay on the bed. Now, though, she cradled the framed photo to her chest.

A photo of Dio, smiling, alive, his arm draped around a much younger Luliana.

"Mom," the girl said softly, placing a hand on her shoulder. "Uncle Dio is here. Can you hear me?"

Weary blue eyes cracked open. "Dio?" Luliana asked, her voice frail and barely audible.

Dio released me and slowly approached the bed. "Luliana. It's me."

"I knew it. I knew you were alive," she whispered, reaching a shaking, withered hand toward him. "My darling *frate*. You haven't changed one bit."

Dio didn't move to take it. I gave him a nudge in the back, and he stumbled forward, lifting his hand to hold hers. "Luliana, I'm sorry that you have to see me like this—"

"I never gave up hope. I searched for you my entire life." Her eyes clouded with tears as she gazed up at Dio. "Thank you for coming home."

Dio knelt beside the bed, now clutching her hand in both of his. "I'm sorry. I came too late."

"Not too late." She lifted her other hand to touch his cheek, but it fell away quickly, her strength giving out. "Never too late. I was afraid to die, knowing you were out there somewhere alone, but now I can rest peacefully knowing you're alive and well."

"I left you alone," Dio whispered. "I'm sorry. I'm so sorry. I was scared you'd hate me for what I turned into."

"I would never hate you. You are my family," she responded, her eyes falling shut, breathing deeply. "You are my precious brother. I have missed you terribly. And I am so happy I got to see you again in this lifetime."

Dio's shoulders shook, and when a soft sob left his lips, my chest clenched. "We'll meet again, Luli."

"Live well until then," she said, her voice scarcely more than a breath. "I want you to be happy, Dio. That's all I ever wanted. And for you to know that I lived happily as well. As happily as I could without you."

Dio leaned forward, wrapping his arms around her carefully and with a tenderness that had me choked up. His body shook with silent sobs, his forehead resting against hers. I had to look away, tears welling in my eyes, and the pendant on my chest suddenly grew hot. I reached for it, pulling it off my skin, looking down to see a new piece of ruby materializing. I stared at it in disbelief as it attached to the original piece, creating a slightly bigger shard.

What the...

The newly formed ruby still didn't fill up even a quarter of the pendant's setting, but it was definitely bigger than before. I blinked, confused. What caused it? Something with the labyrinth? But that hadn't happened before, with Neima.

It pulsed, and I turned my head, seeing a door made of shadows form, signaling my return to the castle. I'd have to figure out the pendant later.

"Dio," I said, keeping my voice soft. "It's time for me to go."

He pulled back from his sister, tears coating his cheeks. "I didn't get to repay you for what you've done for me, Nell."

"I didn't do anything," I denied.

"You gave me courage. You helped me find a reason to live again. How could I ever repay you?"

"Repay me by doing as your sister said. Live happily. Find yourself again," I said, glancing over at Luliana, watching her chest rise and fall. Slow. Ragged.

"Someone needs to take over the bakery, too," Luliana's daughter said quietly, tears streaming down her cheeks. "Mamă always said if you showed up, you'd have to teach me to make her favorite cozonac."

Dio let out a watery chuckle. "She begged me to make it every day when we were young." He stood up, keeping a tight hold on Luliana's hand. "Thank you, Nell."

I smiled at him. "Enjoy your time together."

"I will. I just wish we had more," he whispered, his voice catching in his throat.

The pendant pulsed again, and I brought my hand up to my chest, hovering over it. "For what it's worth, I don't think you're a monster, Dio. And I know Luliana doesn't either. Live your life knowing you deserve to. That you deserve it."

"I will. I promise," he responded, glancing back at Luliana. "I'll become someone I can be proud of. That Luliana can be proud of."

I paused. "Dio, what did you long for? What did Enver promise you?"

Dio gave me a half-smile. "I was desperate to feel anything again. But perhaps I should have been more specific. I forgot how staggering grief is. But... this isn't all bad. I'm sad, but I feel happy too. It's bittersweet. I forgot just how confusing emotions can be after so long without feeling anything. I'll figure it out, though. Go on. Before you get stuck here forever."

I blinked. That could happen? "Then I should go. See you, Dio."

"Bye, Nell. *Noroc*."

I turned away then, heading to the door, and giving him one last wave before stepping into the darkness.

10

Never had the sight of stairs brought me more relief than now—although these stairs differed from the ones I'd appeared in front of last time. These were crumbling and chalky, the carpet over them frayed and faded. It was as if the castle had deteriorated even further in the time I'd been gone. The stained-glass windows lining the walls had cracks, leaving shattered glass scattered everywhere. Rain sheeted against the windows, spraying me with a cool mist. I started my ascent carefully, using the dismal light from the cracked windows to find the safest spots to step. The pendant on my chest was suspiciously cold and dormant.

Something felt off. The castle had always given off an unsettling feeling, but this was different. A heaviness in the air threatened to make my knees collapse under me with every stair I climbed. The kind that reminded me of how I felt when I'd seen Veronica and Julian sitting together in front of me. Something was wrong.

Enver's words echoed in my head. *This labyrinth is as much a part of me as I am of it.*

My pace quickened, and I took the stairs two at a time, no

longer caring about the glass. What happened while I was gone? Why was the castle in such a state? Had something happened to Enver? But even if it had, why did I care?

Still, I didn't stop moving, panting as I reached the top. The light from the windows could not touch the landing, leaving it covered in darkness. I didn't hesitate to step into it, searching for the door waiting for me amidst it. My hand wrapped around a cold doorknob, and I twisted it, pushing the door open.

Thunder rolled overhead as I walked into a room that immediately set me on edge. It emitted a tense atmosphere. One that made my heart pick up and my feet slow. Floor-to-ceiling windows dominated the towering walls, their glass panels rain-streaked, shedding a shadowy overcast over everything. The streams of water also distorted the view of the outside, and I couldn't make out how high I'd gone up. But judging by the way the ceiling pinched together at its highest point as I looked up, I thought I was in one of the castle's towers.

A flash of lightning nearly blinded me, and I turned away. The burst echoed in my eyes, blurring my vision for a moment. I blinked rapidly, trying to clear the afterimage. Another streak of lightning lit up the sky, and my gaze caught on a figure in the center of the room, his dark silhouette unmistakable.

Enver.

As the lightning faded, shadows obscured him again, but not before I witnessed him dropping to his knees, hunching over himself.

My body moved before my mind caught up. I rushed across the carpeted floor, thunder crashing so hard around us that the windowpanes shook. "Enver!" I called, a fear I shouldn't have felt for him rising in my chest.

As I approached, more shadows manifested, lunging at me. I gasped, throwing my hands up to protect myself, but they halted inches away from crashing into me, dematerializing under the glow of a lightning strike. I looked at Enver, seeing more swirling tendrils surrounding him.

Protecting him.

"It's okay," I breathed, holding out a hand. "I want to help him."

I moved forward cautiously, and they didn't attack again. I knelt in front of Enver as I reached him, my hands going to his shoulders. I took in the way he held his fist to his chest, fingers tangled in the silk of his shirt. His black hair fell into his face, concealing his features from me. His breath came out in ragged gasps, his shoulders quaking.

"What's wrong?" I asked, my pulse hammering. "Are you hurt?"

He didn't answer, pitching forward, and the hand not currently clenching desperately at his chest shot out to brace himself on the floor beside me. His head rested against my collarbone, right where my dress had torn, and I froze, feeling something wet against my skin. Blood? Was he injured?

"What's wrong?" I repeated more urgently. "Enver—"

He lifted his head, and my voice died in my throat. Tears glistened on his lashes, briefly illuminated by another streak of lightning. His gaze, normally stoic and impenetrable, betrayed an agony so raw and vulnerable it took my breath away. It was as if a century of pain coalesced there.

His lips parted, a shaky breath escaping from them. "What have you done?" he demanded, and a tear dripped from his lashes, sliding down his cheek.

He made no move to brush it away. My gaze followed its path down his perfect skin to where it dropped off his chin, onto the hand pressed against his chest that seemed to cradle an invisible wound—right over where his heart should be. Another chased it, splashing onto his bone-white knuckles.

"What is this?" he demanded, his desperate gaze searching mine. "I feel..."

My eyes widened. Enver *felt*. "Dio completed the labyrinth," I breathed, my voice nearly drowned out by the relentless rain hammering against the windowpanes. Which meant that, after a century of being devoid of it, Enver was being consumed by...

"It is agonizing," Enver admitted hoarsely, more tears spilling down his cheeks. "This sadness."

Something inside me broke at the sight of his sorrow. He reminded me of myself the night at the club. Desperate. Hurting. I threw my arms around him, pressing myself close to him, crushing his hand between us. The muscles in his back tensed under my tight embrace, but he didn't make any move to push me away. I clung to him, feeling his body tremble against mine.

Seeing him unravel before me like this pulled at an empathy I didn't want to feel for him. At that moment, Enver seemed human. Being crushed by the weight of misery, unable to do anything but suffer through it. "It's okay," I murmured, soothingly running my fingers through his hair.

Eventually, Enver's hand snaked out from between our chests, releasing the death grip he had on his chest to loop around my waist. He tucked his chin in the curve of my neck, inhaling deeply and exhaling slowly. I closed my eyes, my fingers stroking from the crown of his head down to his neck, over his shoulders and back, comforting him until his breathing gradually steadied and the storm outside lulled to a faint drizzle.

When he finally drew back, I released him, looking into his red-rimmed eyes. Wetness lingered on his cheeks, and I raised my hand to brush it away. His eyes closed, and he leaned into my touch as if savoring the warmth of my palm. I caressed his cheek with my thumb, much like he'd done to me the night he found me in the club. When he'd soothed my sadness with gentle touches and kisses.

Before I could stop myself, I rose on my knees and leaned forward, kissing the high point of his cheek, replicating the memory. His lips parted in a soft exhale as I repeated the motion on the other side, kissing away the saltiness of his tears.

He tilted his head up, and the heady haze of his half-lidded eyes took my breath away. "Again."

My pulse quickened. "I can't," I said, forcing myself to release his face but unable to convince myself to move away from him altogether.

"Stay," he rasped, taking my hand in his and pressing it back against his cheek. Our shadow rings materialized, their tendrils curling together, binding us. "Kiss me. Distract me from this agony. It is more than flesh and blood can endure. I fear I will shatter without your touch."

Whether I should didn't matter anymore. His plea resonated with my heart. I knew that hurt. That pain. That want for distraction. I couldn't deny him. I wouldn't. He had never denied me.

Our lips found each other's, and Enver sighed into my mouth, his immediate respite audible. His lips were warm and pliant against mine as I kissed him slowly, wrapping my arms around him again, feeling the tension leave his body with each soft breath he let out. I traced the seam of his lips with my tongue before parting them, making him shudder. I explored the contours of his mouth with unhurried strokes, and he moaned softly, his back tensing under my fingers. He suddenly rose on his knees, pushing gently on my shoulders. I let him go and allowed him to guide me onto my back on the carpet. He settled between my thighs, his own thigh catching the underside of my knee, spreading my legs further as he moved up my body, creating space for him to press flush against me. His weight was a warm, welcome familiarity, and I wound my arms around his neck as he slid one hand under my back, his other coming up to cradle my jaw.

He deepened the kiss, delving into me with a fervor that set my blood on fire. Every brush of his tongue against mine had me arching into him, wanting more. His hand at my back pushed up, forcing us even closer, as if being crushed together still wasn't enough for him. I could hardly think, swept away by the taste of him, the heat of his touch, and then understood why he considered this a distraction. I only thought of him. He took over my senses completely.

And as he pulled back to give me a moment to catch my breath, scattering sweet kisses across my nose, cheeks, forehead, and all the spaces between, I knew he only thought of me, too.

"I need you," Enver murmured against the corner of my lips.

His words sent a rush of desire through my body. And at that moment, I wanted to cling to them, to believe them. I wanted him to need me. I wanted him to treat me as his lover, like he promised so many times before. But I knew he couldn't. I knew I needed to say no. A kiss was one thing, but I couldn't give him my body again. Not as a distraction. Not when he didn't really want me.

My throat worked, but no sound came out as his gaze met mine, burning with desire. Directed toward me.

It speared through me, piercing my fragile resistance. Would it be so bad? To only be desired? I could pretend he loved me. Hadn't I been doing that my entire life, anyway? Pretending people loved me when they never did, to begin with? How would this be any different?

I wouldn't ever have a love like Neima and Paloma shared. I wouldn't ever have a loving relationship with Veronica, as Dio had with Luliana. I didn't even know if anyone would ever love me. So why shouldn't I just take what I could get? At least Enver wanted me in some way. That was more than I'd ever received from anyone before.

I let my head fall back, surrendering to Enver's false affections.

He indulged me, kissing under my ear. "You are so beautiful," he murmured against my skin. "So lovely, my little lover. The way you give in to me fills me with irresistible desire. I want to make you mine. To make every part of you succumb to my touch the way you do to my words."

I closed my eyes, his beguiling words washing over me and leaving a yearning in their wake. He nipped at my ear, and my fingers clutched at his shoulders. "Enver."

"Be mine," he coaxed, voice dropping into a velvety caress. "Stay with me. Let me possess you, and not a day will pass where you will not know my desire for you."

Something in the back of my mind gnawed at me, warning me, but Enver's lips returning to mine made it fade into the background. I gave into him completely, malleable under his touch, lost in the sensations of his touch and kiss. He trailed his lips down to my throat, and I flinched as his lips passed over a sore spot.

The pain confused me for a moment until I remembered Dio had bitten me there.

Enver drew back, and I opened my eyes, seeing him staring at the mark on my neck. "What is this?" he asked.

"Um," I began, not sure what to say or how to explain that I let a vampire bite me.

His gaze swept down my body to my chest, taking in the torn fabric. Within a split-second, light flooded the room, sconces and lanterns I hadn't seen in the dark sparking to life. Enver's expression hardened as he took in the wound on my neck and the blood on my dress. I tried to hide the claw marks on my arm by keeping it looped around his neck, but he leaned back until he straddled my waist, forcing me to release him. His eyes narrowed, and he seized my wrist, bringing my arm closer to him.

"Who did this to you?" he said, his voice unsettlingly steady, given the cold severity of his gaze.

I hesitated, his intensity throwing me. Why did it sound like he cared?

His fingers loosened their grip on my arm. “Tell me,” he said, his tone becoming softer.

“In the labyrinth,” I said. “I ran into Dio, and we were attacked.”

“You ran into Dio?”

“Yes. Can I, um, get up? Then I’ll explain the rest.”

Enver took in my prone form, then nodded, rising to his feet and helping me up off the floor. I smoothed out my dress, taking in its soiled state. Dirt and blood stained most of the bodice, and torn strips of fabric fluttered as my chest rose and fell. “Sorry about the dress,” I apologized, grimacing.

Enver seemed distracted for a moment, his brows slanting together, lips curved down into a frown. “It is true,” he murmured. “Dio completed the labyrinth. That explains this pain. But why were you with him?”

“I’m not sure. I just showed up there,” I explained.

“Strange. That should not happen.”

“I was in Neima’s as well.” I paused. “Has she not completed it yet?”

He closed his eyes briefly before opening them again. “No. She has not.”

Hopefully, it was still by her own doing. I didn’t know what it meant for me if she ended up failing. I went to rub a hand over my chest and flinched as I touched one of my wounds.

Enver’s gaze flared with renewed intensity as he stared at my torn dress. “How did you get hurt?”

“Another vampire attacked me.”

Enver’s hand shot out, and shadows formed before us, taking the shape of a door. He immediately stalked toward it.

“Where are you going?” I asked, startled by his abrupt movement.

“I am going to end the life of the one who hurt you.”

For a second, I was too taken aback to respond. The steadfast determination in his voice had my heart racing. How could he consider killing someone simply because they hurt me? I gathered myself before he stepped through the shadowy corridor, lunging forward and snatching his wrist. "Wait!"

"Do not stop me," he warned, his voice dropping to a dangerous level.

"He's already dead," I said. "Dio killed him."

Enver stopped, glancing down at me with suspicion in his eyes.

"There's not even a body," I continued. "He burned up in the sun. Dio almost did, too, saving me."

"So, you allowed him to bite you?"

My cheeks heated. "He was dying."

Enver didn't look impressed, but then he sighed, the door behind him dissolving into the air. "I suppose I, too, would let myself come near to death if it meant I could be that close to you."

My heart fluttered, and I lowered my gaze. "Anyway, I think that's how Dio completed his labyrinth challenge. Getting his revenge on the vampire who turned him."

"No, it is not that."

I looked back up at him. "It's not? How do you know?"

"Revenge is not an emotion in itself. It is an action taken when driven by emotion," he explained.

"Then how did he complete it?"

"He chose to live," Enver said. "He embraced his pain instead of letting it consume him."

I considered that. Neima had also chosen to embrace her pain. "Then what is my labyrinth challenge? Neither Neima's or Dio's had anything to do with me. Why was I even there? How do I complete mine?"

Enver shook his head. "I cannot say."

"Why?"

"Because you are still in the midst of the labyrinth. I cannot offer you any guidance for your own challenge."

I folded my arms over my chest. "Can't? Or won't?"

"I cannot," he said. "Unless you would like to remain here with me? Because that would be what awaits you should I help."

My heart skipped a beat. "I would automatically fail if you helped me?"

"Yes." He cocked his head to the side, eyes lighting up with mirth. "Hm. Perhaps I should help you after all. You—"

I stood on my tiptoes to press my hands against his lips to silence him. "That's okay! I'll figure it out on my own!"

I could feel him smirk against my fingers. He pulled my hands down. "You are full of contradictions."

"What do you mean?"

"When I am touching you, I feel as though you might agree to stay here with me. But when I am not, you are still determined to leave."

I didn't answer. I knew why. Because with him, in the moments when his caresses made my body burn, I wanted to stay. I couldn't deny that. I couldn't get enough of the way he yearned for me. But when the temptation of touch didn't cloud my mind, reality set right back in. Nothing he felt toward me could be real. Not the desire, not the want, not the need. I had to leave before I lost myself to him.

"The idea of never seeing you again strikes me with a deep ache," Enver said, pulling me from my thoughts and carefully placing a hand over his chest. "Right here. Why?"

I didn't want to know the answer to that. Why would he feel pain when thinking about me? To feel pain, he would have to care, wouldn't he? It had to be a lingering pain from the sadness he'd regained that he mistakenly associated with me—the sorrow that had hurt him so badly.

My chest squeezed at the memory of the tears in his eyes.

"Do you remember what could have caused you to feel so sad?" I asked.

His eyes closed, his fingers digging into his skin like before. "No. Nothing comes to mind. For as long as I can remember, I have been ruling over this labyrinth. Carrying out its demands and remaining distant from those who challenge it."

A distance that didn't seem to exist between us. I hesitated before asking my next question. "Could it be from when you lost your heart?"

"This is not a physical pain. It runs deeper than that. I can feel it in the core of my being. As if it has always been there, as if it is a part of me, and I just have not remembered how to feel it until now."

"Do you remember why you lost your heart?"

Enver shook his head. "No. Perhaps I never had one."

I doubted that. Not judging by that brutal scar that marred his beautiful skin. Something tore his heart out. Just as something stole his emotions from him. Could it have been the labyrinth itself? He spoke of it as if it was animate, but he also said it was a part of him. And as unsettling as his castle was, it didn't seem capable of physically injuring someone.

I thought of the shadows that resided within the castle. While terrifying, they'd never harmed me. Sure, they'd dragged me further into the labyrinth, but they had also led me to where I needed to go so far. They hadn't plunged into my chest and ripped my heart out.

"I should continue the labyrinth," I said, drawing myself from my thoughts, coming too close to becoming more curious about Enver.

His dark eyes opened, and he brushed his fingers against the tattered neckline of my dress. "Let me clean your wounds first. And perhaps find you something more suitable to wear."

"Okay," I agreed. It wouldn't be wise to turn down first aid.

Now that I knew I could get hurt and maybe even die in the labyrinth, I didn't want to risk infection.

Enver took my hand and led me to the door I had used earlier. As we stepped through, we arrived in his bedroom. I gasped as I took in the sight before me—shattered windows, torn curtains, deteriorated furniture strewn about. The canopy over his bed now hung in shredded, shimmering ribbons.

"What happened?" I asked him, looking at the flickering sconces that fought to stay lit despite being nearly cracked in half.

"I told you I have a connection with the labyrinth. When I am in disarray, it is as well," he told me, unaffected by the scene.

I didn't move as he tried to lead me to the bathroom, unable to tear my gaze away from the destruction.

He frowned. "Your distraction, while divine, could only lessen my reaction for so long. The sorrow remains."

That wasn't what struck me about the scene in front of us. I knew my kiss couldn't heal his hurt. But if his sadness destroyed the castle, what did its usual darkness represent? What caused the gloom of his castle's halls? The stretching shadows that enveloped the timeworn walls, the frayed carpets, and the worn decor. If everything changed because of Enver's feelings, then how did he normally feel? What caused such melancholy?

He tugged on my hand, and I forced my feet to move, following him into the bathroom. Once luxurious, now dismal. Cracks tore through the tub, the plants dead in their pots. This was how Enver felt inside right now. Broken. Torn apart.

He brought me to the chipped porcelain counter and set me on it. I watched him as he went to the rotten wardrobe in the corner of the room, retrieving a small basket of medical supplies.

His gaze met mine as he walked back over, frowning at whatever he saw on my face. "What is it?"

"Dio reminded me of you," I said, my throat feeling tight. "When he turned into a vampire, he forgot how to feel."

Enver tensed. "I see."

"But when I saw him, I didn't see a monster. I saw someone forced to become someone they never wanted to be. Someone suffering terribly."

Enver's gaze turned hard. "Then I must be quite loathsome to you to deserve such a title."

"No," I whispered, grasping onto the edge of the counter. "You're not."

He stayed silent, picking up a cloth and turning on the faucet to wet it. Neither of us spoke as he cleaned the blood off my arm, his movements gentle and cautious. He moved to my chest next, pushing aside the dirty scraps of fabric. His eyes remained focused on what he was doing, and mine never left his face.

The perfect curve of his jawline. His rosy lips curved down in concentration, full and kissable. The way the faint glow from the lamps caught on his cheekbones and caused shadows to form under his lashes. His coal-black hair nearly touched his eyebrows as he slanted his head down to inspect my wounds.

I reached out, sliding my fingers through the silky strands, pushing it out of his face.

He made a noise of contentment, as if my touch was everything he wanted, and straightened out. Gripping my thighs, he spread my legs so he could move between them, stepping closer and bringing the cloth up my neck to clean the bite marks Dio left on me. "Seeing this makes me have improper thoughts," he mused.

My hand detangled from his hair. "Like?"

"Wanting to leave my own marks on you," he said, his voice

dropping lower, deeper. "So anyone who dares to come this close to you again will know you are mine."

The image of him marking me, sinking his teeth into my neck, leaving love bites all over me, entered my mind. Arousal followed soon after, and I had to fight to keep my voice steady. "I'm not yours, though."

"Not yet," he said decidedly, leaning closer to me.

His hips pressed against my lower stomach as he forced me to lean back against the counter, my hands going behind me to keep myself propped up. "You sound so confident."

His lips pressed against the opposite side of my neck from Dio's bite. "Because I know you find me hard to resist," he murmured before scraping his teeth along my throat lightly—an unvoiced question.

One that I answered with a nod.

His teeth sank into my skin, and I had to hold back my moan. It was different from when Dio bit me. Dio's teeth were sharp and painful. A deadly weapon. But Enver's were blunt and thrilling. A source of pleasure. Pleasure that shot through me as he nipped and sucked at the spot, determined to leave his imprint on me. I trembled as my head fell back, giving him better access, and he released me, only to move lower and repeat the act.

His fingers gripped my thighs tight, and I adjusted myself, trying to press into him more, a moan escaping me as I felt how much this turned him on, too. I didn't try to resist my instinct to grind against him. I put my weight on my hands and lifted my hips to move against his erection, closing my eyes and savoring the feeling of his desire for me. His teeth suddenly bit down too hard, making me gasp, pain intertwining with the pleasure. He let go immediately, soothing the spot with a gentle kiss.

And then he moved back completely, breaking all contact. My eyes snapped open, and my ass fell back to the counter without him to use as leverage. "What's wrong?"

"I am supposed to be cleaning your wounds. Not this," he said, although his arousal strained at the fabric of his trousers. "I am only creating more work for myself."

I took a steadying breath, my neck throbbing from his attention. I wanted to pull him to me again, but the distance he put between us cooled down my need enough for me to think straight again. "Right."

We fell silent as he brought the cloth back to my neck, keeping a healthy space between our bodies. After finishing with the cloth, he washed his hands and then picked up a glass jar of something that emitted an herbal and medicinal scent as he opened it. He scooped it onto his finger and applied it to my now clean wounds. I expected it to hurt like disinfectant, but it didn't, only producing a cooling sensation. After treating all the injuries on me, he also rubbed some over the fresh marks he'd left on me.

"There," he said, cleaning off his hands again and putting everything back into the basket. "Now, let us find you a new dress."

He cupped my waist as he helped me down from the counter. I looked down at the dress I was currently wearing and frowned. Aside from that first strange feeling I'd had when I put it on, which still lingered, it hadn't been the best thing to wear while fighting for my life. What if I ended up in danger again? "Could I actually have a pair of pants? And a shirt?" I requested.

Enver raised an eyebrow. "You want clothing meant for a man?"

"Clothing doesn't have genders," I said, frowning. "I just want to wear something comfortable."

"It will have to be mine." His gaze raked down my body, then dropped to his own, the difference in size obvious. He stood over a head taller than me. "I will find something that will fit you."

We went back into his bedroom, and I followed Enver to his clothing wardrobe. Inside, though, mostly held dresses. Each floor-length and beautiful, but forgotten. Dust covered their hangers, not a fingerprint in sight. Curiosity bit at me, but I held it back. He reached to the shelves above the dresses, pulling down a thin, long-sleeved shirt. He unfolded it and turned to hold it against my torso. It hung to my mid-thighs, but I still took it from him.

"Can you turn around?" I requested.

"I have seen you naked before. I have tasted everywhere you feel shy to expose to me—"

"Just turn around!" I said, flushing. "Please."

Enver smirked but started digging through the closet again, putting his back to me. I quickly slipped out of the dress, letting it slide to the floor, and then pulled on the shirt. The sleeves went far past my wrist, but I folded them up, happy to be in something that wasn't a dress for the first time in days. I'd never been a dress person, anyway. I only wore them to make Julian happy.

I bit my lip, looking at the ground. What was Julian up to now? Was it possible he hadn't realized I was missing yet? Or maybe he had and was searching for me now. Maybe it scared him into realizing he had genuine feelings for me. And maybe my disappearance made Veronica realize a man wasn't worth losing her sister over. If I never returned, would they miss me? Would they look for me for decades like Luliana had looked for Dio?

No, a cruel voice answered for me—my own. I knew the truth and couldn't pretend otherwise. If anything, they'd be happy I disappeared. So that they could be together without feeling any guilt. If they even felt anything to begin with. They would forget about me and have their happily ever after. And I...

"Oh, my little lover," Enver murmured, lifting my chin up

with his finger so I faced him. "Do not let your thoughts of him consume you."

"How do you know what I'm thinking of?"

His finger trailed down my neck to my breast, just over my heart. "I can feel your desperation, remember?"

"I'm not desperate," I said, although my chest constricted.

"You cannot lie to me," he responded, eyes locking onto mine. "While your desperation only whispered to me before, it resonates within me now. It is so closely tied to your sorrow."

"I just..." I shook my head. "Never mind. I'm fine."

Enver's finger traced back up to the hollow of my throat, then up to the aching marks he'd left on my neck. "There it is. Your despair. Shall I distract you?"

"No," I said quickly, falling back a step, away from his touch. "If you kiss me again, then I don't know if I can stop myself from taking things further."

His gaze darkened with desire. "Oh?"

My cheeks flushed. Why had I said that?

"Then perhaps I *should* kiss you," he said, advancing toward me.

"No," I repeated, my words firmer than my resolve, though if he tried to kiss me, I wouldn't stop him. "I need to continue the labyrinth."

He hummed his disagreement but faced the wardrobe again, retrieving a pair of linen pants. He held them out, and I kicked my shoes off before slipping the pants on. I was surprised they fit much better than his shirt did. Then I considered his narrow waist and wondered how I'd even got them over my hips. I tucked in the oversized shirt, relating it to his broad shoulders.

"You look endearing with my clothing on," he said. "But now I want to take everything off you."

"You're insatiable."

"You are irresistible," he countered in a murmur that sent

my pulse racing. "But fear not. I will resist the urge to touch you. For now. I am quite an accommodating enemy of yours, no?"

Enemy. I'd said it so confidently before, yet given right into him when he kissed me. I had no self-control.

I put my shoes back on, the wound on my chest stinging as I bent over, scrunching the skin there. I paused. "Wait, how is telling me about Dio's labyrinth not helping me?" I asked as I straightened out. "Why did that not make me fail?"

"I wonder that myself," Enver responded.

A chill ran through me. "You didn't know if it would cause me to fail or not when you told me?"

"No," he answered nonchalantly.

My stomach dropped, and I stared at him. His expression was calm, and his posture relaxed. He didn't see the issue with what he'd just revealed.

Because he *couldn't* see it.

My hands trembled. "I'm going now."

He nodded and gestured to the wall beside us, where shadows climbed up to form a doorway. "Be careful. I do not want to see you hurt again."

No, you don't care what happens to me, I thought as I moved toward the portal. *You can't care what happens to me.*

Enver couldn't care about me. Something I needed to remind myself of constantly. He was not a good man. I paused before I entered the shadows, glancing back at him one last time.

Hurt laced his features. Crumpled his forehead, drew his mouth down, and gave a depth to his eyes that hadn't been there before.

Hurt I knew was real because he could feel sadness now.

It was then I realized I'd accidentally said my thoughts out loud. But before I could say anything else, the shadows swallowed me whole.

11

The betrayal in Enver's expression drove me to twist around and try to fight my way back through the darkness to him. "No, wait, bring me back—"

Light suddenly enveloped me, and I blinked to adjust my vision, my mouth falling open as I took in the grand ballroom I'd ended up in. Chandeliers sparkled above me, casting a golden glow against polished marble floors and stained-glass windows. An enchanting melody filled the air, and my gaze turned toward an orchestra of musicians dressed in elegant attire. Past them, a sea of finely dressed men and women in beautiful ball gowns twirled around on a dance floor, a myriad of colors blending together as they gracefully glided around each other.

"Woah," I said, their effortless dancing distracting me from my previous panic.

"You don't belong here."

A deep, commanding voice from behind me caused me to startle, and I turned away from the swaying couples on the ballroom floor toward the direction of the sound. Standing before me was a young man with soft features that were offset by the way his deep brown eyes narrowed at me in suspicion and how his lips twisted into a frown. His jet-black hair fell around his face in an unruly manner, reaching down to his broad shoulders, a section of it tied back with a ribbon. Pointed ears poked out from behind his mane, sharper, wider, and longer than a normal human's, covered with... *fur*?

I blinked, wondering if I was seeing things, but then they rotated, much like a fox's ears did when it was listening intently to something. Actually, his ears resembled fox ears entirely. Then, a motion behind him caught my attention, and I noticed a fluffy tail. I nearly jerked backward but managed to keep myself still. Was he some sort of fox creature? Was I the only human doing the labyrinth?

When our gazes met, his expression faltered momentarily. Distrust melted into disbelief, his eyes widening. "Cas?" he whispered, a swirl of emotions clouding his tone. Hope. Sorrow. Confusion.

"Cas?" I repeated.

And then suddenly, it was all gone, tension creeping back into his body. "No. You're not Cas. How did you get here?" he demanded, a gloved hand subtly moving down to the hilt of a sword.

My eyes followed his movement, and I brought my hands up immediately, trying to show I was harmless. "The labyrinth!" I said quickly, hoping that the labyrinth had deposited me amid someone else's challenge like before. "I'm also doing it!"

His hand didn't move from the hilt, but he also didn't make a move to unsheathe his sword. "No one else has ever appeared here before."

"I don't know why I appeared here either," I told him.

I didn't think it was a coincidence anymore, though. This was the third time I'd ended up in someone else's labyrinth. And most likely, my challenge would be tied with this man's again. What was my goal in them, though? To help the others? Based on the last two, it seemed that way, but I couldn't say for sure. Or why it would be that way. Enver had said the labyrinth would give me what I craved most in the end—*love*. Yet, I wasn't finding love in these challenges. Was I supposed to be finding something else instead? If so, what?

The suspicion in the man's eyes didn't let up, but he let his hand drop back to his side. "I suppose I will believe you. Introduce yourself."

"I'm Nell," I said, holding my hand out to him.

He didn't move to take it and instead gave me a curt bow. "Aki."

Not knowing what to do, I gave a bow back before straightening out. Maybe handshakes weren't the custom here. As I stood upright again, I took in his outfit. Every piece he wore was white as snow, from the tailcoat adorned with pearls on the lapel to the pristine trousers tucked into ankle-length boots. It contrasted against his black hair and ears.

While I inspected his clothing, his gaze traveled my form, too. "This won't do," he said shortly.

I made a mental note to add that to the things I never wanted to hear after someone clearly checked me out. "Um, sorry?"

"I won't have someone dressed as a beggar at my ball."

"A what?"

"Come," he demanded, turning his back to me. "Everything needs to be perfect. And that includes you."

I grimaced but followed him. So far, following the other participant ended up with me succeeding in my challenge, so I'd continue to do that. But...

Now that I thought about it, Enver hadn't received any emotion when I'd completed my first challenge. Had Neima not actually completed her labyrinth? Had she not found her happiness and ended up leaving Paloma after all? What did that mean for me? I'd gone up a floor in the castle, so that had to mean I passed, right? Did the other participant not have to complete their challenge for me to succeed?

Nothing made sense about this damn labyrinth.

I frowned as Aki led me out of the ballroom and down a marble hallway to a tall set of double doors. We entered, and he brought me into a walk-in closet that left my mouth open in awe. Suit after elegant suit lined the walls in varying colors and fabrics. Other pieces filled the space between—shirts, slacks, coats, vests. Aki put a hand on his chin as he considered me for a moment, then dug through the finery.

"Do you collect these or something?" I asked, touching a midnight blue coat with shimmery crystals beaded into the trim.

"They're a gift for someone."

My eyebrows raised. "All of these?"

"I create one every time I miss him," he responded, his voice softening.

"You must miss him a lot," I said, running my fingers over a velvet suit vest as I took in the sheer number of pieces in the closet again. "You're also very talented. These are beautiful."

Aki plucked out a suit and returned to my side, handing it over. "Here."

From the feel of the velvet, I could tell it was something expensive. While he wore all white, the suit he handed me was pure black—even the barely noticeable embroidery stitched on the lapel of the tailcoat. "You want me to wear this?" I asked.

"Yes. Take off that drab attire. I'll wait outside."

He exited the closet before I could get another word in. I stared down at the suit in my hands for a moment before sighing, deciding to do as he said. I peeled off the clothing Enver had given me and stepped into the smooth slacks. They fit better than Enver's, which I considered a plus. I slipped my arms through the dark shirt, swiftly buttoning it up, and placed the vest on top. It fit tight against my chest, and I could feel myself already growing warm from the velvet. I debated leaving the jacket off but finished the ensemble.

I left the closet, trying to smooth out my hair. "All set."

Aki looked at me, not saying anything.

"No good?" I asked, frowning.

"No. You just remind me of him a bit," he said, stepping closer to me, his hand rising from his side, then quickly dropping back down. "Aside from that gaudy hair."

"Gaudy?" I repeated, offended. "It's white. You're literally wearing an entirely white outfit."

Aki upturned his nose. "That's not possibly natural."

"Of course, it's not," I told him. "I dyed it."

"Why?"

"Because—" My voice caught in my throat, the reasons for changing my hair color hitting me harder after everything that had happened. I swallowed. "I wanted to set myself apart from someone. Not that it mattered in the end, I guess."

"And you chose white?"

"It was the most drastic thing I could think of," I muttered.

Aki leaned in closer to me, staring right into my eyes. "You two have the same eye color," he murmured. "The delicate blue of blooming hydrangeas. My favorite flower."

I gazed back at him, the fondness on his face doing little to mask the longing in his eyes. Whoever he was waiting for was clearly near and dear to him. "Your eyes are beautiful, too," I said.

Aki's lips quirked. "I'm aware, thank you."

I smiled wryly, watching as he moved over to a desk in the corner of the room, opened the drawer, and pulled out a dark blue ribbon. He returned to me, gesturing for me to turn around. I did, and he gathered the top layer of my hair, tying it into a half updo.

His fingers paused for a moment. "My, your lover is quite voracious."

My blush burned my cheeks as he released my hair.

"Let us return," he said, his eyes glinting in amusement.

We walked back into the ballroom, and I noticed the same couples still dancing across the floor, spinning and dipping to the unchanged song. "The song hasn't ended?" I asked myself out loud.

"The song will never end," Aki told me. "Not until my love returns to me."

"What do you mean?"

Aki held his hand out. "Care for a dance?"

"I don't know how," I said.

"I will lead us."

Nodding, I placed my hand in his. We made our way to the dance floor, seamlessly merging into the other dancers. Aki guided my free hand to his shoulder before he placed his own above my waist. He began moving, and I immediately stepped on his toes.

"Sorry!" I blurted.

"It's fine. Just follow my steps."

I nodded again, trying to focus on his movements. His hand exerted pressure on my waist, helping direct my steps. The other guests danced around us effortlessly, paying us no mind. Aki spun me, and vibrant colors whirled as my vision blurred. I clutched onto him tighter as he picked up the pace, repeating the same steps, his tail swaying behind him.

The music swelled, and I caught glimpses of the other dancers as we waltzed across the floor. They moved in eerie synchrony, never pausing, their gazes locked onto their partners. Despite their constant motion, no one broke a sweat nor increased their breathing. Dead smiles plastered their faces, and distant looks glazed their eyes. My pulse quickened, and the same unsettling feeling I felt in the room with Enver's mindless servants sank into me. I recognized these mechanical movements.

"What's going on here?" I asked, facing Aki again, trying to break free from his grasp.

Aki didn't stop, tightening his grip on me, forcing me to continue dancing. "We're enjoying a dance."

"Something's wrong," I responded. "These people are—"

"My guests," Aki interrupted, "are enjoying the ball."

"What did you do to them?"

"I told you. The song will never end until my lover returns to me. That means this dance will never end until then, too."

A chill ran down my spine, and I tried to pull my hand from his again. "Aki, let me go."

"No, our dance isn't over," he said.

I tried to stay calm, although my heart pounded against my ribs. "Why are you doing this?"

"I held this ball for my love. I planned on proposing to him, surrounded by our closest friends and family. And then I watched him die in front of me," Aki told me, his grip on me tightening into an almost painful hold.

I nearly stumbled as he abruptly spun me again, then clutched me back to his chest. "He died?" I asked, feeling a little dizzy.

"Right on the steps to my castle. Slain before me by someone I loved and trusted. And he cursed me."

"Who cursed you?"

"My love," Aki answered softly. "As he died in front of me, and I begged him to stay with me, he promised he'd return to my side. After that, I suddenly found myself unable to age. To die. No matter how hard I tried to follow him in death."

I gasped as Aki suddenly dipped me so low I thought I would fall, but he easily hoisted me back up. "How long has it been since then?" I asked, my breath growing heavy as I exerted myself, the velvet of my suit suffocating my skin.

Aki glided across the ballroom, keeping me close. "Decades? Centuries? I do not keep track anymore, nor does it matter. I'll wait for him no matter how long it takes. The labyrinth provided an opportunity for me to meet him again by bringing me back to that tragic day, and I don't intend to waste it."

"The labyrinth brought you back? But you couldn't stop your love from being killed?"

"Unfortunately, it did not bring me back before he died, only the seconds following. Right after the curse was set upon me."

"Have all these people remained trapped here since then? Are these your friends? Your family?"

"Yes. They must be here when he returns," Aki said. "Everything will be perfect for him. Even if I have to keep them all here for centuries."

"What if he doesn't return?"

Aki's gaze hardened. "He will return. He promised. I will find him again and complete my labyrinth."

I panted now, sweat beading on my forehead. My muscles were tense, and every step felt heavier than the last as we danced. How did it feel for the people trapped? Did they even feel? Or were they like Enver's servants? Oblivious and at peace? But this felt more sinister. There was a difference between Enver's servants and Aki's guests. Enver wasn't the one who directly cursed them. He had no choice but to obey the labyrinth and keep them trapped. Aki had the power to release his guests from their torment at any moment.

"Do you think if your partner returns, you'll be free of the labyrinth?" I asked, my legs shaking in their effort to keep up with Aki.

Aki's hands cupped my waist, and he swept me off my feet. "I know it. Because I'll have everything I want again."

"But are you sure this is what he'd want?"

Aki abruptly let me go, and my feet dropped back to the ground, my ankles protesting in pain. Taking on my weight again nearly made me collapse, but I kept myself upright, holding a tight spot on my side as I tried to catch my breath.

"Don't you dare assume you know what he'd want," Aki hissed at me, his jaw clenched. "Figure out why you're here and then leave. I don't need you ruining my night."

He stalked away before I could respond, leaving me in the middle of the ballroom, surrounded by the swirling couples. I made my way through them, nearly thrown off my feet as a pair slammed into me. They didn't react, never breaking their pace or sequence. I hurried to the safety of the refreshments table.

Three people stood near it, plates of sweets in their hands, deep in a lively conversation. Except they spoke no words. Their mouths moved, and their eyes crinkled in laughter, but no sound came out. I watched, horrified and intrigued, as a cycle seemed to repeat. Laughter, chatter, a quick gesture, laughter, chatter, a quick gesture...

I tore myself away, switching my gaze back to the refreshments. A glass punch bowl held a wine-red liquid that had my dry mouth aching to taste it. I cautiously reached out to scoop myself a glass. I'd eaten Enver's food and hadn't been trapped then, so surely now would be no different. But as I picked up the ladle and dipped it into the bowl, the image of it dematerialized in front of me. Instead of a pristine glass bowl, it was now cracked and dirty, coated with black dried sludge. I gagged as a putrid scent filled my nose, stumbling back, taking in the rest of the table. The air shimmered, the sight before me morphing between the polished table filled with sweets I'd first approached, and a rotten table littered with rusted, dirt-crusted platters.

"What the hell?" I whispered, watching the air ripple until it settled back to the depiction of the pristine table, with no sight of the decayed horrors it veiled.

"Glamour," a strained voice said, and I turned to see a young woman in a server uniform approaching me.

"Glamour?" I repeated, confused.

She held a silver tray of sparkling champagne, her blonde hair tied in a bun on the top of her head. Her lips twitched, stuck in a frozen smile, until they formed words. "A magic of illusion."

Magic?

The air shifted, and the champagne in the glasses disappeared, leaving nothing but cracked crystal stems. My eyes flicked toward the woman again, and I had to bite my tongue to keep from screaming. White skin had faded to ashen bone, revealing a skeletal face with hollow eye sockets that stared directly at me, the preserved smile remaining even in death. I turned away, fear constricting my heart, and I nearly stopped breathing.

The ballroom had turned into a macabre nightmare. Skeletons replaced the party guests, their decaying bodies draped in decomposed clothing as they continued their eternal waltz. Grass and weeds grew from the rotten boards that made up the floor they moved on. The music intensified as I slowly faced the orchestra, seeing bony fingers conducting decayed instruments, the sound now out of tune, piercing, and eerie.

"Help us," the woman in front of me whispered, and my gaze snapped back to her. The air contorted, and she was flesh again, lips and cheeks a lively red as she beamed at me. "Drink?"

"No, thank you," I said, slowly backing away from her.

I forced myself to stay calm and put as much distance between us as possible. My skin crawled. Was everyone here dead? Was Aki? I hadn't noticed any glamour on him, so maybe he was still alive. Was he the one casting the magic? Either way, I wanted to leave. I needed to figure out what this challenge of the labyrinth wished me to do. And I needed Aki to do so.

Steeling myself, I made my way back over to the sulking man. "Aki," I started, keeping my voice gentle. "I'm sorry. You love him a lot, don't you? I shouldn't have questioned your motives."

Aki gave me a brief glare before relaxing his posture. "I love him more than I can put into words. More than I thought I could ever love someone. I would do anything for him. Surely you understand? You must have someone you love."

My mouth opened, but I couldn't form the word *yes*. I loved Julian. I loved him with my entire heart. I would have done anything for him. I *had* done everything for him. I'd thought my feelings for him would never change, but now...

Now, as I looked into Aki's eyes, so intensely full of love and brimming with a burning longing that made even *my* heart ache, I wondered if I'd ever truly experienced love. No one had ever looked at me like that. No one had ever waited for me. I'd been the only one to be so desperate. I was the one to wait endlessly to receive back the love I gave freely and unconditionally.

"There is nothing I wouldn't do for Cas," Aki stated, boldly and without reservation. "As I know, there is nothing he would not do for me."

I couldn't confidently say Julian would do anything for me. That anyone would. I wrapped my arms around myself. "What do you think your challenge in the labyrinth is?" I asked, deflecting.

"Waiting for Cas," Aki answered without hesitation. "I know it is."

"But haven't you been doing that already? Even before Enver showed up?"

Aki frowned. "Enver?"

"The lord of the labyrinth," I clarified. Did Enver really never introduce himself to anyone else? Why not?

Aki's lips morphed into a scowl. "Oh. *Him*."

I grimaced. "I take it he didn't leave a good impression?"

"He promised to give me what I wanted, and he's yet to deliver after all this time. So, no. He didn't leave a good impression, as you put it. But alas, I do pity him."

"You pity him?"

"There's a dark, terrible magic surrounding him. One I do not envy," Aki said, turning his head skyward. "A grim and hostile curse."

A numbing sensation crept down my spine at his revelation. "How can you tell?"

"I know magic, human. I *am* magic," Aki responded, looking at me again. "And I know that whoever, or whatever, cursed him is not something to be messed with. It's powerful and foreboding."

I held myself tighter. "Can a curse take someone's heart?"

"In what way?"

"Physically. Out of their chest."

"Perhaps it could, but a curse is never without the one who invokes it," Aki mused, his voice low. "I imagine whoever cursed him is responsible for taking his heart—if you're saying that the lord of the labyrinth is missing his heart. He must have done something quite unforgivable for someone to go so far."

I thought of Enver, of the savage scars marring his chest. What could he possibly have done to deserve that? He said he only ever remembered ruling the labyrinth. Had an unhappy victim of it taken revenge on him? But the way Aki spoke made me think it was more than that. Someone powerful enough to cast a curse that strong surely wouldn't let Enver trap them in his labyrinth in the first place.

"I sense magic on you, too," Aki said, pulling me from my thoughts, oblivious to my unease.

"What?"

He frowned. "It's strange, though. It doesn't feel like yours."

"What do you mean?"

He shook his head. "I don't understand it myself. Perhaps it is the labyrinth leaving traces of its magic on you, too, or perhaps the ruler himself is. What are you seeking from the labyrinth, anyway?"

It took me a moment to respond, still thinking of how I had traced the smooth scars on Enver's chest, wondering who had hurt him so terribly. The person who had cursed him. I cleared my throat, trying to loosen my posture, putting my arms back at my sides. "Um. Love."

Aki blinked at me, then laughed. "Then we're more alike than I thought."

"You're seeking love, too?"

"Is that not obvious?"

"But you have love."

"I *had* love," Aki corrected. "Until he was taken away from me. That's why I believe completing the labyrinth will bring Cas back to me."

I turned toward the brightly lit chandelier in the center of the room. "Who killed Cas?"

Aki's hand curled into a fist. "*Aniki,*" he admitted.

"*Aniki*?"

"My brother," Aki translated.

My head whipped toward him again in surprise. "What? Why would your brother kill your lover?"

"He believed my negligence led to the deaths of his wife and children."

"Why would he think that?"

Aki paced the floor in front of me, running a hand through his hair. "Back then, a terrible disease ran rampant throughout our country. It mainly affected the folk who lived on the outskirts of our city. While I moved to the inner city as soon as I could and prospered here, my brother remained in the outer city. His family caught the disease, and he sent me letters asking for help, but what could I do? It was too late.

There was no cure then. Nothing I could have done would have helped."

I stared at him, stunned. "You didn't even try to help?"

"Cas had fallen ill with it, too," Aki said, coming to a stop in front of me. "I couldn't afford to be distracted."

"But it was your family—"

"I know," Aki interjected sharply. "I should have done more. I should have cared more. Because maybe if I had, he wouldn't have murdered Cas."

Aki's lips trembled, and he turned away from me again. I reached out and put a hand on his shoulder. "I'm sorry. That whole situation is terrible."

"It is."

"Do you think if we find your brother and you resolve your issues, it'll complete the labyrinth for you?"

Aki shook his head. "No."

"Why not?"

"Because he's already dead. I killed him the moment Cas went cold."

I froze, my hand slipping off Aki's tense shoulder. "Are you sure it wasn't your brother who cursed you?"

"No, I'm sure it was Cas. I never knew humans could hold such power, but Cas was always different from the other humans I knew. Strong in mind and heart."

"Cas was a human?" I asked. "Then do humans have magic too, here?"

"No. He shouldn't have had magic. But yet, he managed to curse me, so he must have."

I frowned. A human without magic powers had placed a curse strong enough to stop time for decades or more on someone? That didn't sound right. "What happened again? When he cursed you?"

"I'd gone out to escort him inside when I heard news of his arrival," Aki told me, gazing toward the entrance to the ballroom. "As he approached, my brother struck him down from the shadows. It does not take much to kill a mortal. One perfectly aimed stab through the heart, and Cas crumpled." His voice caught, and his gaze went to the spot on the floor, as if reliving the memory in his head. "We barely had a minute with each other before I lost him. I needed him to stay, but he didn't. No matter how much I begged, he still slipped away. It was in his dying breath that he cursed me. He promised to return to me. I told him I'd wait. Forever, if I had to. Time hasn't moved in this place since then."

Aki turned his chin down, his shoulders shaking, and I bit my lip. Why would Cas cast a terrible curse on the person he loved? How did that make sense? "What exactly did Cas say when he promised to return to you?"

Aki took an uneven breath. "He told me not to wait. To be happy without him until he made his way back to me. But, how could I? I lost myself when I lost him. I knew I would never move on. I would only love him. I swore I would wait for him here. That I'd keep the celebration going, so he knew where to return."

That didn't sound like what someone who wanted to curse someone else would say. Cas hadn't wanted Aki to wait for him, so why would he curse him with that exact affliction? Cas wouldn't have. I thought back to Aki's earlier revelation—*a curse is never without the one who invokes it.*

Suddenly, it hit me.

"Aki... Cas didn't curse you."

Aki's jaw jutted. "Yes, he did. How else do you explain my state of being?"

"You cursed yourself with your love for him," I said, turning toward him. "Your desire to wait for him to return to you must have manifested it. And now you are trapping all the people you and Cas ever cared about by keeping them locked in this endless dance—yourself included."

Aki stiffened, his dark gaze slowly returning to my face. "What did you just say?"

"You cursed yourself," I repeated softly. "Cas wouldn't want this for you. He told you not to wait. He would never curse you to decades of torment, Aki. He loved you, didn't he? He wouldn't want you to suffer like this."

"No, that's..." Aki shook his head. "That's not possible."

"Aki," I said gently.

"I cursed myself?" he whispered, staring down at his hands, his fingers curling inward.

"And I think I know how to undo the curse," I told him.

Aki lifted his chin again, tears glistening in his eyes. "How?"

"You have to let all this go."

"But Cas—"

"Is gone," I told him, my throat tightening. "He's gone, Aki. No amount of glamour can change that. Keeping up this illusion won't bring him back to you. You need to let it all go."

"But if I let go, then I'll lose him forever," Aki said, tears falling down his cheeks. "I can't lose him again. I promised him I'd wait for him."

I reached out, cupping his face in my hands, wiping away his tears. "He wants you to be happy, Aki. I know he does. He... he loved you."

My words tripped over themselves despite how I wanted to sound confident. I wanted to believe Cas loved Aki as much as Aki loved Cas. I wanted them to share the love I yearned for, to prove it at least existed. But part of me was afraid—afraid that Aki had cursed himself for someone who hadn't been worth the wait. That Aki had done so much for someone who hadn't felt the same way about him.

Like I had with Julian.

I shoved the thought aside. I couldn't let my own heartbreak affect how I helped Aki. I couldn't let my own experiences taint his. He didn't deserve to suffer any longer.

Aki sobbed softly, cheeks wet with tears. "Cas, no..."

I swallowed the lump in my throat, pulled Aki toward me, and wrapped my arms around his tall frame. "Cas wouldn't want the people he cares about to suffer, either. Let them go, Aki. They don't deserve this. Think about what you've been doing to them. Please. For Cas."

Aki didn't respond, trembling in my arms, but the world around us began to change. Gold and elegance peeled back to reveal grey and decay as the glamour dissolved. The ceiling crumbled away, bathing us in moonlight, and the floors gave way to overgrowth and dirt. The stained-glass windows cracked, scattering their remnants along the ground. The melody that had filled the air faded, replaced by the haunting sound of wind whistling through the gaps in the castle walls.

The guests finally stopped dancing. In unison, they turned toward Aki and me, bowing one last bow, before disintegrating. Their bodies dispersed into particles of light, floating up and dissipating in the air until only Aki and I remained.

Maybe, I thought as I watched Aki's heart break all over again, *love itself is a curse.* A curse that took on a hundred forms —from trapping someone in an everlasting ball to remaining in a relationship that slowly destroys you. From the feeling of abandonment when someone you love disappears to the pain of being unable to let go.

I held onto Aki, looking over the ruined ballroom. The moon was bright enough to illuminate every broken part, and the decay filled me with a deep sadness. Aki had been here waiting for Cas in ruin and isolation for decades, with only the memories of his lost lover to keep him company.

And now he was letting it all go.

His weeping continued long after the curse lifted. I continued to hold him, my hand sweeping over his back soothingly.

"He's gone," Aki rasped into the newfound silence, the pain

in his voice making my chest tighten. "Cas, my love. My heart. My everything. How can I go on without him?"

"I'm so sorry," I whispered.

"We were supposed to be together forever. I was supposed to keep him safe. I failed him. I couldn't save him. Why couldn't I save him? Why do I have to live without him? Why? Why him? Why not me?"

I could only hold him, my tears mingling with his.

"I can't breathe," Aki gasped. "I—"

"See! I knew I wasn't imagining things! I finally found this place. After all these years."

I jumped at the sound of a masculine voice cutting across the desolate ballroom. Aki pushed away from me, his head snapping toward the voices.

"How did you even know this was here?" another voice responded, high-pitched in amazement. "How has no one else discovered it? I thought you were crazy when you talked about seeing a castle!"

"I told you I wasn't crazy," the first voice said, footsteps growing closer to us. "Something kept pulling me toward this place. I can't believe I finally found it. It's like it appeared out of nowhere. There's something here for me. I know it."

Aki and I shared a startled glance, and I yanked on his collar, dragging him behind the remnants of a collapsed stone column. We squatted low, watching as a man and woman emerged between the cracked open doors of the ballroom.

Aki inhaled sharply.

I watched as the man froze at the threshold of the ballroom. Even from the distance I sat at, I could see his blue eyes grow round. A shade so much like my own.

"This place is insane!" the woman exclaimed, hiking a backpack over her shoulder and slapping her friend on the back. "We've gotta film—dude, are you crying?"

The one with the same color eyes as me brought a hand to his cheek, brushing away a tear. "What? Why am I crying?"

His friend set down the backpack, her excitement fizzling. "Are you okay? Did you hurt yourself?"

"I don't know. This place feels so familiar to me." He brought his hand over his heart. "It's making my heart hurt. Like it's remembering something I can't."

Aki stood then. I tried to stop him, my heart racing as I realized who this man was—or could be a reincarnation of.

Aki strode out from behind the pillar, advancing on the pair.

"Holy shit!" the woman cried, snatching up her backpack and stumbling backward in fear. "Who are you? Stop right there! Wait, are those *fox ears*?"

Aki didn't stop. The chestnut-haired man didn't move. His blue eyes were trained on Aki, the tears he'd brushed away replaced with new ones.

"Casey!" the woman said, grabbing his hand. "Run—"

"No," Casey said, ripping his hand free of her. "I know him." More tears streamed down Casey's face as he moved toward Aki, closing the distance between them. "I know you. Don't I? You're the one I've been searching for all my life. You're my heart. My everything."

Aki came to a halt as Casey approached, his steps hesitant but determined.

"And you've been waiting for me," Casey breathed.

I couldn't see Aki's face, but from how his entire body trembled, I knew he was crying again. "I have. For so long. You promised you'd return."

"I'm here now," Casey said, his hand cupping Aki's neck. "Please don't cry anymore. I finally made it to you. I'm here."

"I'm sorry," Aki said, his voice thick with emotion. "I'm sorry. Everything is all my fault. I should have protected you. I should have saved you. Instead, I—"

"No," Casey responded, his hand running over Aki's jaw. "No. Whatever happened to me wasn't your fault. Don't blame yourself. I can't stand to see you like this. I want to see you smile. It's been so long, hasn't it? Thank you. Thank you for waiting for me. For loving me."

The sound of Aki breaking down into sobs again made tears spring to my own eyes. He had his love again. His love that he had endured decades of self-imposed torment to see again. What was it like to love like that? To be loved like that? Would I ever know?

I took a shaky breath, trying to calm myself, watching Casey hug Aki to him even closer. "I'm here. I'm here," Casey kept repeating soothingly. "I won't leave you again. I'll love you again. It's okay."

His friend looked around, absolutely bewildered. "Uh, Casey? What's going on? Who is this? Holy shit, he's got a tail, too?"

I pushed myself to my feet, wanting to meet Cas properly—to meet the person Aki loved so profoundly and who returned that love. But as I stepped toward them, shadows rose in front of me, the pendant flaring with heat. My eyes widened. "Wait, no, I want to—"

My voice disappeared in the air as they engulfed me.

12

I appeared in a ballroom that starkly contrasted with the one I had been in with Aki. Where Aki's gleamed with gold and light, midnight and shadows drenched Enver's. Black pillars stretched high in a line, creating massive arcs as they connected to the vaulted ceiling. Black mullioned windows let moonlight filter across the enormous, empty room.

"There you are, my little lover. I have been waiting for you."

I jumped at Enver's voice, spinning around to find him leaning against a tall windowsill, his frame silhouetted by the moon's soft glow.

His smoldering gaze swept over my suit before he approached me. "I take it you were in no danger this time around? Though, the change of clothing displeases me. I preferred you in mine."

"I was fine," I responded as a tear slid down my cheek.

His eyes narrowed, his steps quickening as he closed the distance between us within a heartbeat. "What is wrong?" he asked softly, taking my face in his hands. "Did something happen?"

I shook my head, another tear falling. I was just happy for Aki and Cas. Happy they found each other again.

"Or would you prefer I not inquire since you believe my concern is insincere?" he continued.

I bit my lip as he reminded me of our parting words from before. "I didn't mean to say that out loud."

He brushed his thumb along my cheek, wiping the wetness away. "But you meant it."

"That's—"

Enver released my face, moving behind me to wrap his arms around my waist, pulling me back against his chest, his warmth bleeding into me. He leaned down to rest his chin on my shoulder, and I tried to ignore how his breath tickled my neck as he spoke. "You are not wrong. I say the words, but cannot mean them how you want me to. I would be sad if I lost you, but the thought of you being in danger only insults my pride. Nothing more."

"Your pride? Why?"

"It offends me that someone would dare touch what I view as mine."

My heart tripped, and I couldn't find a response to that.

"Aki escaped the labyrinth."

I whirled around in Enver's arms. "He did?" I glanced at the heart pendant, finding what I'd already figured—that another piece of the ruby had formed, the gemstone now filling a third of the setting. Was it some kind of sign of a labyrinth being completed? If so, then what happened to Neima? "Then did you get an emotion back?"

"I believe so," Enver said, keeping one hand on my waist, the other moving up to fiddle with the end of the ribbon Aki had tied into my hair, his fingers brushing my neck as he did so. "Something is different within me, but..."

My heart pounded with our proximity. I hated how easily he affected me. "You don't know for sure?"

"It is not as strong as the last. It is faint," he elaborated. "Seeing you makes my chest ache in the same way it does with sadness, but it is also different from that. It makes me want to embrace you. I want to wipe away your tears and take away your pain. To comfort you and tell you I understand."

"Understand what?"

"Being trapped," he answered, and it seemed to surprise him as much as it surprised me. He let go of my ribbon, his brows furrowing together as he stepped back from me. "Losing something precious."

I tilted my head, unsure of what the emotion he was describing could be. "Aki wanted love, so it must be an emotion related to that, right?"

Enver shook his head. "Aki did not want love."

"He said he did."

"He wanted *his* love back. But in order to have that, he needed to understand how he was going about it wrong. Just as he did not help his family because of his love for Cas, he also disregarded the lives of the poor souls trapped in his ballroom because of his love for Cas. It was that which prevented Cas from returning."

Although now I knew he could tell me about other participants' challenges once they finished them, I still tensed, afraid he would say too much and doom me, but then my brain caught on Enver's word choice. *Poor* souls.

And I knew what emotion he had gained back.

"It's empathy," I told him, eyes widening.

"Empathy," he repeated. "It does not feel like much. Just a heaviness that has joined the ache in my chest."

I frowned at him. Regaining sadness made him act like he was dying, but empathy barely affected him? I knew people held different amounts of empathy, but witnessing it was something else entirely. I was the type to cry if someone else cried in front of me. Had Enver really gone a century without any empathy for those he preyed on for his labyrinth? "What about your servants? Don't you want to release them now?"

"No. They chose to be here," Enver said. "I have shown you that."

"But—"

"Do we need to have that demonstration again?" he asked, his voice hardening.

I shook my head immediately. "No. What about me, then?"

"I still wish to keep you by my side. That will never change, my little lover."

I tried not to be swayed by him, but my heart skipped a beat. Still, I held my ground. "Is that why you told me about Dio's labyrinth, despite knowing revealing too much could keep me trapped forever?"

Enver's expression faltered before he glanced away. "Perhaps."

His answer hit me in the gut, even though I already knew it was the truth. I turned away from him, attempting to walk away. He gripped my wrist, stopping me and attempting to pull me back to him. "Let go," I said.

"If I could take it back," he said quietly, "I would."

"Why?" I asked, keeping my back to him. "It's what you want, isn't it? For me to stay here with you forever?"

"I will not deny that. There is nothing I want more than that."

I tugged on my arm, but his hold didn't loosen. "Then why not just force me to stay? Interfere with my labyrinth challenge and get it over with. Make me yours forever."

"You do not mean that," he said. "Do not tempt me, my little lover."

"I—"

"Ask again though, and I will not hold back," he pressed on, voice low and husky as he tugged on my wrist.

I finally faced him again, stumbling closer, my heart racing. "No, I didn't mean that."

His gaze softened, and whatever he saw on my face made him release my arm. "As I did not mean to hurt you with my actions."

I lowered my eyes again, finding myself placated by his words. Were they a product of his newfound empathy? Or...

"Allow me to make amends," he offered.

"Amends?" I asked.

"It would be a waste to have you in my ballroom and not share a dance."

"I think I've had enough dancing for a lifetime," I responded, shuddering.

"Do not deny me," he murmured, taking my hand.

Our fingers interlaced, his long fingers entwining with mine, and I knew I couldn't resist him. Even after everything. "Okay," I acquiesced in a mumble.

"First, though, I will not have you wearing the clothing of another man." He leaned in, his lips brushing my cheek. "Although you always look lovely."

Shadows converged on us, pitching me into complete darkness. Tendrils peeled at my clothing, and I gasped, struggling to push them off me, remembering the ones that had dragged me through the castle before.

"You are all right," Enver whispered soothingly into my ear, his hand cupping my neck. "Let them."

I made myself relax, allowing them to strip me and then help me into a dress that fit tightly to my torso. It tightened even further, and I grunted, making Enver chuckle. The shadows slipped my shoes off me, replacing them with heels that made me feel unsteady. A moment later, the shadows retreated, and as my eyes readjusted to the brightness of the ballroom, I looked down at my new attire.

A sheer corset bodice explained the tightness around my

torso. It clung to my skin, enhancing my curves, embellished with flowers, lace, and gemstones, all different shades of burgundy. Lace filigree, the color of plum, layered the cups over my breasts, providing a bit of modesty. The adornments continued down the boning of the corset before ending where the beautiful tulle skirt ran the length of my legs, ending just above the floor. It was beautiful.

Yet, again, something tickled at the back of my mind. The wrongness of the dress. I brushed it off, though, deciding it was just because of how weird it was that it fit perfectly.

Enver's eyes narrowed as he caught sight of the pendant on my chest, now cool against my skin. My hand immediately shot to hide it from sight, but I let it go after a second, revealing it to him again, confused about why I would want to hide it from him. "Do you recognize this?" I asked.

He shook his head. "No. Where did you get it from? You were not wearing it the night we met, as far as I remember."

"It was in my pocket," I lied and subtly moved closer to him, trying to see if the pendant would react to him.

It remained cold and unresponsive, and I let it fall back against me, frowning. Maybe it didn't have anything to do with Enver but only the labyrinth itself.

"I see. A shame it is fractured. It suits you," Enver responded, reaching up to touch it, his fingers brushing against my breasts. "As does this dress."

"I'm guessing you like me wearing dresses the most, huh?" I said, smoothing my hands down the skirt, then swaying my hips to watch it swish around me. "I've never been a fan of them myself."

"I love you wearing nothing the most," he responded, a hint of teasing in his tone.

I pressed my lips together, looking up at him and seeing a pleased smirk grace his face. It was then I noticed he had also changed. My eyes roamed over the sharp lines of his new attire, admiring how the silky fabric molded perfectly to his body, outlining the muscles in his arms as he stretched them out to give me a better look. I couldn't quite name what he wore—it resembled an elongated blazer of luxurious black silk, draping down to his mid-thigh. A satiny belt across his waist cinched the two sides neatly together. Enver wore no shirt underneath, and the jacket's lapels dipped low, exposing a good portion of his sculpted chest. The blazer separated again just under the belt, and his black slacks sat low on his hips, revealing a tantalizing glimpse of his toned abdomen.

I didn't understand how he could be so beautiful. He was strength, elegance, and allure wrapped in one breathtaking masterpiece—a living sculpture of perfection. My hand reached out to touch him subconsciously, and when I realized what I was doing, I pulled it back, clearing my throat. "You don't like wearing normal shirts, do you?" I said, trying to suppress the heat rising to my cheeks.

The muscles on his chest rippled as he tensed, lips flattening. "I dislike the feeling of being confined."

My eyes shot back up to his face, surprised by his earnest answer, but he quickly recovered, masking his sincerity with his usual aloofness before bowing before me.

"May I have this dance?"

My heart fluttered, and I held my hand out to him. "Yes."

I didn't miss the lust that mingled with his amusement at my word choice while he took my hand in his, bringing me in close until our chests came together. His other hand pressed against the small of my back firmly, and we danced, with only the sound of our shared breath and the beating of my heart to lead us.

Enver's touch differed significantly from Aki's. While Aki's had felt impersonal and practical, Enver's held a possessiveness that made me tremble in anticipation. His fingers stroked along my back, tracing the curve of my spine and leaving behind a heated trail through the thin fabric of my dress, sending goosebumps scattering across my arms.

When I gathered enough courage to look him in the eyes, my heart nearly stopped at the intensity I found there. Molten desire flickered in their depths—a hunger so raw it left me breathless. His grip on me was unwavering and unyielding as he moved us with an effortless grace, guiding my every step. He curved my body into a dip, leaning down to kiss my throat, his lips lingering on my pulse point before bringing me back up. We glided across the ballroom floor, dancing to a silent, slow waltz just for us.

With a flourish, he spun me outward, and the dress of my skirt billowed around me. But as he twirled me back, I lost my footing, falling against the solid warmth of his chest. Flustered, I tried to push away, but his arm encircled my waist, keeping me against him as he steadied me. "I have you."

I nodded, allowing him to set us up again and continue to lead the dance. As he lifted our hands to shoulder level, I caught sight of my shadow ring, its tendrils reaching out for its mate, the one on Enver's hand on my waist.

"Beautiful, are they not?" Enver asked, catching my line of sight.

"Yes," I responded honestly. "But these aren't like shadows you control, are they? They feel different."

He watched me for a moment, his fingers pressing against the small of my back, an unreadable expression on his face. "No, my shadows did not create them," he said after a moment. "But mine can be just as beautiful."

The air rustled, and shadows appeared around us. Their ethereal forms took the shape of faceless dancers, tangling together as they whirled and twirled around us in perfect synchronization. Startled, I lost my rhythm, stepping on Enver's shoes. He easily corrected me, guiding me back into the flow of the dance and sweeping me across the floor to join the swirling shadows.

"They are beautiful," I breathed, meeting Enver's gaze and the muscles feathered in the corners of his mouth.

We entered a series of dips and spins, and I lost myself in the darkness that cloaked us, letting Enver have complete control. The shadows danced alongside us, their movements hauntingly beautiful and fluid. I didn't know how long we danced. I felt weightless and graceful in Enver's firm hold, his hands moving me effortlessly. His eyes never left mine, and the world seemed to fade around us, leaving me to drown in his ever-captivating presence and beguiling shadows.

Eventually, he pulled me closer, our movements coming to a lull. His lips grazed my ear as he leaned into me. "You are beautiful as well, of course."

I let out a soft exhale. "Enver."

"My name sounds so sweet from your lips," he murmured, nuzzling my neck. "I will never tire of it."

I didn't know if I was out of breath from his words or the dancing. Either way, my heart raced, and I knew I had to clear my head before I did something I regretted. "Why don't you tell anyone else your name?" I asked, trying to keep myself from falling into his magnetism again. "No one ever recognizes it when I talk about you."

Enver's grip on my hand tightened momentarily before it loosened again. "It is unnecessary for them to know it. I wish you would refrain from speaking it so freely in front of others."

"Why?"

"It betrays our intimacy."

"W-we are not intimate," I stuttered, now attempting to break free from his hold.

He moved swiftly, his arm snaking around my waist, dragging me close again. "No? Is that not why I can remember the taste of you on my tongue? Why I desire to taste you again? To kiss and adore every inch of your body?"

My cheeks burned, and I averted my gaze. "No. That's not intimacy. That's just lust."

He bent his head down to kiss my jaw. "I will not deny I lust after you."

My skin tingled under his lips. "How can you lust after me? I thought—wait." I sucked in a sharp breath, angling my head up to face him again. "Is that one of the emotions you already had when we met? Lust?"

"I longed for passion, specifically," Enver told me, confirming my suspicions. "But you are correct. It is one of the three."

Three? I thought briefly, but then my brows furrowed. "Wait, what? Then how can you feel lust? Passion is—"

"A strong, overwhelming desire toward something," Enver described, his hand sliding up my back, fingers teasing at the lace of my bodice. "That desire manifested in me toward you. I have never felt it so strongly before. It burns through me. You do not know how much I covet you. How torturous it is to resist you when you are within my reach."

That would explain the way he looked at me all the time. The hunger in his eyes. The desire. Heat pooled low in my stomach. "Then you really slept with me that night at the club because you wanted to?"

"Yes," he said, his fingers now trailing a path around my ribs, over the curve of my breast, and up to my neck. "I told you so before. I wanted that as much as you did. There was no other reason behind my bedding you."

"Then why did you ask me to agree to the labyrinth when we were... you know," I asked, resisting the urge to duck my head. "Why not wait until after?"

The corners of Enver's lips curved up. "The moment was

fitting. Your begging and pleading do wickedly satisfying things to me, after all."

Blood rushed to my cheeks again, and this time I did try to hide my face. "Enver—"

"Do not turn away," he said, his fingers moving to my jaw, holding me in place. "I cannot get enough of the blush that kisses your cheeks when it is caused by me."

I swore my heart would burst with how hard it beat. His words played havoc with my feelings, stirring up a whirlwind of conflicting emotions. Relief that not everything was manipulation. Self-reproach for being *relieved* about that when he'd still essentially abducted me and forced me into this nightmare. But worst of all, I felt elated. Elated by the fact he wanted me, even if it was driven by sexual desire. Elated by the fact that his passion was genuine and elicited by me.

Enver wanted me. That was real. He wanted me in ways Julian never had. Never would.

"Nell," Enver spoke, both his tone and expression now subdued. "Do not let my lust for you mislead you. Do not mistake it for love."

The elation drained from me at his warning, and I jerked back from him, a pit forming in my stomach, hollow and uncomfortable. "I wouldn't."

His gaze softened in a way that didn't suit him, and he let me go, ending our dance. The shadows dissolved around us, and I wanted to flinch away from the sudden brightness in the room.

"I'm not mistaking it for love," I said, hating how my chest constricted. It just felt good to feel wanted for once.

"Good," he said, and it only made my heart hurt more.

"Why are you telling me that, anyway?" I asked, wrapping my arms around myself and directing my gaze toward my feet. "Don't you want me to stay with you? Why not let me be swept away by your words like before?"

"You have proven you will not be swayed by my words again." He paused, reflecting. "Or at least, so I had thought."

My fingers dug into my biceps. "I still plan on completing the labyrinth and leaving."

"You still have a long way to go," he informed me. "I may not have to rely on persuading you to stay with me after all."

"What do you mean?"

"Your time runs short."

"Wait, what? What do you mean? How much time has passed?" I asked, my heart leaping into my throat. "How much do I have left?"

Enver held out his hand. Shadows swirled together until they formed a dark hourglass. Sand trickled down, each grain a visual representation of my time slipping away. "Twenty-three hours. Then, you will be mine."

"It's already been over twenty-four hours? How is that possible?" I asked, anxiety creeping up on me.

I measured the amount of sand in each globe, realizing they were almost even. Enver was telling the truth. I quickly scanned the ballroom, rushing over to the nearest window. I put my hands on the windowsill, peering out into the night. The clock tower Enver had pointed out before loomed above me, still several stories higher.

I spun toward Enver again. "How many more challenges do I have?"

He said nothing, observing me, the hourglass still in his hand, letting time fall away.

"Tell me," I said, a pressure in my chest making it hard to breathe. "How many?" When he still didn't respond, I went back over to him, clutching his arm tightly. I tried to judge it by the shards of the pendant I'd found, but what if my challenge didn't end when it filled up? "Please, Enver. Just tell me!"

His gaze went down to my shaking hands. In a split second, the hourglass vanished into a plume of darkness, and Enver took hold of my hands, prying them from his arm but not releasing them. "Five."

"Five?" I repeated, suddenly feeling dizzy, struck by the reality that my time was running out. It'd taken me twenty-five hours to finish the first three layers of the labyrinth. Now I only had twenty-three hours left and five layers of the labyrinth yet to go. There was no way I'd make it. There was no way. My hands quivered in Enver's grasp. "Let me go."

His hands slid to my wrists, keeping me in his viselike grip. "No."

My eyes widened, and I tried to jerk away from him. "What are you doing? Let me go!"

"No," he repeated, firm and unwavering.

"Let go of me! I'm not going to make it!" I cried, my voice rising, struggling to free myself. Images of his soulless servants flashed in my mind, taunting me. Of Aki's guests, trapped in their never-ending waltz. Lost to themselves and the world around them. "Don't do this to me, please! I can't become like them. I *can't*—"

Enver's tone turned sharp. "Look at me."

Panic crashed into me. My heartbeat thrashed in my ears as I fought against him, desperate, but his grip was unyielding. "Let go!"

One of his hands wrestled both my wrists into its grip while his other moved up to grasp my jaw. "I said, look at me, Eleanora."

I didn't have a choice but to obey as he tilted my head back, forcing our gazes to meet. I didn't try to pull away, instead letting out a resigned plea. "Please..."

"You underestimate yourself," he told me, his voice low and silken. "You have come this far, have you not?"

"Yes, but—"

"You have already achieved what countless others could not. You have completed three challenges of the labyrinth when most are unsuccessful in their first attempt. You can continue to surpass the odds."

I tried to shake my head, his hold on me making it hard to do so. "No, you're wrong. It's not possible for me to complete them all. I only have—"

"Do not let your fear decide your fate," he cut me off, his dark eyes piercing into mine, familiar and grounding, cutting through the chaos of my mind. "Do not give in to despair over something so small as a grain of sand."

I stared at him silently, letting his commanding tone wash over me.

"I will not let you give up now, Nell," he murmured, stroking calming circles into my cheek with his thumb. "You have already come so far."

I let out an unsteady breath. "Why are you trying to reassure me right now? Shouldn't you be trying to get me to give up on escaping so I become yours?"

His expression shifted, revealing a flash of vulnerability that made my heart skip a beat. "While I still desire to claim you as mine, I no longer wish to subject you to a fate you fear. I am finding I cannot bear to see you like this."

"Like this?"

He released my wrists and retracted his hand from my face, falling back, a shadow falling across his face. "Afraid of me."

I stood still, watching the hand that had been on my cheek curl into a fist at his side. His gaze dropped to the floor, his jaw clenching. Before, I wouldn't have believed him. Would have thought he was just going through the motions to fool me into something. But now he carried sadness. He possessed empathy. He could understand a small fragment of what I felt and experience it for himself. Now he meant what he said. He truly understood my despair.

But he still didn't understand my fear.

"I'm not afraid of you," I said before I could stop myself.

Enver looked up, still tense. "Then what do you fear?"

"Losing myself," I confessed quietly. "I don't want to become like the rest of those who've failed the labyrinth. I can't."

"Then become mine," he said. "You would not have to lose yourself."

"You were just telling me not to give up, and now you're telling me to become yours," I responded, shaking my head. "Which is it?"

The corner of his lips twitched, amusement dancing in his eyes. "I suppose I still cannot help but endeavor to get you to agree to stay here with me willingly."

"Even when I'm actively trying to escape?"

"Even then. I want you."

I paused, the gravity of his declaration stealing my breath. "You said if I attempted to leave your labyrinth and failed, you wouldn't keep me by your side, though. Is that because that wouldn't be me agreeing to be yours willingly?"

"Yes."

"Is it because it would hurt your pride?"

He frowned. "Yes, I suppose it is," he admitted after a moment. "But remember, I also said if you changed your mind at any point, I would still have you as my equal."

"Then, if my time was about to run out, and I agreed to become yours right as the last grain of sand fell, you wouldn't force me to become your servant?"

I didn't miss the dark spark that ignited in Enver's eyes, turning them into smoldering pools of obsidian. He stepped toward me, the raw hunger in his gaze keeping me rooted in place. His hand rose, fingertips ghosting along my neck. "If you agreed willingly, even in those last moments, you would become mine in every sense. My forever lover. My eternal consort," he said, tracing a line of fire down to my collarbone. "My sempiternal beloved. Never anything less than my everything. Never my servant."

"How do I know you'd keep your word?" I asked, fighting against the intoxicating pull of his presence as his fingers danced down my arm. "That you won't turn me into one of your servants if I fail, even if I say I'll be yours?"

He captured my left hand in his, raising our palms between us, and our shadow rings swirled together again. "Should I make an oath for you?"

"An oath?"

"Yes. A sworn promise bound by the oldest of magics. Unbreakable and eternal."

A chill ran through me. Considering what I knew of this world's magic, whatever he was about to offer would set my fate in stone. "What would the oath be?"

"I will swear to keep you at my side as my lover and consort for eternity," Enver stated. "You will swear to become mine."

"You keep saying lover," I said, "but you can't even love me."

"No," he agreed softly, "but that does not mean I cannot long to love you. I would make you feel wanted. I would offer you intimacy in every other way. I would make that enough. I would be enough for you."

The way his words made me want to give in to him immediately scared me. I needed to take my hand back. Needed to walk away and continue the labyrinth. No matter how much I feared losing myself, I couldn't do this. This was losing myself, too, only in a different way. I needed to distance myself from his intoxicating words and magnetic presence. Giving in to him would lead to my ruin.

"You would come to love me, and I would requite your love with my entire being, in any and every way I can," Enver coaxed, bringing our hands up to his lips, where he placed a tender kiss onto the top of mine. "I promise you this."

I closed my eyes as he kissed each of my knuckles in turn, his lips lingering on the last.

"Do not be scared," he murmured against my skin. "Take

comfort in knowing that I am what awaits you should you fail. Being mine is far more preferable than the alternative, is it not?"

The image of his servants entered my mind again. That was the alternative. What was worse? To lose myself like them, or lose myself in Enver's arms?

Was that even a question?

"Promise me I will be in control of myself if I fail," I said, opening my eyes again, my voice shaking. "That you won't mess with my mind or whatever you did to all the other people who failed your labyrinth."

"I will do better than a promise. I said I would make an oath on it," he responded, bestowing another kiss on my hand before lowering himself onto one knee. "One the labyrinth will bear witness to."

Now was my only chance to stop this. To pull back and walk away.

I kept my hand in his.

His long lashes rested on his cheeks as he inclined his head over our entwined hands. "I vow that, should you fail my labyrinth, no manipulation of your mind or soul will befall you. Your autonomy will remain untouched by my influence and that of the labyrinth forevermore."

My hand trembled in his grasp. I didn't miss the allusion to the fact that if I failed, I'd be trapped here for good, never able to return to my old life again.

But what did my old life even have for me? More hurt? More betrayal? What did it offer that Enver did not?

"And your vow?" Enver's voice was velvet-soft yet carried an undercurrent of dominance that made my heart pound. He tilted his head, his eyes glittering in the golden light. "Go on."

"I vow to become yours," I whispered. "Forever."

Possessiveness rippled across his features once more at my words, his gaze darkening, pupils dilating with desire. A muscle in his jaw twitched as if he was physically restraining himself, and when he spoke, his voice was lower, rougher. “I would suggest being more specific, my little lover. Are you aware of what you promised me just now?”

My eyes widened as realization hit me. “If I fail!” The words tumbled out, high-pitched and breathless. “If I fail, I’ll be yours forever!”

“Very well,” he said, sounding vaguely disappointed that I’d corrected myself, even though he was the one who let me. “Then do you accept this oath?”

I braced myself and nodded. “Yes.”

The air shifted, and an unseen current, electric and alive, flowed between Enver and me, causing the hairs on the back of my neck to stand up. A shadowy mist materialized, coiling around our joined hands like ethereal ribbons. It seeped into our skin, causing a sense of comfort to wash over me, chasing away the lingering chill of uncertainty. I released a soft breath, letting the sensation take hold.

Enver rose to his feet in one fluid motion, his free hand finding the small of my back. With a gentle yet insistent pressure, he erased the distance between us, drawing me flush against his body. “It is done. Now, a kiss to seal it.”

My mind spun, our sudden proximity sending a jolt of warmth through me. “What? Really?”

“No. I am merely desperate to kiss you.” His hand moved up my back, fingers skimming across my neck before coming to rest on my chin so he could brush his thumb against my bottom lip. “I have been holding back this entire time. May I?”

I didn’t understand how he undid me so easily. I couldn’t resist him. I nodded.

His lips descended onto mine, soft and slow, kissing me in a way that left me wanting more, but he didn’t give it. His kiss remained delicate and teasing, ending too soon.

I looped my arms around his neck, stopping him as he tried to pull away. "No. I need more," I whispered.

"Oh, my little lover. You know just how to tempt me," he murmured. "How could I say no to such a pretty plea?"

But he didn't lower his head. He remained where he was, looking down at me, a mischievous glimmer in his eyes. The distance between our lips tormented me as I stared up at him, waiting for him to close it.

"Well?" he prompted. "Come on, then. Kiss me."

I knew my time was running out. I knew I couldn't fail. I was just terrified, wasn't I?

But now...

Now, I *wanted* him.

Not just his kiss, but everything he offered—the danger, the unknown, the promise of belonging.

I threw away all my rationality, lifting myself onto my toes while pulling him down toward me to kiss him fiercely. I could feel his lips curl into a smirk before he brought both of his hands to my hips, pulling me flush against him, our bodies molding to each other as our lips and tongues clashed together. His scent and taste chased away all thoughts of reason and doubt. I wanted nothing more than to lose myself in him and the heat consuming me.

Now that I knew his desire for me was real, I couldn't stop myself. Desire was all it was, but it was still genuine. And it ignited my lust for him in return. And as long as lust was all it was, who was I to deny that to myself when I wanted it, and he did as well?

His hands moved under the straps of my dress, sliding them off my shoulders so he could kiss the newly bared skin there before he captured my lips with his again, kissing me so fervently I found it hard to keep up. I had to pull away to breathe after a moment, only for him to draw me back to him almost immediately, not giving me a moment to catch my breath. He sucked my lip into his mouth, licked at the sensitive underside of it, and caressed me in a way that had me squeezing my thighs, trying to ease the arousal between my legs.

Just as I got dizzy from lack of air, Enver grasped my jaw, tilting my chin up so he could lay hot kisses on my throat, letting me breathe. My mouth parted in a moan, my bottom lip brushing against the tip of his pointer finger as I did so. My tongue darted out from my mouth to lick it, and he paused his actions for a moment and then slid his finger up higher on my jaw, allowing me easier access. I took his finger into my mouth, sucking on it lightly. His harsh inhale in response did ungodly things to me. I mimicked the way I'd taken him in my mouth before, and he groaned.

His lips returned to their path to my collarbone. "I only asked for a kiss," he said between nips, pulling his finger free from my mouth. "But you seem so eager to take it further. Tell me, what is it you want, my little lover?"

I should have said nothing. I should have stopped it here. There was so much I should have done when it came to Enver.

But I didn't care anymore.

"You said you wanted to taste me again," I breathed instead, the need in me too strong to deny.

He straightened out, gazing down at me with a mix of hesitance and hunger in his eyes. "I would never deny myself the pleasure of tasting you again if you allowed it," he told me. "I want nothing more than to savor every inch of your beautiful body."

"I want you to do that, too," I said, anticipation making my stomach flutter.

13

Leaning in, Enver placed a gentle kiss on my forehead. "We do not have the time for that."

The horrible, humiliating feeling of rejection washed over me. My entire body turned hot again, now in the wrong way, as memories of times with Julian slammed into me. I never asked him to do anything for me because he always refused. I'd quickly learned not to. I should have known better with Enver. I should have kept my mouth shut and—

"Even forever would never be enough for me to enjoy you to my content. But we have time for me to worship you where you want me the most," he continued, his voice almost a purr as he slid the skirt of my dress up my thighs until it gathered around my waist. Lazily, he trailed a finger over my hip bone, dipping lower until he brushed against the fabric of my underwear. "This is where you really want my tongue, is it not?"

He didn't even have to ask. We both could feel how wet I was by the way cool moisture clung to the lace as he pressed his finger further into me. I reached out and grasped his arm, unsteady on my feet from his touch.

"I..." I trailed off, the whiplash of my emotions getting the better of me, discomposed by my self-imposed memory of Julian. The arousal I'd felt faltered slightly, now combined with an echo of abashment. Even though Enver agreed to my request, I couldn't push away the persisting humiliation of previous rejections from Julian that had popped into my mind. To be denied intimacy again and again—and not just sexual intimacy. Everything.

Enver abruptly withdrew his hands, letting my dress cover my thighs again. "What is it?"

"Nothing, sorry," I said, refusing to look him in the eye. "We can continue."

"Tell me what you are thinking," he said, cupping my face and tilting it up, forcing me to meet his gaze. "If you have changed your mind, then I will stop. I want you to enjoy my touch, not endure it."

"No, that's not it."

"Then tell me."

"Julian wouldn't really ever do anything for me," I admitted after another moment. "So, when you said we didn't have time, it felt like a rejection and reminded me of him. That's all."

Enver released my face, a flicker of irritation crossing his face. "I see."

I quickly grabbed his hand in mine, my heart sinking. "I'm sorry. It's not fair of me to compare you to Julian. I shouldn't have—"

"I take no offense at being compared to someone so inconsiderate and inadequate when the comparison is irrefutably in my favor," Enver told me, shaking his head. "I take offense that he would deny you at all. You should know how you deserve to be treated and understand how he never deserved you. You should be cherished, adored, and pleasured. Never denied."

I shivered at the steadfast glint in his obsidian eyes as he gazed down at me. "Enver."

He took my hand that held his and brought it to his lips,

gazing down at me over it. "I will never deny you any pleasure nor deny myself the joy of giving it to you. Remember that."

I would. I would remember nothing but Enver for the rest of my life. I knew now that even if I escaped his labyrinth, he would always be at the back of my mind, invading any intimate moment I'd ever share with another. He would be the standard that I compared all my future lovers to. The thought should have unnerved me, but I couldn't bring myself to be anything but overcome with want and affection for the man who so easily undid me.

"I intend to show you just how deserving you are," he murmured. "Until you will not forget it. Do you want that?"

"Yes," I whispered back. "Please."

"Turn around," he ordered.

I did as he said, and his hands touched my neck, moving my hair to the side so he could untie the ribbons of my corset bodice. The dress fell off me to the polished floor, and Enver helped me step out of it, pressing in close to me. He kissed the back of my neck and the curve of my shoulders as he unhooked my bra, letting it drop to the floor as well. I closed my eyes as his fingers slipped into my underwear, pushing it down my thighs as he kissed along my spine.

Being naked in the middle of the grand ballroom with Enver fully dressed beside me had me breathless with arousal. He continued to plant a trail of kisses down, lowering himself into a kneeling position behind me, and I nearly jumped as his lips brushed against the curve of my ass cheek. I tried to move away, but his hands gripped my thighs, keeping me in place.

"Do not move," he commanded, kissing me again.

My hands clenched, wishing I had something to hold on to as he descended further, licking a hot stripe across the back of my thigh before nibbling at the soft skin there. He continued to litter my thighs with kisses, and then his hands left my thighs to squeeze my ass, and he made an appreciative noise.

"Lovely," he said before rising to his feet again.

My face flamed, and he moved to stand in front of me, his eyes sweeping across my nude form.

"Spread your legs for me."

I adjusted my stance obediently, and his pupils dilated with desire.

"Good," he praised, his hand tangling in my hair, pushing my head forward into a kiss. "So obedient for me."

When he released me, he pushed me back harder than I was expecting. I gasped, losing my balance, but instead of falling to the floor, I fell onto something cool and firm. I immediately recognized the peculiar sensation of his shadows. Umbral armrests were on either side of me, and a backrest pressed against my shoulders, rising above me. Tendrils crept over my wrists, winding around them, keeping me bound to the dark throne the shadows had formed beneath me.

Enver loomed over me. "Keep your legs spread."

My thighs parted as I shifted into a more comfortable position on the throne.

"Wider."

I spread them until they bumped against the base of the arm supports, preventing me from stretching any further. More tendrils materialized, wrapping around my thighs and the legs of the throne, snaking all the way down to my ankles, binding me completely.

"You are so beautiful like this," Enver said, drinking in the sight of me for a moment before reaching down and pinching my nipple. "Tied up and docile, ready to receive whatever I decide to give you."

I moaned, and his hand slid around to cup my breast, massaging it with his long, slender fingers. "Please. *Fuck*."

"You say that word often when I touch you," Enver remarked. "What does it mean?"

I tried to focus on his question as he toyed with me. He was asking this *now*? "Fuck? It depends," I said through a groan. "You can use it as an exclamation or noun... or verb."

"A verb?"

"Yes. When I use it with you, it's because I want you inside me. When I want you to fuck me."

His lips twitched into a smirk. "Is that so?"

I arched my back, wanting more. "Please, Enver."

"Still so eager for me," he all but cooed. "Tell me what you want."

I closed my eyes, my head falling back. "You."

"Be specific, my little lover."

"*Anything*."

He tweaked my nipple again as he leaned over me, his voice a low rumble against my ear. "Anything? You should know better than to say that to me by now. What if I wanted to keep you tied up here forever? Spread open and helpless, entirely at my mercy?"

My hands twitched in their restraints. His response should have intimidated me, but it did the opposite, sending arousal flooding through me. "Enver, please," I tried again.

"Or... what if I were to have my shadows fuck you while I watched?" he murmured, his breath hot against my neck. "Would you like that?"

My breathing stuttered. His shadows? I shuddered, my mind inundated with images of his shadows writhing against me, using me in a way that both intimidated and excited me.

"Oh, I think you would," he said, his hand trailing over the swell of my breast, over my stomach, down to the dripping apex of my thighs. "Do you want to find out now? How it would feel to have my shadows fill you until you cannot think of anything else? I would love nothing more than to watch you come undone by my creation and command."

I lifted my hips, trying to press myself harder against him. "No, I want you," I said.

"You said anything," he responded, and a shadow brushed against my inner thigh, nudging in closer. "Remember?"

My eyes shot open again, my mouth opening to protest, but as soon as our gazes locked, the pad of his thumb swiped across my clit, and the notion left my mind. I barely managed to hold back a whimper, melting back into the throne as he repeated the action, rubbing slow circles into my sensitive skin.

"Are you ready to tell me what you want now?" he asked, his thumb moving lower, his shadow inching closer to my entrance, causing my hands to clench in response.

"I want you to taste me," I whispered, my cheeks flushing, but the shadow dropped away from my thigh.

"Taste you how?"

I stared at him, and he gave me an expectant look in return. My tongue felt heavy and useless in my mouth as I struggled to form the response he wanted to hear, unconfident in voicing my desires. "I..."

"Is it too hard for you to say? Would you like me to help you?" he offered, lifting his hand to tuck my hair behind my ear.

I nodded, falling into his touch.

"Repeat after me, then," he said, pulling his hand back. "'I want you on your knees before me, Enver.'"

I took a steadying breath. "I want you on your knees before me, Enver."

"Good." He obeyed my echoed command and knelt in front of me, his breath fanning across my navel as he gazed up at me. "Now say, 'I want you to fuck me with your tongue until I come.'"

My heart skipped a beat. He'd picked up on how to use the word fuck quickly. "Enver—"

"Say it."

The demanding, husky edge to his voice had me complying

immediately. "I… I want you to fuck me with your tongue until I come."

"Very good," he responded lightly. "You are so desperate for pleasure. Is there anything else you would like me to do? Do not be shy now. Remember, I will not deny you."

I knew he wanted me to come up with something on my own this time. His breath teased me as he waited for my answer, and I squirmed on the throne. "I want more than just your tongue on me. I want your fingers on me. In me," I said, hot embarrassment creeping up my neck even though what was about to happen would be far, far more unreserved.

Enver smirked. "It would be my pleasure. Or, should I say, *your* pleasure."

I let out a moan in response as his fingers dug into my hips, tugging me forward on the throne until his mouth hovered over my wet, throbbing center. His tongue darted out, tasting the moisture there, and he hummed in satisfaction before flattening his tongue against me, licking up and down in broad strokes.

I gasped at the contact, arching my back, straining against the shadows holding me down. His tongue delved deeper, greedily pushing into my folds, then moving down to circle my entrance, dipping in teasingly before retreating. I bucked my hips up, and he pulled back briefly, only to move in again and lick a path up to my clit, which he then sucked into his mouth, focusing all his attention there. His tongue flitted over it again and again, sending jolts of pleasure through me that had my toes curling.

My thighs shook, and he released my clit, opting to take a moment to kiss my inner thighs, his lips ghosting over the sensitive skin there, leaving behind a damp trail of my arousal. "You taste even better than I remembered," he told me, his thumb moving to tease my clit again, making me moan. "And sound even sweeter. I cannot get enough of your lovely little noises. Do you know how hard they make me?"

God, I didn't think someone's voice could turn me on so much. Yet Enver's words alone had me aching, his thumb's slow caress almost paling in comparison to the need his words evoked in me. "Enver, please."

"Are you enjoying yourself, pet? Am I pleasing you?"

"Yes," I breathed.

"Then I want to hear your appreciation and encouragement," he said. "Let me know how much you love what I can do to you with my tongue and fingers, or I will stop. No more sounds out of you unless it is you praising me. Understand?"

A rush of excitement followed his demand, and I looked down at him, letting out a shaky breath, trying to gather my courage. He stopped his teasing circles as he waited for my response, his cheek pressed against my thigh. "You make me feel so good, Enver. Like no one ever has before," I told him, grasping at the shadows of the throne to steady myself, my voice sounding strange to me, speaking words I'd never usually say. "I-I could come by the sound of your voice alone."

He rewarded my obedience by returning his mouth to its previous position, his lips replacing his thumb, his tongue flicking against me in quick succession.

"That feels good," I moaned, struggling to speak when the only thing I could focus on was the way his mouth moved against me so perfectly.

He pulled back, glancing up at me from between my thighs. "You can do better than that. Praise me, my little lover."

My mind scrambled to find the right words as he went back to sucking, then trailed his tongue lower to plunge inside me, fucking me with it as I'd demanded before. My hips rocked against every thrust, trying to feel him deeper. I let myself get lost in the sensation, letting go of my inhibitions. "I love your tongue," I whimpered. "I love the way it feels inside of me. You feel so good. I don't want you to stop, please..."

He brought his thumb back to my clit, and I jerked against my bindings, the dual sensations causing my head to spin. I wouldn't last long. Not like this. My hands clenched and unclenched as I tried to fight off the pleasure building in me. I didn't want it to end yet. But, as if sensing I was close, Enver redoubled his efforts, his tongue and thumb working together to bring me over the edge.

My head fell back, and I moaned loudly. "E-Enver, you're going to make me come," I gasped, my eyes fluttering shut.

Praise, I reminded myself. He wanted praise and encouragement.

"I love what you're doing to me. Please don't stop," I continued, my breath coming in short bursts as heat and tension coiled in me, making the words slip out unabated. "Keep going, just like that. I love it. I—*ah*—I can't..." My words died on my tongue, pleasure getting the best of me, a moan ending my attempt at praise.

Enver let out a low groan against me, his tongue retreating from inside of me. Before a whine of protest could even form in my throat, he sunk two fingers in instead, thrusting deep as his mouth found my clit again, his lips sealing over it, tongue encircling it as he sucked.

A choked gasp left my lips as his fingers curled inside me. My legs quaked with pleasure, and I tossed my head back and forth, biting back a moan. "I-I'm so close. Please, Enver. *Please*—"

My voice broke off as the pleasure building inside me crested, waves of pure ecstasy crashing over me as his fingers continued to push into me as I came, feeling myself pulse around him. My body arched up against the shadows that held me to the throne as his unrelenting tongue and fingers continued their ministrations, drawing out my orgasm until I whimpered with the overstimulation.

"Wait," I gasped.

"Again," he demanded.

I fell against the backrest of the throne, pleasure burning through me, my body quivering as he pushed a third finger inside of me. "Fuck!" I cried, unable to catch my breath, every nerve in my body on fire. Torn between wanting to come again and wanting him to stop, I twisted against my bonds. Sweat beaded on my forehead, and a low whine escaped me, my toes curling as his fingers pumped in and out of me. I wasn't sure if I was going to come again or die.

Then his tongue swiped over the perfect spot, and the tension inside me snapped again. I choked on a cry as stars flashed across my vision.

I slumped against the backrest when his touch finally receded, my eyes falling shut. My pulse pounded in my ears, my body twitched from the strength of my orgasms. Fabric rustled as Enver stood, his hand appearing on my jaw, turning it upward to pull me into a searing kiss. I sighed into it, tasting myself on his lips, and he groaned in return, his teeth finding my lower lip, giving it a gentle nip before pulling away.

"And?" he prodded. "Did I pleasure you well? Judging by your cries, I believe I did, but I desire to hear more of your voice as you tell me exactly how much I pleased you."

"Don't be greedy," I mumbled, worn out.

He chuckled, stroking my cheek. "Why not? I believe you would love it if I were. I am insatiable, remember?"

I suddenly wanted nothing more than to sleep. I shifted to sit up again, reluctantly opening my eyes. My gaze zeroed in on the bulge in Enver's slacks as I did so. I swallowed, looking up at him, seeing his chin still glistening from my arousal, his dark hair a mess over his forehead.

He shook his head as if reading my thoughts. "This was only for you. I expect nothing in return."

"But you're..."

"I can take care of it myself," he told me. "I have over a century of experience in that respect, after all."

I blushed at his implication, but he didn't seem bothered by it. "And where did you get the experience for everything else?"

My question seemed to throw him. His brows furrowed for a moment before he answered. "Natural talent," he said, but his voice lacked the confidence it usually held.

"Oh, I wasn't saying it was bad or anything—"

"No, your enjoyment was apparent," he said, cutting me off, still sounding distracted.

He fell into silence, and I studied the way his lips pulled down into a frown. "Um, can you have your shadows release me?" I asked, suddenly feeling exposed.

"Oh." He cleared his throat, and a second later, I could move my arms and legs again. "My apologies."

I pushed myself onto my shaking legs, reaching down for my dress. Weariness wore on me, as if the relaxed state I entered after orgasming reminded my body that I hadn't slept in over twenty hours. My eyelids felt heavy, and I struggled to pull my dress over my hips, nearly falling to the side.

Enver grasped my hips, holding me steady. "Are you all right?"

"I'm just a little tired," I told him, letting myself rest against his body as he moved closer to me.

"You need to sleep."

"I can't. I have to continue the labyrinth before I run out of time."

"Your time is not running at this moment."

I inhaled sharply. "You can do that?"

"Only when you are with me," he explained.

"Then—"

"I cannot use it to help you," he reminded me gently. "Remember what I told you would happen if I helped you?"

I tensed. I'd fail if he helped me. "Isn't letting me sleep helping me, technically?" I asked, worried now.

Enver shook his head. "No. It is acting on my desire to keep you close to me."

"Aren't you the one who set my time limit in the first place? Why can't you just get rid of it?"

Enver scooped me up into his arms, my dress sliding off my hips as he did so, leaving me bare again. Startled, I clung to him, wrapping my arms around his neck. "I..." He hesitated, frowning down at me. "I have something to confess to you."

My heart sank. "What is it?"

"Let me begin by saying I now wish I had not done it."

"What is it?" I repeated, arms tightening around his neck as we exited the ballroom, reappearing in his bedroom.

I glanced around, no longer seeing the destruction caused by Enver's previous emotional state. Everything had been reconstructed and mended, returning to its normal extravagance.

"I created the time limit for you even before you insulted me," he said.

I lowered my gaze at the reminder of when I'd called him a monster. "That's it? Why did you make it sound like you had something serious to say?"

"When I created your time limit, it was bound to our contract. That is why I cannot change it now."

For some reason, hearing this didn't upset me that much. "What's done is done," I said slowly as Enver carried me over to his bed, "but why did you create a time limit for me when you haven't done that for anyone else?"

"I hope you believe me now when I say it is because I wanted you from the moment I first laid eyes on you. You are the first person I have truly desired. The first person I have wanted to claim. The first person I have wanted to keep as my own. I created the time limit to ensure you would fail and be forced to remain by my side as my lover."

Instead of terror, a thrill rushed through me—one I tried and failed to nip in the bud. I shouldn't have felt so intoxicated by the idea Enver wanted me so badly that he planned to manipulate me and keep me captive from the moment he saw me, but I did.

My heart beat faster, my hands tangling in Enver's disheveled hair. "You really wanted me that badly?"

"Yes. I still do. Very much so. How much more do I have to convince you of that? Your mere presence drives me to the brink of insanity with the desire I feel toward you. Every moment you are away from me, I am left with an emptiness that I feel more profoundly than the one created by my absent heart."

I stared up at Enver as he laid me on his bed, and my breath stuttered as his body followed mine, caging me in.

"And even when you are here with me, that ache does not go away," he confessed, gazing down at me with a look that was full of both longing and heat. "While your touch can lessen the pain of wanting you, knowing you do not belong to me is a constant torment."

"Enver," I whispered, left breathless by his admission.

No one had said things like that to me before. He offered me the things I'd always wanted to hear so willingly. No hint of hesitation, no hint of deception. It made me wonder what it would be like if he could feel love. If he could care for me as intensely as he wanted me. If he would love me the way I always wanted to be loved.

"Only having you completely will ease this torture you cause me, my little lover," he said, cradling my jaw in his hand. "Only when you are mine will I feel whole once again."

"I don't understand," I said. "Why me?"

It was never me.

Never.

Not until him.

"I do not have the answer you are looking for," Enver responded, his hand sliding down and behind my neck, cupping it. "I am simply drawn to you. Something inside me tells me I need you. As stars need darkness to shine. As shadows need light to cast them. I need you to exist."

The answer I was looking for? What did he mean by that? Before I could ask, his lips descended on mine, capturing them in a tender kiss. My eyes fluttered shut, and I tried to pull him down, wanting his weight on me as our mouths moved against each other's leisurely.

But the muscles in Enver's arms flexed as he resisted my efforts. He broke our kiss to press his lips against the shell of my ear. "You should sleep."

"I want you to kiss me more," I said.

He obliged, scattering kisses down my ear and onto my neck. The puncture wounds Dio had left stung dully as his lips passed over them, moving to the ones he'd left on me in return, and deep down, I finally felt a flicker of recognition of the danger in Enver's confession. He would do anything to have me. I needed to remember that. I needed to make sure I didn't get too swept away by his words and actions to forget it.

Even if staying here sounded more and more tempting with every minute I spent with him.

My exhaustion crept up on me, even as Enver's lips sent heat coursing through my body again as he littered my collarbone with kisses. He didn't stop moving, meticulously covering every inch of my skin with his kisses, leaving no part unclaimed.

"What are you doing?" I asked, fighting to keep my eyes open.

"I told you earlier forty-eight hours would not be enough

time for me to worship you the way I wanted to," he responded, his lips now brushing against the tops of my breasts.

"Why is that?"

"Because I would lay kisses upon every inch of your beautiful body," he murmured, kissing the hollow of my throat. "Caress every curve and contour. Taste every expanse of sweet skin. I would take my time unraveling you."

I swallowed, and his gaze found mine, full of fervor. "You said we don't have time for that."

"I meant only forever would provide me with enough time to worship you the way I crave to," he responded. "I should have told you that your time stops with me and fulfilled my promise immediately rather than letting you believe, even if only for a moment, that I was denying you."

A yawn escaped my lips. "Did you say that because you didn't plan on telling me that my time stopped when I was with you?"

"Yes."

"I saw the grains of sand falling through the hourglass, though."

"An illusion, so it seemed like time was still moving," he told me. "Although I did not deceive you about the amount of remaining time."

I didn't have the energy to be mad. "You went that far to hide it, but you still ended up telling me?"

"You need rest. I feared you would continue the labyrinth in your state and collapse somewhere I could not find you. Then, your time would undeniably be wasted."

"Now you're the one full of contradictions," I murmured, his lips kissing a trail down between my breasts and across my sternum. "You want me to fail, yet you keep helping me so I can succeed."

"I do not understand it myself."

As I didn't understand why I couldn't convince myself Enver was the enemy. Not my friend. Not my lover.

He placed his relentless kisses along my ribs, and I sighed sleepily. "Then, are you trying to make good on your promise now?"

I could feel his lips quirk up against my skin as he continued his path. "Consider it a preview."

"Enver, I'm tired."

"Then sleep," he responded, but didn't stop his attentions. "Fall asleep to my kisses and dream of my touch."

He pulled his blankets over us, disappearing under them. As his lips pressed against my lower stomach, we lapsed into silence, and his quiet breathing and gentle caresses slowly lulled me to sleep.

14

The bed was missing Enver's warmth when I woke up. I rolled over, tangling myself more in his comforter. I blinked a few times groggily, scanning the room for the enigmatic man and finding him standing by the window. A living sculpture framed by the velvet curtains that fluttered around him. He stared out the window, unmoving, wearing nothing but loose cotton pants that rode low on his hips. Even after all this time, the sight of him stole my breath away. The broadness of his shoulders. The elegant lines of his well-defined back. The way it tapered down to his trim waist. The way the morning light kissed his flawless skin. He was too beautiful. Too perfect.

And I was helpless to resist the draw he had on me.

He seemed lost in his thoughts, standing as still as a statue as I shifted to slide out of the bed, keeping the sheet wrapped around my naked body.

The moment my bare foot hit the floor, Enver turned toward me, as if pulled by an invisible thread connecting us. All the tension in his body visibly melted away as his gaze landed on me.

And then, he smiled.

I froze.

It wasn't like his normal smiles. Not the usual arrogant twist of his mouth or the typical teasing smirk that so often made an appearance. No. This was something new. Something full of emotion. It started as a gentle curve of his lips, gradually unfurling until it blossomed into something tender and intimate.

Something *real.* Devastatingly, heart-achingly real.

It lit up his face—softening his normally sharp features and causing my pulse to quicken as he drew closer. "Enver?" I asked cautiously, perched on the edge of the bed, looking up at him.

"Good morning, Nell," he greeted, stooping down to kiss the crown of my head, the blinding smile still playing on his lips as he straightened. "I hope you slept well."

"What...?" I trailed off, unsure of how to phrase my question. "What's wrong?"

His eyebrow arched, eyes glimmering in amusement. "Nothing is wrong. Why do you ask?"

"You seem... different," I ventured.

He laughed.

Laughed.

"Do I, my little lover?" he asked, his voice a silken purr. "How so?"

I rose from the bed, keeping the sheets swaddled around myself, and he immediately closed the distance between us, tucking me against his bare chest and dropping another kiss into my hair. "Did something good happen?" I asked cautiously.

"Only good things happen when I am with you." His smile still hadn't faded as I looked up at him. His eyes crinkled as he tucked a strand of my hair behind my ear. "You are adorable when your hair is a mess."

I just stared at him, growing more and more confused and

concerned. Was this one of his shadows impersonating him? "Do you feel okay?"

He tilted his head, his smile shifting to something more playful, his thumb caressing my cheek. "Yes, but I know how I could feel even better. Care to indulge me, my dearest Eleanora?"

Before I could respond, his hands slid under the sheets covering me, grabbing hold of my bare waist. I jumped at the coolness of his touch, and he chuckled, bringing his head down to nuzzle his nose into my neck.

I didn't move, still disconcerted by his demeanor. It was almost as if he was...

Happy.

I pulled back from him, pushing against his chest, looking up into his eyes again. His smile faltered a bit at my rejection, but another easy one replaced it soon after, and he released me, adjusting the sheets so they covered me again.

"Enver, did Neima complete her labyrinth?" I asked, letting the sheets slip down so I could see the pendant on my chest.

The ruby nearly filled half of the setting now, another piece having appeared while I was sleeping. Even without Enver saying it, I knew Neima had completed her labyrinth. It had to be true, then—a piece of the gemstone appeared with each completed labyrinth layer. But why? How? What did it mean? What would happen when it became complete?

"Hm." Enver closed his eyes briefly. "She has. I suppose that would explain the new feeling within me."

"What do you feel, exactly?"

"Warm, when I look at you," he murmured. "As if you are in my veins, running through me, filling me with a warmth that seeps into my very bones, staving off the cold I have grown accustomed to." He paused, seeming to search for the right words. "I feel... weightless, too. As if the world is not as heavy a burden to bear as I previously thought. Not when you are here with me."

My heart lurched as my mind latched on to a thought before I could stop myself—*what if it isn't happiness?* What if it was love that had returned to him? Why hadn't I thought about that before? That *love* could return to him. That the way he felt when he looked at me could be more than just happiness.

I couldn't stop the way my stomach knotted. The way my pulse picked up. The way hope bloomed in me.

My voice carried that hope as I spoke. "Do you only feel that way about me?"

Enver thought about it for a moment, then shook his head. "No. Seeing the sun shining across my garden also evokes the same feelings in me. Although, it is not as intense as it is when I look at you. Nothing compares to that."

I faltered. Neima had wanted happiness. That was most likely the emotion that had returned to Enver, not love. His description of happiness made sense, too, but it didn't ease the swift disappointment that swept through me, leaving me feeling hollowed out. It squeezed the air out of my lungs and burned my throat.

Enver's brows drew together, his expression growing concerned. "You are upset," he said. "Why?"

I lowered my eyes, unable to find my voice, the sincerity of his concern only making everything hurt more. I'd only let myself believe it for a second. Imagined only for a moment that he could love me. That he would. Yet the pain of disappointment cut deeper than it should have.

And it'd led me to a harrowing realization.

It wasn't only lust that drove me toward Enver. It was something more. Something that planted its roots deep in my desperate heart and grew every time he touched me, threatening to blossom into something dangerous and terrifying.

Something that would only lead to my own heartbreak in the end.

Enver couldn't love me. I couldn't forget that. But I did. Over and over again. I *let* myself forget it. Let myself fall deeper into his arms.

I was doing what I always did. Giving myself up to someone who would never love me in return.

Enver placed a finger under my chin, tilting my face up to meet his probing gaze. I turned my head, taking a step back from him. I needed to leave. To put distance between us and dig up these unwanted feelings before they bloomed into something uncontrollable. My muscles tensed, eyes scanning the room, searching for an escape.

"No. Do not run away now," Enver said, his voice soft and entreating as he reached to take my hand. "Stay with me. I want to feel more of this." His fingers skimmed up my wrist to my shoulder, where the slipping sheet had revealed my skin. "More of you."

"No," I said, and he paused. My pulse raced, and I swallowed hard. "I don't want to."

His hand retreated, and this time, my rejection had a flash of hurt crossing his face. "You do not want me to touch you?"

"No," I repeated, lowering my eyes. "I don't."

My words were a lie. I longed for him to touch me, to kiss me. But I knew that was exactly what would tend to the emerging feelings inside me. The more he held me, the more they'd flourish. They'd flower until their thorns pierced me and left me bleeding and raw.

I couldn't let that happen.

"But that is everything I..." he trailed off, his jaw setting. "Very well."

I refused to meet his gaze, focusing on the hollow of his throat instead. I didn't want to see what his eyes held. I attempted to move around him. "I'm going to continue the labyrinth now."

He blocked my path but kept his distance. "Stay with me," he said again. "Just a little longer. I will not touch you. You have my promise."

I stopped, now glancing up at him. The smile had vanished from his face, replaced by the impassive expression he'd worn when we'd first met. He stood stiffly, tension radiating from his frame, having lost the ease from before. My chest tightened in response, guilt coursing through me. I was why the happiness he'd felt for the first time in a century had already waned.

I hated myself for it. I needed to suck up my insecurity—just for this moment. So Enver could feel happy for the first time in a hundred years.

"Okay," I said softly. "I'll stay."

His shoulders relaxed, and his expression turned fond. "There is somewhere I would like to take you. But first, have a bath. I will have a meal prepared, too. You must be hungry."

Food was the last thought on my mind, but I nodded anyway. I didn't know what the labyrinth would hold for me next, and it would be better to eat in case it would be awhile before I had another chance to. Enver gestured toward the bathroom, but he didn't follow me in, allowing me privacy as I relieved myself and started the bath. I washed myself thoroughly, using the floral scented soap from before. As I glanced down between my thighs, the memory of Enver between them had heat rising to my cheeks. I clamped them together and put it out of my mind.

No more. I needed to focus on completing the labyrinth. I needed to get home before I trapped myself here forever.

I climbed out of the bath, found a clean towel in a wardrobe, and dried myself off. The door creaked open, and I whirled toward it, finding a shadow sliding inside, a set of clothing hanging over a corporeal tendril.

I watched it cautiously, remembering the night before, how the shadows had held me in place so Enver could—

No.

Out of my mind.

I reached for the clothing, surprised to find my underwear and bra in the pile, now clean. The idea of the servants being forced to clean my clothing didn't sit well with me, but I was grateful not to have to go about the day commando. I slid into the pants, Enver's again, and pulled the shirt over my head, tucking it in. I still swam in his clothing, but it beat wearing another dress. I didn't like how they made me feel like I was stealing something from someone.

"Thank you," I said to the shadow.

The shadow seemed to bow at me. Or maybe I was crazy.

When I followed it out of the bathroom, it led me to a small table I hadn't noticed before, now placed in front of a window in Enver's bedroom. Enver was nowhere to be seen as I sat at it, feeling the warmth from the sun outside on my back and shoulders.

The sight of the food in front of me had my mouth watering. Toast, jam, eggs, potatoes, sausage. Maybe I was hungrier than I thought.

Enver suddenly appeared across from me, materializing from the shadows of the curtains. I jumped, banging my knee on the table. I grimaced, my hand going to the sore spot, rubbing it soothingly. Enver raised an eyebrow as he took a seat. "Did I startle you?"

"No," I lied.

A hint of a smirk crossed his face, but he said nothing, lifting an empty plate and filling it with an assortment of the food in front of us. I relaxed, seeing him at ease with me again, our earlier exchange seemingly put aside. He was dressed now, wearing a loose shirt that showed off a good portion of his scarred chest. I averted my gaze, feeling like I was invading his privacy when I looked at his scar.

He buttered two slices of toast, adding them to the plate, and then slid it over to me. "Here."

"Thank you," I said, taking it from him. Our fingers brushed and Enver quickly retracted his hand, placing it in his lap. I hesitated when he didn't move to make a plate for himself. "Are you going to eat?"

"I never have much of an appetite, but I suppose I can."

I watched him pick up a plate for himself, taking some potatoes. His response confused me. He never had an appetite, yet all the times I'd been in his dining room, the table had been lined with enough food to feed dozens. Thinking about it, though, I'd never seen him eat anything besides the peach he'd tasted. Did he even need to eat? If not, then what was with all the food?

I slid the plate of sausages closer to him as he scanned the table, deciding what else to take. "Here."

He shook his head. "That is for you. I do not consume meat."

"You don't? Why not?" I asked. "Oh, wait, I'm not judging you or anything. I'm just curious," I added quickly.

"I..." Enver trailed off, shaking his head. "I cannot seem to recall why."

I chewed on a piece of my toast, watching his grip on his plate tighten before he set it down on the table, his jaw tight. The food I'd seen before made even less sense now, unless he had considered what I might eat even that first morning together. There'd been a variety of meats on the table. But maybe he didn't choose what his servants cooked?

"I suppose my memory has faded with time," he said after another moment, his voice terse and distant.

He didn't touch his food after that. I ate quickly, feeling like I'd brought down the mood again. When I finished, I stood up from the table. His gaze followed my movement, a frown still on his face. "Finished?" he asked. "Shall we go?"

"Um, do you happen to have toothpaste?" I asked.

"Toothpaste?"

"Like to clean your teeth? Is that a thing here?"

"Ah," he responded, nodding. "I have something for that. In the bathroom, you will find a black jar by the sink. It might not be quite what you are used to, though."

I stood up from the table. "I'll take anything at this point."

Especially if Enver ever wanted to kiss me again.

I blinked. *No*. I couldn't have thoughts like that. What was wrong with me? What didn't I understand about not letting him touch me again? I shouldn't even be entertaining the thought. I shoved it out of my mind as I made my way back to the bathroom, finding the jar in question. Inside was some kind of salt scrub. I did the best I could with it, scrubbing my teeth with my finger until they felt clean.

I rinsed out my mouth, my gums feeling assaulted by the scrub. Never again would I take modern-day amenities for granted. I caught my reflection in the mirror, leaning closer, inspecting my skin. It looked dry and dull, with the effects of stopping my skincare already visible. My hair looked just as dry as I picked up a wavy lock and sighed.

I watched Enver appear in the bathroom doorway through the mirror's reflection. He casually leaned against the door frame, folding his arms over his chest. "Something wrong?" he asked.

"No," I said, turning away from the mirror to face him. "I'm ready to go now."

"You are beautiful."

His unprompted compliment made my cheeks burn. "I'm average," I said because I was incapable of accepting any compliment.

He pushed away from the doorway, approaching me with

slow strides. I held still, my knees going weak at the look in his eyes. The one I so often saw in his eyes before he kissed me—one full of longing and desire.

"No," he said softly, lifting his hand to my cheek, but not touching me. His fingers hovered centimeters away, and the heat radiating off them made me ache for his touch. "You are anything but average. You are beyond what I can put into words. You are my fantasies brought to life. My wishes fulfilled, and my dreams realized."

"You're good at saying pretty words," I said, my voice coming out breathless, his proximity leaving me light-headed.

His gaze swept my form, taking in my nervous state, the corner of his lips curling up into a small smirk as he stepped back, his hand returning to his side. "That is not the only thing I am good at, my little lover."

I couldn't stop the heat pooling in my lower stomach at his response. "D-didn't you want to show me something? Let's go."

He continued to smirk as I brushed past him, heading for the bathroom door. Sunlight blinded me as I stepped through and found myself outside. For a moment, I thought I'd returned to the garden with Neima and Paloma, but as my eyes adapted to the brightness, I recognized Enver's flower garden. We were in the same area where I'd met Isla for the first time, and I could hear the water flowing from the fountain I'd found before.

I looked at Enver behind me, surprised to see the hedges of the garden maze had started to grow again, green sprouting from the once brown limbs. "Are your gardens also affected by your connection to the labyrinth?" I asked.

"It would seem so."

"But this part of the garden has always been..." I trailed off, remembering how Isla had said Enver didn't let anyone come here.

But it was too late. Enver had already realized what I was

about to say. He gave me a sharp look. "You have been here before?"

"By accident," I explained. "I got lost in the maze."

"Were you alone?"

I hesitated. Isla had helped me out, and I didn't want to throw her under the bus, but I didn't want to lie to Enver. His gaze burned into mine, waiting for an answer. "Yes," I said.

He continued watching me for a moment, a frown flitting across his face, and I got the feeling he didn't believe me. "Well, now I understand how you passed so much time in the maze if you ventured out this far," he said. "Your sense of direction must be poor if you ended up here."

I looked back up at him, my mouth falling open, indignant. "What? My sense of direction? Your maze literally has *illusions*! I don't think anyone would have a good sense of direction when you're supposed to walk through dead hedges! Those things are thick!"

He chuckled, and I realized he was teasing me. "That is quite unfair of me, I suppose," he conceded.

I could feel myself flush, and I stubbornly turned my head away from him. "If you think about it, it's your fault the maze led me here. So, you can't be mad."

"I am not mad. Perhaps if it was anyone other than you, I would be. But not you."

Enver began walking away, and I trailed behind him, fighting off the warmth his words left me with. "Why don't you want anyone to come here, anyway?"

"There is no significant reason. Only that this garden is where I spend the majority of my days. It is a personal place for me. A private sanctuary of sorts."

"Really? Why here, out of your entire castle?"

Enver slowed his pace, allowing me to fall into step beside him as we moved through the garden together. "I feel calm when I am here. There is a familiarity within this garden that soothes me, though I cannot place it."

I remembered the feeling of safety that had washed over me when I'd fallen into the fountain. Was that how Enver felt? What caused it?

"It reminds me of how you make me feel."

I glanced at Enver, my heart skipping a beat. "In what way?"

"The warmth you fill me with," he continued, his voice dropping lower, eyebrows drawing together. "I remember feeling it before here. A long time ago."

"You must have enjoyed gardening," I said, bending over as we passed a patch of carnations. Their sweet aroma wafted up to me, and I took in a deep breath, savoring the scent.

Enver stooped over next to me, snapping one off its stem and handing it to me. "Perhaps I did."

I took it from him, running a finger over its delicate petals. "I think this is the first time I've received flowers from anyone."

He considered me for a moment, then knelt next to the flower patch, gathering a dozen more carnations. I watched as he bundled them together with a vine before straightening out and presenting them to me. "Take these as well."

A smile broke out across my face as I took the makeshift bouquet from him. "Thank you."

He paused, staring at my face.

I frowned, suddenly feeling self-conscious. "What is it?"

"Your smile."

"What about it?"

He curled a lock of my hair around his finger before setting it aside. "It makes me... happy. I wish to see you smile again."

My breath caught, and he brought his hand down to press his thumb into the corner of my mouth, pushing my lip up. I wasn't sure if it was because of the weird grimace he'd forced my mouth into or my dumbfounded expression, but whatever it was drew another affectionate chuckle from him. I didn't say anything, didn't move. Didn't breathe.

"Beautiful," he murmured, the amusement on his face turning to something intimate. His eyes locked on my lips as his hand slid to my neck.

A wave of heat swept through me as he leaned in. My eyes fluttered shut, but a moment passed, and nothing happened. When I opened my eyes again, Enver's eyebrows had pulled together, and he had straightened out. His hand dropped, his back turning to me, bending over to pick up another flower.

Disappointment welled in me, but I had no right to feel that way. I was the one who told him not to touch me. I was tired of myself and my conflicting feelings, but he made it so hard to resist him.

"Even if I gave you every flower in this garden, it would not be as many as you deserve," Enver said as he tucked the new flower into my bouquet.

I clutched the carnations to my chest, the sincerity of his words making my heart race. "Then you'd ruin it. You can't give me everything."

"I would try, nonetheless. And it would be worth the effort. There is nothing I would not do for you."

Our gazes met, and I knew from the look on his face that he wasn't only talking about the flowers anymore. I turned away again, focusing my attention on the garden. I needed to change the topic. "If you can leave your castle, why can't you just abandon the labyrinth?"

"I told you before that I am tied to it," he responded and started walking down the dirt path of the garden again. "I cannot leave for long periods of time."

I stayed at his side. "What happens if you do?"

Enver hesitated before answering. "When I am gone, the labyrinth decays. The longer I am away, the more I can feel its pain. An ache forms in my bones until it becomes unbearable. I can feel the labyrinth pulling at me no matter where I go, trying to wrest me back to it."

"What if you didn't return?"

"The labyrinth would drag me back."

"It would?" I repeated, alarmed.

He shrugged. "It would seem my connection to the labyrinth runs deep. I am willed to remain here and maintain it as much as I am willed to find the poor, desperate souls who sustain it. Should I venture too far or for too long, I would be forced to return."

"I don't understand. The labyrinth really feeds on people's desperation?"

"It would seem so," he answered.

"What happens if you don't bring anyone here?"

"I face losing my remaining emotions."

"How do you know?"

His shoulders tensed. "I have learned the consequences of noncompliance firsthand."

I fell silent, my fingers curling tighter around the stems of the carnations. So he'd once tried to go against the labyrinth and had been punished for it. He sounded as trapped as I was —no. It was worse than that. I at least had a chance of escaping the labyrinth. He couldn't leave at all. He'd been stuck here for over a century and would continue to be for who knew how long. Endlessly forced to do the labyrinth's bidding while risking losing what little he had left of himself if he defied it.

My heart squeezed as we continued through the garden. I pitied him. But how could I pity someone who'd trapped countless people in his labyrinth? Even if he had no choice, it didn't make up for all the suffering he'd caused.

Enver's steps came to a halt, his gaze crossing the garden, falling on the statue of the beautiful woman. My eyes followed his line of vision, watching the water flow down her marble body. Enver remained quiet, preoccupied with his thoughts, as my own drifted away from his plight. They went to the hands that had sunk me into the water, leading me to the heart pendant that now rested in the valley of my breasts. I remembered feeling the same way then as Enver said he felt here. Calm. Serene.

Even now, gazing upon the statue, I could feel a weight lifting off my shoulders. Her beautiful features shimmered as the sunlight reflected off the water that trickled over her body.

"Does this statue mean anything to you?" I asked Enver. "Do you know who she is?"

"She has been by my side throughout these unceasing years," he responded. "I am fond of her, but if you are asking me why she exists here, I do not have an answer. I do not remember."

Enver had been alive for over a century. It made sense he would forget things, but I didn't understand how he could forget so much. Especially important things—like how he'd become part of this labyrinth. Or why his heart had been torn out. Not remembering the statue or how the garden made him feel wasn't anything compared to those two things, but he didn't even seem to question his memory loss. He just accepted it. Accepted it the same way he accepted his fate.

I suddenly remembered Aki's words.

There's a dark, terrible magic surrounding him. One I do not envy.

A grim and hostile curse.

How could I have forgotten? I inhaled sharply, twirling toward Enver. "Enver, Aki told me you're cursed. Could it be that a curse is keeping you here?"

Enver didn't outwardly react to that. His attention was still on the statue. "Yes, I have considered that before."

"Why do you sound so unconcerned?" I asked, startled by his nonchalance. "What if the curse is what's keeping you tied to the labyrinth? What if it's why you lost your heart and your emotions?"

"Even if that is the case, there is nothing to be done about it."

"What? That's all you have to say? Can't you break the curse?"

He didn't answer, his jaw clenching.

"Aki said he felt the magic within you," I pressed. "He was sure someone cursed you. If you agree it could be a curse, why haven't you tried to break it? You've never tried to? In all the time you've been trapped here?"

A muscle in his cheek twitched, but he still didn't respond.

His silence only fueled my incredulity. "Why aren't you saying anything? What if you're a victim of the labyrinth just like I am—"

"And if I am not?" he cut me off, finally meeting my gaze, his eyes now hard and cold. "What if this is not a curse? What if I am the monster you have accused me of being before?"

My voice caught in my throat at his change in demeanor. "I don't—"

"What if I am the reason the labyrinth exists in the first place?" he demanded, advancing on me, the space between us rapidly diminishing. "I could have cast out my heart, my emotions, and my memories myself and created this nightmare. I could be the reason you and everyone else are trapped here. I could be the cause of everything. What then, my little lover? Would you still consider me a victim?"

I stared at him, refusing to flinch away. Even as he loomed over me, the carnations crushed between our chests. "Enver."

"Do not make the mistake of thinking me innocent. It will only lead to disappointment."

"You didn't do this to yourself," I said, shaking my head.

"How can you be so sure?" he responded, voice sharp. Accusatory.

I didn't blame him. He couldn't remember why he'd become like this. He had no reason to believe what I was saying. No reason to trust my instincts. I couldn't imagine how often he'd grappled with his forgotten past or current predicament over the years. I couldn't imagine what it was like not to remember who you were. What you'd done. How you'd ended up where you were. Why you were trapped and torn apart.

But still...

"I've seen your pain," I told him, the words tumbling out of me. "Both physical and emotional. Even if you couldn't feel it before, it has always been there, like the scar on your chest. I felt your empathy when you told me you understood what it was like to feel trapped and then reached out to console me—when you encouraged me to continue the labyrinth despite wanting me to stay with you."

Enver went still. "That does not mean anything."

"Yes, it does," I said softly. "You may have lost your emotions, but you didn't lose your humanity. I'm sorry for ever calling you a monster, Enver. The labyrinth may be cold and unfeeling, but you aren't. I know that now."

He stepped back, giving the carnations space to breathe again, but his expression didn't change, remaining stony. "Even if I did not bring the labyrinth on myself, and I truly have been cursed, I am still undeserving of your misplaced compassion."

"What do you mean?" I asked, watching as he lifted a hand to the carnations, his touch light as he brushed his fingertips over them, reminding me of the way he so often caressed my cheek.

"I must have deserved it."

His words caused my heart to sink. "You think you deserved to be cursed?"

"A curse strong enough to bind me to this labyrinth and cause my immortality is not one set upon me for nothing," he said. "I must have done something unforgivable that I cannot remember."

"Immorality?"

"I cannot die," he said icily.

I couldn't bring myself to ask how he knew that. "What if you didn't deserve it?" I argued. "What if you didn't do anything? Why are you so quick to take the blame?"

"Why are you so quick to absolve me of it?" he returned, his eyes narrowing. "Why are you now so intent on believing I am anything but the cruel monster you once thought I was? I am still your heartless enemy who has taken you here against your will and has not allowed you to leave. You seem to have forgotten."

My pulse quickened. "I gave you my consent."

I thought my response would have allayed his belief he was the villain here. Made him realize the point he was missing—that he *hadn't* forced me to do anything. Something he had been so adamant about before. And I understood why now. Enver was the only one truly trapped here, forced into a situation he never wanted within the labyrinth.

But my words had the opposite effect of what I wanted. His shoulders tensed, and his hand fisted around some of the carnations before he jerked them back to his side. Their fragile petals fluttered to the ground between us as he stared at me with a growing, cold awareness. The muscles of his jaw worked beneath his smooth skin, and when he finally spoke, his voice was low and strained. "You are beginning to care for me."

My stomach lurched, and a rush of adrenaline shot through me. It wasn't a question. It was a statement. And I couldn't get myself to respond. To deny it.

My silence answered for me.

Enver fell back, creating more distance between us, his face becoming an unreadable mask. "Leave. Continue the labyrinth."

The abruptness of his order sent my heart racing. "Enver—"

"You forget yourself, my little lover. I am not a kind man. I am not the victim you wish me to be. Leave before you mistake my manipulation for kindness again. Before your desperation for love becomes your downfall."

"I..." I couldn't speak, my pulse thundering in my ears. I couldn't understand why he was saying this. He wanted me, didn't he? So why was he pushing me away? Why was he rejecting me so harshly? "I'm not forgetting," I finally got out. "I just don't believe you are what you think you are. Is it really that wrong to want to reassure you—"

"Leave," he repeated roughly. "This is who I am in the end, Nell. Who I am cursed to remain. Trapped, forgotten, and alone."

Alone.

Despite his rejection tearing through me, I focused on that one word. A feeling I knew so well yet failed to recognize when it was laid right out in front of me. "Alone..."

Enver's eyes widened a fraction of an inch as I spoke, and he turned his head away, attempting to hide his face.

But it was already enough. My heart nearly stopped. Because now I knew how to describe the hollow atmosphere that haunted Enver's castle. How to explain the darkness and melancholy etched into the stone walls. To explain the dust on the unused furniture. The dozens of seats at the dining table that only ever hosted one occupant. The chill that clung to every corner. The stillness that permeated every corridor. The quiet that blanketed the air.

Loneliness had cast its dark shadow over every possible inch of his castle, transforming it into a shell of what it should have been. A loneliness reflected from the man who ruled over it.

Enver was lonely.

A lump rose in my throat as I looked at him, the way his dark form stood out against the sea of bright flowers beyond him. "You're lonely," I whispered.

His gaze snapped back to me, his eyes flashing. "No. I am not lonely. Do not tell me how I feel."

"I've seen it. In your castle. Your garden. Your eyes."

"You are overstepping, my little lover," he warned, tension radiating from his broad shoulders. "Stop there."

I ignored him, a flutter of nerves building within me as I moved closer to him. He'd said before that he'd had three emotions when we'd first met, but only two people had completed the labyrinth. I'd thought it was a slip of the tongue, but it wasn't. It meant one of his emotions had always been with him—that *loneliness* had always been with him. "I don't understand. Why is it loneliness? Why have you always had that emotion when you've been forced to remain alone for so long? How could someone be so cruel? It's... It's..."

"Stop."

"No wonder you're so desperate to keep me," I whispered. "You don't want to be alone anymore."

"That is *enough*."

The fury in his tone left me breathless. His nostrils flared, and I paused for a moment, swallowing. I'd never heard him speak like that. I didn't know why what I was saying was making him so upset. It wasn't his fault he was lonely. There was nothing wrong with feeling lonely, either.

And now that I was here...

A rush of determination coursed through me as I pushed on. "You said you feel happy because of me. Then maybe I can lessen your loneliness the same way—"

"Ah, you are right," he interjected, his gaze turning deadly. "Perhaps you can lessen this feeling of isolation the same way you gave me happiness."

A jolt of unease washed over me at the new mocking edge in his voice. "I want to help you."

He smiled, and it held none of the warmth it did earlier, replaced with a cold emptiness. "Then have sex with me," he said. "Come back to my chambers with me, spread your legs, and allow me to take what I want from your body."

I froze, my pulse stuttering.

"You want to lessen my loneliness, do you not? Then allow me to bury myself deep inside you. Give me the warmth of your skin as I fill you. Allow me to use your body as my new private sanctuary until I feel less alone."

The carnations slipped from my hand, falling to the ground at my feet as my hands trembled. "What?"

"You will allow me to, will you not?" Enver continued, his voice turning imploring now, a false sweetness lacing his words. "You want to ease my loneliness the same way you gave me happiness after all, no?"

I fought to speak over the lump growing in my throat. "You were only happy because I had sex with you?"

"What else would it have been?"

I took a shaky breath, my eyes searching his face, and the indifference displayed there made my chest ache. "That's really all it was?"

"Yes. I do not have it in me to feel anything else for you." His smile dropped, his expression hardening. "Or did you forget that, too?"

"You... You said..." This wasn't good. The lump in my throat grew more prominent. It burned.

He regarded me coolly. "I said what I had to in order to convince you to stay with me. I did not know it would work so well. That you would give yourself so freely to me in exchange for the illusion of a happily ever after."

Something stabbed into my chest, and I retreated back from

him, finding it hard to breathe. My eyes stung, and my lips quivered when I tried to speak again. "I don't believe you."

"What reason do I have to lie to you, my little lover?" he asked, the breeze tousling his black hair, gentle where his words were not. "I have you trapped here, and now it seems you are quite fond of me. There is no reason for me to deceive you anymore. If I asked you to lay with me right now, to give yourself to me so I could feel happy and less alone, you would. Am I wrong?"

I didn't say anything. I didn't move. My body felt heavy and cold.

"I need you, Nell," Enver murmured, his voice softening, attempting to lure me in with a soothing tone. He held his hand out to me, palm open and inviting. "Let me have you. Come to me, my little lover, and let me find solace within you."

Despite the nausea in my stomach, despite knowing I shouldn't, I still reached for him.

Something akin to anger flashed in his eyes, and his hand dropped before I could take it within mine. A storm brewed in his gaze as shadows formed around us, rising from the grass, blacking out the garden. "I see you have learned nothing from the labyrinth," he spoke as the shadows swirled around us. "Still so desperate for love. Even from someone who cannot love you back."

The lump in my throat choked me as I tried to respond, and all I could do was stare at him as the shadows surged on me. I didn't fight them as they dragged me into their darkness.

15

Heartache settled in as the shadows melted away, and unshed tears blurred my vision. My shaking hand was still stretched out in front of me, reaching for Enver. His harshness left me with a feeling I knew all too well. The sting of rejection I'd felt over and over again. The familiar pain of knowing no one would love me how I wanted them to.

But I didn't expect that of Enver. I knew he couldn't love me. I knew he only felt desire toward me. It shouldn't have hurt to hear it was only sex that made him feel happy, but I'd let myself believe there was something more between us. That when he said he wanted me, it went deeper than just physical pleasure. That when he promised me he would love me in any way he could, he meant it. That when he said he'd felt happy because of me, it wasn't only because I'd let him touch me.

I blinked rapidly, refusing to let the tears fall. I should have known better.

I *did* know better. But once again, I would have given up every part of me for a chance at love, even if it wasn't real.

As my vision cleared, I looked down and realized I was now

wearing a tight black dress—the same one I'd worn to the club the night Enver came to me. My head snapped back up, and I inhaled sharply, finding myself in my front yard. In front of my house. The sight of it stole the air from my lungs. I was... home?

I glanced around me, seeing the familiar sight of my lilac bush beside my front door, its branches dead, the cold air having defoliated it. I forced my feet forward, unable to trust my eyes, and reached out to touch it. Its limbs were cold and hard, and one scraped along the back of my hand, causing a twinge of pain.

I still didn't believe it. My heart hammered in my chest. How had I come back? Had Enver sent me back? Had he had the power to set me free the entire time? Or had I somehow completed the labyrinth without even realizing it?

I climbed the steps to my front door, found it unlocked, and pushed it open. I wanted to cry at the sight of my kitchen. I was home. I didn't know how, but I was home.

I kicked off my heels, taking in the familiar scent of my home, and feeling the overwhelming heat that I always cranked when the temperature dropped outside. I moved further into the kitchen cautiously, as if expecting it to dissipate into shadows. My favorite candle sat on my kitchen table, filling the room with its familiar and comforting scent.

I paused, frowning at it. Had I left a candle burning when I'd left? I didn't think I would. House fires had always been a fear of mine, and I wouldn't have risked it.

A noise suddenly came from the living room. I turned toward it, my heart jumping into my throat.

"Nell? Is that you?"

I froze at the sound of Julian's voice. He appeared seconds later, his blond hair disheveled and his eyes wide with shock. I noted his wrinkled maroon T-shirt. It looked like he'd slept in it for days.

"Nell!" he cried, and the next thing I knew, I was in his

arms. They wrapped around me, pulling me to his chest. "Where the hell have you been?"

Stunned, I went stiff in his hold, my forehead pressed against his collarbone.

"Nell, why didn't you answer my calls?" Julian continued, taking my face in his hands, wrenching my head up to face him. "Do you know how worried I was? How could you ignore me like that?"

I stared at him, at the concern etched into his expression. It couldn't be for me. Why would he care if I'd disappeared?

"Are you okay? Why aren't you saying anything?" he asked, pulling back so he could run his eyes over my body as if checking for injury. "What happened to you?"

"How long have I been gone?" I asked shakily, still trying to process the fact I was home.

"Nearly three days," Julian answered, his lips pressing into a tight line. "Where have you been? I thought something happened to you! You can't just disappear like that! I almost called the police to report you missing."

"Why would you do that?"

Julian gave me a look of disbelief. "Why? Because you're my girlfriend and you went missing! I was worried sick about you."

I blinked at him. "I'm your girlfriend? What does your fiancée think of that?"

His expression fell, regret crossing his face. "Nell. Listen—"

I tried to shrug out of his hold. "Let me go."

"No," he said, hugging me closer, his hand sliding to the back of my head, tucking me into him. "Nell, I made a mistake. I broke it off with Veronica."

I stood there, leaving my arms limply at my side, but my heart leaped into my throat. "What?"

"I've been an asshole. No, I've been worse than that," Julian said, crushing me to him. "I'm so sorry. I should have never done that to you. You have been nothing but perfect to me, and

I betrayed you in the worst way. I didn't see what I had in front of me. But when you disappeared, I thought my world ended."

I didn't want to hear this. Tremors wracked my body. He didn't mean it. "Julian—"

"Please listen to me," he said, pushing me back so he could see my face again. His eyes were red-rimmed and wet.

"No," I said, although my voice came out strained. "Leave me alone."

"These have been the worst days of my life. Knowing you were missing. Knowing it was because of my stupidity and selfishness. The idea of never seeing you again has been killing me. I haven't slept. I couldn't eat. I could only think about you. It made me realize how much I care about you." Tears slipped down his cheeks. "I'm sorry for what I said before. You are more than enough, Nell. You're everything to me. I'm sorry for everything. I really am."

I could only watch him, my heart pounding. His skin was gaunt, and dark circles stained the skin under his eyes. I'd never seen him like this before. He never cried—especially not over me.

My fingers twitched, instinctively wanting to reach out to him, to accept him again, but I forced myself to keep my hands at my side. I couldn't give in to that instinct. Enver said I hadn't learned anything, but I *had*. I knew I didn't want to be desperate enough to be with Julian again. Knew he would never love me.

"Please, Nell. Say something," he pleaded.

I slowly shook my head, trying to pull myself free from him again. "No, I..."

His fingers dug into my arms. "Don't leave me, Nell. Please. Don't leave me again. I promise I will be better. I don't want to lose you. I can't. I..."

Everything blurred around me. I couldn't hear anything but Julian's voice. I couldn't see anything but his lips moving, forming the only words I'd ever wanted to hear from him.

"I love you."

All the air left my lungs.

I love you.

I love you.

I staggered into him, my knees giving out, his words echoing in my mind. He caught me, pressing his face against my neck.

"I love you, Nell. I always have. I'm sorry for not saying it sooner. For lying to you and saying I never did. I love you," he whispered into my hair. "I love you so much."

He loved me. *He loved me.*

I couldn't believe it. I could barely breathe, clinging to him. This couldn't be real. It had to be an illusion. But Enver's promise flitted into my mind—that if I completed the labyrinth, I would get what I wanted. Love. And being here, being home, meant I'd succeeded. Enver and Isla both confirmed that.

This was real.

But was it even what I wanted anymore? After everything Julian had done to me? What if he was lying? Did he even deserve to be forgiven?

"Nell, I'm sorry it took me so long to realize it," Julian said, pressing a kiss against my neck, sending a strange pulse through me. "I'm sorry I hurt you so badly. I was an idiot. I took you for granted. I didn't deserve you before, but I promise, if you give me another chance, I'll treat you the way you deserve to be treated."

"How can I believe you?" I whispered, my mind feeling fuzzy.

He held onto me tighter. "I know I haven't given you a reason to trust me, but I will spend the rest of my life making it up to you. I've found a job. I'll support myself. I'll support you so you can quit your shitty job. Just stay with me, Nell. Please. I love you."

My quivering hands seemed to have a mind of their own as they slid around Julian's waist, hugging him back. Heat radiated off him. His body formed to mine, solid and real. Tears blurred my vision as I listened to him confess his love for me again and again. What I had wanted for so long was finally happening. Julian loved me. Why was I trying to refuse it?

"I love everything about you, Nell. Your kindness, your dedication to our relationship. I love the small things you do for me, even if I never acknowledged them before. I promise I won't ever betray you again. I will love you the way I should have this entire time."

I clung to him tighter, trying not to sob. This was all I ever wanted to hear. All I ever hoped for. Even if Julian had made a mistake, I could forgive him, couldn't I? I'd wanted this for too long to throw it away. He'd apologized. He'd promised to be better. I wasn't perfect, either. From here, we could grow together.

I would forget the one who could never love me. Forget his labyrinth.

Yet when I tried to speak, the words felt laden, clinging to my throat. "I... I love you, too," I whispered, forcing them out, feeling like I was going to choke on them.

Julian's breathing stuttered, and he pulled back again, his hand coming to cradle my cheek. It felt cold and unfamiliar. His palm was too rough, scratching my skin. Not soft like Enver's.

My heart skipped a beat, and I pushed the thought aside. I wouldn't think of Enver anymore. Julian gave me what Enver couldn't. Where Enver wanted me for sex, Julian wanted my heart and offered his in return. A heart I would gladly take in exchange for my own.

Julian leaned down, his lips hovering over mine. I closed my eyes, allowing him to kiss me. He pressed too hard against me, his lips crushing mine forcefully. Nothing like the way

Enver's lips had caressed and molded to mine as if we were made for each other.

I stiffened. *No*. I wasn't going to think about Enver anymore. It was over.

Julian kissed me deeper, hungry and rough, and I fought off the urge to shrink back, trying to lose myself in his taste and touch. Julian was who I wanted. Who would make me happy. I could tell from the way my body seemed to feel alive under his hands. His fingers tangled in my hair, tugging painfully, and I gasped. Revulsion rolled through me at the taste of his tongue against mine, but I ignored it.

This was what I wanted.

Julian was who I wanted.

Julian walked me backward, his lips never leaving mine. I gripped his shirt for support as he guided me into the living room, the back of my knees hitting my couch. We broke apart as he pushed me down, and I landed on the cushions with a light thud. He climbed over me, his hands trailing over my body, groping me.

I couldn't relax under his weight. I tried to lean back and enjoy it, but my heart raced for the wrong reason. Everything felt off. His touch, his kiss, his body. He didn't notice my hesitation as he kissed along my jaw, his hands sliding to my thighs, inching up my dress. As he mouthed across my neck, he stopped.

"What is this?" he asked, his lips pressing together.

My eyes widened when I realized he was seeing the marks Enver had left on my neck.

"Did you sleep with someone else?" Julian asked.

"I..." I couldn't think quickly enough to lie. "Yes."

I expected Julian to be pissed. Instead, he sighed. "I'm sorry. I drove you to do that, didn't I? I can't blame you. I didn't give you enough attention."

"No, I'm sorry," I apologized, my heart swelling with hope.

Julian was already acting differently than before. He was already keeping true to his promise. "I won't sleep with anyone else again."

"Good," he murmured, kissing my neck. "I won't either. You're mine. And I'm yours from now on."

The possessiveness in his voice reminded me of the way Enver had made the same claim, but instead of filling me with desire as Enver's did, it left me uneasy. Julian crashed his lips against mine again, shoving my dress up to my waist. My hands moved to stop him, but they were so heavy they were almost impossible to lift off the couch cushions.

"Let me love you," Julian said as he spread my legs. "Let me make everything up to you. I want this. Don't you?"

No, I thought.

But I did want this. I wanted Julian. We loved each other. "Yes, I do," I said.

Julian unzipped his jeans, his mouth meeting mine again. He pushed my underwear aside, and my eyes shot open in bewilderment. We were doing it like this? Face-to-face? He'd never wanted to see my face before.

His eyes were still closed as he moved back to adjust our positions, helping me wrap my legs around his waist. My gaze dropped to his erection. Completely hard. I didn't even have to suck him off first.

He wanted me. This proved it.

I reached up and brought his face back to mine, kissing him hard. He moaned, and I finally felt arousal beginning to build in me. His tip nudged against me, and I tried to calm my racing heart.

Without warning, he pulled back, breaking our kiss. Before I could ask what was wrong, he grabbed my waist, rolling me over so that my knees were now on the cushion. My stomach dropped as his fingers dug into my hips, yanking me closer to him. I glanced over my shoulder at him, my chest tightening at the sight of his head tilted down, eyes focused on my ass.

"Julian, wait," I said, trying to push away from the back of the couch. My next words caught in my mouth, but I managed to get them out, hesitant and quiet. "I don't want to do it like this. I want to see you."

One of his hands slid between my shoulder blades, not forcing me back down, but halting my movement. "You know how much I like it like this, Nell. Just relax."

My heart pounded in my chest as he bore down on me, sinking my chest and face into the back of the couch. "Julian—"

"*Shh*, you'll enjoy it like you always do."

Enjoy it? Did I ever enjoy it?

Enver appeared in my mind again. His dark eyes trained on mine, never letting me turn my face away from his, always wanting to see me. His deep kisses and his soft touches. How he treated me like I was the most precious thing to him. The way he never seemed to get enough of giving me pleasure. Of me. Even if it had only been about sex to him, he had still treated me better than Julian ever had. Than Julian ever would.

But Enver wasn't here. Enver didn't love me.

Julian did. Wasn't that enough? Wasn't that what I wanted? Wasn't this what the labyrinth had given me for completing it?

Julian lined himself up with me, his hand moving up my back to my neck, applying pressure, pushing my face down.

I squeezed my eyes shut, my hands shaking as I held onto the back of the couch. This had to be enough. It had to be what I wanted. Wasn't it?

But why wasn't I happy? Why did I feel as though a weight was bearing down on me, threatening to crush me? Why did Enver's words and promises fill my mind?

You should know how you deserve to be treated and understand how he never deserved you.

Why did I think I'd hate myself if I went through with this despite my body screaming that it wanted him?

Julian halted his movements. "Oh darling, you're quite conflicted, aren't you?"

My eyes flew open, and I glanced over my shoulder at him. "What?"

"This is quite the surprise," he continued, an amused look crossing his face. "This man is not the center of your desires after all, yet you'd still consider accepting him?"

"What..." I trailed off, nausea creeping through me. I wrenched myself away from him, shoving myself off the couch and fixing my dress. "You're not Julian."

"Obviously."

Julian's form shifted, his body becoming taller and less bulky, his light blond hair turning jet black, his jaw becoming sharper, and his hazel eyes darkening to a familiar charcoal color. Enver.

No, not Enver. Whoever had taken the form of Enver.

"My little lover," they crooned. "Come. Let me show you how you should be treated."

"Who are you?" I asked immediately, my skin crawling.

They tilted their head. "You caught on so quickly with him. Not so much with the first one. Perhaps you would have succumbed to me more easily in this form. You put up quite the fight, even with my influence. I almost got you, though. Seems your mental fortitude is strong, even if your resolve isn't."

Their words sank in, and I could feel the blood drain from my face. I was still in the labyrinth. Julian hadn't forgiven me. He hadn't claimed to love me. Everything had been a trick. One I nearly fell for because my emotions had been missed with. "Who are you?" I whispered again, my throat feeling tight.

"I have many names," they told me, and my living room melted away around us, revealing a dark forest. Dead trees stretched overhead, and snow covered the ground, muting all sounds. "I also have many forms."

I gasped as their form changed from Enver to Aki in the blink of an eye, then to an employee of a cafe I frequented, then to Neima, and finally to Veronica. The image of my sister made me recoil, nearly slipping in the wet snow.

"Oh, isn't she a catch?" Not-Veronica commented. "What beautiful hair. Why is yours already greying?"

"It's not grey," I said, still reeling but needing to defend my hair. "It's white. I dyed it on purpose."

"Hm. Interesting choice."

"What are—" I cut myself off, trying to think of a better way to word my question. No one deserved to be referred to with the word *what*. Even if they lured me into labyrinths or tried to sleep with me using my boyfriend's form—ex-boyfriend's form. "You're not human."

They laughed, the sound an exact replica of Veronica's laugh. It made my stomach roll. "You're so observant!"

I flushed, irritation seeping through me. "What is this? Why were you pretending to be Julian?"

They morphed again, resuming Julian's form. "I showed you one of your deepest desires."

My deepest desires? Being with Julian? "I desire him still?" I asked.

"Not quite," they said. "Your desires have changed, but that man lingers in your mind." Julian became Enver again, and they stepped closer to me. "You desire him now. But you don't want to. You know you can't have him, and it hurts you. Yet you can't help but long for him. How tragic."

I stared at them, clenching my jaw. I couldn't deny what they were saying this time. "What do you want?" I asked.

"Do you know what you do to him?" They smirked wickedly, the look unnatural on Enver's face—his lips stretched too wide, too thin. "Do you know how you make him feel?"

"Stop," I said, my pulse picking up.

"He wants you, too, you know."

My heart stuttered. "What?"

"But it's not the same way you want him. He wants to keep you. Possess you. He can barely control himself around you. Barely rein in the darkness. He has to restrain himself every time you come near. But his desires are misplaced."

"What do you know of what he wants?" I asked, shivering in the frigid air.

"I can see people's desires," they responded. "I feed off them." They took on another new form—my mom. "Ah. There's always trauma brought on by someone's parents, isn't there? You want to know why she decided to abandon you but not your sister. Why she came back into your life only to use you."

"No," I responded, my voice wavering. "You're wrong."

"*Why is it always me?* That's what you ask yourself, isn't it?"

My pulse thudded in my ears. "No. Stop it..."

"Poor little human. Insecurity can be oh-so debilitating. I almost feel bad. Especially because I have no answer for you. Cruelty does not always have an explanation. Sometimes, it simply is."

I watched as they transformed once more, now taking the shape of a slender person with midnight blue hair tied in a loose ponytail over their shoulder. Their skin turned from white to a pale white, their eyes becoming a beautiful jade color. They stretched their arms out, letting their neck roll from side to side as if getting more comfortable in this form. A tail flicked in the air and swayed, batting away snowflakes.

I tried to calm myself down, my fingernails digging into my palm. "Are you some kind of... sex spirit?"

They laughed, the sound echoing through the silent snowy forest. "Well, you could certainly put it like that in your case, but not everyone's desires are sexual in nature. I actually prefer when they're not. I feed of desire in general. I do tend to find some humans refer to me using the term incubus, although I don't always appear as a male. You're not picky about someone's sex though, huh?"

"Stay out of my head," I warned.

They cocked an eyebrow. "You sure? I could answer a few questions for you."

I didn't know whether I could believe them. Yet, one question still came to the tip of my tongue. "What do you mean Enver's desires are misplaced?"

Snow fell harder around us, and they brushed some flakes off their shoulder. "You should never trust someone who has no memory of themselves or their past. You do not know who he was before. What he could have done."

I frowned. Enver had said the same thing. "I'll make the decision to trust Enver or not myself."

"Suit yourself. You're free to break your own heart. You're quite good at it, it seems."

"Are you doing his labyrinth?" I asked, shivering again and ignoring their jibe. The frigid air burned at my skin, and I could barely feel my hands. "I am, too."

They didn't seem surprised by my question. "I am."

"I'm Nell," I said needlessly.

"Morgan."

I watched them warily. Judging by the way the other layers of the labyrinth had worked, for me to complete this one, I would need to help them in some way—even if they'd tried to deceive me. I also wanted to know what would happen when all the pieces of the gemstone in the pendant were together again. "Is there somewhere warmer we can go?"

Morgan considered it for a moment. "Sure."

I blinked and suddenly found myself in a cabin, warmth enveloping me as a fire blazed in a fireplace tucked into the corner of the room. I glanced around, startled to find a man sleeping in a nearby bed. My head jerked back to Morgan, who stood beside me.

"Who is that?" I whispered.

"A… friend," Morgan said, walking over to the man's side.

I studied him for a moment, seeing him struggle to breathe, a sheen of sweat on his forehead. "What's wrong with him?"

Morgan hesitated, glancing at me, a frown twisting on their lips. "I fed off him, and he's been like this since."

"Isn't feeding off someone taking their energy?" I asked, trying to remember any knowledge of incubi I had. It was mainly from fiction, but maybe it held true here. I'd read a few succubus romances.

"I suppose. I consume their desires, and it gives me my life force."

"That's what you planned to do to me?"

"Yes," they responded casually. "You happened to appear at the perfect moment. I couldn't take from Karim again. Not when he's like this."

The gauntness in Karim's face and the pallor of his brown skin were evident. "Does feeding off someone leave them like this?"

"Not if it's only once. They won't even remember it. It would be like a pleasant dream," Morgan told me.

"How many times have you fed off Karim?"

Morgan tensed a bit. "He's been my only energy source for a while now."

"Isn't that dangerous?" I asked, turning back to Morgan, worried. "If you're taking someone's energy constantly, how will they replenish it?"

"That's not my concern."

"Did Karim agree to this?"

"He doesn't need to. He doesn't remember anything."

"Morgan, that's—"

"How I survive," Morgan cut me off, narrowing their eyes.

"It's no different from how you humans slaughter an animal for food. They did not consent to that, either. At least those I feed on don't die. I have no choice but to do this. It's how I survive."

I couldn't argue that point. I was trying to rush into figuring out how to complete this layer of the labyrinth without considering Morgan's situation. "I'm sorry. I spoke out of turn. I don't know your circumstances."

Morgan eyed me, but their expression relaxed. "For what it's worth, most human's desires are more forthright than yours. I don't have to deceive the majority. Karim welcomes me every time. I'm even in my own form when I go to him."

"Why have you only been taking energy from him?" I asked.

"His energy is powerful. Addicting. And he is very receptive to me," Morgan said, a small smile pulling at their lips. "I've never met a human like him before."

A moan came from Karim, concern replaced Morgan's amusement, and they hurried to his side. "Karim?"

I followed them, stopping by the bedside, seeing Karim's eyes squeezed shut as if in pain, another groan escaping his dry lips. "Is there anything we can do for him?" I asked Morgan.

"No. I don't think so."

"So, he's just going to suffer?"

"There's nothing I can do."

"You caused this," I said.

"And?"

The indifference in their response threw me. "He could die because of you. Because you decided his desires tasted the best. And now you don't care that you hurt him?"

Morgan threw me a harsh look. "You're speaking about something you don't understand again."

"I understand that you used Karim, and it ended with him harmed, whether you intended that or not. We can't just leave him like this—"

"What do you want me to do?" Morgan snapped, spinning

around to face me. "I didn't know if I took this much, his life would be in danger! I just... felt comfortable with him. Happy. I didn't want to lose that connection. I didn't know it'd end up this way."

I stayed quiet for a moment, my gaze shifting back to Karim. Maybe Morgan wasn't as nonchalant about Karim's state as I thought. They seemed to care about Karim. "What did you want from the labyrinth?" I asked.

Morgan hesitated before speaking. "I wanted to have a real relationship with Karim. To come to him as myself, not only in a dreamlike state. Normal humans can't see my kind. But then the labyrinth showed me how it might be possible. If I only fed from him, we'd form a connection, and he would one day be able to see me. I think it's been working, too. He's been desiring *me*—even before I go to him. Desiring to talk with me, to simply spend time with me. But he has only grown weaker and weaker."

"Why didn't you stop, then?"

Morgan gritted their teeth, throwing me a glare. "Because I thought this was the only way. I just wanted him to see the real me. I didn't know it'd become like this."

They hunched their shoulders, their gaze returning to Karim. I studied them for a moment, unsure of what to do. It was clear they cared about Karim, but their desires blinded them. Like the other participants in the labyrinth, they were going about their challenge in the wrong way.

As I thought about it, I realized it was true. Everyone so far had been about to make the wrong decision until I showed up and helped point out what they couldn't see. To become their voice of reason.

Maybe the labyrinth tricked people into making the *wrong* decision, and that's why so many had failed before. It showed its participants what they desired, leading them astray to claim them forever. Those who faced it alone couldn't see past their desires and failed.

Maybe there *was* a reason I was appearing in everyone else's challenges. Maybe it wasn't an accident, and I was actually supposed to help them.

Or was it to show me I was the same as them? That I was making the wrong choice? But what was my choice about? Julian? Or Enver?

I shook my head. This wasn't about me right now. I had the chance to help save Morgan from becoming one of Enver's servants and return an emotion to Enver, and I wouldn't waste it.

"I understand that desperation for a real relationship, but Morgan, what you are doing could never create one," I started, keeping my voice kind and blameless. "You are still manipulating Karim. You have to stop feeding on him."

"Our connection hasn't formed yet," Morgan responded, shaking their head. "What if it only takes one more? I can't..."

"What if one more kills him?" I countered. "What then? Is it really worth it?"

"I'm so tired of feeling lonely," Morgan whispered, looking at me again. "I just wanted someone to stay by my side. Am I really so evil for wanting that?"

My chest tightened, and I couldn't help but think of Enver, trapped and alone for so long. I didn't know how long Morgan had been alone, but I couldn't imagine their loneliness. If the physical representation in Enver's castle was anything to go by, I imagined Morgan's loneliness was just as all-consuming.

But it still wasn't right to have someone innocent suffer for it.

"You're not evil, Morgan," I said softly. "But wouldn't it be even more lonely if the last memory you have of Karim is him dying?"

Morgan flinched, and a shaky breath left their lips. "I..."

“This isn’t the way, Morgan.”

Karim moaned loudly again before Morgan could respond, his body shuddering, and Morgan bent over him, grabbing his hand and holding it tightly. They dropped to their knees beside the bed. “Karim, I’m so sorry. What have I done to you? I never meant for this to happen. I didn’t want to hurt you. I only wanted to stay near you.”

“Can’t you help him?” I asked them. “Is there no way to return energy to him?”

Morgan bit their lip, glancing up at me. “I’m not sure. I have heard it’s possible, but it requires taking energy from someone else. I don’t have enough.”

“If I wanted to offer you energy, would we have to have sex?”

“Not necessarily,” Morgan said. “A kiss would suffice in your case.”

“You kissed me earlier, though. You didn’t get energy from that?”

“Well, I thought we would go further, so I was saving it for that.”

I grimaced. I didn’t want to be reminded of that. “Then let’s transfer some of my energy to Karim.”

“Why would you want to help us?” Morgan asked, but pushed themselves to their feet again, gazing at me uncertainly. “What do you get out of being so nice?”

Their question threw me off guard. “What?”

“What’s the point? What do you expect from others if you’re kind to them? Do you think I will love you if you are nice enough to me?”

I went still. “Is that what you think I’m doing?”

“I can’t figure it out based on your desires,” they replied.

“I don’t need an ulterior motive to want to be kind.”

“No,” they agreed, “but most humans do, regardless of whether or not they realize it.”

I opened my mouth to argue but then fell silent as I realized

I *did* have an ulterior motive for helping them—to escape the labyrinth. The same could be said for all the other layers. My actions weren't purely selfless.

But...

"I do think it's part of my labyrinth to help others," I answered truthfully, "but I also just want to help you. Maybe I do expect something in return for being kind sometimes, but I wouldn't stop being kind even if I never received it. I want to be kind because the world is cruel. I want to be kind because it's the one thing I know how to do. Everyone deserves kindness. You included."

Morgan's eyes were wide and shimmering. "But why...?"

I took a step closer to them. "It must be so difficult to be alone and cut off from everyone else. I understand your desperation for a connection."

Morgan inhaled softly, and their hand moved to cup my neck. "I know you do."

"But Morgan, if I help you, you shouldn't keep doing this to Karim," I said, making Morgan pause, their face inches from mine. "Don't make the same mistake twice."

Their lips trembled, and they nodded. "I know. But I can say the same to you."

I swallowed. "I know."

We leaned closer to each other, letting our lips meet. There was no passion in it, only the motions of a chaste kiss. An odd, tugging sensation spread through me, and I could feel the energy being drawn out of me. Morgan pulled away a moment later, moving to Karim and pressing their lips to his.

My head felt light as I watched them, and I wondered how much energy Morgan had extracted from me. I reached for the headboard of the bed to steady myself.

Karim's eyes snapped open a moment later, and he drew in a sharp breath. Morgan straightened out, watching him. His gaze went to them, and he tried to push himself up into a sitting position. "Morgan? Is that you?"

Morgan froze. "You can see me?"

"Am I dreaming?" he asked, and when Morgan tried to pull their hand away, he grabbed it again, enclosing it within his. "I can feel you."

"No, you're not dreaming," Morgan said, their eyes wide. "You can really see me?"

Karim stroked the back of Morgan's hand. "Yes. Does this mean all the times you visited me were real?" he asked, his voice weak, eyes scanning over Morgan as if he couldn't believe they were real. "I had hoped, but everything always felt so foggy after waking up. I thought I was losing my mind. Your touch felt so real. Just like this."

"How is this possible?" Morgan whispered. "You shouldn't be able to see me."

"Well, I'm glad I can," Karim said with a smile. "I thought I'd never be able to see you if it wasn't in my dreams."

Morgan fell back a step, ripping their hand back. "You shouldn't be happy to see me. I almost killed you."

"You did?" Karim asked, blinking. He grimaced a bit as he tried to get out of the bed. "I guess I have been feeling weak lately. I thought it was just from a lack of sleep. But, my gods, was it worth it to be able to see you. I haven't had a single nightmare since you came. I used to be plagued by them every night."

"Don't sound thankful to me. I'm not who you think I am," Morgan said roughly, putting more distance between them.

"I know who you are," Karim stated, standing on shaky legs, using the bed for support. "You're Morgan, the one who protects me from my nightmares and gives me the sweetest dreams instead."

"I took from you. I feed off the dreams I give you."

"Then we both benefit from them, don't we?" Karim asked, breathless. "I'm glad. I thought I was being selfish."

Morgan's mouth fell open. "What? How? *I'm* the one being selfish, not you!"

"I prayed you'd visit me every night. I didn't want you going to others," Karim responded sheepishly. "I selfishly hoped you would only ever come to me. No one else. I wanted your company all to myself."

"But I..." Morgan trailed off as Karim tried to take a step forward and nearly collapsed. Morgan quickly caught him, holding up his weight. "Hey, don't try to walk. You're still weak. You could hurt yourself."

"Is it okay if I hug you?"

Morgan swallowed audibly before nodding. "Yes."

Karim wrapped his arms around them, hugging them. "You feel even better when I'm not dreaming. I can't believe this. Please, let me stay like this for a while. I just want to be near you, nothing more."

Morgan flushed, and our gazes met. I couldn't help but smile. Morgan had completed their labyrinth. I didn't need to see if Enver had received a new emotion or wait for the ruby shard to know it this time.

"Thank you," Morgan said to me, holding Karim tightly in their arms. "I'm afraid of what I would have done without you."

"You would have made the right decision," I said.

Morgan shook their head. "No. I don't know that I would have."

A shift in the shadows tucked in the corner of the cabin caught my attention, followed by the familiar burning of the pendant tucked against my chest. "I think it's time for me to go," I told Morgan.

"Good luck with your labyrinth," they said. "I wish I could help."

"Can you answer a question for me again, then? About Julian. Is it true? Did he never love me?"

Morgan's face fell, revealing the answer before they spoke. "I don't want to hurt your feelings."

"It's okay," I said tightly. "I already know now. I hate to admit it, but you've helped me open my eyes."

"I'm sorry, Nell."

Somehow, hearing Morgan confirm Julian's feelings didn't hurt as much as I thought it would. I reached for the pendant, feeling the newly formed piece of ruby and holding onto it, letting it soothe me. It resembled a broken heart now, with the gem filling the setting a little more than halfway. "Thank you, Morgan," I said as I turned to leave.

"Nell, wait."

I glanced back at them. "Yes?"

"It is easy to be misled in the labyrinth. And it's easy for kindness to be taken advantage of. Be careful."

I nodded, the shadows creeping up on me. "I will."

"It's also easy to be misled by feelings," they added. "Keep that in mind."

The shadows swarmed over me before I could ask what they meant, and Karim and Morgan were gone.

16

Every corner of Enver's castle seemed to be plunged into darkness once more when I returned. I frowned at the deteriorated carpet that lined the crumbling stairs, avoiding the glass as I ascended to the next floor. Knowing the decay represented Enver's loneliness left me with an uneasy feeling I couldn't shake. My feet felt heavy as I climbed the staircase. I wasn't ready to face Enver yet. I hoped the castle would just lead me to the next layer of the labyrinth instead of bringing me to him like last time.

I held my breath as I pushed open the door at the top and let it out in relief as it revealed one of the empty hallways. I closed the door behind me and eyed the shadows that clung to the stone walls. They didn't make any attempt to grab me, so I turned my back on them, heading down the hallway. I'd find the next layer myself.

I opened the first door I came across, blinking in surprise as I stepped into a massive room—a library, I realized. It was well-lit, a rare occurrence for Enver's castle, and lined with floor-to-ceiling bookshelves, all filled with books of varying sizes. A staircase on either side led up to a second floor, where I could see even more towering bookshelves. I moved further into the room, the scent of old paper and dust meeting my nose. Walking up to a bookshelf, I plucked out a leather-bound book, marveling at its craftsmanship. Hand-bound and nothing like the books I found at my local bookstore. I flipped it open, not recognizing the language that lined the pages. It looked well cared for despite how ancient it appeared to be.

I tried not to get too excited looking at all the books. I probably couldn't read many of them, nor would I have time to. I needed to escape the labyrinth.

But I couldn't deny it was tempting.

"Nell?"

The sound of my name made me jump. I snapped the book shut, whirling around to find Isla behind me, her eyebrows raised. "Isla, hey," I greeted, putting the book back in its place. "What are you doing here?"

"I was going to ask you the same thing." Her lips curved down. "No luck making it out of the labyrinth yet, huh?"

"I'm still working on it," I said, grimacing.

She gave me a half-smile. "Same."

"Still couldn't find what you're looking for?"

"No," she said with a sigh. "This castle is huge. I swear I've looked everywhere."

"It is huge," I agreed. "Even this library. I wonder if Enver has read all these books. Is a century even enough time to read this many?"

Isla stared at me, going silent.

I smiled awkwardly. "Oh, right. It's weird that I call him by his name."

"Actually," she said slowly, "I was just thinking you could help me."

"How?"

"There's a throne room in this castle that you can't access without knowing how. I haven't been able to figure out how to get in there. Do you think you could get him to tell you?"

I hesitated. "Um. I'm actually trying not to see him right now."

"Why?"

"I just want to finish my labyrinth and leave."

Isla leaned against the bookshelf, folding her arms over her chest, her gaze piercing into mine. "What if I told you what I'm searching for would help us both escape the labyrinth?"

"Is that possible?" I asked, standing straighter.

"It is. But I need to find what I'm looking for first. There's a possibility it's in the throne room."

"What is it?"

Isla pursed her lips, watching me for a moment. "I guess it doesn't hurt to tell you. It's a key."

"A key?"

"Yes. It'll help us leave this place."

I furrowed my eyebrows. "How? Aren't we trapped here by magic?"

"You'll just have to trust me," Isla said. "Once I get that key, I promise I will help you get home. But I need that key."

A thought hit me, and I tensed. "Is this key a physical object?"

"Not exactly. That's what makes it so hard to find."

I relaxed a little. It wasn't the pendant, then. "Are you sure it's in the throne room?"

She slumped a bit. "No, but it's one place I haven't searched yet, so I'm hoping it's in there."

I fiddled with the sleeves of my shirt. Isla was a participant in the labyrinth. So far, helping the participants led to them completing it. It could be the same for her. "Maybe I could help."

Her eyes lit up. "Will you? Really?"

"I can try, but I can't promise he'll tell me."

"I thought you were close to him?" Isla asked, putting her hands on her hips, frowning.

"I thought that, too," I mumbled, lowering my gaze. "But I was wrong."

A hand on my shoulder had me lifting my head again, and Isla gave me a sympathetic look. "It's in his nature to be manipulative, Nell. It's not your fault. I told you before—we're just pawns in his games. But that doesn't mean that we can't beat him."

I nodded but knew I didn't feel that way about Enver, even after what he'd said to me. He was just as much of a pawn as we were.

"Although, perhaps we can use his own tactics against him," Isla said, pulling her hand back.

"How?"

"Do you think you could manipulate him? Can you use whatever you had between you to your advantage?"

I thought about it. What we had between us was just sex, apparently. My heart clenched at the thought. *Just sex.*

But... I *could* use that to my advantage. Exactly as he had done to me the night he'd found me at the club. "I have an idea," I told Isla. "It might work."

She beamed. "Really? Great!"

I tried to smile back, but anxiety filled me at the thought of what I was about to do. I had wanted to avoid Enver. This would be the exact opposite, but if it led to a chance of escaping without needing to complete the labyrinth, I had to do it. I didn't know how much time I had left, and my vow with Enver gave me no comfort now, either. I couldn't spend forever with a man who only wanted my body.

"I'll go now," I said, trying to steel myself.

She reached for me again, squeezing my shoulder. "Good luck, Nell. Let me know how it goes."

I nodded and turned to exit the library. My fingers trembled as I reached for the doorknob. *I can do this.*

A faint scent of vanilla and amber wafted around me as I stepped through the door and into a new room. My eyes landed on Enver almost instantly, and my traitorous heart jumped at the sight of him. He sat behind a dark oak desk, leaning back in his chair, his eyes closed, his black hair tousled as if he'd been running his fingers through it. He looked relaxed, but the frown that twisted his beautiful lips told me otherwise.

"I didn't have to try very hard to reach you," I said.

His charcoal-grey eyes opened, meeting mine, and their intensity had my steps faltering. "You may seek me out whenever you wish to," he murmured, not moving from his sitting position, his hands resting on the chair's armrests. "The castle will always bring you to me, be it this chancery or my chambers. Though, this still does not count as completing the labyrinth."

"I didn't think it would."

He remained quiet for a moment, his unwavering regard feeling like a physical weight on my shoulders. My pulse thrummed in my ears as I gathered the courage for my plan. I didn't have to fake my attraction—even now, my fingers longed to tangle in his hair and pull him close.

My body didn't care he only wanted me for sex. Only my mind did.

"Nell," he began, his tone unexpectedly gentle. "I—"

"Stop talking," I interrupted, hating the tremor in my voice.

His brows pinched together, and his dark gaze followed me as I crossed the room to him, his head tilting back slightly to keep eye contact with me as I stopped at his side. Even seated, his height was impressive, my shoulders level with his chin. "What do you desire of me?" he asked.

I didn't respond, trailing my fingers down the side of his face, feeling the roughness of his jaw. For a heartbeat, he froze, but then his eyes drifted shut, an almost imperceptible sigh escaping his lips as he surrendered to my touch. His cheek pressed into my palm, his warm breath feathering my skin. The way he let me caress him so easily made my mouth go dry. At that moment, I knew he would let me do whatever I wanted to him. Was this how he'd felt when he'd first approached me? Did he know he could do anything to me at that moment, like how I knew I could do anything to him right now?

I straddled his lap, and his muscles tensed under me, but he didn't resist. Instead, he spread his legs, providing me more space to settle onto him, his hands leaving the armrests to settle against my lower back. My arms wrapped around his neck, and I brought myself even closer to him, my chest pressed against his. I leaned in, kissing his neck softly before pulling back.

His eyes opened, and he looked at me through his long lashes. "What game are you playing right now, my little lover?"

I kissed him again, this time on his jaw, and his breathing grew shallow.

His hands flexed against my back. "Nell—"

"Be quiet," I ordered. "If you don't like what I'm doing, stop me, but if not, don't say anything."

His gaze grew dark with desire, and he said nothing else.

My hands found the thin strap holding the edges of his silk top together, undoing it, letting the slippery fabric fall on either side of his sculpted torso. His muscles grew taut as I pressed one of my hands against his scarred chest, noting the absence of his heartbeat, before slowly dragging it down to the waistband of his trousers. I kept my eyes locked on his face the entire time, watching him react to my attention. His tongue darted out, wetting his bottom lip in anticipation.

His hands encircled my waist, using me as leverage to tilt his hips up, grinding against me.

"No," I said, taking my hand away, but my voice lacked strength as I felt how hard he was.

I'd only planned to tease him. To not cross any lines, only tempt him enough to make him slip up. I didn't plan on having sex with him again. But I couldn't deny the arousal growing in me. I couldn't deny how good his body felt underneath mine. I wanted his lips on mine. Wanted him inside me, making me mindless with pleasure like the last time we'd been intimate together.

This time would be different, though. This time, I would be the one in control. The one taking from him. I would use his body for my own self-indulgence while getting the information I wanted from him.

"I'm going to ride you," I told him. "And you're going to sit there quietly and keep your hands to yourself."

His fingers dug into my skin momentarily before he released me, returning his hands to the armrests. I pushed myself off him to undress, starting with the shirt I'd borrowed from him, slipping it over my head, then moving to my pants, bending over in front of him tantalizingly. I stripped until I was bare, and his heated gaze never left my body.

"You're going to stay dressed," I said, my fingers moving to the ties of his trousers, undoing them, and trying not to react as his erection sprang free, hot and thick against my hand.

It shouldn't have surprised me that he wore no underwear, not with the way he never seemed to wear a proper shirt since the night at the club. But I couldn't hide my reaction in time, my lips parting, a blush coloring my cheeks.

Enver smirked in response, clearly pleased with how his body affected me.

He shifted in his chair, bringing himself to the very edge of it, and I was about to scold him before I realized he was adjusting his body to make it easier for me to ride him. This way, the armrests wouldn't be impeding my movements.

I turned away from him, backing up over his thighs to line myself up above him, but his hands were suddenly at my waist, stopping me. I glanced over my shoulder at him. "I told you not to move—"

"Face me," he demanded, his voice husky.

I was supposed to be the one in control, but I obeyed his command. His hands returned to the armrests again, releasing me. I placed my hands on his shoulders, using him for balance as I straddled him again, my legs on either side of him. His erection rubbed against my inner thigh, and I let out an unsteady breath, feeling the moisture of his pre-cum spread across my skin.

My gaze caught his again, the black of his pupils nearly eclipsing the grey of his eyes, revealing the extent of his desire for me.

I reached between us, grasping his erection in my hand, and guided it to my entrance. For a moment, I teased him, rubbing his head against me, letting my wetness slick him. His length twitched in my hand, and he let out a low, impatient groan.

I sank onto him, taking him all the way inside me in one go, ignoring the burn of the stretch. Once fully sheathed, I squeezed myself around him, making him inhale sharply. He throbbed inside me, eager for movement, and I half-expected him to thrust up into me, but to my surprise, he remained still. I gave myself a moment to adjust. The way he filled me so completely had my legs shaking already.

"So obedient," I whispered, lifting myself.

He moaned in response, and it sent a new rush of arousal through me. I hadn't expected him to be so vocal. The past times we'd slept together, he'd barely made a sound if it wasn't dirty talk.

Once only his tip remained inside of me, I slammed myself back down onto him, and he rewarded me with another sultry sound. Encouraged by this, I used his shoulders as leverage as I increased my pace, sliding myself up and down his length, panting softly from exertion. His head fell back, his lips parted as he breathed shallowly, fingers gripping the armrests tightly.

My thighs burned as I took my hands off his shoulders, my legs bearing all my weight now, but I wanted to touch him. I brushed my fingertips against his pecs before pinching his nipples. He bucked his hips, making me moan as it caused him to hit even deeper inside of me. “Don’t move,” I reminded him breathlessly, tweaking his nipples once more.

His body trembled, the veins in his arms bulging with his restraint. The sight had me moving faster, needing to watch him unravel under me more and more. I couldn’t believe I had this much of an effect on him. I wanted more.

“Kiss me,” I commanded.

He wasted no time in crashing his lips against mine, kissing me roughly and desperately. My mind clouded with pleasure as his tongue teased mine, sending tingles down my spine as I ground down on him, trying to take him deeper and deeper. I spread my thighs more, leaning forward, pressing my clit against his pelvic bone, grinding it there, using him to please myself as I held him inside me.

He responded by letting out a hoarse groan, his teeth catching on my bottom lip, and biting down. I started moving again, his kisses becoming frantic and messy as I collided with him again and again, the sound of our skin slapping together filling the room.

Enver’s breathing became more labored, and he panted in my mouth between kisses, his quiet moans increasing in frequency as I rolled my hips. He twitched inside me, and his muscles tensed, signaling he was close.

“Enver,” I said, breaking our kiss and wrapping my hand around his throat to get his attention. “Look at me.”

He obeyed, his gaze finding mine, half-lidded and heavy

with desire. His lips were shiny and swollen from our kisses, and the sight nearly made me lose control.

"Tell me how good I feel. Tell me how much you enjoy having me like this. Riding you," I demanded.

He let out a broken moan. "You have no idea what you are doing to me. You feel... exquisite."

"You can do better than that," I panted, using his own words against him, keeping my hold on his neck to support myself as I continued to move on top of him. "Stop with the pretty words. Tell me what you really think. Are you enjoying me using your body for my pleasure?"

"Yes," he ground out. "Use me. Take what you want from me. I am yours. Only yours. Yours to use. Yours to take. *Always* yours—"

His words caused a fresh surge of arousal to course through me, slicking him further, and I took him even deeper, a small whimper escaping me.

I didn't expect to enjoy this so much. To enjoy taking control. I would never have done this with Julian—too afraid to voice my wants, let alone demand he do exactly what I wanted. But with Enver, confidence flooded me. With Enver, I had nothing to fear. No doubts. No insecurity. I felt sexy, powerful, and desired.

The way I should have felt with all of my past partners.

"I cannot get enough of the way you take me," Enver groaned. "How wet you are for me. How well I fit inside you. So tight and—" he cut himself off, his hips bucking up, his restraint cracking.

"Stay still," I breathed.

His head fell back, lips parting, his Adam's apple moving against my palm as he swallowed. It was then that I noticed shadows—his shadows, curling around his wrists, keeping him bound to the chair, preventing him from breaking my command. Holding him back as pleasure wracked his body.

Fuck.

The sight had me clenching around him. So, this was what he saw when he made me fall apart. No wonder he never wanted me to face away from him.

"Enver, I need to know where something is," I said, forcing myself to focus, too close to giving into the pleasure and giving up my plan.

His only response was a slight nod of his head.

"How do I get to your throne room?"

His brows furrowed, a sign he was pushing through the haze of his pleasure. I tightened my hand around his throat, and his hips jerked again. I slowed my movements to an agonizing pace, keeping him from finishing, and making him savor every roll of my hips.

"Speak," I ordered.

"You cannot get in by yourself," he responded, voice strained.

I used my free hand to pinch his nipple. "Then how do I get in?"

"Nell—"

I started moving faster again, leaning in to lay kisses on and nip at the base of his neck, right under where I had my hand wrapped around it. "Tell me, and I'll let you come."

"You—" he began, but his words turned into a strangled groan, the noise vibrating against the pressure of my hand as I squeezed his throat even tighter. "Oliver," he gasped. "Find him. He will bring you there."

I pulled my head back, my thighs on fire as I quickened my pace again, riding him for all I was worth. "Where is he?"

"The kitchens," he groaned. "Gods—"

"You can move now," I said, feeling like my legs were about to give out.

"Tell me I can touch you," he rasped.

A shudder of pleasure rolled down my spine. "Touch me, Enver."

One of his hands shot to my ass, gripping it tightly, and he rose from the chair, keeping himself inside me as he roughly swept everything off his desk. He all but threw me down onto the smooth wood, causing him to slip out. He grasped my calves and shoved them up toward my head, forcing my knees to bend. My legs quaked, but he didn't give me any time to rest, nearly folding me in half as he leaned over me, dragging me closer to him. "Do not think I did not know what you were doing," he murmured into my ear.

My eyes widened in realization. "You let me do it."

A faint smirk ghosted across his lips as he lined himself up with me. "Just like you are going to let me fuck you until all you can ever plot in that pretty little head of yours again is the next way you can feel me inside of you."

I let my head fall against the desk, whimpering as he thrust back inside me with an intense snap of his hips, burying himself deep. His teeth skimmed my earlobe before dropping to my neck, digging into the same spot I'd bitten him as he began to pound into me. I cried out at the intensity of his pace, only feeling pure pleasure as he took complete control.

He suddenly adjusted me so his left hand held both my legs over my head, driving into me at a new angle that had me keening with every thrust. His now free hand encircled my neck, and I stared up at him, my breath hitching.

"I did not give you permission to choke me," he said, his fingers splaying against my skin, my neck feeling small and fragile compared to the size of his hand. "But I am not so discourteous. Would you like me to choke you?"

Although my body shivered with anticipation, I shook my head, already overwhelmed by every other sensation. My legs wouldn't stop shaking, so much so I felt self-conscious, unable to control them. They were strained in their position, my body contorted, but I also didn't want him to let me go.

Enver rotated his hips, hitting the spot inside me that had me gasping as he trailed a finger down my throat, finding the chain of the heart pendant. He slid his finger under the chain, tugging it taut. "No? Then answer me."

"No," I managed to get out, my breath coming so rapidly it made me light-headed, the chain biting into the back of my neck.

"Another time, then," he decided, releasing the chain and gathering my wrists in his hand instead, pinning them above my head. "For now, lay there and accept the consequences for attempting to deceive me."

I didn't think I could do anything else, anyway. My body was on fire, and the heat only grew as he continued to drive into me, his hand slipping between us to rub at my clit. I writhed under him, looking above me, seeing that his shadows had replaced his hand, trapping my hands within their tendrils.

"You do not mind, do you?" he asked, noticing where I was looking.

I should have minded. I knew I should have.

"No," I said instead. "I like it."

I liked his shadows. I craved his control.

He rewarded me with a heady kiss and more shadows. They curled around my breasts, teasing my nipples.

I closed my eyes, trying to breathe through the onslaught of sensations, feeling my orgasm building up, knowing it would be as powerful as every other one he'd given me before. My back bowed as it washed over me, the intensity leaving me breathless. No sound came from my lips as they parted in a silent cry.

"There it is," Enver said, not slowing his pace. "Again."

My eyes flew open. *Again?* "I can't," I panted, wiggling my hips to get away from his touch.

"You can. You will."

"Enver!" I cried as he continued playing with my clit.

"You are going to come for me again," he said, then took his hand away from me. "You are going to beg for it. And then you are going to thank me for it."

My cheeks flushed. I couldn't do that. "Enver—"

"That was not a request," he warned, eyes narrowing, slamming into me hard enough to shove me further up the desk.

My heart stuttered. "Please," I whispered.

"Good," he grunted and then pulled out to adjust our positions again so my ankles rested against his shoulders. My legs still quivered, but at least this position wasn't as strenuous. "Again."

I sucked in a quick breath as he sunk back into me, this position allowing him to reach so deep I found it hard to breathe. "Please make me come," I pleaded, my words slipping into a moan as he moved within me.

"You can do better than that."

"Please make me come, Enver!" I tried again, my voice rising as he returned to a brutal pace, punching gasps out of me. "Please!"

"Louder."

I gritted my teeth together, swallowing a whine.

"I said *louder*," he said, and my eyes rolled back with the force of his next thrust.

"Oh—fuck!" I cried helplessly, my hands clenching into fists reflexively. "Enver, please!"

His hand returned between my thighs and he stroked me once, twice, and on the third swipe, I came around him, feeling on the verge of passing out as my body convulsed. I fought to get air in my lungs as I moaned again, my toes curling. He didn't stop, continuing to fuck me through it, and the overstimulation quickly had me writhing against the desk, unable to stop the feeble noises spilling from my lips.

"Say thank you," he ordered sharply.

I struggled to get the words through my moans. "T-thank you."

"For?"

A deep stroke had me keening. "For making me come."

"Good. Do you want me to come?"

I nodded, unable to catch my breath long enough to form any more words.

His thrusts became shallow, staying deep inside me. "Say it. Beg me to come inside you."

He teased a finger against my clit again when I hesitated, and I jolted. "Please come in me!" I cried, knowing I couldn't take any more.

His jaw tightened, and his going still was all the warning I had before he released inside me, filling me with his cum. He let go of my legs a second later, letting them fall to the desk on either side of him, and he leaned over me, resting his weight on me. I closed my eyes, and he pressed mindless kisses to my collarbone as he continued to leisurely rock inside me as he softened. I went limp under him, exhausted.

"I have decided if you would like to deceive me again, I will allow it," he murmured against my skin, letting the shadows dissolve.

I didn't have it in me to give him any response to that other than a weak grumble.

He chuckled, pulling out of me and tucking himself back into his pants. "Care to explain why you needed the information about my throne room?"

"No."

"Hm." His hands slid under my thighs and lower back, lifting me from the desk and holding me up against him, my legs wrapping around his waist. "Well, I suppose it does not matter to me whether or not you know how to enter the throne room."

I knew I probably should have protested and demanded that he let me go, but I let him hold up my weight, pressing my face into his balmy neck, breathing in his scent as I looped my arms around his neck.

"I will warn you, though. If I catch you there, you will not like the consequences." He paused, adjusting his grip on me, and one of his hands sliding to my backside, squeezing it. "Or perhaps you will."

My body reacted to his words in a way that made me wonder if I was also insatiable around him. I certainly had no self-control. I pushed my face harder into his neck, embarrassed by myself.

"Come, bathe with me," he said, leading me toward the door to his chancery. "Your legs are still trembling. The warm water should help."

I pulled back, clarity suddenly filling me. "No, I'm going to continue the labyrinth."

He stopped. "What?"

I struggled to get out of his arms. "Put me down."

His arms around me tightened. "No."

"Enver, put me down. I'm leaving."

"What is this? You fucked me, and now you are done with me? You took what you wanted, and now you plan on leaving?"

"And if I am? What does it matter to you?" I demanded, shoving against his chest, a bitterness rising in me. "The only thing you want from me is sex. You said it yourself. And I just gave you what you wanted. I don't owe you any more of myself than that. I hope this at least made you happy. I spread my legs for you, just like you wanted me to."

His arms loosened around me. I slipped out of his grasp, my legs feeling weak as I walked over to my clothing. I only managed to throw my underwear and his shirt back on before he grabbed my wrist, pushing me against the wall behind his desk. I glared at him as his hands went to either side of my head, keeping me trapped. My mouth opened, ready to lay into him, but his expression made me fall silent.

"Nell," he began, his voice becoming soft again, his gaze locking on me. "I am sorry."

My heart tripped in my chest. "What...?"

"My words were callous and untrue. I lost my composure and intentionally caused you pain," he confessed, his fingers sliding up my wrist to entwine with mine. "It was cruel and uncalled for."

"Then why did you say it?" I asked, refusing to let his sincere tone disarm me.

A flash of vulnerability crossed Enver's face, and his lips curved down. "Because you are correct. I am lonely. I have endured this loneliness for over a century. It ate away at me at first—the isolation, the quiet, the longing for touch from another. But eventually, I resigned myself to being alone. I convinced myself that the loneliness did not affect me since I accepted my fate. That I did not feel alone—therefore, I was not lonely. And I remained that way. Until you appeared. Then, that devastating loneliness brewed within me again, and when I tried to brush it aside once more, it only festered and grew every time you came to me and left again."

My mouth felt dry when I went to speak again. "What does that have to do with what you said to me?"

"I spent decades denying that loneliness inside me. It took you mere seconds to undo that repression," he said. "I told you before one of the other emotions I possess is pride. When you tried to comfort me about something I wanted to continue to refuse to acknowledge, it wounded my pride, and I lashed out. I did not want to admit to feeling alone. Not to myself nor to you. Yet you persisted, and I took what you said at that moment and twisted it into something to use against you as a means of deflection. For that, I am deeply sorry."

I swallowed, thinking back to the moment in the garden.

He'd tried to get me to stop. I'd pushed. "What is wrong with feeling lonely?"

"To feel lonely means you desire not to be alone. I assured myself that I was content in being alone so that I would not suffer from the alternative."

"Why can't you convince yourself of that anymore?"

The hand not holding mine dropped from the wall, coming to rest on my cheek. "Because of you. You are a reminder of all that I am missing, all that I long to have again, and all that I stand to lose. I want to have you by my side. I do not want to be alone anymore. I cannot deny it anymore."

I didn't move to pull away from his touch. His palm warmed my skin and caused my blood to thrum under my skin. "How do I know what you're saying isn't more of your manipulation?"

"It is," he murmured, his hand sliding up to tuck a strand of my hair behind my ear. "I am manipulative by requisite. No matter what I say, there will always be a part of my words designed to convince you to stay. That is a part of me I cannot change. I conditioned myself to manipulate, coerce, and deceive for so long it has now become second nature. However, there is no deception in my apology. I am truly sorry. You are worth far more to me than just sex. Far more."

When I didn't respond, his hand fell away from my face. I caught it in mine, my fingers tightening around his. My stomach knotted, and I stared down at our joined hands. "Then when you felt happy before...?"

"It was because of you," he told me. "The way your smile lights up your entire face. The way my scent lingers on your skin. The sound of your voice. The endearing sight of you curled up in my bed, tangled in my sheets, the morning sun illuminating your hair. I will not lie and say I do not enjoy sex with you—I do, very much so—but my happiness lies in any of the instances when you are near enough for me to simply savor your presence."

My chest tightened, my heart beating wildly. I wanted to believe him. I did believe him.

His thumb brushed against the inside of my wrist. "I want you by my side. I desire it. Even if it is only the time between the challenges of the labyrinth, I crave those stolen moments with you."

"Why did you seem upset when you realized I was starting to care for you?" I whispered, unable to meet his eyes.

"Because I am full of contradictions," he said. "I want to trap you here, yet I also want to set you free. I want you to myself, yet I know I cannot keep you. The more you care for me, the greater the guilt inside me grows, but at the same time, your feelings feed my pride because I know my words have swayed you."

"Guilt?" I repeated, going still, my blood running cold.

He nodded. "Yes. I recognize the emotion Morgan returned to me. It is guilt."

"Is that why you're apologizing?" I asked, dreading the answer. "Because you feel guilty now?"

"No," he said firmly, pulling his hand free from mine to take hold of my chin, tilting my face up to meet his. His eyes bore into mine, unwavering. "I am apologizing because I was wrong. I wanted to apologize even before Morgan completed their labyrinth. Guilt did not drive me to do this. The despair I felt upon seeing your pained expression did. Knowing I caused it. I do not expect your forgiveness, but I ask for it all the same."

The knot in my stomach unraveled, but the dread did not fade. If he hadn't apologized—if he'd remained distant and cruel—I could have convinced myself to finish the labyrinth and forget about him. My feelings could have been buried away along with the hurt he caused me, and I could have left him behind and never looked back. I could have returned to my world and gone on with my life without ever thinking about the ethereal man who ensnared me in his castle and arms. I could have forgotten him and saved myself. Saved myself from heartbreak. From a love I knew couldn't be but couldn't stop myself from wanting.

But now…

Now, I couldn't. I couldn't forget him. I couldn't walk away. I couldn't stop the warm affection that continued to grow inside me. I couldn't shake the fierce longing that ached in my heart. I couldn't stop falling, even though I knew how it would end. I couldn't save myself. Not from him.

"I forgive you," I breathed.

17

Warmth spread within me as Enver leaned forward, pressing his forehead against mine. His breath mingled with mine as he spoke, "Thank you."

"I'm sorry for pushing you, too," I apologized, my eyes fluttering closed.

"Do not apologize, my little lover," he said, leaving butterfly kisses on my eyelids and cheeks. "I know your intentions were for my benefit."

"I can't stay here," I said, pulling back, and I didn't know which one of us I was trying to convince.

His lips ghosted across mine. "I know," he responded, and without warning, he lifted me into his arms again, this time so my legs wrapped around his waist, our bodies pressing flush together. "I will not stop trying to persuade you otherwise, though."

"I know," I responded, and I couldn't help but smile. "You could try saying please once in a while, though."

"I do not beg," he reminded me, kissing my nose.

"I bet I could make you."

He gripped my ass roughly, supporting my weight. "I assure you. You cannot."

"What if I rode you again? Made you beg me to let you finish—"

"Keep talking, and you will be the one begging me to have mercy on you."

I immediately closed my mouth. I was too sore for any more right now.

He smirked. "Wise decision. Now, let us make the most of our time together, regardless of what will happen between us in the end."

"Okay," I said, threading my fingers through his hair as he carried me out of the chancery. "My time isn't running, right? Maybe I want to take a bath after all."

"Your time will never run when you are with me."

"It's still impossible for you to get rid of the time limit completely?" I hedged. "Then I wouldn't really need to be in a rush, and maybe I would be okay with spending even more time with you than trying to finish—"

Now, it was his turn to smile as he caught my gaze before pressing his lips to my jaw. "Still impossible. Though I have to say, the time limit has yielded some unintended but pleasurable results."

"What do you mean?" I asked, my heart fluttering at both his smile and his kiss.

"I am referring to the... *enticing* method of yours that you used to get information from me," he said, his lips skimming against my ear.

I blushed, hiding my face in his neck as he carried me through the chancery's door and into a dimly lit washroom. "Oh."

"Although I may have recognized your intentions, I admit I would have been incapable of stopping you, anyway."

"You could easily have stopped me with your shadows."

"You misunderstand me," he said. "I am unable to resist *you*. Powerless against the temptation of your touch. Your kiss. Your voice. You have become my sole weakness, my inevitable undoing, and my relentless obsession."

I pulled back, searching his gaze, a quip about his pretty words dying on my tongue at the unbridled desire I found in his eyes.

"You have a dangerous amount of power over me, yet I find myself craving more of your control," he murmured.

"That doesn't scare you?"

"Perhaps it would if I were capable of feeling fear."

I winced. "Oh. Right. Sorry."

"It does arouse *other* feelings in me, though, so I would like to experience it again."

"We'll see," I mumbled.

Enver chuckled, and without him even moving a hand, dozens of candles burst to life, their flickering flames lighting up the washroom. This one was smaller than the other I'd been in, but not any less luxurious. The subtle scent of lilac filled the space, originating from the oversized golden tub in the middle of the room, already filled with steaming water.

He placed me on the tiled floor, and I allowed him to help slide my shirt over my head, and then I stepped out of my underwear. Enver held out his hand for support as I stepped into the water before he stripped off his own clothing. My eyes roamed over his body, taking in his broad shoulders and sculpted torso, lingering on his scar before being distracted by the way his muscles rippled as he moved toward the tub. He climbed in, sinking into the water beside me, and grabbed my waist, pulling my back against his chest. I tensed a bit, but then his hands were on my shoulders, massaging them back into a relaxed state. My eyes fell shut, and I melted into him as his fingers dug into my neck expertly, making me hum in contentment.

"What was your labyrinth like this time?" he asked me.

My eyes cracked open, and I turned my chin to look up at him. He'd never asked me about any of them before. Of course, this one would be the one he asked about. I hesitated, not wanting to bring up Morgan tricking me. Or me convincing myself to go back to Julian.

"Tell me," he coaxed, pressing a kiss against my cheek. "Since you have already completed it, it will not put you in danger of failing."

"Morgan took the form of Julian, deceiving me into believing I was home, and that Julian was apologizing and telling me he loved me."

Enver stilled, then his arms wrapped around my waist. "That was cruel of them."

"No, Morgan was just doing what they had to do to survive," I said, biting my lip, and looking down at our blurry legs under the water. "But I went back to Julian so easily. You cut me off, and I went to the next person who would accept me. Just like the real Julian said I would do. I can't even use being under Morgan's influence as an excuse. I still gave in."

"Why would you return to that substandard excuse of a man?"

"I love him," I said, defensive, but then I realized what I'd said. "No, I meant I *loved* him."

His arms tightened around me. "Did you?"

"Yes—"

"Do you remember when I asked you what love means to you?"

"Yes, but I don't know if I believe that anymore," I said hesitantly. Now I'd seen *real* love. True, unconditional, and undying love. Between Paloma and Neima. Dio and Luliana. Aki and Cas. Morgan and Karim. When I thought of them and compared my relationship with Julian to theirs, then... "I don't think that's what love is anymore."

Enver rested his chin on my shoulder. "If you based love off what you used to believe, and that belief has changed, then did you ever love him? Or did you convince yourself you loved him simply because you were desperate to love someone and be loved in return?"

My lips parted, trying to form a response—trying to claim that I had loved Julian, fully and truly—but the words wouldn't come out.

Had I loved Julian? Or had I given him all of me because I was desperate for someone to want me?

"Why are you so desperate for love, my little lover?" Enver breathed into my neck, his voice softening. "Why do you place your self-worth and happiness in the hands of another?"

"I don't—"

"It is a dangerous thing to do," he warned. "You cannot control whether they will cherish what you offer or use it against you—whether they will protect or break you."

I swallowed hard. "I have to offer all of myself. It's all I..."

It was all I had, yet it never seemed to be enough.

"It is cruel, is it not?" Enver contemplated quietly. "To want something so desperately while knowing you are incapable of obtaining it. Incapable of offering what you truly wish to give."

My throat tightened. His words hit too close to home. I was tired of never being enough, yet incapable of being anything else. After so many years of being treated as disposable, how could I believe I was worth more? Worth anything at all? I knew I was putting my self-worth in someone else's hands, but I didn't know any other way to feel like I was worth anything.

I didn't want to feel that way. I didn't want to struggle with such insecurity. But I didn't know how to stop. Didn't know how to do things the right way. I didn't even have a single positive reference for a healthy relationship until I entered the labyrinth.

And seeing the others... it made me want to be like them.

To be happy. To be loved. To just have the confidence in myself to do so.

"I would cherish you," Enver murmured against my ear, fingers splaying across my stomach. "I would cherish and adore every part of you, my little lover, no matter how small the piece is, if only you would let me."

"What if I can't offer you anything in return?" I whispered. "What if I don't know how to yet?"

He kissed the soft skin below my ear, sending a pleasurable quiver through me. "Then you are far from the only one."

I turned my head, the warmth in his eyes and the gentle curve of his lips filling my chest with an ache that was both familiar and unfamiliar.

"But do you truly believe you have not already offered a part of yourself to me?" he asked, his fingers sliding lower, making me hold my breath.

"Are you talking about my body?" I breathed out, turning my head away from him again, too afraid to see his reaction.

His hand stopped its descent, thumb resting on my hip bone. "Nell," he started, voice low and gravelly by my ear. "You mentioned owing me earlier. You do not owe me anything. You will never owe me anything. Especially not your body."

"I know," I admitted. "I guess the idea that you only wanted me for sex hit me deeper than I thought it would."

Enver's breath tickled my neck as he exhaled. "I deeply regret my words, Nell. Know this—I would have you with me even if we never had sex again. Being near you is enough. I promise."

My hand found his, lacing our fingers together over my lower stomach. "But you said it's hard to even control your lust around me."

"It is," he confirmed, "and that lust only intensifies the closer we become, but it is no longer the only feeling you kindle within me. Now, it is only one among many. And if denying it meant you would stay with me, then I would do so for as long as you asked. There are many other ways to show intimacy."

As if to prove his point, Enver started to wash my hair and body with warm and soothing hands, and I wondered what he would be like if he had even more of his emotions back. If he were this attentive and tender while going through the motions of how he believed a lover would act, how different would he be if he could actually love me?

Enver trailed kisses down the back of my neck, and I inhaled shakily. If he loved me, then...

I stopped myself there. He didn't, and wouldn't. *Couldn't.* I could allow myself to enjoy my time here with him, but I couldn't let myself believe he could love me. No matter how much I wanted to, it was the one line I couldn't cross. I didn't want to be desperate anymore. I didn't want to be desperate enough to settle for some kind of pseudo-love.

I abruptly pushed away from him, scooting myself to the other side of the tub, causing the water to slosh between us. Enver looked at me with a curious expression, his eyes darkening with an unspoken question, but I avoided his gaze, knowing if I stared for too long, I would lose my resolve and fall back into his arms.

"What is wrong?" he asked.

"I should go," I said, standing from the water and moving to get out.

Enver's hand shot out, stopping me. I gasped as he tugged on my wrist, causing me to fall down across his lap, splashing water out of the tub and onto the tiled floor. I didn't resist as he positioned me to straddle him, our faces nearly level with each other. "What is it, my little lover? Why so apprehensive all of a sudden?"

"I just don't think I should be wasting time here," I lied, turning my head away from him.

A hand on my jaw guided my face back toward him, his eyes brimming with an intensity that made my heart ache. "How can it be a waste of time when your time is not passing?"

"Still," I protested weakly as he angled my chin up toward him. "I need to complete the labyrinth. I need to go home."

His thumb caressed my cheek as he leaned in toward me. "Is that so?"

"Yes," I responded, swallowing as his breath swept across my lips.

"Will you say no if I ask to kiss you right now?" he murmured.

"No."

Enver closed the remaining distance between us, his lips melding to mine so perfectly it was as if they were formed just for me to kiss. I let my eyes shut, losing myself in the delicate way his lips moved against mine. Tortuously languid and unbearably soft. The kiss of a lover. His tongue dragged against my bottom lip, and I allowed him entrance into my mouth, moaning as his tongue teased mine, tracing slow circles onto it that had goosebumps breaking out across my skin.

I buried my fingers in his hair, raking my fingernails across his scalp slowly as I tilted my head to allow him to kiss me deeper, drawing a sound of satisfaction from him. His hands explored my body lazily, mapping out every dip and curve. He kissed me slowly, as if we had all the time in the world to indulge in each other. I supposed to him, we did.

When I broke away to take a breath, he chased my lips, refusing to let our connection break for too long. I pushed myself up on my knees, using his hair to guide his head back, kissing him roughly before laying wet, open-mouthed kisses down the column of his throat, the taste of his skin almost familiar at this point as I licked and nipped at him. A deep rumble came from his chest and he gripped my waist, dragging me closer, his erection digging into my stomach.

"If I asked you to become mine, would you say yes?" Enver whispered, nuzzling his nose into my neck.

I shuddered in his lap, my hands dropping to his shoulders, my fingers curling around them as he traced the shell of my ear with his tongue. "I can't."

"Why not?" he asked, his voice a soft hum. "Am I not enough for you, my darling?"

Darling. That was new. I didn't say anything for a moment as he pressed small kisses to every inch of my skin he could reach, from my throat to my collarbone to my breasts. Ceaselessly. *Lovingly*. Except it couldn't be. I took a deep breath, pushing away from him again, and he raised his head, watching me with a heavy-lidded gaze that had my breath stuttering.

I wanted to tell him that I wanted more than just physical pleasure. That I wanted his heart, not just his body. But how could I when he didn't even have a heart to begin with? Only a hollow spot remained in his scarred chest where it should have resided.

"I need more than what you can offer me," I said instead, finding it hard to speak through the lump forming in my throat. "I need more than this physical relationship between us. That's why I can't be yours, Enver. That's why I eventually have to leave your labyrinth. I can't do that to myself. Not again."

His body became taught beneath mine, his mouth setting into a straight line. For a long moment, neither of us spoke, and my heart pounded so hard it hurt. I flinched when he suddenly moved, but he only lifted me from the tub, carrying me out with him. He retrieved two towels from a wardrobe, handing one to me as he put me down. "I will find you fresh clothing," he said. "Stay here."

I did as he said, drying myself off, and he returned shortly, dressed in one of his silk tops that only closed with a thin strap along his stomach, leaving most of his torso bare. He carried a flowing gown—powder blue, with white flowers embroidered into the skirt. Delicate and light, with only thin straps to hold it up on me. He approached me, holding it out, and I quickly put it on, struggling to get the smooth satin over my damp skin. Before I could reach for the ties in the back, Enver was already carefully moving my hair to one side of my neck so he could lace me in.

"I will have my servants wash your undergarments and return them to you," he told me, placing a pair of flats on the ground for me to slip my feet into.

Fortunately, the dress held my chest rather well, but I did feel a bit exposed without my underwear. The idea of servants washing them made me cringe, but I didn't want to make any demands of Enver at the moment. "Thank you."

His gaze lingered on me for a moment, sweeping over the way the dress clung to me. "That suits you quite well."

His compliment warmed my cheeks despite the eerie chill the dress left me with. "Where did you get all these dresses?"

"My wardrobe," he answered.

"Why do you have so many?" I asked, considering him for a moment. From what I'd seen of his style, he enjoyed wearing loose clothing, but he hadn't worn any type of dress in front of me.

Enver frowned, staring hard at the bodice of my dress, before turning his scrutiny to my bare arms. "It is missing something."

"It is?" I asked. "What?"

"I do not know," he answered, his voice dropping into a lower pitch as his brows pinched together. "The dresses I have been giving you have been in my wardrobe for as long as I can remember, yet I do not know why or how they came into my possession."

A chill ran through me despite the balmy air in the washroom. I had to fight the urge to take the dress off. Who knew the history behind it? "You really can't remember anything?"

"No matter how often you ask me that, my response remains the same. I cannot."

"I feel weird when I wear these dresses," I told him. "Like I'm taking something that belongs to someone else. Does what you wear ever make you feel like that?"

He glanced down at the black silk shirt he had thrown on. As with the rest of his outfits, it fit loosely and revealed the scar on his chest. "No. I am sure this is mine."

"How do you know for sure if you can't remember anything?"

"In the same way that I know my name is Enver, and I know there are foods I do not eat. There are some things I know, even though I cannot explain why I do. I remember how to comfort and pleasure someone, even though I do not remember ever having someone to do so for before you."

I looked back down at the dress, and the unsettling feeling surged. I hadn't let myself entertain the thought before, but now it hit me full force—I wasn't Enver's only lover. There wasn't a question about it. Enver knew how to please someone. He knew exactly how to touch and tease me, skillfully taking me over the edge again and again. He was too comfortable in the role of a lover to have never had one before.

And now that I accepted the thought, I understood why I didn't like the dresses. I had no way of knowing if they belonged to one of Enver's ex-lovers.

I didn't like the thought of him being with someone other than me.

I pulled at the neckline of the dress, regretting having brought anything up. I didn't want to think about it. I didn't want to think of him touching someone else. *Loving* someone else, back when he was still capable of feeling the emotion. Knowing someone could have had his full affections, his heart entirely, made mine clench.

I didn't like it. I didn't like the jealousy that coursed through me. The want to claim him as mine when I knew I couldn't.

"I am sorry I do not have a better explanation for you," Enver apologized quietly. He covered my hand with his, stopping my anxious fiddling. "I wish I did."

Surprised, I looked at him, seeing the remorse on his face. "Huh? Oh, no, you don't have to apologize. It's not your fault. I was just curious."

"You seem upset."

Dang it. Why did he have to feel empathy so strongly? I waved him off. "No, I'm not."

"Tell me what you are thinking. I want to ease your mind if I can."

"I'm..." I turned my face away from him, ashamed to admit it, but his hand squeezed mine encouragingly. "I'm thinking about how I'm selfish and full of contradictions, too."

"In what way?"

"I want to leave, but I want to stay. I crave your touch, though I know I shouldn't. I don't want to be yours, yet I want you to be mine."

"Oh, my little lover," he murmured, stepping closer to me and cupping my cheek. "Do you not know? I am already yours. I was yours from the very moment my gaze first fell upon you. I am yours now, even when you will not offer yourself back to me. And I will continue to be yours even after you leave me. There will never come a day when I am not yours entirely and irrevocably. I may not be able to love you, but I am yours nonetheless."

My lips parted, but I couldn't think of a response or even remember how to breathe. What he couldn't offer me in emotion, he would with devotion. He would give me everything in any way he could, just as he had promised before. Now, though, more than ever, it felt like a true promise—a vow. A vow as compelling as the oath we made that tied my fate with his. He was *mine*.

"Why?" I whispered.

"Because being yours is something I know I am instinctively, no matter how little I can recall," he said. "You are something my soul recognizes. Something familiar and precious. I cannot explain it, but I cannot deny it either."

"That doesn't make any sense. We just met," I said, hyperaware of his proximity, aware of how I only needed to lift myself onto my tiptoes to be able to kiss him.

"It does not," he agreed, his tone softening as he dipped his head toward me, "but it also does not change the fact it is true. I am yours."

Our noses brushed, and my mouth found his, unable to stop myself. My fingers twisted into the front of his shirt, keeping him close, and I kissed him hard, trying to show him everything I couldn't bring myself to say. His hands cupped my jaw, matching my passion as his tongue sought mine.

I moaned, and his grip tightened as he deepened our kiss, stealing my breath away as he always did, be it with his words, his touch, or his very existence.

I understood how he could be so sure he was mine. Something in him called to me too, drawing me to him, and leaving me helpless to resist. He was a stranger, yet the pull I felt toward him was unmistakable. Undeniable. Being with him felt right despite our circumstances. When I thought no one would ever make me feel the way he did before, I hadn't fully recognized the truth in the words, not like I did now.

No one would ever be able to make me feel this way again. No one would ever be Enver.

And that terrified me.

He broke away from our kiss, gazing at me with a faint smile, and my chest clenched. How would I be able to walk away when all this was over? How could I forget him when I wanted him so badly? My body begged for his touch, but my heart yearned for his love, and only one of those was a possibility. I would love him with all of me and receive only a part of him in return. I would break my own heart every time I remembered he didn't have one.

"I can't do this," I said, forcing myself to release his shirt. "I'm sorry. I—"

"I know," he responded, brushing my damp hair out of my face, "but I will never stop wanting you. Never stop endeavoring to keep you. Not until you can no longer deny what lies between us, just as I cannot."

"Until I say I am yours."

Enver hummed in response, brushing my hair back from my face. "Until then."

"I'm scared that you already have a part of me," I confessed. "A part I don't think I can ever get back."

Another hint of a smile appeared on his face. "You do not know how much it pleases me to hear you say that. You should be more cautious."

"Cautious? Of what?"

He leaned in, his lips skimming across my ear as he spoke. "Of me. You have admitted a part of you is mine, and now I know it is possible for me to take more. I want all of you. Every beautiful, precious part. And I am tempted to steal the rest right now."

With more effort than it should have taken, I forced myself to move back, away from his warmth and the pull of his magnetism. "Y-you can't!"

"Is that a challenge?" he asked, eyes glittering with mirth.

"I'm going to continue the labyrinth now," I said, retreating slowly.

He advanced, matching my every step, until my back hit the washroom door. "And if I told you I am not finished with you yet? That I want more of you and am not willing to let you leave until I am satisfied? Perhaps for the remaining sixteen hours straight so you run out of time to complete my labyrinth?"

My pulse skyrocketed as his hand grazed the fabric of my dress by my thigh. "Enver," I said, my voice too high-pitched and breathy.

He chuckled, and his hand moved to the door handle, opening it for me. "I will be waiting for you to return to me, my little lover."

I refused to react outwardly, even as my disloyal heart raced and my skin tingled in anticipation. My arm grazed his as I turned and stepped out of the washroom, back into the castle hall. It was brighter now, lit up with polished sconces. The carpet was no longer decayed, now lush under my shoes as I started down the hall, searching for one of the shadowy doors that would transport me to the labyrinth. Daylight filtered in from intact, arched windows. It was strange to see the castle so put together.

I paused. Did this mean Enver felt happy right now? Was it because of me? I could feel a smile pulling at my lips, and I tried to bite it back. I couldn't be happy that he was pleased because I was giving into his advances. I needed to get it together. He'd said I only had sixteen hours left.

"Nell!"

Isla's voice caused me to startle, and I twirled around toward the sound of it, finding her coming out of a door I hadn't noticed before. "Isla, you have to stop appearing out of nowhere and nearly giving me a heart attack."

She grinned, stepping up to one of the windows, and the sunlight made her black hair shine. "Sorry. Did you get the information?"

"Yes, but..." I said haltingly.

"But what?"

"There has to be a reason why the throne room is so hard to get into, right?"

"I agree," Isla said. "That's why I need to get in there. The key could be in there. We could be out of here in no time."

I fiddled with my fingers, looking down at them, suddenly unsure if I wanted to share the information with Isla. It felt like betraying Enver. "Right."

Isla folded her arms over her chest, resting against the windowsill. "You *do* want to leave, don't you?"

"I..." Why was I hesitating? I wanted to leave, and this was a way to do it.

"Nell," Isla said, setting her hands on my shoulders. "I don't know what kind of hold the lordling has on you, but—"

"He doesn't have a hold on me," I said immediately, looking up at her.

She pursed her lips. "It's obvious he does."

"No—"

"His scent is all over you. That's not your dress. The marks on your neck certainly weren't there the first time we met."

I flushed. "That's..."

Isla's fingers dug into my skin, her brow furrowing. "Nell, he's manipulating you. Don't you see that? He wants to trap you here like the rest of us."

"I know that."

"I don't know that you do."

Was it that obvious that I was torn? I hated the shame that flooded into me. "I know I can't stay here. I know I need to go home. But—"

"It's not your fault," Isla said, her voice softening. "He does this. He gets into your head. Under your skin. He gets you all turned around and twisted up. All to get what he wants from you."

"But he's just as trapped as we are!" I burst out, unable to stop myself.

"Is that what he told you?" Isla asked, her voice turning cold, releasing her hold on me. "That he is the victim here?"

"He's cursed," I told her.

"A curse he is deserving of," she snapped. "You do not know him, Nell. You know what he wants you to know of him. I know the real him. *I* know what he does to people. I know all the terrible things he has done and why he ended up here. And that's why I am asking you to trust me on this. Let me save us both before it's too late. Tell me how to get into the throne room."

"You know him?" I asked, my eyes widening. "From before you came to the labyrinth?"

"Yes," she said. "I am one of his very first victims. Because I so desperately wanted to undo everything he did back then. I still do. So please, tell me. I will get you out of here. I promise. You'll be free."

I didn't know what to do. I didn't know what to believe. Who to believe. I shook my head. "I—"

Isla's jaw clenched. "You're going to trust someone with no memory over his victim?"

A knot formed in my stomach. I knew it could be possible that my gut feeling about Enver's innocence was wrong, but I didn't want to face it. I didn't want to choose between who to believe. But Isla was still a victim of Enver's labyrinth. She had helped me before, and I owed her at least this much, especially if I needed her to complete her challenge in order to complete mine.

"Enver said Oliver will bring you to the throne room. He's one of his servants," I told her.

A spark of recognition appeared in Isla's eyes. "I know exactly who that is. Thank you, Nell. I'm sorry if I came across as harsh."

I forced a smile onto my face. "No, it's okay. I understand. I hope you can find the key."

"When I do, I will come find you right away, okay?"

"Okay."

She threw me another smile before heading down the hall, pulling open a hidden door.

I watched her for a moment. “Isla?” I called before she stepped through.

Stopping, she glanced back over her shoulder at me. “Yes?”

“What did Enver do to deserve this?” I asked.

Her expression turned dark. “He took the heart of someone he should have never touched in the first place.”

18

Ominous and heavy, Isla's words lingered even after she vanished into the darkness. I didn't know if she meant that literally or figuratively, but thinking about Enver's scarred chest and his missing heart made me believe it was the former. Could Enver really have killed someone? Had he ripped out someone's heart and had his own taken in return? Why? What happened in the past he couldn't remember?

A shiver rolled through me as shadows under the window climbed up it, opening a doorway for me.

When I exited through the other side, I came to a dead stop, my mouth falling open at the sight before me. Golden orbs of light floated in the air in front of me, surrounding a chandelier that also hovered in the air, nothing attaching it to the ceiling. Or, what I thought was a ceiling. Black stretched on until it met the four walls of the room, creating a live tapestry of a starry night. As I looked, a star shot across the fabricated sky.

I took a cautious step forward, my gaze sweeping across the cluttered room. To my right, a wooden bookshelf held plants that emitted a soft blue glow. Books bound with leather levitated all around me, their tan pages slowly flipping back and forth, as if someone was reading them. Crystals were strewn across every open space, radiating a rainbow of colors. An armored suit stood a few feet in front of me, a humming sound coming from it. I approached it, smiling a little. It reminded me a little of Paloma.

Its head turned toward me, and I nearly screamed. Spectral eyes burned into mine and I stumbled back a step, crashing into a table full of jars of bubbling liquids.

"Silas!" a voice suddenly cried, covering the sound of my impact, and then came the sound of a fist pounding on a door. "You can't keep me in here! Let me out! Where the hells are you?"

A crack of what looked like blue lightning shot through the air and I instinctively ducked. I crept around the animated suit of armor and tried not to be weirded out when the helmet rotated to watch me pass. A young woman with curly dark brown hair wearing magenta robes entered my vision, banging her head against the oak door, groaning in frustration. She then straightened out and kicked the door, only to hiss in pain, pulling her knee up to grab at her foot.

"*Ow*. That stupid jerk. I'll make him pay for this," she muttered, setting her foot back down and crossing her arms over her chest.

I cleared my throat.

She gasped and whirled around, her eyes widening. "What in Star's name?" She lifted her hand, a white magic gathering in it. "Who are you? How did you get in here? Speak now, or I will end your life."

Her voice was high-pitched with the hint of an accent I didn't recognize, but full of a deadly threat that had me throwing my hands up in front of myself defensively. "I'm Nell!" I squeaked. "I'm doing the labyrinth! It brought me here!"

"The labyrinth?" she repeated, the magic still swirling viciously in her palm. "How do you know about that?"

"I'm also a participant. I swear!"

Her eyes narrowed suspiciously. "Does Silas know you're here?"

I shook my head. "No. I don't even know who Silas is."

She watched me for another moment before she finally lowered her hand, the magic fizzling out. "He's the owner of this castle. He's also doing the labyrinth."

"Wait, were you brought here too, then?" I asked, surprised. "I haven't met anyone else who ended up in someone else's labyrinth for their challenge. I thought it just happened to me."

"No, this is my home," she said, folding her arms over her chest. "Well, this tower I'm trapped in isn't my home, but this kingdom is. What is left of it, that is."

I deflated a bit. "Oh." Then I perked up again. "Wait. If there are two of you doing the labyrinth, maybe that counts as two layers for me. Maybe there is hope for me finishing it on time."

She stared at me, blank-faced. "Sorry?"

"Oh, nothing," I said dismissively, walking up to her. "Let me introduce myself again. I'm Nell." I offered her my hand.

"Rielle," she answered, shaking my hand, her grip firm despite the softness of her skin.

"I think I'm here to help you," I told her, getting straight into it. "Not to sound like I have a savior complex or anything—I just think that's my challenge for the labyrinth. Helping others. I should be able to help you with yours."

Her brows raised. "You think you can help me?"

"Sure," I said, confident. It'd worked out with everyone else so far. "What's going on?"

She laughed, bitter and mirthless. "Come here."

I followed her as she guided me across the room and up a spiral staircase that led out to a balcony. Wind whipped around us and I shuddered, walking over to the railing and peeking over it. A thick spectral mist covered the ground, bathing the land below in an eerie incandescence. Gnarled, dead trees jutted out from the mist, blackened and bare, their limbs stretching out toward the sky like they were trying to escape the haze. Wisps of the mist curled around dilapidated structures scattered about, and it took me a moment to recognize that the chilling scene before me had once probably been a castle town.

My gaze zeroed in on unrecognizable shapes moving around in the mist, and I inhaled sharply, my heart skipping a beat. “What are those?” I asked, horrified.

Shadowy creatures with long, thin limbs and sharp claws stalked through the haze. Their forms shifted and contorted, reminding me of the shadows Enver controlled. Except, I didn’t fear Enver’s shadows. But these sent a chill down my spine and sent my heart racing. How they moved with lanky, jerky steps, and how their heads swiveled back and forth as if on the lookout for something, unnerved me.

“My people,” Rielle said, her voice strained. “Cursed to become monsters.”

I couldn’t stop staring at the creatures, resisting the urge to back away from the nightmarish sight. “Those are people?”

“They were. Now they are shadows of their former selves. Their sanity stripped away by the mist.”

“How?” I breathed, forcing myself to turn away, looking at Rielle.

“Silas,” she answered, her hands clenching into fists. “He was once a prodigious sorcerer. His magic was powerful, but uncontrollable and violent. My father, the king of this kingdom and one of the oldest living wizards, took him under his wing to help him rein in his magic and learn how to control it. But then Silas betrayed him. He betrayed all of us. He killed my father, cursed my entire kingdom, and kidnapped me. I’ve been locked in this tower for months now, watching everyone and everything I’ve ever known wither away.”

I swallowed, glancing back at the roaming shadow creatures. "I'm sorry."

"What's done is done. I just need to fix it. To save everyone," she responded.

"No, I mean, I'm sorry for that, too, but also for speaking so offhandedly before. Treating your problem as if it were something I could easily solve to complete my labyrinth," I explained, shifting uncomfortably. "I didn't mean to minimize what you're going through. This is awful."

A small smile tugged at her lips. "It is. And thank you for your apology. I didn't think you had any ill intentions, but I appreciate it."

"Is what you want from the labyrinth to save your people?" I asked.

"Yes," she answered. "That, and I want my revenge on Silas. I don't understand how he could do this to me. After everything we've been through, I thought..." she trailed off, her throat bobbing as she swallowed. "I have no choice anymore. If he refuses to break the curse, I have to myself. Even if it means killing him. I must choose myself and my kingdom."

"What—killing him?"

She averted her gaze. "I will do whatever it takes to save my kingdom. I will end him, even if I break my own heart in the process. That is my consequence for loving him."

"Is that really the only choice?" I asked. "Revenge?"

"It's not just revenge. It's doing the right thing for my kingdom," she said, an edge to her voice now. "If he has to burn to save it, then I will light the match. I will not allow him to lock me up here. I will let go of our past and fight for myself and my people."

Anger tightened her features, and my stomach flipped with unease. Could that be the wrong path that would lead her to failing the labyrinth? Killing Silas? "I won't pretend to know what you've gone through, Rielle, but if you kill him, you won't ever be able to take it back. Be careful with decisions born from anger—they could haunt you later."

Rielle studied me for a moment. "Are you an Oracle?"

"A what?"

"Never mind," she said. "Still, I will take your advice into consideration. You must have appeared in front of me for a reason."

I relaxed a little. "You said Silas is also doing the labyrinth? How do you know?"

"The lord of the labyrinth came to us at the same time," she explained, placing her hand against the railing, frowning. "I don't know what Silas wishes for. What he's wanted so far, he's simply taken by force. No one can stop him—not that there is anyone still around to do so. Everyone has been turned into shadows. My father, our guards, the townspeople. Even Xander."

"Xander?"

"Silas's mentor and my father's right-hand man," she said. "Silas cursed them all."

I studied her for a moment as I took in her words. Her brown skin was free of blemishes, her features soft and delicate, but dark rings encircled her chestnut eyes, and she hunched in on herself, her shoulders curling forward as if the weight of the plight of her kingdom rested on them. I knew in a way it did.

She puffed out a short sigh before looking at me. "So, still think you can help?"

"I'll do everything I can," I assured her. "There has to be a way to break the curse, right?"

"There always is," she said. "There is no such thing as an unbreakable curse. That is the only thing that gives me hope. My magic may not be as strong as Silas's, but I know it is enough to break the curse if I can find out how."

The wind suddenly picked up, whistling in my ears and

causing Rielle's robes to whip around her. A deep, rumbling sound echoed through the air, vibrating through the stone tower beneath our feet. I froze, glancing at Rielle, who stared up at the starless sky. The rhythmic noise grew louder, sounding almost like...

Wings.

"He's coming," Rielle said steadily.

Before I could ask who, a massive shadow loomed over us, blotting out the moon. My gaze shot upward, and I gasped.

Not just a shadow.

A *dragon.*

"Holy fuck," I whispered, caught between terror and awe.

Its black scales gleamed in the moonlight as it circled the tower, each shimmering plate the size of my entire torso. Its wings spread out from its body as it soared, its wingspan rivaling the horizon. A long tail swished behind it, the spiky tip nearly colliding with the top of the tower as the dragon suddenly banked left and fixated its glowing, icy blue eyes on me.

An earth-shattering roar erupted from its massive maw, and the force of it was strong enough to make my ears ring and the tower quake. It flapped its wings once before descending toward us in a steep dive.

Rielle grabbed my arm, yanking me out of the way as the dragon landed on the balcony with a thunderous crash. The railing crumbled under its weight, and its claws dug into the stone crenellation.

"Silas," Rielle hissed, somehow not intimidated by the dragon at all.

I could barely stand with how hard my legs were trembling. I clung to Rielle, unable to tear my gaze away from the beast. It lowered its head, thin pupils narrowing into slits as it regarded me.

This was Silas?

Then its form began to shimmer and shift, scales melting away to reveal white skin, wings and tail receding until they disappeared completely, and the creature standing before me was no longer a dragon, but a man. My heart leaped into my throat at the sight of him. Silas stood at least seven feet tall, clad in dark leather armor that formed to his sturdy build. He'd tied half his blond hair up into a knot at the top of his head, the rest falling just below his shoulders. A faded scar crossed from the top right of his temple to the bottom corner of his lips, marring the otherwise smooth skin of his face. His icy blue eyes bore into mine as he grew closer, his nostrils flaring.

I didn't have a chance to speak before an unseen force wrapped around my neck, squeezing tightly. I gasped, my fingers clawing at my neck, unable to find the source of the pressure.

Rielle whipped her head toward me. "Nell? What's wrong?"

I struggled against the invisible force, falling back a few steps, my breath coming out in harsh rasps.

"Who are you?" Silas demanded, his voice deep and threatening. "How did you get here?"

"Silas! Let her go!" Rielle snapped. "Stop it!"

"Speak," Silas commanded.

"Nell," I rasped, my air supply dwindling.

"You dare to invade my home and approach what is mine?" Silas continued, undeterred, his eyes blazing.

Rielle seized the front of his leathers. "Yours? I'm not yours, Silas! Let her go!"

"Silence, Rielle. Do not move," Silas said, and Rielle went unnaturally still, as if frozen in place.

When she spoke, it sounded muffled, as if her jaw was locked. "She's a participant in the labyrinth!"

This caused Silas to pause, his gaze flickering between me and Rielle. I wheezed, wondering if I was about to die here. Of all the ways I'd thought I would die, being strangled to death by *magic* hadn't been one of them. What would Enver think if I didn't return? Would he be worried? Would he be sad?

Why was I worrying about what Enver would think while I was being strangled?

As the lack of oxygen weakened my body and I staggered into the wall for support, the pressure on my neck suddenly disappeared. I barely had time to take in a breath before Silas's hand slammed into my shoulder, pinning me to the wall as he loomed over me. "I suggest you speak quickly. Why are you here?"

"I..." I hesitated, trying to think of what to tell him. Something told me saying that I wanted to help Rielle break the curse on the land wouldn't end well with him.

"Well?" he prompted, impatient.

"I'm here to help you get what you want from the labyrinth," I decided on. It was mostly true—if Silas was another participant, I would probably need to help him, too. Although what I would do for him depended on what he wanted out of his challenge.

He sneered at me. "I don't need your help. Try again, or I will cast you out into the mist.""You don't have much time," I blurted, and his eyes narrowed, but I clung to the lie forming in my mind. "The lord of the labyrinth sent me to help you. Your time is running out to complete your challenge."

"What lies do you spew?"

I tried to keep my expression straight, although inside I reeled. How did he figure out I was lying so easily? "I'm not lying. You only have hours left. If you don't complete the labyrinth, you'll lose the thing you want most."

His gaze flashed to Rielle before returning to me, his fingers digging into my shoulder. "If I find you are lying to me..."

"I'm not," I squeaked.

"She's telling the truth," Rielle insisted. "She's here to help us. I saw the lord of the labyrinth bring her here."

I nodded furiously. "See? You can at least believe her if you can't believe me—"

"Come," he suddenly ordered, grabbing my arm and dragging me back inside the tower.

I tossed a glance back at Rielle, who could move again, and she rushed after us. "Silas, wait."

We descended the spiral staircase and walked through the trinket-filled room until we reached a doorway with no door. As we grew closer, though, I noticed a faint, white sheen covering the entire opening, and my feet halted on their own.

"It's a magic barrier," Rielle explained, noticing my apprehension. "Designed to keep me trapped in here like some sort of caged familiar."

"To protect you," Silas corrected in a flat voice.

"I don't *need* protection."

"I won't allow anyone to hurt you."

"Anyone other than yourself, right?"

Silas's fingernails dug into my arm, and I winced. "I would never hurt you," he said.

Rielle crossed her arms over her chest. "You already have. By taking away my freedom, my family, my friends. My *kingdom*—"

A low growl rumbled in Silas's chest and he yanked me forward through the barrier. An electric pulse jolted through my body, radiating from my chest and spreading outward. It hurt, but only lasted a moment, gone before I could do more than inhale sharply. Rielle pressed her hands against the magic barrier, her brown eyes filled with worry. "Nell! Are you okay? Silas, you could have killed her! What if she had magic?"

Silas ignored her, hauling me away. I offered her what I hoped was a reassuring smile before Silas pulled me through another door, this one physical, and shut it behind us. He let me go, and after giving me a stern look that commanded obedience, started down a long spiral staircase. I carefully followed him down it, my pulse racing.

"You have no magic," he surmised. "The barrier didn't react."

"I don't," I confirmed, although my chest still tingled.

"Yet you expect to help me?"

"I'm going to try. What is it you were desperate for?"

He didn't answer, and I didn't press, focused on navigating the winding staircase. As we reached the bottom, my foot slipped, sending me careening forward. I floundered, my arms shooting out, and Silas turned and immediately caught me, his large hands encompassing my waist.

"Careful," he said as he set me back to my feet.

"Sorry," I muttered, sheepish.

"If you can't even handle a staircase, I have little faith in your ability to assist me."

"Hey, this staircase is insanely steep and the steps are short," I defended myself. "It's a safety hazard at best and a death sentence at worst."

Silas raised his eyebrows, looking amused. "A death sentence? Are stairs so dangerous where you come from that they warrant such a title?"

I pursed my lips at him. "People can die from falling down the stairs in *any* world."

"You are quite pathetic, aren't you? I'm having less and less faith in you."

"Why are you keeping Rielle trapped?" I asked, trying to steer the conversation away from insults toward me.

The humor disappeared from his face, his features hardening, before he turned and strode down the hall. "I'm not keeping her trapped. I'm protecting her."

I wanted to question his definition of protection but figured it was best not to antagonize him. "Protecting her from what?"

"Everything."

"The curse, too? But aren't you the one who cast it?"

"I cast it to save her," Silas said, sweeping open a door at the end of the hall, leading us to a dimly lit corridor. "I had no other choice. She didn't know the danger she was in. What the king plotted against her."

I struggled to keep up with his long strides, frowning. "Her father? He planned on doing something that would harm her?"

"Yes."

"So, you cursed the entire kingdom? Did you try talking to her about it first?"

Silas suddenly stopped, and when he whirled around to face me I froze, my mouth snapping shut. He scowled. "What do you think? That she would believe the poor beggar she took pity on over her own father? Of course I tried. She brushed me off every time until it was too late. I had no choice. I will let the kingdom burn to save her."

"But keeping her locked up isn't fair to her," I said. "Even if you feel it's the only option, don't you think it's cruel to take away her freedom? If you love someone, shouldn't you want them to be happy above all else? She isn't happy—"

"What do you know about love?" he snarled, his eyes like shards of ice.

I swallowed hard. "More than I ever have before. Enough to know how much it can hurt, and how much it can heal. And enough to know that even the best intentions can become the worst ones, if you let fear consume you."

"Fear?" he scoffed. "I fear nothing. Rielle is safe with me, and I will never let her go. Never risk her life. Never—*never*—lose her."

His jaw clenched, shoulders heaving as his breathing grew heavier. My brow furrowed as I regarded him. His anger, his possessiveness, and his unwavering determination to keep her... Maybe his actions were rooted in love, but they came across more like an obsession.

But in a way, I could understand Silas. I'd been obsessed, too. Obsessed with being loved. Enough so that I would give up everything to obtain it.

But obsession *wasn't* love.

"Silas," I started, keeping my tone soft. "I understand you don't want to lose her, but if you keep something too tightly in your grasp, it will shatter and scar you both."

Silas said nothing, his body rigid.

"I know you want to protect her, but you also have to trust her," I said. "Trust her to protect herself and trust her to make her own decisions. What you're doing now will just make her hate you."

"Enough," he said roughly. "If you keep on with your foolish prattle, I will send you out into the mist without a second thought."

The threat was enough to shut me up. The last thing I wanted was to become one of the shadow monsters. Even less so than becoming one of Enver's mindless servants. At least with Enver, I would still be human.

I needed to navigate this labyrinth challenge carefully. Three fates rested on my shoulders this time—Rielle's, Silas's, and mine. And time was running out.

19

Regarding Silas warily, I walked behind him silently through the halls until we reached a set of wooden double doors with a swirling purple sigil emblazoned between them. Silas reached out, muttering a few unintelligible words, causing the sigil to disappear and the doors to swing open by themselves. I entered the room after him, shivering as the temperature dropped. It was dark and bare, save for a pedestal in the center where a glowing orb the same eerie green color of the mist sat. It pulsed and flickered ominously.

The air felt thick, like something was pressing in on my lungs, and I glanced at Silas. "What is this?"

"A conduit," he said shortly, walking over to it. "I channel my magic through it to maintain the curse on the land. Without it, my magic would run wild. My master offered it to me to help control both my magic and the curse."

I approached the orb cautiously, wanting to keep my distance but also drawn to it. As if the malevolent energy wanted to pull me in, envelop, and devour me. A chill raced down my spine, but I couldn't stop myself from getting closer.

Literally.

My feet moved on their own accord. I tried to stop but couldn't. I lifted my hand, stretching it out toward the orb. A tugging sensation similar to the one I felt with Morgan came over me as if the orb was trying to steal my energy.

Cold fingers encased my wrist, stopping my hand only inches from the orb. "I would not do that if I were you," Silas warned against my ear.

The spell broke. I jerked back from him, pulling my wrist free. My heart hammered in my chest as I faced him. "There's something weird about that."

"You have no magic. How would you know?"

"I've felt something similar before. Are you sure it's a conduit?" I looked back at the orb, unsettled. "It feels more like it's trying to absorb something than channel it."

Silas considered me for a moment before turning toward the orb. His fingers hovered over it, his eyes closing. The glow surrounding the orb reacted to his presence, pulsating faster, almost frantic. It seemed eager for his touch, stretching out to close the distance between them. I didn't miss how Silas flinched when he brushed it, either, or how it took effort for him to pull away.

The orb seemed to glow brighter as he backed away, casting an eerie, green pallor over his face and deepening the dark circles under his eyes.

"Are you sure it's channeling your magic?" I asked. "Where did you find it?"

"My master gave it to me," Silas replied in a clipped tone. "To help me protect Rielle."

"Your master? Isn't he lost to the curse?"

"No," he said, eyes narrowing. "Why do you say that?"

"Rielle told me that—"

"Who is this?" an unfamiliar voice suddenly asked, resounding and accusing.

I twirled around as Silas stepped forward. "Master Xander,"

he greeted, a hint of uncertainty in his tone.

Xander?

Xander stood at the door's threshold, resting against the frame, his eyes narrowed at me, crow's feet creasing the corners. Black hair streaked with grey framed his square jaw and fell to his chest. He wore a black robe that billowed around him as he stepped further into the room, a gnarled, wooden staff in his hand. "What is the meaning of this? How has she escaped the mist?"

Rielle's voice filled my head. *Xander. Silas's mentor and my father's right-hand man.* Was this that Xander? But how? Wasn't he supposed to be lost to the mist?

"She claims she was sent here to help—"

"She's lying," Xander said sharply. "She's a sorceress trying to deceive you."

My mouth dropped open. "What? No. I don't have any magic—"

"I can sense it," Xander continued, cutting me off.

Silas glanced at me, frowning. "She got through the magic barrier protecting Rielle, though."

Xander's eyes narrowed briefly at Silas before he smoothed out his expression. "I'm more attuned to the specific nature of her magic. It seems she's able to mask it at will."

"I don't have magic!" I repeated, a knot forming in my stomach as Silas's icy gaze bore into me. I focused on him instead. "Silas, listen to me, something's weird here—"

"Silas, I leave you alone for two days, and you put Rielle at risk once more," Xander said. He lifted his staff, and the same green glow began to emit from it. "How do you let a threat so close to your love? We must rid ourselves of her at once."

My pulse quickened. "Wait, please, I'm trying to help—"

"Not yet," Silas said. "I wish to question her more."

"She will only try to deceive you."

"Then brew me a truth potion," Silas suggested calmly, but

the muscles in his arm flexed as he balled his hand into a fist behind his back.

Xander scowled for a moment before nodding. "If that is what it will take for you to see that I am right. As I always am."

"I want to see if what she claims is true."

"And what does she claim?"

"That she is from another world," Silas said, but his eyes flickered to the glowing orb again before switching to me.

"I will need your assistance," Xander told Silas. "The flower root I need grows in the Northern gardens. You will have to enter the mist for it."

"Very well," Silas said before facing me again. "Come with me. You'll be imprisoned until the potion is finished."

I didn't argue. I would rather be with Silas than Xander. Silas steered me out of the room, his large hand clamped down on my shoulder. We retraced our path through the castle, and he stayed close to me as we climbed the narrow staircase back to the room where he had confined Rielle.

"Silas," I began, but he gave a swift shake of his head, making me fall silent.

He ushered me in, undoing the magic barrier, but did not follow after me. "Stay here," he said, sounding distracted. His eyebrows pinched together. "Do not leave until I return."

"But—"

Silas twisted on his heel and stalked away as Rielle rushed toward me, her voice breathless. "Nell! What happened?"

"Didn't you say the curse also claimed Silas's master?" I asked.

"Yes," she replied. "He was with my father when the curse claimed them both."

I frowned, folding my arms over my chest. "I just saw him. Xander, that is. He is free of the curse. I also saw what is hosting the curse. It's some kind of orb."

Rielle's face crumpled in confusion. "How is that possible?

Xander was also a victim." Her gaze went past me, and she gasped. "Wait. Silas forgot to put the barrier up."

"Are you sure?" I asked, but as Rielle said, the shimmering magic in the doorway was missing.

She moved forward, tentatively sticking a hand into the hall, and then she gasped, fully stepping out of the room before twirling back toward me. "Is this a trap?"

I considered how preoccupied Silas had seemed. "No. I think something I said unsettled him. The orb hosting the curse appeared to absorb his magic."

"Can you show me this orb?"

"I think I can remember the way back."

Again, I made my way down the treacherous stairs and hoped I led Rielle in the correct direction. "Xander and Silas went to retrieve a plant from the gardens, so they shouldn't be in there."

"Are you sure it's Xander?"

"Silas called him master," I said, only able to offer her that.

Her lips twisted, falling silent, and we finally reached the room that held the orb. She went in first, flinching as she swung the door open. "What?" she started, her voice wavering, shoulders stiffening.

"That's it," I said, stepping beside her and pointing at the orb. "Silas said it was a conduit—"

"No," she said, putting out her arm, preventing me from getting closer to it. "I know this orb. It's supposed to be locked away in my father's vault. How did Silas get ahold of it? This isn't a conduit, Nell. It's a vicious artifact. It absorbs the magic of anyone nearby, draining them until nothing is left, and then stores that magic for the one who summoned it to harness."

"What happens if it completely absorbs someone's magic?"

"They die," she said, her voice low.

Horror washed over me. "What?"

"But it should not be draining Silas's magic if he summoned it," she told me, her lips curving down.

"Acute as always, Miss Rielle," a voice said behind us.

I jumped, but Rielle tensed, her face paling. She turned slowly, her hand going to her chest. "Xander?"

Xander smiled cruelly, and the door slammed shut, trapping us in the room. "How did you get out of your room?"

"I-I don't understand. How are you here? I saw the curse take you," she spluttered.

"You were always clever, but not quite clever enough," he responded, advancing on us.

Rielle grabbed my wrist, forcing me to fall back with her. "What is the meaning of this?"

"I have no quarrel with you, my girl. Do not be afraid." His creepy eyes slid to me. "You, on the other hand, are an unwanted interloper. You will not wreck what I have worked so hard to accomplish. Your interference ends here."

He raised his staff and a burst of magic shot out. Rielle reacted before I could, her magic deflecting Xander's, clashing in the air together, sending scalding particles showering over us. "What are you doing?" she demanded, sparks of blue flowing from her fingertips.

"If you protect her, you will leave me no choice but to eliminate you both," Xander warned. "I can find other ways to manipulate Silas for his magic if I have to kill you. I can blame your death on her."

Rielle pulled me further behind her, shielding me, and my heart skipped a beat at her willingness to protect me. "It was you," she said. "You're the reason Silas set the curse. But why?"

"Come now, you already know why," Xander answered, his lips curling into a sneer. "Power. Control. I should have been chosen as your father's successor, but then that pathetic sorcerer showed up. Your father took him in and ignored all the years of service I provided him. I had no choice but to put an end to it."

"Successor?" she repeated. "But Silas is not next in line to the throne. He has no blood relation to us."

"Your father planned to offer your hand in marriage to him," Xander snapped. "I will never allow Silas to take my rightful spot. Once his magic is absorbed, Silas will die. Then, I will undo the curse and be hailed as a hero. I planned on asking for your hand in marriage as a reward, but perhaps it will be better to kill you after all. Silas's magic will be mine and I will be unstoppable."

Rielle's expression hardened. "You tricked Silas into thinking my father was the one with nefarious plans, but it was you all along."

"And he will never know better. I am sorry things have to end this way."

I searched the room for an escape. We were in danger. But Xander struck again, his magic a powerful bolt that sent Rielle crashing back into me, throwing us both to the floor. Rielle grunted as she landed on me, both the fall and her weight knocking the wind from my lungs, but she was quick to push herself back to her feet. Her hair whipped around her as magic flowed from her hands, deflecting a second blow from Xander.

I didn't know what to do. I didn't have any magic to defend myself with. I was only a liability.

But I couldn't let Rielle fight alone.

Rielle sent a blast of magic toward Xander, which he reflected, shooting it back at her. I yanked her out of the way before diving to the side myself as Xander sent another blast out. This one went straight through the stone wall, obliterating it. Rielle and I coughed as dust filled the room, lowering the visibility. Another shot sideswiped Rielle, making her stagger closer to the orb, causing it to pulse violently. Its green glow enveloped her immediately, draining her magic. I hauled her away, putting myself between her and the orb.

Xander shot more magic toward her, and this time she wasn't quick enough to defend us, the blow knocking us both back. I managed to keep myself upright, but Rielle flew across the floor, smashing into the stone wall. She groaned as she fell to her knees, struggling to push herself back to her feet.

"Such a waste," Xander tutted before lifting his staff.

"Stop!" a deep voice roared as Silas appeared at the door, his eyes blazing with fury.

Xander cursed, spinning around to face him. "Silas—"

"I heard everything," he snarled. "You deceived me. You betrayed me. You betrayed us all."

"I will do much worse if you stand in my way," Xander promised.

"No. You will not hurt her." Silas reached a hand out toward the orb, and its green light flared to life, shooting out at him.

"Silas!" Rielle cried.

But Silas didn't recoil. The magic swarmed him, causing him to glow with the same eerie color. His head bowed, his shoulders hunching. "Ugh."

"Your magic will be mine," Xander said, laughing darkly. "It's already begun. It will consume you. It will be mine—"

"No," Silas spoke, his voice calm, his body straightening out again. "You have underestimated me, Xander. It will not consume me. This magic is *mine.* And it will never be yours. You forget I am not human. And human-made artifacts will never be strong enough to overpower me."

The green mist disappeared, sinking into Silas. Then it shot out from Silas's hand, striking Xander in the chest, and sending him flying backward. Silas did not stop there. More and more magic erupted from him, burning green lighting up the room, making me shield my eyes in fear of being blinded.

"Silas, wait," Rielle called, fighting to be heard over the explosions of magic. "Wait! Don't kill him!"

"Don't stop me, Ri. He deserves a fate far worse than this for everything he has done. To you. To *us*. To the kingdom."

"He doesn't deserve for it to be over so fast," she responded, and the coldness in her tone sent a chill down my spine. "I will make sure he suffers for what he's done."

Xander lay unconscious on the floor, his face bruised and battered, his clothing still smoking. Silas didn't look like he wanted to listen to Rielle, but the magic surrounding him began to wane.

"Are you okay?" Silas asked her, his voice becoming gentle.

Rielle hesitated, keeping a few feet between them. "Silas, how did you fall for his lies?"

"He said you were in danger. He told me how I could protect you."

"He's the reason you once told me my father was a danger to me," she concluded.

Silas glared down at Xander. "He used my fear against me. I was too desperate to save you to see it."

"You thought cursing the entire kingdom was the answer?" Rielle asked, anger now lacing her tone. "You thought imprisoning me would save me? You *killed* my father—"

Silas's head whipped toward her. "Your father is not dead."

"What do you mean?"

"I did not kill your father. I simply placed him under the curse along with everyone else."

"But Xander said..." Rielle trailed off, taking in a shaky breath as realization hit her. "He lied to me. Then, my father is really alive?"

"I will lift the curse. You will be reunited with him again," Silas said, casting his gaze toward the orb on the pedestal. "Then I will accept my punishment for my crimes. I am sorry, Rielle. Truly."

"I don't understand," she said. "Why did you go so far?"

"I was scared," he murmured. "I thought I would lose you. I have lost everything in my life. When I met you, and you saw more than just an orphan in me and gave me a home, I knew I'd spend my life protecting you. I only honed my magic to be able to keep you safe. I was too focused on that to see that Xander was taking advantage of that fact. My fear grew to something twisted. All I could see was a world where you were lost to me if I didn't do everything I could to protect you."

"Taking away my freedom is an interesting way of protecting me," she responded dryly. "You took away my agency, my choices, and my power. I take pride in myself, Silas, and you belittled me with your actions."

"It was all I could think to do," Silas said, rueful now.

"You never thought to trust me to protect myself?" Rielle demanded, her shoulders back, her hands balling into fists. "I was born to lead this kingdom, Silas. I have an obligation to protect myself and my people. You should have trusted me to make the right choices. I don't need to be protected. I need to be trusted."

"I'm sorry," Silas apologized again, and it was strange to see the man who had been so intimidating earlier shrink in on himself.

"Lift the curse," Rielle ordered, her gaze lowering. "We will speak more later, after I see my father is alive and well."

Silas walked over to the orb, bowing his head and placing his hand over it. A ripple seemed to move through the air, then another, and the muscles in Silas's back flexed as the green light grew brighter and brighter before shattering. I covered my face, but there was no physical impact.

When I opened my eyes again, the orb was gone, and I could feel a subtle shift in the air. It no longer felt oppressive, no longer weighed down on me. Rielle strode toward the window in the room, and I followed behind her, gazing out at the once mist-covered town. Now, it dissipated, revealing a beautiful countryside and a village. The gruesome monsters were gone, and confused and scared humans appeared in their place.

Rielle turned to me, a fierce determination on her face. "I have to go to my people now, Nell. They're waiting for me. They need me more than ever." She took my hands in hers, squeezing. "Thank you."

"I didn't do anything," I said.

"Your actions here saved my kingdom," she told me. "Do not dismiss it so easily."

"What will you do about Silas? Do you still want to kill him?"

Rielle chewed on her bottom lip. "No, I don't want to kill him. I know Xander manipulated him, but he still did terrible things. I don't know how to proceed from here."

"What does your heart say to do?"

"My heart remembers when he first came to my castle. A dragon a quarter of the size he is now. We were only children then. Dragon shifters are a dying breed, and poachers hunt them for their bounty. Silas was scared and alone, and my father and I welcomed him with open arms. He kept me safe all these years, and I fell in love with him. But then he turned around and cursed the kingdom that took him in. I don't know what to think or do. I was so angry before, but now..."

As she held my hands, shadows formed from under the windowsill, created by the sunlight now filtering in as the mist outside continued to fade. I smiled at Rielle, letting her go. "You don't have to decide right away. You'll make the right choice. I know it. I can only wish to have as much confidence in myself as you do in yourself."

"Do you want to know the secret to it?" she asked.

"What's that?"

"Believe in yourself," she said. "Believe in the person you

want to be, and you will get there. Believe in the strength you have, and it will grow. Believe in your heart, and it will guide you in the right direction." She paused, looking down at her hands before curling them into fists. "And if there are times when you don't believe in yourself, that's okay, too. We are all works in progress."

I took in her words, letting them wash over me and settle. *Believe in myself. Follow my heart.*

"Anyway, thank you, Nell," she said, smiling back at me. "I think I would have regretted killing Silas despite feeling like it was the only way to save my kingdom. I'm glad it didn't come to that. Your words guided me in the right direction."

"Go to your people," I said. "They're waiting for you. I have to go, too—someone's also waiting for me. I'll keep your advice in mind."

"Return home safely," Rielle responded, leaning forward to kiss my cheek.

The skin on my chest prickled, and the shadows grew taller, opening a portal for me. A glance down at the pendant proved my theory true—both Rielle and Silas counted toward completing my labyrinth. The gemstone was now over three-quarters of the way to becoming whole again.

I held back before leaving, turning to Silas, who looked exhausted and worn. "Silas, curses can always be broken, right?"

"Yes," he answered, "but the magic that breaks it must be stronger than the curse."

My heart sank, and the shadows curled around my wrist, tugging me toward the portal. "There's really no other way to break a curse?"

He gave me a grim look. "The only other way is the death of the one who cast it."

The shadows converged before I could say anything else.

20

Lost in pitch blackness the moment I returned to Enver's castle, I barely had time to process my surroundings before shadowy hands seized me. I shrieked as they knocked me off my feet, holding onto me so tightly it was painful. "Get off me!" I cried as they dragged me through the dark. "Stop it!"

I tried to grab at the shadows, but more hands circled my wrists and forearms, forcing me still. My pulse raced in alarm, but I gave up fighting, letting the shadows take me wherever they were leading me. The familiar nausea from the shadow portals rushed through me, and a moment later, cold air met my exposed skin. I blinked, trying to get my eyes to adjust to the moonlight that nearly blinded me, such a sharp contrast to the dark nothingness.

The shadows still didn't release me, adjusting my position and making me kneel on the ground of what appeared to be the top of the clock tower. Each tick of its hand shook the stone under my knees. They twisted my hands behind my back, looping around my wrists to bind me. The wind whipped my hair around, a howling echoing around me as it swept through the stone pillars and columns of the castle.

I went still as my gaze fell upon a figure standing on the battlement of the tower.

Enver.

He watched me silently, his face cloaked by shadow, his posture tense and coiled, like a predator ready to strike. Physical shadows like the ones keeping me captive curled behind him like a dark aura, twisting and swirling. His silk top billowed around him, the strap at his waist now undone, leaving his chest bare. His pale scars glowed under the moon, and the shadows at his back looked almost like wings. He shifted, and the moonlight revealed the darkness of his expression. The fury that burned in his eyes. The hard set of his jaw.

My heart skipped a beat. Something was wrong.

He no longer resembled the statues of gods I once thought he did. No, he was something different—something darker, more dangerous. Terrifying, but devastatingly beautiful at the same time. I didn't know whether I wanted to run away or move closer.

"There you are," he said.

"Enver, let me go," I said, feeling too vulnerable with my hands bound when he was acting so off.

"No."

My eyes widened at the sharp edge of his tone. "What?"

"You heard me. Do not make me repeat myself," he said, his voice cold, his words clipped.

My skin prickled with unease. "What's wrong?"

He stepped off the battlement, his footsteps soundless as he crossed the roof to me. "I grow weary of this, my little lover."

"This?"

His hand came to my jaw, roughly gripping it, forcing my gaze up to meet his. "This chaos you cause within me. I have had enough. This will end. Now."

I tried to pull my face away, but his grip only tightened. "Enver—"

"I have tried to play fair with you and allow you to try for your freedom, but I am tired of it all. Tired of the way you tear me apart with every layer of the labyrinth you complete. Tired of how I am driven mad by every moment I must wait for you to come back to me, plagued by the thought you may never return at all. I did not ask for you to come here and bring out these wretched emotions within me, yet here you are, turning my sequestered world upside down, making me want things I cannot have and feel things I do not wish to feel."

My throat felt tight as I watched his jaw work. I'd never seen him like this before. I didn't understand what could have changed from the time I'd left for my challenge, and now. "Enver, what—"

He cut me off with a squeeze of his fingers. "You are mine. I will not let you leave my side again. I will not let you ruin me further. And if I have to force you to stay here with me, then so be it."

Fear trickled into my blood at the threat in his words. "No, you can't keep me here," I whispered.

"I can, and I will," he said icily. "You cannot escape me. You will remain here at my side."

"Why are you doing this?"

"It is time you realize I am everything you claim I am. Heartless. Cruel." His grip on my jaw tightened. "Yours. Forever."

The dark promise in his words made my breath catch. "Enver..."

His thumb grazed my bottom lip. "And you are mine, even if you despise me for it."

"No," I started, my voice dying as his eyes narrowed threateningly.

"Yes," he responded, releasing me, and sweeping his arm out.

The shadows holding me pulled me down so I was flat on my back against the cold stone. They curled around my bare legs and slid up to my thighs, smothering me in darkness as they engulfed my body. "Enver, wait!" I cried, trying to break free, panic rising in me as the shadows continued to rise higher. "Stop it! What's wrong? You can't do this! I need to finish the labyrinth!"

He gazed down at me, cold and unforgiving, and his words carried a deadly clarity when he spoke. "You have already lost."

I lost?

Tendrils wrapped around my throat and over my mouth, leaving me unable to speak. They covered me completely, sinking me back into the darkness. Tears pricked at my eyes as a suffocating feeling came over me, the shadows pressing in on me from all sides. I couldn't breathe. My mind raced, wetness coating my cheeks. Was I about to die? Could I drown in his shadows? My lungs burned as I fought to take in air, and I fully believed I could. If Enver could tear someone's heart out, who was to stop him from suffocating me?

Just when I thought I would pass out, the darkness receded, and I choked in my rush to take in a breath. My hands shot to my throat, finding it freed as the shadows slid off me. I was still on my back, but inside now, looking up at a vaulted ceiling with intricate plasterwork.

Enver entered my line of sight, offering me his hand.

I scrambled back, sliding across the smooth onyx stone of the floor. A second later, shadows wrapped around me again, forcing me back to my feet. "No, let me go," I said, attempting to wrench myself free of them.

Not expecting the shadows to actually let me go, I used too much strength, nearly throwing myself off my feet again as they freed me. I fell into Enver, and he steadied me with a firm grip before bringing his thumb up to my cheek, gathering the moisture that lingered there with his thumb. "Do not cry, my little lover. You must have known it would end like this—with you bound to me forever. Now you have nothing to worry about. I will take care of you."

I stilled under his touch. "What do you mean I lost? Did I run out of time?"

A moment passed before he answered. "You did not run out of time. Not yet."

"Then why did you say I lost?"

"Because I will not allow you to face the labyrinth anymore. I will not allow you to continue to torment me. It is over. Accept that you have lost, and I will forgive you for the chaos you have wreaked upon my existence."

My eyes widened in disbelief. "What? No! You can't do that. You can't decide that for me—"

"You seem to forget who holds the power here."

"Enver, what's going on?" I demanded, jerking out of his grip. "Why are you acting like this?"

He allowed my escape, watching me with an icy gaze. "I have already told you. I am tired. Do not fight me on this. You will only make it worse for yourself. I have lost everything once before. I will not lose it all again."

"No," I said, a surge of anxiety gripping me. "No. You can't keep me here like this. I'm finishing the labyrinth. I'm going home—"

"*No*," he snarled, and the shadows rose behind him again, his rage stirring them. "You will not leave me. You will *never* leave me. Do you understand? You are mine."

The possessive ferocity of his words caused me to tremble. Anger hardened his features as he glared at me, and I suddenly recognized the expression on his face—it was the same look of obsession that Silas wore around Rielle. The same desperation and desire. The same need and want that had led him to lock her away.

Now Enver wanted to do the same to me.

Except Silas's feelings had manifested over months, giving him time to adjust to the intensity of his emotions, to have some level of control over them.

Enver's emotions must have hit him in full force the moment Silas and Rielle completed their challenges, and the reaction was explosive and immediate. Obsession wasn't an emotion, though, so what awakened in him that drove him to such extremes? Anger? I'd seen it on his face, but did anger lead to obsession?

Either way, I had to tread carefully.

"I asked if you understood," Enver said, voice dangerously low.

I swallowed, my hands balling into fists, resisting the urge to fight back. "I—yes."

His shadows receded. "Good."

I glanced around the unfamiliar room we were in. There were no windows, making the room feel enclosed and isolated. The only light came from a sole chandelier hanging on the ceiling. My eyes followed an onyx-colored carpet adorned with black embroidery up to a raised dais where an imposing throne sat. Made of black marble, it shone under the light of the chandelier, its high back adorned with carvings of roses and vines. Black leather cushioned the seat, plush and luxurious.

My gut sank. Enver had brought me to the throne room. I had asked him how to get inside. I never asked him how to get out.

I was trapped.

"The throne forged by my shadows was a poor mockery of the one it sought to replicate," Enver spoke, his voice now a seductive murmur as he circled behind me and pressed his lips against my ear. "Perhaps you would like to sit upon the real one while I taste you as before?"

Goosebumps broke out across my skin. "No."

"No? Would you rather I sit upon it with you on my lap? Naked and writhing against me while I drive into you again and again?"

"No!" I repeated, twisting away from him, my stomach rolling. "Stop it. Don't talk to me like that."

"What is wrong, my little lover?" he asked, reaching out to encase my wrist in his grasp. "We have shared pleasure so many times before. Why deny us both the same now? When we can enjoy each other here for eternity?"

"Enver—"

"Quiet," he commanded, drawing me back to him. "Do not forget, I know what you desire. How you crave and yearn for my touch. How you convince yourself it could be enough for you time and time again."

I drew in a shaky breath, tensing.

"How *I* could be enough for you," he breathed, his fingers curling around my neck. "And I will prove to you I can. I will worship you. I will give you everything. *Be* everything you ask of me, so long as you belong to me, and me alone."

"No," I said. "I'm not yours."

His gaze darkened. "You *are* mine. You were mine from the very beginning, and you will be mine forever. Mine to touch, to hold, to taste, to fuck..."

I trembled, turning my face away from him, knowing what his next words would be. "Stop it. Don't say it."

His fingers moved up to dig into my jaw, forcing me to meet his gaze again. "To love."

Love. The word tore through me, leaving a hollow ache. "No," I whispered.

"Yes," he said. "You want this. You want me."

"No—"

"You want me to love you," he murmured. "So, let me love you. I will love you, Eleanora."

His words, spoken so softly, felt like a knife through my heart. It hurt because I did want that, no matter how much I told myself I didn't, that I couldn't. I wanted Enver to love me. Wanted to love him. I wanted his touch, his kisses. His smile. His laugh. His heart. I wanted him. All of him. So badly that it ached.

But I didn't want him like this.

My hands shook as I brought them up to Enver's face, cradling his jaw. He let go of my chin to cover my hands with his, lacing his fingers through mine, and leaning into my touch. The anger in his expression faded as he gazed at me. It made a lump form in my throat, but I swallowed it down. "Enver," I started, keeping my voice even and gentle. "This isn't love. This isn't what I want."

He went still, his shoulders stiffening.

I forced myself to press on. "You can't ever give me what I want, no matter how much I wish you could. You said yourself how not having all of me won't be enough for you, and it's the same for me. I can't have all of you, and that's not enough for me. It will never be enough. We both know this."

"I can be enough," he said, and the desperation in his hoarse voice made my soul ache. "Let me be enough."

"You can't," I said, shaking my head, feeling my throat tighten. "You can never be enough for me. So, stop this and let me go."

"No," he whispered, his hands clutching mine desperately. "Stay here with me. Do not leave me alone again. I cannot lose you."

My breath hitched as I watched his expression crumble, his mask of anger breaking and revealing the shaky vulnerability underneath. Everything suddenly made sense—the way he lost his temper, his obsessiveness, his need to possess me.

Enver was terrified.

I could see everything clearly now. His fear. The anger he used to mask it. The overbearing loneliness fueling them both. Every beautiful groove of his face and every strained line of his body revealed his emotions now. So different from the usual stoicism he displayed and so heartbreakingly raw.

But even as I recognized his new emotions, the fear quickly veered to anger again. He yanked his face free of my hold, his hand moving to wrap around my throat. "Why do you do this to me?" he demanded, his voice low and raspy. "Why do you force me to feel these emotions I cannot control? Why do you bring out these desires in me that I cannot satisfy? Why do you make me want things that cannot exist? I am exhausted by it all. I never asked for this—"

"I never asked for this either!" I cried, grabbing his wrist and digging my fingernails into his skin. "I never asked you to bring me here! I never asked to do your labyrinth! I never asked for you to do this to me!"

"You are ruining me, so why should I not make you suffer the same fate?" he responded sharply, his thumb pressing into the hollow of my throat.

I sucked in a shallow breath, his hold restricting my airflow. "Do you think I'm not suffering too?" I gasped out. "From the fact that I know deep down I want to stay with you despite knowing I will lose everything in the process? That I constantly go back and forth, torn between wanting you and wanting to be free? Between choosing you or choosing myself? That no matter what I choose I will never have all of you? That I will suffer either way? What I want is something I can't have, and it's tearing me apart. You are ruining me, too, Enver. We are ruining each other, and neither of us asked for it, so just..." I struggled to breathe, to speak. "Let. Me. *Go*!"

His grip slackened.

And then his entire body jerked violently. He didn't make a

sound, but his eyes widened, his gaze dropping to his chest as his hand slipped from my throat. I looked down, too, to the scar that marred his flawless skin. Sharp metal glinted under the lights. Metal that protruded from his pale skin. Sharp metal coated in crimson.

Blood.

His blood.

21

Dread turned my blood to ice as I dragged my gaze from the dagger in Enver's chest to his face. "Enver…?"

"Nell, *run*!" a voice cried out.

The blade moved further through Enver and he grunted, staggering forward. I let him fall into me, too stunned to react, feeling the tip of the blade against my sternum as I tried to hold him up. I looked over his shoulder and found Isla standing there, blood on her outstretched hand.

"I-Isla?" I could barely speak, barely register what was happening. "What—"

"Get out of here!" Isla cried, throwing her arm out. "Run! Now! I'll take care of him!"

Warmth seeped into my chest, and I looked down to see Enver's blood staining my dress. Enver wrapped his hands around my biceps, steadying himself. He rose to his full height, fury taking over his expression as he turned to look at Isla, his body straining to stay upright. "How did you get in here?" he demanded.

The sight of the blood covering Enver had me stumbling

back, horrified. There was so much of it. His shirt tore where the dagger had stabbed through it, aimed perfectly at where his heart would lie if he still had one.

"Nell helped me," Isla told Enver, glaring at him.

The muscles in Enver's back went rigid.

"No," I whispered, my heart beating frantically in my chest, my body shaking. "I mean, I did, but I didn't know—"

"Nell, we don't have much time," Isla said, throwing me an impatient look. "He won't stay weak forever. Get out of here!"

Enver tried to take a step toward Isla but collapsed to his knee, blood splattering on the ground below him. "What have you done?" he rasped.

I didn't know which one of us he was talking to. My hands shook as I reached for him. "No, Enver, no..."

"What are you waiting for, Nell? Go!" Isla snapped, the impatience in her tone growing.

I fell to my knees beside Enver, my hands hovering over his body, too scared to touch him. I didn't know how to help. "Isla, what are you doing?" I asked, fear making my voice crack.

"What am I doing? Saving us both!" she responded in disbelief. "Ending this madness. Giving him what he deserves. Don't protect him."

I shook my head, looking up at her, my eyes stinging. "No, I didn't know you were going to do this!"

She scowled at me. "Nell, get the hell out of here. I have waited too long for this moment to let you ruin it. And if you try to stop me, you can share his fate."

"Isla—"

"I'm not above striking you both down," she said coldly, the threat in her voice clear. "Either get out of here, or I will kill you, too."

Enver suddenly reached for the dagger's handle embedded in his back and ripped it out.

"Enver, don't," I choked out, knowing doing that would only exacerbate the bleeding.

More blood seeped out as he pushed himself back to his feet, his body shaking with effort. He stepped forward, putting himself between Isla and me. With a practiced flick of his wrist, he deftly flipped the dagger into a more secure grip in his hand. "Your mistake was not coming here, Isla."

She narrowed her eyes at him. "What?"

"I could have allowed it to pass—both your intrusion and your attempt at killing me. I know you harbor a hatred for me warranted by something I have done that I cannot remember. Your desire for revenge drives your actions here. I am aware of that."

Her mouth tightened, her nostrils flaring.

"Your mistake was daring to threaten her," Enver continued, his voice lowering, a dangerous undertone lacing it. "It is not my fate you have sealed here, but yours. I will not allow any harm to come to Eleanora, even if that means ending your life to ensure her safety."

My heart stuttered, and a chill ran through me. I had no doubt that Enver meant it, especially with him in this state. His emotions were already running wild, his control over them slipping further and further.

He would kill Isla.

Isla sneered at him. "Protecting isn't in your nature. Killing me, though? That makes more sense. You finally showed your true self—the fiend who took her away from me. You might not remember, but I do. Let me show Nell exactly how much of a monster you are. You play the victim now, but she'll soon learn what you've done. And she'll hate you as much as I do."

"You know so much about me," Enver said evenly, "yet you use a steel dagger to try to weaken me?"

A flicker of confusion crossed her features, but she quickly recovered, scowling. "Shut up. I'm going to take everything away from you like you took everything from me."

"Use iron next time, then," Enver suggested.

"A dagger to the heart is still a dagger to the heart," Isla responded, retrieving another dagger from behind her back.

"I do not have a heart," he said. "Or have you forgotten?"

"You don't," Isla said, "but *she* does."

The veins in Enver's arm strained as his grip on the dagger tightened. "I have warned you against threatening her. If you dare to touch her, it is your heart that will be torn out this time."

"You took someone precious away from me, so I'll take someone precious away from you. Then you'll understand my pain." Her expression darkened. "Although monsters don't feel, do they?"

She moved quicker than I expected. She flicked out her hand, and the blade flew toward me with deadly accuracy. I tried bringing up my hands to protect myself, my movements feeling too slow and clumsy, closing my eyes as I braced myself for it to strike me. Instead, though, Enver grunted.

My eyes snapped back open to see him rip the second dagger out of his shoulder, more of his blood spilling. "Enver, no—"

"Stay behind me," he ordered.

My mind was reeling, an intense panic setting in. I couldn't think clearly. Not with Enver injured in front of me. *Because* of me.

Isla didn't waste a moment before lunging toward us. Enver didn't move, staying in front of me, ready to protect me. His posture remained tense, but his expression stayed unnervingly collected. As if Isla was nothing but an inconvenience to him.

Once Isla was less than a foot away, his shadows shot out from the ground, crashing into her with enough force to send her flying backward. She landed hard, her body skidding across the floor, hands dragging along the floor to stop her momentum. As she came to a stop, she easily leaped back to her feet, glaring at Enver.

"So, you are going to rely on your shadows. And to think I thought you would fight me fairly for a second there."

"There is nothing fair about me," Enver answered her.

"Then let me even the playing field."

She plucked out another dagger, bringing her arm back. This time, I was more prepared. I forced myself to my feet, ready to dodge if it came to it, but instead of launching the blade at me, she launched it up toward the ceiling.

I followed its trajectory, noticing that this dagger looked strange, a faint orange tinging the metal. Almost like it was glowing. I watched as it soared straight into the chandelier chain, and as it hit, severing its chain entirely, I realized what she was doing. I reached out for Enver in a blind panic, my fingers digging into his injured shoulder as I yanked him backward, making him fall to the ground with me just as the chandelier collapsed. Enver rolled over me, protecting me as it crashed into the floor.

Everything went dark, and the deafening sound of shattering glass and twisting metal caused my ears to ring, but otherwise, I was uninjured. "Enver?" I whispered into the darkness, feeling his weight pinning me down but being unable to make out any of his features.

Isla's voice rang across the room. "You can't use shadows without light."

Enver moved quickly, dragging me to my feet with him. "Do not leave my side," he ordered quietly, his fingers wrapping around mine, pulling me into his chest. "Do not speak."

I stumbled a bit, disoriented and unsteady. My heart beat so loudly I feared Isla would hear it.

Footsteps approached from our side, glass crunching as Isla moved over the broken chandelier. Enver didn't move, listening.

Something whizzed by my ear, causing my hair to shift, and then Enver's grip on me tightened, a quick breath escaping his lips. Dread coursed through me as I reached my free hand up, touching his shoulder and finding a new dagger lodged there.

Enver shifted, one of his hands going to my neck, wet with his blood, pressing my face against his chest, the other splaying out on my back. I realized he was trying to cover as much of me as he could with his body. He planned on taking every blade Isla threw at us.

"I know where you are," Isla said, her voice appearing right beside us.

Enver twisted us around, and this time, I heard the blade sinking into him. A horribly, fleshy *thunk*. He didn't react. Instead, he scooped me up, my knees under one arm, his other supporting my back as I wrapped my arms around his neck. He took off into the pitch-black, holding me close to him, leaving only silence in his wake.

He wouldn't try to defend himself if it meant leaving me defenseless.

A sharp sting exploded in my upper arm, and I couldn't stop myself from crying out in pain. Enver's breath came out in an exhale against my neck. "I'm okay," I whispered quickly.

The air whistled.

He jolted, a groan escaping him as he faltered, barely setting me on my feet before his arms fell away from me.

I steadied myself, hearing his footsteps as he moved away from me, short and uneven. "Enver—"

"Stay silent and run," he ordered roughly.

"I can't leave you," I said, reaching for him.

His breathing sounded heavy as his hand found mine in the dark, holding it tightly before letting go again. "You can. I will not stop you this time. Leave me."

Fingers tangled in my hair and yanked my head back before I could respond. I fell backward, into Isla, crying out as she threw me to the ground onto the shattered glass. I gasped as Isla's foot slammed into my chest, a moan of pain escaping me.

"Nell!"

The way my name seemed to rip from Enver's throat, frantic and hoarse, was unlike anything I'd ever heard from him before. The visceral panic and fear in it hurt more than the glass that cut into my exposed skin.

I suddenly didn't care about my safety. Something burned hot in my chest at his fear. Something dark and fierce. An instinct I didn't recognize. I had to protect him. My hands fumbled on the ground, and I ignored the sharp bite of glass, my fingers finding a piece of twisted, broken metal and gripping it. I swung it blindly in Isla's direction with as much force as I could muster.

It must have surprised her because her foot disappeared off me. I scrambled to my feet, hearing either Enver or Isla approaching me again. I didn't decide to wait and find out, barreling further into the inky darkness. "I'm over here!" I shouted, hoping Isla would follow me.

"Nell, no!" Enver called after me, before I heard him crumple to the ground again.

"That one had iron," Isla taunted.

"Nell," Enver repeated, the sound of glass scraping against the stone floor reaching my ears.

As if he were trying to crawl after me, dragging himself over the jagged shards.

I ignored Enver's plea, slamming my feet hard with every step I took so Isla would follow me, and I could lead her as far away from Enver as possible. I didn't have a plan—I just knew I needed to separate them. Protect him.

"You're brave." Isla's voice appeared behind me again, and suddenly, I was falling to the floor again, my foot tripping over something I couldn't see. "But you waste your bravery on a monster like him."

I caught myself before my face hit the floor. "He's not a monster!" I snapped, rolling onto my back and swinging the metal out again.

This time, though, Isla was more prepared. She caught it, attempting to wrangle it from my grasp. "You don't understand, Nell. I tried to warn you. He will kill you."

"You're trying to kill me right now!"

"Because you're interfering!"

"Enver would never hurt me like this—"

"You're wrong!" she screamed, and it startled me enough that my grip slipped on the metal. She ripped it out of my hands, and it clattered somewhere far off to our side. "Do you know what happened to his first love? He killed her! He dragged her to this castle and murdered her all because she turned him down! He would have done the same to you. But at least when I kill you, it won't feel like as much of a betrayal."

Her words hit me hard. The brutality of her accusation. The confirmation of something I already knew deep down. Enver had loved someone before. Yet Isla said she turned him down? And he'd killed her for it?

That couldn't be true. It couldn't. She had to be misunderstanding something.

"Isla, there has to be something else," I said, attempting to climb to my feet.

Her foot connected with my torso again, forcing the breath out of me. "Stay down."

My mind raced as pain blossomed in my chest. Isla had come to the labyrinth for revenge. She truly believed what she was saying. Yet, so did all the other participants. They all thought they were doing the right thing, but they weren't. Isla had to be the same. I needed to get her to understand that before she lost herself to the labyrinth.

Isla's fingers found my neck, and then the sharp edge of a

blade pressed against me. “Wait,” I said, finding her wrists in the dark and clinging to them. “Isla, you can’t do this—”

“This will be quick,” she promised. “I only regret that he won’t be able to watch you die. But don’t worry. I’ll kill him next, and maybe you can reunite in the afterlife.”

The tip of her dagger dug into my skin, and I struggled to pry it away, failing to do so. “Isla, please listen to me! I’ll help you find out the truth. I promise. I want to help you—”

“Shut up,” she hissed, the blade sinking deeper, and something wet and hot dripped down my throat.

My blood. I tried to twist away again. She was going to kill me. She was actually going to kill me, and I couldn’t stop her. “Isla, if you do this, you will lose the labyrinth. You’ll lose yourself—”

“I don’t care,” she said, her voice shaking, the dagger digging further into me. “I don’t care! I have waited a century for my revenge. You will not stop me. I’m doing this for her. It won’t bring her back, but at least I can give her justice and peace.”

“Is that what she’d want—”

“Don’t pretend you know anything about her, Nell! Don’t you pretend you know anything about *him*. He killed her and felt no remorse. He never has. He never will. He needs to pay!”

“Isla,” I said, my thoughts a panicked mess. I didn’t know what to say to her. How to stop her. “We can figure something out. You don’t have to do this. You don’t have to lose yourself. Let me help you!”

“I don’t want to be helped,” she said, her voice trembling, but the pressure on my neck lessened slightly. “I want to get my revenge and leave this pain behind. This is the only way.”

“It’s not. I can help you. I’ve helped everyone else. People are completing their challenges. You can, too!”

Her voice cut through the dark, fierce again. “I never said I wanted to complete it. I only came here to get my revenge.”

"You can't kill him!" I cried as a last resort. "The labyrinth won't let him die!"

"Then I will make him suffer until the end of time instead," she promised.

My eyes focused on nothing in the darkness as I tried and failed to search for Enver. I would die, and he would blame himself. He would lose me in the worst way and be trapped here with his regret, guilt, and despair. He would be alone again.

I couldn't let that happen. I wouldn't let him suffer anymore.

"Help me," I choked out into the darkness. "Please."

"He's not coming," Isla said, and she pulled the dagger back, holding my neck still. "I'm sorry, Nell, but goodbye."

The air rustled behind me. I used all the strength I had to shove Isla away from me, using her momentary surprise to twist around. I reached my hand up until I touched a door handle. My fingers curled around it, yanking the door open.

Light flooded over me and Isla.

And then shadows erupted around us.

They wrapped around my shoulders, dragging me backward as they slammed into Isla, forcing her to release me as they crashed her down onto the floor. They curled around me, enveloping me, cradling me. Protecting me. Isla fought against the tendrils that coiled around her, making her let go of her dagger as they dug into her skin. One tendril circled her neck before abruptly constricting, her breath coming out in a strangled gasp.

Another shadow fell over us, this one solid and imposing, and I turned my head up to see Enver towering over us, shadows spilling from his body. Icy rage twisted his features, and the sclerae of his eyes were streaked with black as if his shadows were bleeding into them. Blood drenched his pale skin, and his body shook with fury.

"I warned you what would happen if you touched her," he said, low and lethal. "Now, there is nothing that can save you from me."

He stepped over her body, crouching beside her, his hand joining the shadows around her neck. The minute he squeezed, she stopped struggling, only staring up at him, her expression contorted with fear. Gone was the anger, the hatred, leaving only terror as her skin turned blueish, the shadows preventing her from defending herself from him.

He was going to kill her.

"Enver, stop," I breathed, but he disregarded me, the shadows around him thickening as his grip tightened.

Isla's body twitched, her eyes falling shut.

"Let me go," I whispered to the shadows sheltering me. "Please."

They retreated, and I threw myself at Enver, wrapping my arms around him in an embrace. He stiffened under my touch, and the shadows clinging to his form withdrew to allow me closer.

I buried my face in his neck. "Don't do this," I pleaded against his skin. "Don't kill her. Don't be the monster you think you are. You aren't, Enver. Let her go."

"She hurt you," he rasped.

"You saved me," I told him, pressing a kiss against his neck. "Please. Stop."

He shuddered under my touch, his hand loosening on Isla before he retracted it completely. The shadows lifted from her neck, and she drew in a ragged breath. I fell back from Enver, meeting his gaze as he turned toward me. The shadows in his eyes melted away, revealing their beautiful obsidian. He reached up, his thumb brushing against the wound on my throat. "I cannot bear to see the sight of you hurt. She must pay for what she has done to you."

"She is," I said. "Look."

Isla had gone still, her expression distant. "Ev, I..." A tear slipped down her cheek, her eyes meeting mine briefly before turning empty, glossing over. I trembled as I watched the labyrinth claim her.

She had failed. And now she'd become like all the others who failed—a servant of the labyrinth.

Enver watched her for a moment before attempting to climb to his feet. He staggered and then fell forward. I tried to stand and catch him in time, but he was too heavy, and we sank back to the ground beside Isla. "Enver," I started, feeling how hard his body shook as he tried to push himself off of me. "What's wrong?"

"I will be fine," he assured me in a tight voice. "I am just weakened momentarily."

"You're covered in blood!"

"I will heal," he said, gritting his teeth and pushing himself to his feet.

I shook my head as he offered his hand to me, too afraid I'd pull him down again. I stood, and Isla rose as well. My heart stuttered in fear, but all she did was look at us obediently.

"Gather the others and clean this mess," Enver ordered. "And be grateful this is all that will happen to you."

Isla bowed. "Yes, my lord."

I watched as Isla crossed the room, her movements robotic and unnatural. My heart ached. "Isla."

"She is no longer your concern, Nell," Enver said. "She chose her fate."

"I know, but she thought she was doing the right thing. She just wanted to protect someone she loves," I said, the words burning in my throat as Oliver appeared next to her to guide her out of the throne room. "I failed her."

"She made her own choice."

I half-expected to fail my labyrinth challenge, but the air

was still around us. What did it mean for me now that Isla had failed?

I gasped as the pendant suddenly flamed, looking down to find a new piece of the ruby forming, melding with the rest of the gemstone. It was nearly complete now. How? Hadn't Isla failed? Was I wrong to have thought I received a piece of the ruby every time I helped someone conquer their challenge? What did it represent, then?

Enver released a long breath once Isla disappeared, and I turned back to him. I let out a muffled cry as he suddenly gathered me into his arms, my face flattening against his chest. "Enough about Isla. Let me hold you for a moment."

"Wait, your wounds!" I said, attempting to pull away from him.

His hold was unyielding as he buried his face into my hair. "Stay," he breathed.

"I don't want to hurt you—"

"Even if you do, I will not complain. It is worth it to have you this close to me. Safe. Alive." He kissed the top of my head. "Let me have this moment. I need..."

I nodded, not needing him to finish his thought, and I relaxed into his embrace, my arms looping around his waist. I could feel the stickiness of his blood against my cheek, but I ignored it. I wanted to hold him. I wanted to be held by him. I didn't want to let go. He didn't seem to want to either because his arms tightened, pulling me even closer.

"I am sorry," he whispered.

"For what?"

"Many things. Letting my emotions get the best of me. Attempting to keep you here by force yet again. Speaking to you in a degrading way."

I curled my fingers into the silk of his shirt. "Enver, there are people who can't control emotions they've had their entire life. I won't blame you for losing your composure when a century's worth of them hit you all at once. I also reacted emotionally, anyway."

His arms loosened around me, but he didn't let me go. He leaned back to look at me, lips tilting down. "That is not an excuse. Do not forget what I have done to you. Do not forget, I am the one who trapped you here—the one who put you in this danger in the first place. The one who took away your freedom."

"But you are also the one who brought me to you," I told him, raising my hand to cup his face. His eyes closed as he nuzzled his cheek into my palm. "And I don't regret that. I would go through all this again just to have met you."

"Nell—"

"I was scared, too," I admitted quietly. "I was scared that you would die."

"If I died, you would be free," he murmured, eyes still closed, soaking in my touch.

"That's not a price I'm willing to pay for my freedom," I whispered. "I thought I feared being trapped here the most, but I was wrong. The thought of losing you is more terrifying. I can't lose you. You can trap me here, Enver. You can keep me—as your lover, as your prisoner, as your anything."

His eyes opened now, half-lidded and full of an emotion I couldn't place. He turned his head, his lips brushing against the inside of my wrist, right against my pulse point. "Do not make such promises, my little lover. You do not know what temptation lies within them. Especially now, when my need for you is overwhelming."

"Then have me," I said, my breath hitching as his head dipped down, his lips finding mine. "Take me. Keep me. I don't care if you ruin me anymore. Make me yours."

"No," he said as he pulled back. "Your emotions are heightened. You are not thinking clearly at the moment, and I will not take advantage of you again."

He released me, and I bit my lip as he stepped away. I knew he was right. Adrenaline still pumped through me, keeping me on edge. But I also knew the truth of my words. I would be his. Whether I remained in the labyrinth or left didn't matter anymore. I couldn't deny it any longer. I no longer feared the chance of failing the labyrinth. Maybe I hadn't feared it in a while. I only feared I wouldn't have the strength to leave when the time came.

"Come," Enver said, entwining his fingers with mine. "I need to tend to your wounds, and I do not enjoy the feeling of blood coating my skin."

22

From the void of a shadow, a door materialized, and Enver led me through it. "Thank you," I breathed into its darkness, and I swore it held me for a moment, responding to my gratitude before spilling us into Enver's washroom.

I helped Enver strip out of his shirt, carefully peeling away the bloodied fabric, my heart skipping a beat at the wounds on his chest and shoulders. The bleeding had already stopped, but the damage was still evident, his skin swollen and red around the puncture wounds left by the daggers. Somehow, they had all already closed, the edges knit together, crusted with dried blood.

He caught me staring, tilting my chin up. "Do not worry," he told me. "I cannot die. The curse of the labyrinth can benefit me from time to time. It has already begun healing me."

"I thought you were weakened."

"I suppose your touch has mended me."

I frowned as he smirked. "Enver."

He sighed. "I cannot explain it, even if you ask. A wound caused by iron does not heal as swiftly. It weakens me momentarily. Even the labyrinth struggles to heal the effects of it at the same rate as wounds caused by other means. I do not have an explanation for why. It is something else my memory fails me on."

I didn't respond, and he retrieved a small cloth and a wooden bowl before returning to the tub. He turned on the faucet, adjusting the temperature until satisfied, and then took a seat on the edge of the tub, pulling me to stand between his thighs as he filled the bowl with water.

"Fortunately, the cut does not appear too deep," he said as he mixed some kind of herb into the water and cleaned the area where Isla had pressed her dagger into my throat.

I bit the inside of my cheek as my wounds stung from the mixture. Isla had more than one chance to kill me when she had me pinned, and she hadn't. I didn't know what to make of that. Would she really have if it came down to it? Or...

Enver's touch was gentle as he took my hands in them, picking the smallest shards of glass out of my palms with tweezers before disinfecting the cuts. When he finished, he didn't release me immediately. His gaze remained focused on my palms, and then he brought them up to his lips, kissing them softly before letting go.

Then he dumped the old water and found a new cloth for me to use on him.

I filled the bowl with water again before emptying it over his back. Red ran in streams down his skin before cascading to the tub floor and washing down the drain. I poured more water over his chest, trying to wash away as much blood as possible before filling it once more and adding the antiseptic herbs. He tensed as I dampened the cloth before gently cleaning the drying blood from his back and shoulders, rinsing every few moments until his body was clear of the crimson stains.

"Are you okay?" I asked as I moved the cloth to his chest,

watching as he adjusted his position so the water would fall into the tub, not the floor.

He groaned, his eyes squeezing shut as I brushed the cloth over his pecs, across the fresh wound there. "Wait."

I stopped immediately. "What's wrong?"

"I am still sore."

I pulled back and examined the stark reminders of the daggers once embedded in his torso. "Then—"

He caught my hand and brought it back to his chest. "Not there. I believe I know how you could make me feel better, though."

"Where does it hurt?" I asked, worried now. "How can I help?"

He cracked an eye open, tapping his lips. "Here. A kiss from your lovely lips should soothe the ache."

I scowled at him, pushing the cloth harder against his chest. This time, his groan was real. "You must be feeling better if you can joke around."

"Perhaps not as much as I thought," he said, his fingers enclosing around my wrist. "I am in great pain. So much so that I fear I could die without your kiss. I might even expire on the spot, full of regret for not having tasted you one last time before I fade from this world—"

"Enver," I cut him off, my voice tight, my hand shaking against his scars. But the image was already in my head. His lifeless body, bleeding out on the throne room floor. All alone. "Please. Don't joke about you dying when I thought you just were. I..."

Enver rose from the edge of the tub, all traces of humor gone from his face. My throat felt thick as he cradled my cheeks in his warm hands. "Forgive me, Nell. I did not intend to upset you. I am fine, I promise. I will not be going anywhere."

"I am, though," I said, taking an unsteady breath.

And I realized why I imagined Enver dying alone just now.

Because I was leaving.

I would no longer be here with him. If any danger came to him again, he would face it alone. He would face everything alone the minute I escaped his labyrinth.

"If what happened with Isla counted as a layer of the labyrinth, then I only have one left," I told him, trembling. "I'll be gone soon. You won't have me, and I won't have you. If you get hurt again, how can I heal you?"

His thumb traced circles on my cheek. "I was always aware of the threat Isla posed. It was only a matter of waiting until she struck. It will never happen again. You need not worry about me."

My hands shot to his wrists, and I clung to him. "How can I not? What will happen when I leave? When you're all alone again? What if something happens to you?"

"That is not something for you to worry about. Do not concern yourself with me after you leave."

"If," I said, my pulse stuttering.

"When," he said, firmly.

"Enver—"

"Nell," he interjected, his tone harsh, making me fall silent. His demeanor softened a moment later, his voice turning gentle. "You are not gone yet. For now, you are still here. With me. We can still enjoy our time together. Put to rest the thoughts of leaving and what could happen to me when you do. Only think of us. Of now."

I clenched my jaw, trying to calm myself. His lips brushed across my forehead. My nose. My lips. Each kiss unraveled me a bit more, the tension slowly leaving my body, replaced by a welcome warmth. "I'm sorry," I said after he finished kissing me.

"Do not apologize, my little lover. I..." he trailed off, his fingers digging into my cheeks briefly before he let go. "I believe you are forgetting you could still fail my labyrinth and thus be forced to remain here with me. Do not let overconfidence become your undoing."

I waited for his words to instill fear in me like they had done so many times before, but as I thought, it never came. Overconfidence wouldn't be my undoing. He would.

I finished cleaning the blood off Enver, and then he double-checked the cut on my neck, treating it with so much tenderness and care it made my heart squeeze in my chest. He then filled the bath and dragged me close as we both settled into the hot water. He took his time washing my hair, and when I glanced over my shoulder back at him, I caught the content smile on his face. Like there was nothing else in the world he would rather be doing.

I forced myself to look away from him. The way he took care of me and the way he treated me continued to open my eyes, making me realize how poorly I'd allowed myself to be treated in the past. He and everyone else I'd met during his labyrinth showed me how things should be. How I now wanted them to be.

I knew that when I returned home, I would not be the person I'd been when I left. I would be a woman who no longer accepted anything less than what she deserved. And I would learn how to love and be loved. Properly this time.

But for now, I was with Enver. I would enjoy the time we had left together and face my last challenge with everything I had.

I would.

My stomach knotted.

I would, wouldn't I?

Enver would always remain in my memories. I would at least have him there. I would cling to that thought, but I still wanted to know more about him. I wanted more to remember him by.

After Enver finished washing me, I turned to him, straddling his lap and dispensing some of the floral-scented soap into my hands. He made a satisfied sound as I massaged his neck and his eyes closed. "Enver?"

"Yes?"

"Do you remember when your birthday is?"

He cracked an eye open. "My birthday?"

My hands moved to his shoulders, working the muscles there. "You said there are some things you remember. Is your birthday one of them?"

"No," he said, relaxing further into my touch.

"I'm sorry."

"Do not be. It is not your fault. But what about you, my little lover? When is your day of birth?"

"It's actually really soon," I answered. "October 16th."

"I see. We are under the Ember Moon now. Your day of birth falls right before the Frost Moon rises."

Ember Moon? His answer threw me for a moment until I realized the calendar system here was probably much different from the one in my world. "You can remember what your months are called?"

Enver leaned toward me, his face pressing into my neck as my hands slipped around him to wash his upper back. "Not exactly. I have come across that information over the years of searching for participants for my labyrinth. I pick up on things from time to time."

"Is that why you speak so formally?"

"Do I?" he responded, his voice muffled by my skin.

I couldn't help but laugh. "Yes. Very much so."

Enver pulled back at the sound of my laughter, surprise flickering in his eyes before he cupped my cheek, thumb caressing my bottom lip. "I thought nothing could rival your smile, but your laughter captivates me just as deeply."

I pressed a kiss against his thumb. "There you go, saying pretty words again."

"They are not merely pretty words. They are the truth."

"Have you ever heard of contractions? Slang?"

Enver dropped his hand, water splashing up on us as it broke the surface. "I have spent most of my years here reading through the books stored in my library. It is possible that is how I formed this habit of speaking formally, as you put it. Does it bother you?"

"No," I told him. "You just sound like me when I was in college trying to hit the word count needed for an essay. It's actually pretty cute."

"Cute?" Enver repeated, tilting his head, his nose scrunching up. "Is that supposed to be a compliment?"

"Yes. Is there something else you prefer?"

"Handsome?" he offered. "Charming? Irresistible? The most desirable lover you have ever laid eyes on?"

"You're so full of yourself," I teased.

"And soon you could be full of me," he murmured, his fingers sliding to my inner thighs.

I splashed water on him, blushing. "Stop it."

He chuckled, his hands going to stop mine from spraying him with more water. "Very well."

"Let's move on. Do you have a favorite color?"

He straightened, the corners of his lips tugged up into a smile. "I can answer this one. I may not remember what my favorite color was originally, but now I am torn between two colors. White." He delicately lifted a strand of my hair before letting it slip through his fingers like silk. "Or perhaps blue." His thumb traced the curve of cheek, lingering just beneath my eye. "The vast sky, the shimmering stars... neither could ever contend with the radiance of your beauty."

My heart skipped a beat. "You're exaggerating."

"Let me add pink to that," he said, eyes trained on my blushing cheeks. "What is your favorite color?"

"Black," I responded immediately, causing his smile to change into a smirk.

"Perhaps you enjoy my shadows a little too much."

I playfully pushed against his chest. "Or maybe you enjoy using your shadows on me a little too much."

"Never enough. I have more plans for you and my shadows, my little lover."

A rush of excitement went through me. "You do?"

"Mm. But that will have to wait. I am enjoying this. Keep asking me questions," he encouraged, closing his arms around me again, chin on my shoulder once more. "I might not be able to answer, but the longer you speak, the longer I get to enjoy your voice."

I smiled. "Favorite food?"

"I am partial to peaches. And your—"

"Don't even."

He chuckled again, and I couldn't help but join in, too. I loved the sound of his laughter. The vibration in his chest. I loved seeing him relaxed and happy. It was something I wished I could experience every day.

I considered my next question, aiming for one he could answer without reminding him of his missing memories. "Favorite place in your castle?"

"Any place where you are."

"Enver," I chided, earning another lovely rumble of laughter.

"Very well. If it has to be inside the castle, then the observatory."

Where I had found him after completing Dio's labyrinth. "It was beautiful there." Even in the middle of a thunderstorm.

"I will bring you back there."

"So then, the garden is your favorite place outside the castle, right?"

He nodded. "Correct. It is also the only place outside the castle I can go, but that does not make it any less special."

"Do you have any questions for me?" I asked.

He hummed. "Do you have any pastimes?"

"Reading," I said. "That's pretty much it."

"Ah, something we have in common," he responded, eyes crinkling. "I also enjoy literature."

"I kind of doubt we read the same kind of things," I muttered, thinking of all the... *mature* books I preferred to read.

"We will have to share recommendations."

I briefly wondered if Enver would like reading about alien sex or vampire sex more. Did those kinds of books even exist in this world?

"Do you have a profession?" he asked, changing the topic.

"Yes," I said. "I do design work, but I hate it. It pays well, but I'm miserable doing it. The money is the only reason I stay."

"Is there something you would rather do?"

I hesitated. "I'm not sure. I used to have other interests but never pursued them. It was easier to stick to something safe and comfortable, even if it left me unhappy and unfulfilled."

Like my relationship with Julian.

"You deserve to be happy, my little lover," Enver said, the sincerity of his words seeping into me, filling my chest, and warming my heart.

I breathed out shakily, trying not to feel the weight of his statement. It would only lessen my resolve to leave further. "Do you think you have family somewhere, Enver?"

He shook his head, his hair tickling my skin. "I cannot remember. If I do, though, I wonder if they have lost their memories of me as I have lost my memories of them."

My hands slipped around him again, feeling the muscles of his back ripple under my fingertips as he adjusted his position to move away from the edge of the tub. Was someone waiting for Enver? Like Aki waited for Cas? Was someone looking for him desperately, as Luliana had searched for Dio? Would I be that person to Enver once I left here?

"Your family must be missing you," Enver said.

"No," I responded, my chest tight. "I don't think they are."

"How could someone not miss you?" he asked, pulling back to look me in the eye, his brow furrowed. "I crave your presence again within moments of you leaving me."

I looped my arms around his neck and slid closer to him, our chests pressing together, my chin tucking into his neck. "My dad left when I was sixteen, and my mom decided it was my fault. She kicked me out as soon as she legally could. But only me. Not my sister. Only me."

His fingers stroked my hair, his other hand on my lower back, long fingers splayed against my skin. "Your mother is a fool, then, to deprive her life of someone as precious as you. As is your father."

"I don't think my dad was happy, though," I said. "I remember I didn't blame him for leaving. I still don't. My mom used him for his money. She cheated on him multiple times, and he eventually got fed up and left. We never heard from him again. I… I just wish he hadn't left me behind."

I tensed as I said the words, not intending to reveal so much. I'd never told anyone that before. Any of this. But with Enver, everything seemed to slip out. I didn't feel embarrassed to tell him anything. And now that he had some of his emotions back, I knew he could understand me, and we could have conversations like this.

But Enver didn't speak. He simply held me, our bodies molded together. But it was enough. The comfort. The support. The safety. A lump rose in my throat. How could someone who emotionally couldn't care for me, who could never love me, make me feel more cherished than those I'd known for years?

I breathed in his scent, letting it wash over me. "My sister was the only constant in my life."

"Was?"

"The night you found me at the club is when I found out Julian was cheating on me with her, remember? That's why I was so desperate. They both betrayed me. I thought Veronica cared about me, but who does that to someone they claim to care about? And worse, my mom knew all about it. And is *okay* with it. I don't understand why they would do that to me. What I did to deserve it. They were using me..." I bit my lip to keep myself from saying more, afraid of admitting more things I didn't want to face.

Enver was silent for a moment. "If I could take away your pain, I would," he said quietly. "You deserve to be surrounded by those who cherish you, not those who take you for granted. You are not a thing to be used, Eleanora. You are a treasure—one worth fighting for. One worth keeping forever. One worth loving unconditionally. And I am sorry you have been hurt by those who are undeserving of you."

"No, it's okay," I said, putting space between us again so I could cradle his cheek in my hand. "I don't regret it happening. Not anymore. Everything that's happened to me has led me here. To the labyrinth. To you."

"Eleanora."

"I now realize I wasn't happy before," I said, my voice wavering. "I accepted what I thought I deserved. I was desperate to be wanted and needed. By family, by lovers. But I know better now. I won't let it happen to me again. Whether it was your intention or not, you've changed me by bringing me here. For the better."

His eyes met mine, soft and affectionate. "You have changed me as well. Forever, my little lover. Much as the scar upon my chest marks my flesh, you will be forever branded upon my soul."

"I won't forget you," I promised. "I won't forget what you've done for me—*to* me."

"I will ensure you do not," he responded, before his lips descended on mine.

It took us a long time to leave the tub between stolen kisses and touches. Once we did, Enver scooped me up into his arms, carrying me back to his room, where he retrieved fresh clothing for us.

Seeing a dress in his hand made my stomach churn, but I ignored it, allowing him to dress me. I couldn't stop the realization lingering in the back of my mind, though. That these dresses more than likely belonged to Enver's past lover. The one Isla claimed he killed.

I had to resist the urge to tear it off my body. I wouldn't ruin my remaining time with him by feeling jealous of a ghost.

"I am an archery master," Enver said abruptly.

I raised an eyebrow at him, watching as he pulled a pair of cotton pants over his hips, the fabric clinging to him in ways that made my pulse quicken. "What?"

He frowned, seemingly as surprised by his random statement as I was. "The thought suddenly came to me. I remembered I am an excellent marksman."

"What were you thinking about just now?"

"My frustration at how powerless I felt when Isla attacked you," he responded, his brow furrowing. "Something prevented me from fighting at my full potential. I am missing something, but I cannot quite figure out what."

"Like a bow and arrow?"

"No," he answered, "but perhaps my line of thought prompted that memory to resurface." He stretched out his left hand, looking down at it, his shadow ring shimmering on his finger. A ball of darkness materialized above his palm a second later, then morphed into an arrow. "This curse may have taken more from me than just my emotions and memories."

Anxiety settled in my chest. "What will you do about the curse when I'm gone?"

His silence answered my question, and the shadow arrow dissolved into the air.

"Won't you at least try to break it?" I pressed.

"I am willing to make an attempt right now," he said, walking up to me. "Care to assist me, my little lover?"

I nodded vigorously. "Of course—"

He kissed the words from my lips, his arm snaking around my waist to hold me to him. I parted my lips, welcoming the kiss, and deepening it. A groan rumbled in his throat when I sucked his bottom lip into my mouth, nipping at it lightly. He pulled away, forcing me to release his lip, his heated gaze meeting mine.

"Did it work?" I breathed.

"No. I suppose a kiss of true love cannot break a curse when the one cursed cannot love," he murmured. "A pity. I am up for attempting it again, though. And maybe once more after that. Or an infinite number of times more. Until you grow weary of me."

A teasing smile hinted at his lips, but I was too distracted by the reminder that he couldn't feel love to react. I couldn't help but think he'd brought it up on purpose—to remind me not to lose myself to him. It was a reminder I didn't want.

One I always needed.

"I wish to check on the mess in my throne room," he said, when I didn't respond. "Let us return."

Was this a test? He wanted to bring me back to an inescapable room. Did he expect me to say no? "Let's go, then," I said.

A flash in his eyes had me questioning my assumption of his intentions. He didn't seem disappointed in my response. Instead, he seemed pleased. I caught the faintest smirk on his face before he turned from me to form another shadow door.

We returned to the throne room through it, and I blinked, stunned by its appearance. Light flooded it again, revealing no evidence of what had transpired. A new chandelier hung from the ceiling, pristine and bright. The floor was clear of broken glass and debris—not one single blood stain or crack tarnishing the glossy marble.

"The servants are as efficient as always," Enver commented, wandering around the room, his hands clasped behind his back. "Good. I worried the mess would be a distraction for you."

I glanced at him. "For me?"

He turned toward me, a smirk now fully on his lips. He slowly approached me, steps measured and purposeful, and my stomach swooped in anticipation. "Yes. For you. Nothing could distract *me* from what I am about to do to you."

23

As I stumbled back a step, my heart began to pound, but not from fear. "What are you saying? You can't possibly mean..."

"Oh, but I do," he confirmed, continuing to stalk toward me.

My cheeks burned. "But, your wounds—"

"I have been patient thus far," he said dismissively, his hand shooting out to grab my wrist when he was close enough, halting my retreat. "Your kisses and voice and how your body settled onto mine in the tub have left me wanting more."

I pushed the fabric of his top away from his chest as he came to a stop, so close to me his breath fanned across the top of my head. The new scar left by Isla stood out amongst his other faded ones. "It still looks fresh. The labyrinth can't heal you that fast."

"It does not hurt."

"You need rest," I protested.

"What I need is you," he said, wrapping his arms around my waist. "Just you. Nothing else."

"Enver—"

He pressed his lips to the column of my throat, littering it with soft kisses. "I warned you, did I not?" he murmured.

"Warned me?" I repeated, distracted by the heat of his lips against my skin.

"That I would punish you if you entered my throne room. Do you remember?" My cheeks flushed again as I recalled that conversation and the things we'd done before it. He chuckled at my visible reaction, moving his lips to my jaw. "I see you do."

"Now isn't the time. You were just stabbed," I pointed out, but I also couldn't ignore the heat pooling in my stomach.

His hands slipped lower, squeezing my backside through the fabric of my dress. "A minor setback."

"*Minor*?"

His grip tightened, and he pulled me flush against him. "Yes, minor, especially compared to your transgressions against me."

"Wait, but you're the one who brought me here. Both times now," I said, indignant, even as my breath caught at the feeling of his growing arousal against my stomach.

"Oh, my darling little lover," he crooned, releasing my ass with one hand to grab my chin, tilting my head up to meet his gaze. "Whether you came here by choice or force, your actions are no less deserving of punishment."

My mouth went dry as his face came closer to mine, his hand moving to my neck. "That's not fair."

"I have never claimed to be fair, remember?" he responded, before pressing his lips to mine.

His other hand trailed from my ass around to my stomach and up to one of my breasts, where he pinched my nipple roughly through my dress. It caused me to gasp, and he slid his tongue into my mouth, deepening the kiss to taste me. I leaned into him, moaning as his fingers continued to play with my nipple.

Enver broke away from my lips, moving his head near my ear. "Will you allow me to punish you now?"

"I…" I struggled to get myself to tell him he needed to recover first, but it turned into a losing battle when he started sucking at the hollow spot under my ear, his mouth like a brand against my skin. I wanted him. I couldn't deny that.

And if this was our last chance to be together like this, I would let myself have it. Have him.

"Should I remind you of your other offenses?" he asked before moving to nip at my earlobe. "Why you deserve your punishment?"

My knees nearly buckled. "What other offenses?"

"You told Isla how to enter this room," he told me, fingers leaving my nipple to trail down my stomach before moving between my thighs, pressing the thin fabric of my dress against my center. "Hm. Already so wet for me. Perhaps you require no further convincing."

My hips jerked against his hand. I flushed again, knowing I couldn't argue that point. "Are there more?" I asked instead, breathless.

"Many."

"Tell me."

"You tried to leave me," he accused, slowly circling my clit with a featherlight touch, and although I could barely feel it through the barrier of my clothing, it was enough to have me squirming. "Should I tell you how many times? Or will you acknowledge your wrongdoings?"

I had to steady myself on him, my fingers curling around his shoulders, my legs shaking. "Six," I panted. "Six times."

He let out a low hum. "Then it would be a fair punishment for you to do something for me six times in return."

The implications of his words, combined with his teasing caress, made me moan. "Enver, I can't. That's not possible."

"Let me remind you, my little lover, that the one being

punished does not dictate her own punishment. It is solely up to me. Is that understood?"

My thighs clenched around his hand. His commanding tone did wicked things to me. "How will you punish me?" I asked, my heart racing in anticipation.

The hand on my neck slid into my hair, and he fisted it, tugging it back roughly. "I asked if you understood."

My back arched, pushing my body further against him, and I moaned again. His roughness did nothing to deter my arousal—in fact, it had the opposite effect, making me ache for him even more. His fist tightened, and my scalp stung. "Yes, I understand," I gasped.

"And is this what you want?" he asked. "To be punished by me? To be completely under my control?"

"Yes," I said again, sounding all too eager.

His mouth curved up as his gaze darkened, satisfaction mingling with desire, and the sight nearly brought me to my knees. He was beautiful. "Such a good little lover," he murmured. "So ready and willing for me."

His praise went straight between my legs. I took a shaky breath as his thumb continued to tease me lightly. "Do you want this, too?"

He pressed his erection against my stomach, now full and hard. "Does this answer your question?"

I swallowed. "Yes."

"I always want you," he told me, the heat of his arousal searing through the fabric separating our bodies. "You are the one thing I will no longer deny myself. I will give you what we both want. Let us begin your punishment."

"Please," I encouraged.

"You will tell me if you are uncomfortable or want me to stop," he instructed. "Although this is a punishment, my only desire is our shared pleasure. If you cannot speak, tap any part of my body thrice in succession. Understood?"

I was more turned on than ever before. It was like I was on fire—all because of his words. I didn't know what would happen when he finally touched me in the way I wanted him to. Right now, I could only nod, clinging to him, wanting to feel more of him against me, to have his bare skin against mine.

He pulled on my hair until I had to raise myself on my tiptoes to relieve the pressure, straining against him. "I did not hear that," he murmured.

"Understood," I repeated, trying to grind against his hand, getting desperate.

In response, he drew his fingers away and released my hair, letting me drop back to the flats of my feet. I bit my tongue to keep from complaining. "You will let me do anything I want to you," he mused. "So eager to please me, even though you are being punished. My desirous little lover. How you tempt me."

"Yes, you can do anything," I told him, lifting myself back onto my tiptoes to kiss him.

He took a step back, now breaking all contact with me. A smirk graced his lips as I shot him a frustrated look. "Since you are so desperate for me, I do not believe only one of me will be enough to satisfy you."

My brow wrinkled in confusion, but then a pair of arms wrapped around me from behind, and a chest pressed against my back. I froze, seeing Enver still in front of me. Yet the form behind me felt so familiar. So much like Enver. The same height, the same scent of vanilla and amber, and as I looked down, the same hands that slid up my thighs, bunching my dress up with them as they rose higher.

I swallowed, turning my head over my shoulder to see Enver's face, the same smirk playing on his lips. "What the—" I said, startled, attempting to break free from his grasp.

The Enver lookalike behind me held me securely, not letting me move away. "Do not run, my little lover," he said.

A tremble went through me. He even sounded the same as

Enver, but his breath was cold against my neck, not warm. "What...?" I tried again, but my words were failing me, so I turned back to Enver. The *real* Enver.

Amusement glittered in his eyes. "I seem to be adept at rendering you speechless. Is it not as I said? One of me is not enough to satisfy you. You will have two of me to worship you tonight. Or perhaps more if you are good."

"You can make doubles of yourself? Out of shadows?" I asked, my heart racing with both surprise and anticipation.

Enver closed the distance between us, embracing me again, sandwiching me in the middle of him and the shadow version of him. Two sets of hands touched me now—Enver's stroking my back as the shadow double continued to push my dress up. "Although what stands before you is a likeness of me created by my shadows, I assure you, you will find his resemblance to me entirely thorough," Enver told me, his voice husky. "From my taste to my touch."

I already found it hard to decipher the difference between their touches. "What are you going to do with him?"

"I am still deciding. Perhaps have him fuck you while I watch," Enver contemplated, his hand trailing up the line of my spine before he cupped the back of my neck firmly. "The thought has not left my mind since I last suggested it."

My dress pooled around my waist now, and the soft material of Enver's pants pressed against my bare skin as he and his shadow compressed me between them. His shadow slid his erection against my ass, and I sucked in a breath, shifting forward, only to press myself further against the real Enver. Enver groaned at the friction, his shadow echoing the noise.

"I can feel everything he can feel," Enver informed me, gripping my hips so he could grind himself against me. "He can feel everything I feel, too. When he is buried deep inside you, surrounded by your heat and wetness, I will feel it, too. I could sit on my throne and enjoy a show, watching him fuck you, while feeling it all as if I am the one inside you without ever needing to leave my seat."

The shadow double began to pull my dress up over my head. I raised my arms, my chest rising and falling rapidly as my arousal continued to build, my stiff nipples brushing against Enver's silk top. Now naked between them, I could hardly focus on anything but their bodies against mine.

Enver's lips ghosted the shell of my ear. "I can have you take me between those pretty lips of yours while he thrusts deep inside you, so we can feel your throat and walls clench around us at the same time. Or would you prefer it to be me filling you up while my shadow uses your mouth to pleasure himself? Perhaps we will take turns."

I could feel moisture drip down my inner thigh. I didn't think I'd ever been this wet in my life. This excited. Excited by the idea of sharing my body with two of Enver. The idea of being completely at their mercy. I briefly wondered if I should have been turned off by the idea of a shadow fucking me instead of absolutely dripping with excitement, but I pushed the thought away.

I wanted this.

The shadow double brought his fingers between my thighs, running a finger through my wetness, and I jerked at his cool touch. His thumb replaced Enver's previous spot on my clit, and I fell back against him, panting. Enver's words had already put me on edge. I didn't think it would take much for me to come. Especially not when Enver himself leaned down to claim my lips in a hungry kiss. My eyes closed, and I let him devour my mouth. Our tongues clashed together, the kiss messy and careless.

Their bodies held me securely between them as the shadow double worked me over as easily as the real one. He knew just how and where to touch me, how much pressure to use, what to do to make me writhe between them. I moaned into Enver's mouth, my thighs quaking. The shadow double's teeth bit into the junction of my neck and shoulder, and the unexpected sting of pain brought me even closer. It was too much.

"I'm going to come," I groaned into Enver's mouth.

Then suddenly, the double's touch disappeared. My eyes flew open, and Enver's smug expression greeted me as he broke our kiss. A pleased smirk shaped his lips as he pulled back. "There is your first."

I tried to find the shadow double's fingers again, rotating my hips. "What?"

"What did you think your punishment would be?" he inquired, gripping one of my hips with his hand to hold me still. "That I would give you six orgasms?"

I stared at him, my chest heaving. My arousal seemed to throb through my entire being, in need of release. "I—yes?"

"That would not be much of a punishment. Even if watching you come apart by my touch is always a sight I treasure. You are almost on the right track, though."

"Then what is my punishment?" I asked, my frustration mounting and the need for release intense.

His eyes flashed with desire as he skimmed his thumb across my bottom lip. "I will bring you close, to the very brink of release, only to deny you it right before you finish—six times. Six denied orgasms for your six attempts at leaving me. You will not come until I allow you to."

I shuddered at the prospect. Would I even be able to handle that? Already being denied once had me all twisted up. "You're—"

"Heartless?" he interjected, cocking an eyebrow, but his tone was teasing.

"Yes," I gritted out.

"A monster?" he taunted, throwing more of my words against me. "Allow me to show you the monster you desire. You said before that we ruin each other, but I will show you a new meaning of the word. I will ruin you in the most exquisite way. Until you are completely wrecked, unable to speak, to think of anything other than the need for release. Of the pleasure only I can give you."

I'm already there, I thought, but I still nodded. That seemed to be enough for him. His fingers curled into my hair again, and he brought my face back to his, crushing our lips together briefly before yanking my head back again and releasing me. Both he and his shadow stepped away from me, and goosebumps broke out across my skin at the rush of cool air.

"On your knees," Enver demanded.

I obeyed, sinking to my knees in front of him. The shadow double stepped around me, coming to stand right beside Enver. "Take us out," the shadow double ordered.

I glanced at Enver, searching for permission. Enver gave a curt nod in response. I reached for him, but the shadow double grabbed my wrist, guiding me to him first. My pulse raced as I undid the tie of his pants, letting them slip down his hips and onto the floor. The sight of him stole my breath momentarily. An exact replica of Enver. Same length, same thickness. His tip glistened, and I tentatively reached out to curl my fingers around him, surprised to find him cool to the touch instead of warm.

Enver inhaled sharply, and I looked up at him, slowly stroking the shadow double's length, witnessing the effect of my touch on Enver's face, though I was not touching him yet. Unable to wait, I used my other hand to free Enver's erection as well, not bothering to push down his pants. He was much warmer to the touch. I experimentally stroked them both at the same time.

Both of them grunted in response, twitching under my palms. Encouraged, I leaned forward, flicking my tongue against the tip of Enver's shaft before doing the same to his shadow. Enver groaned in response, his hand coming to my head. "I might have underestimated the effects of having you pleasure two of me at once."

In response to his comment, I moved my mouth over his shadow and took him into my mouth as far as I could. His shadow moaned, and Enver jerked in my hand. I pulled back, releasing his shadow from my mouth. "Again," Enver rasped. "Just like that, my little lover. Take more of me into that sweet mouth."

I swallowed his shadow down again, running my tongue over his velvety skin. I kept my other hand moving on Enver, making both of them groan again. It must have felt good—Enver rarely made this much noise. It urged me on as much as it turned me on. I attempted to take the shadow double all the way into my mouth, my body tensing as I fought against my gag reflex, my grip on Enver tightening as if to brace myself.

"Gods," Enver muttered, his eyes never leaving my form. "You look so perfect like this. On your knees with those delightful lips stretched around me. So beautiful. Swallow all of me, my sweet. I know you can do it." Enver gripped my hair, guiding my head forward. I let him, focusing on my breathing, doing my best to take him completely. "Show me how much you want this. How much you want me."

I managed, taking him all the way in, feeling him hit the back of my throat and move even further. The shadow double let out an approving noise, and when I reflexively swallowed, both he and Enver moaned again. I choked a bit, and Enver released my hair, letting me pull back to breathe for a second. I didn't stay away long, wanting to hear more of Enver's moans, wanting to watch such a normally composed man lose control.

I took Enver's hand, putting it back on my head, before switching my attention to him. I teased his tip with my tongue before taking him to the hilt. Enver gripped my hair again, immediately guiding me into his desired rhythm. I let him use my mouth, loving the way he closed his eyes and clenched his jaw, taking pleasure from me. When I brought my hand to the shadow double, using my saliva to ease the way as I stroked him, Enver moaned deeply, the sound reverberating through his entire body.

"Touch yourself," the shadow version of himself ordered.

I was too turned on to feel self-conscious. I did as he ordered, bringing my hand between my thighs, and beginning to rub myself while I continued to work my hand and mouth over both Enver and his shadow. Enver opened his eyes again, watching as I fingered myself, and his pace became faster and rougher. He slammed against the back of my throat, making me choke again, but I didn't care. It was exhilarating.

Without warning, Enver pulled me off him, guiding my head back to his shadow. I opened my mouth and took his shadow back in, letting Enver direct every move I made. I moaned, and the vibrations caused the shadow double's hips to jerk, moving further into my throat. I gagged, and Enver yanked my head back, saliva dripping down my chin as he brought me back to him again.

I focused on pleasuring myself, my orgasm building quickly. I tried not to show it, closing my eyes, and sucking hard on Enver's length, trying to keep him distracted so I could finish without him stopping me. My climax built and I tensed, my pace stuttering.

Then suddenly something cold encased my wrist, forcing my hand away from me. I whined around Enver, my eyes opening to see him and his shadow glaring down at me disapprovingly. "Did I say you could come yet?" he asked, pulling out of my mouth.

I tried to free my wrist from the inky shadow that now pinned it behind my back. "Please, just let me—"

The shadow double silenced me by burying himself in my mouth again. I whimpered, my eyes still on Enver.

He shook his head. "No begging. You know the terms. I am

not sure I should count that as the second denial, though, since you were disobedient."

I groaned, unable to form a proper sentence, and the shadow double shuddered.

Enver closed his eyes briefly before he steadied himself. "Perhaps I will offer you a deal. If you can finish him within the next minute, then I will count it as your second. I am curious what it will feel like when he spills down your throat."

I didn't hesitate to meet his challenge, immediately hollowing my cheeks and running my tongue down the underside of the shadow double's shaft. He hissed, taking my jaw in his hands, and fucking into my mouth. Enver's hands flexed at his sides, watching me with a heated gaze.

My tongue pressed against the shadow double's slit, and he grunted, sliding his length against my tongue until he reached down my throat, pushing himself all the way in again. I lost my control for a moment, my throat convulsing around him, and it was all it took to send him over the edge. He came with one last thrust and Enver let out a shuddered exhale as I struggled to swallow, surprised to find his release physical.

I panted as the shadow double pulled out of my mouth and then dragged me to my feet by my upper arms. I didn't have time to react before Enver grabbed my face, tilting my head up to meet his, his eyes flashing as he kissed me hard, his tongue sweeping into my mouth, tasting himself. I felt light-headed when he finally released me, but then he spun me, his shadow claiming my lips next. The shadow bit down on my lip and I groaned.

"Two down, four more to go," Enver whispered in my ear.

His shadow walked me backward, and I clung to him, trying to keep my balance as his tongue explored the inside of my mouth. The icy feel of him that contrasted with mine and Enver's warmth. When the back of my thighs hit something hard, I broke away, only to be forced down onto my ass.

Glancing around me, I realized he'd pushed me down onto the throne. Enver appeared at my side, and suddenly, my wrists were bound to the armrests by shadows before I could even attempt to pull them away.

"Shall I make the third quick and easy?" he asked as he knelt in front of me.

Oh, fuck.

"I'm not going to survive this," I told him, breathless already.

He cocked an eyebrow. "Would you like me to stop?"

I shook my head. "Absolutely not."

A slow, devious smile crossed his fast as he spread my thighs. "As I thought. You crave this. Being at my mercy. Being mine. Am I wrong?"

"No," I confirmed. "I love this."

"I will ruin you," he murmured, his breath caressing my inner thigh. "I will take you apart piece by piece until you are a quivering, needy mess, begging me to let you come. Until you know nothing but me. Then, when you are completely undone, completely shattered, I will give you everything you crave and more. I will put you back together with my touch, my tongue, and with the way I thrust deep inside you. And then I will do it all over again until there is no place you would rather be than here—with me. Underneath me. Surrounded by me. Surrendering to me, and only me."

"Ruin me, Enver," I breathed. "Please."

24

Like a man starved, Enver's tongue moved against me, and stars exploded across my vision. A cry tore from my throat, and my legs tried to close reflexively, but his grip on them kept them wide open for him. He didn't take it slow or easy, lapping up my arousal and letting out a satisfied groan. "I could live off your taste alone."

I moaned in response, my head falling back. "Enver—"

"My name on your lips is intoxicating," he murmured against my inner thigh, nuzzling his nose against me and breathing in deeply. "As is your scent and the sounds you make for me."

Another gasp left me as his lips and tongue returned to their previous positions. He traced his tongue along my entrance, but never higher, never where I wanted him the most. "Higher," I urged him.

He pulled back, looking up at me, his charcoal eyes gleaming. "You do not make demands here, my little lover."

"I—" A shadow fell over me, and the shadow double's lips were against mine a split second later, silencing me.

Enver dipped his head down again, his tongue finally

circling my clit, and I gasped into the shadow double's mouth. Neither gave me a break. The shadow double devoured my mouth as passionately as Enver did between my thighs. When the shadow double brought his hands down to my breasts, tweaking my nipples, I whimpered, unable to stop the noises spilling from me, only to be swallowed up by another kiss.

I trembled under their combined attention, pleasure shooting through my every nerve, building until the pressure was torturous. I rocked my hips toward Enver and felt him smile against me before he sucked on my clit. My lips parted in a silent moan, and the shadow double's tongue delved between them, mimicking the motions Enver made between my thighs against my tongue. I was so close. I concentrated on the feeling of their tongues against me, on the orgasm building inside me. My stomach clenched. Just a little more and—

Enver pulled away, rising to his feet, and I jerked against my restraints, my chest heaving as I broke away from the shadow double's lips. "No! Please, Enver, just let me come!" I begged.

"No," he replied. "If you beg again without my permission, I will stop."

"How do you even know I'm about to come?" I snapped at him.

Enver leaned down to kiss me, face wet with my arousal. "I have told you before. You fall silent right before you finish. I know the moment you stop making those endearing moans of yours that you are close."

"Then next time, I won't make any noise," I told him, glaring at him. "You won't be able to tell if I'm quiet the entire time."

He chuckled. "Is that a challenge?"

My glare faltered. "No—"

"Too late," he said, gesturing for the shadow double to take his spot in front of me. "I would rather have given you a break before you become overly sensitive, but I will not turn down a challenge."

"Wait," I said, but fell silent as Enver lifted me off the throne, the shadow restraints falling away.

He took my spot on the throne before settling me down between his thighs. I blushed a bit, feeling his erection against my back. I tried to shift away, but his hands went to my hips, holding me in place. His ankles hooked over mine, forcing my legs apart again as the shadow double lowered himself in front of us.

"I want to feel you writhe against me, crying out for a release that I will not grant," Enver murmured against my ear. "If you think silence will save you, you are wrong."

His chest was warm against my back, and I leaned into him, accepting my fate. The shadow double ran a finger through my arousal, and I lurched back against Enver.

"Yes, like that," Enver said, his lips brushing against my neck.

When the shadow double's finger dipped inside me, I moaned. Enver clamped a hand over my mouth, silencing me. "Quiet, my darling. No noise, remember?"

I groaned against his hand as the shadow double added a second finger into me. I tried to speak against Enver's palm, my voice too muffled to be intelligible.

"Would you like me to help you?" he asked. "Shall I give you something to do with that lovely mouth of yours?"

I nodded, and he released my mouth, only to trail two fingers against my lips. I parted them willingly, and his fingers sank in, pressing against my tongue. He hummed in approval when I sucked on them obediently. The shadow double continued to pump his fingers in and out of me and then added his tongue to the mix, flicking it over my clit. I held back any noise, but I couldn't stop the way my hips jerked.

Enver moved his free hand around my waist, pulling me

closer to him, his erection digging into my back. It turned me on even more to know he was just as aroused as I was. I sucked harder on his fingers, pretending it was another part of him, and he groaned in my ear. The sound went straight through me, and I clenched around the shadow double's fingers. He responded by sucking my clit into his mouth and increasing his pace, curling his fingers to hit the spot Enver could always so easily find. I squirmed against Enver, my body contracting as my orgasm built.

When a third finger entered me, I tensed, arching my back and gasping. It wasn't another of the shadow double's fingers, though—Enver had slid one of his own fingers inside me alongside his shadow's. My legs trembled as I fought off the pleasure and the sensation of being so stretched. I let my head fall back against Enver's chest, my eyes closing, accidentally biting Enver's fingers in an attempt to silence myself.

"Careful," he said. "You would not want me as much if I lost these."

I turned my head to look back at him, and he pulled his fingers out of my mouth, gazing down at me curiously.

"That's not true," I said, reaching my hand up to cup his jaw. "I want you. Even if you could never touch me again, I still want you. I..." My breath hitched, my words giving way to a moan as the shadow double twisted his fingers inside me, sending me dangerously close to the edge again. My fingers dug into Enver's skin. "It's more than this," I panted. "It's more than sex. You mean more than sex to me. You offer me so much more than this. I am happy just to be by your side, Enver. Happier than I have ever been before. I—"

Enver cut off the rest of my sentence, claiming my mouth and kissing me fiercely. His hand left my heat, coming up to cup my breast, his thumb grazing my nipple. I kissed him back, our teeth clashing in our hunger. He pinched my nipple, and my toes curled. I wouldn't last much longer. I kissed Enver, refusing to let any sound escape, feeling my body shake more and more the closer I got to release.

The shadow double adjusted his hand, a third finger of his own replacing Enver's, and then a fourth finger pressed against me. I broke away from Enver, inhaling sharply, my hand moving to stop the shadow double. Enver quickly caught my wrist, preventing me from doing so. "You can take it," he encouraged.

I couldn't catch my breath. The shadow double continued working on my clit, keeping me on the edge as his pinky pushed into me.

"Let me in," Enver breathed against my ear. "Let *us* in, Nell."

His saying my name, combined with his shadow's tongue on me and the burn of his fourth finger pressing into me—the *idea* of taking four of them—was enough to make me lose it. My body locked up, and I threw my head back, slamming it into Enver's collarbone. "*Enver—*"

And then everything was gone. His fingers, his shadows, his tongue, his touch.

"No," I choked out, whimpering. "Please—"

"I thought you understood your punishment by now," Enver said, pushing my hair off my forehead. "Do not beg. I will not remind you again."

I collapsed against him, short of breath, my entire body twitching. The shadow double leaned forward to flick his tongue against me once more, and my hips bucked upward, nearly making me fall off the throne. Enver hooked his arms under my thighs to hold me steady and lifted me up, standing from his seat. I brought my arm back to wrap around his neck awkwardly as he held me against him, my back to his chest. I watched silently as his shadow took his spot on the throne, a smirk on his face as he spread his legs.

Enver moved forward, holding me over his shadow. It took me a second to realize what he was planning. I gripped his hair, shaking my head as he positioned me over him. "Enver, wait," I said.

He held me still. "What is it, my little lover?"

"I want you inside me," I said. "Not your shadow."

"Hmm. Perhaps if you ask me nicely."

"You told me not to beg."

He nipped at the back of my neck. "Do not be smart with me. If you want me, then you will have to ask nicely. If you cannot do that, then my shadow will have you. So, go on. Convince me."

I swallowed, trying to get my thoughts together. The way he held me so exposed made my heart stutter. "I'm yours," I breathed, wishing I could see his face. "I'm yours, aren't I, Enver? So, please, fuck me. Claim me. Ruin me like you promised. Show me how much I belong to you and you alone. I need you—"

Enver's grip grew firmer, and he lifted me higher, his erection pressing against my entrance. When I realized he planned to take me like this, I froze, unable to prevent myself from thinking of Julian, to stop the gut-sinking feeling from creeping into me at the thought of being taken from behind. But this was Enver. This was *Enver*. Not Julian. It would be fine. I couldn't keep comparing him to Julian. I didn't want to. I closed my eyes, gritting my teeth. I could take it.

Enver held me steady, not attempting to enter me. Realizing he'd probably noticed me freezing up, I tried to relax. "It's okay," I said, hoping he didn't notice how my voice shook. "Do it."

He remained motionless for a moment, not saying anything, before gently lowering me to the ground. I knew I'd ruined the moment. My skin felt tight, and I couldn't bring myself to face him, standing stiffly.

"Nell," Enver spoke softly, taking me by my shoulders and turning me around to face him.

"I'm sorry," I mumbled, keeping my head lowered.

He hooked a finger under my chin, forcing my face up. "Do not apologize. You should not have to force yourself. If you do not want this, then we will not do it."

"No, it's not that," I said quickly. "I do want this. I'm just... I'm still struggling a bit with the whole Julian thing, I guess. Even though I already decided to change, I'm still like this."

"Change is a process that takes time, is it not? And there is no set timeline for such things. You must go at your own pace. There is no shame in that. You should never be pressured into anything until you are ready. That includes with me."

"You're not pressuring me," I told him.

"Were you not just pressuring yourself for me?"

"That's—"

"Do not pressure yourself, Nell," he said. "Never do that for anyone. You should always be comfortable, and if you are not, you have every right to tell any of your lovers that. Do not silently bear it. We will only do things when you are ready and willing. And if you are never ready for some things, that is fine, too."

I could feel a tightness grow in my throat. Not trusting myself to speak, I wrapped my arms around him, hiding my face in his chest. He embraced me, holding me securely in his arms. He dropped kisses into my hair as I inhaled his scent, letting it fill and calm me.

Once I settled down, I tipped my head up, and his lips immediately met mine in a sweet kiss.

"Do you wish to stop?" he asked me.

I looped my arms around his neck. "No. I want to keep going. But I don't think I'm ready for you to take me from behind. I need to see your face. I need to see you looking at me. Seeing me."

"Then we will not do that," he acceded. "I am content with

us facing each other. I never tire of looking at your beautiful face, after all."

A smile snuck onto my lips. "You're not half bad, either."

His gaze darkened. "Not half bad? That is all I get?"

I pretended to consider it, and a deep rumbling noise came from his chest as he yanked me flush against him again, his erection regaining its previous enthusiasm, rubbing against my stomach. I laughed, and he spun me around, guiding us back to the throne. The shadow double dissipated into the air as Enver took a seat upon it again. I planted my hands on his shoulders as he steered me over his lap, my knees resting on either side of him.

His hand slipped between my thighs, sinking two of his fingers into me. "You are quite wet for someone you only find *not half bad*."

I rocked onto his hand. "Enver—"

"Feel for yourself," he said, withdrawing his hand to grasp mine.

His fingers slid against mine, his palm against the back of my hand, guiding it between my legs. He sank our fingers into me together—two of his, two of mine—and I gasped at the stretch, then whimpered as he curled our joined digits. His fingers were longer and thicker than mine, touching places I couldn't on my own. The pure intimacy of the act brought the pleasure to an entirely different level. Everything felt so much more intense.

"Perhaps you would find my shadow more to your liking after all?" he contemplated, and a second later, a wintry chest pressed against my back. Chilly lips swept over my shoulder and then down the line of my spine. Then another shadow double materialized, this time at my side, familiar grey eyes drinking in the sight of the way Enver and I pleasured me together.

"They look just like you, though," I argued weakly.

"So, they are also *not half bad*?"

I groaned breathlessly, our fingers thrusting inside me in tandem, stroking against my inner walls. "Enver, I was just teasing you."

"It hurt my feelings," he told me, but his amused expression made me think it did anything but that. Mirth glittered in his eyes. "Tell me what you think of me, my little lover. I want to hear it. The truth this time."

"You're... perfect," I confessed, and he slowed the movement of our fingers, making me tremble. "So perfect, I find it hard to believe you even exist. Every time I look at you, I swear I forget how to breathe. You're beautiful, Enver. No one else could ever compare."

He withdrew our fingers and released my hand to lift me, notching himself against my entrance. My breath came out unevenly as he lowered me onto him, my hands shooting to his shoulders for balance. "Keep going," he commanded, his gaze fixed on me.

"I..." I struggled to speak through the stretch. "Uh..."

He pushed down on me, making me take him deeper, and my eyes fluttered closed.

When he spoke again, his voice was husky. "Keep talking, Nell, or I will stop. Open your eyes. Look at me."

I obeyed, snapping my eyes open again and clinging to him. "You make me forget myself," I whimpered. "You make me forget anyone and anything else. It's only you. I can only think of you. I can only want you. Only need you."

"Good," he said, his hips thrusting up, burying the last of him deep inside me.

My breathing hitched, and the feeling of him finally inside me sent waves of heat through my body. I didn't know if it was due to all the earlier teasing or the position, but I felt more sensitive than usual. I tried to lift myself, wanting friction, but he held me still, keeping me seated on him.

"Let us do the work," he said. "You relax and enjoy."

My brows furrowed, but then another pair of hands grabbed my ass before sliding under the back of my thighs. Startled, I glanced at the shadow double behind me. He moved in closer, then hoisted me up. Enver mimicked the action, fingers digging into my hips, and together, they moved me as if I weighed nothing. Up, then down. I held tighter onto Enver, the feeling of being manhandled so easily making me gasp.

"Is this okay?" Enver asked.

"Yes," I replied, pulse thrumming, and they lowered me back down.

"You feel incredible," Enver breathed. "I cannot get enough of you."

I moaned and let myself fall forward to rest against Enver's chest as he and his shadow presided over my movements. Their rhythm over me was slow and steady. My thigh muscles flexed and extended reflexively but expended no effort. It allowed me to focus on the sensation of Enver inside me, stretching and filling me, brushing against every electric nerve. It felt so good. *Too* good.

Each drag of Enver's thick length made my body tingle. My breathing turned ragged, and I quivered in his grasp. An angle change had Enver's thrusts turning shallower, his tip hitting against a sensitive spot inside me, and I moaned deeply. He kept the same position, and each languid movement set my nerves further ablaze. The buildup was unhurried and unrelenting. I writhed against them, unable to escape the pleasure, only able to give into it.

"Enver," I moaned, threading my fingers through his hair. Every part of me surged with electricity. "Wait, I think I'm going to come."

"Oh?" he murmured. "You are not trying to hide it this time?"

"This is..." My thighs quaked as they kept up their momentum. "It's too good. I—"

"Let me choke you," Enver coaxed, releasing me with one of his hands. In a flash, another replaced his grip, this one's touch chillier, taking over the maneuvering. "Tell me I can, my little lover."

I brought my head away from his chest and nodded.

"With your words," he amended.

"Choke me," I pleaded.

Enver's fingers encircled my throat, and I clenched around him in anticipation. He groaned and his grip tightened. Everything faded out around me as he squeezed, restricting my airflow. All my other senses dulled, leaving me with just the heady sensation of his hand around my throat, the rapture of him driving into me, and the growing ecstasy that threatened to overtake me.

My heart hammered in my chest, my mouth opening and closing in an attempt to get air in, only succeeding in getting the barest amounts. Enver's eyes pierced into mine, entranced with my every reaction. His thumb caressed my neck, the gesture so tender it distracted me for a moment until he fitted it against the hollow of my throat. I couldn't breathe at all now. My legs shook harder and then my muscles tightened. He didn't show any signs of stopping. He was going to let me come.

I gave in to the feeling, my head falling back. Finally—

Then Enver released my throat, and the shadow double lifted me off him. I sucked in air, tears pricking at the corner of my eyes from both lack of air and frustration as my body fought to bring my release. I couldn't, though, not when I was left empty like this. I could only contract around nothing. This had been the worst one yet. I couldn't stop trembling, even as Enver settled me back onto his lap, his erection against my stomach, hot and sticky from our combined arousal.

"You are so good for me," Enver praised, kissing the moisture in the corner of my eyes away. "You are handling this so well."

I took a shaky breath, staring at him, unable to form any words. He let me rest for a moment, allowing me to compose myself.

"You make me want to see you cry because of me," he murmured, brushing my hair out of my face. "To see you shed tears because you either cannot handle my denial anymore or because the pleasure I give you is too overwhelming."

"You're evil," I mumbled.

"I prefer cruel if I have a choice in the deprecating words you describe me with."

"If I cry, will you end the punishment right now and let me come?"

A smirk tugged at the corners of his lips. "No."

I gave a half-hearted sigh. "Worth a shot."

"You recover rather well."

"I've had practice now," I muttered, leaning into him.

"Just once more, my little lover," he reminded me. "Then I will make you come as many times as you would like."

"What about you? You have been basically edging yourself as well. Do you want me to...?" I trailed off, bringing my hand between us and stroking him.

"That's—*ah*." He inhaled sharply, his length twitching against me before he pulled my hand away, clearing his throat. "I am fine. You have forgotten I have already felt one orgasm."

When the shadow version of himself came down my throat. "Oh. Right."

"How fast do you believe I could make you come right now?"

His question caused me to blush as if he hadn't made me almost come five times in the past hour alone. "Fast, I think," I admitted. "I'm pretty wound up."

"Tell me, then. Would you rather have your sixth denial

over and done with quickly, or would you like me to draw it out and take my time?"

I didn't have to think about it. I didn't want to wait any longer. "Quickly."

"What would you like me to do?"

"I think..." I could feel another flush creeping up my cheeks and I avoided his gaze. "I think if you just touch me, it'll be enough."

Enver adjusted me so I sat further down on his legs, creating space for him to dip his hand between us again. "Do not be so shy. The fact that you are like this because of me makes it difficult for me to maintain my self-control. You should know by now that you entice me completely. Every sound. Every expression. I crave all of it. All of you."

His hand cupped my heat before he slid two fingers inside me, his thumb moving to tease my clit. I let out a short breath, closing my eyes. "Yes, just like that, Enver."

"How are you so wet?" he said, curling his fingers. "It is making me think all sorts of thoughts."

"Like what?" I asked shakily.

"Like what you would feel like riding my tongue. Your thighs pressed tight around my head, your weight on my face, and your sweet arousal dripping down my chin. I want to suffocate in your heat and drown in your essence. Your hand fisted in my hair, forcing me deeper as you take your pleasure from me."

I moaned. "Enver..."

"I feel you tightening around me. Do you enjoy that thought? I could do it for hours, my little lover. You could use me all you wanted. I would be content to lie there, pleasing you, letting you grind against my mouth. Taking what you want, for as long as you want. I can think of no better way to spend my time. I wish for nothing more than to be your obedient plaything."

"Keep talking," I groaned, gyrating on his fingers, trying to feel him deeper. "I'm close."

"Oh? Is that what does it for you?" he whispered, his voice low and husky and right against my ear as his fingers plunged in and out of me faster. "The sound of my voice? You do not know the impure thoughts I entertain regarding you. How much I continue to restrain myself every time you are near. How much I long for you to give me a reason to unleash everything I have held back on you."

"Tell me," I whimpered.

"I wish to make a mess of you," he murmured. "Mark every inch of your skin. Claim you in every way possible. Leave no part of you untouched, no place unknown. I want to fill you in every way possible. Take you repeatedly until both my scent and seed cover you. Until everyone in the world understands you are mine."

Holy fuck.

"But even then, it would not be enough," he continued, his voice dropping to a dark and sensual purr. "I would become selfish. I would take you and lock you away so only I could see you. Only I could touch you. You would be a prisoner to my desire. I would keep you here, next to me. Wet and aching. Wanting. Ready to receive me wherever and however I wanted."

I shuddered, clenching around his fingers again.

"You want that," he breathed, his lips grazing my ear. "I can tell. Your body gives you away."

"No—"

"Yes," he said, thrusting his fingers so deep it tore a cry from my throat. "You do. You want me to keep you as my toy—my pet."

I fought to breathe, to speak, his fingers moving relentlessly. "N-no."

"No? Then do not come," he said, the hand on my hip going to my breast, rolling the nipple between his thumb and forefinger. "Prove to me you do not want to be my willing little captive. That you do not want me to tie you to my bed, naked and ready, open to me at all times. That you do not crave me inside you. Using you over and over until all you know is my name and the word '*more*'."

"Enver," I whined.

His breath was hot and heavy against my skin as he shifted to scrape his teeth against the juncture of my neck and shoulder. The movement caused his erection to press into me, hard and leaking against my stomach. He was just as turned on as I was. "And when I have to leave you alone, I will not leave you empty," he vowed, words rough as he rocked his hips up against me to create friction against his own aching need. "My shadows will take care of you in my stead. Keeping you stretched and filled until my return. You will always have a part of me inside you. Always feel me within you. Always belong to me."

Fuck.

The image he painted in my mind and the way he rutted against me was too much. My nails dug into his shoulder, my back arching as my orgasm crested. "I'm—"

Enver let out a soft breath, satisfaction flickering in his eyes. He removed his hand, bringing his fingers up to his mouth to suck my juices off them. I struggled for a moment, my body convulsing, trying to reach an orgasm, but, once again, without his touch, it was useless. Instead, I surged forward to kiss him, the taste of me on his tongue making me want him even more.

He broke the kiss after a few moments but kept his face close, smirking. "So, you cannot deny it. You want to be my pet."

"You..." I began, letting the rest of my sentence die on my tongue, too worn out to argue when I knew he was just teasing me. Instead, I let myself fall against his chest, resting my chin on his shoulder. He chuckled lowly against my ear.

His hands moved to my back, massaging small circles across it, causing me to melt further into him. "That is all six.

You did so well, Nell," he said, his breath falling over my neck, making stirs of desire awaken in me again. "Tell me what you want, my little lover, and it will be yours. All you have to do is ask, and I will fulfill your every desire. Your reward for being so good for me."

It took me a moment to peel myself away from him. Enver tilted his head, sitting up straight and creating space between us again as he waited for my response. A shadow version of himself stood on either side of us, silent and motionless. I considered all versions of him for a moment. "You said you feel everything they do, right?"

"That is correct."

"I want payback," I decided.

Enver raised an eyebrow. "How do you plan to achieve that?"

"Can we go to your bed?" I asked him. "I'm going to need more space."

"As you wish," he responded, standing from the throne and hoisting me up so I could wrap my legs around his waist.

A shadow portal appeared in front of us, and he carried me through it. We appeared in his bedroom, and he carried me over to his bed, lowering me onto the plush mattress. I wiggled back on the bed a bit until my head hung off the edge.

"What are you doing?" Enver asked curiously.

"Bring one of your shadows over here."

One of the shadow doubles materialized by my head. I reached out and grabbed his hard length, opening my mouth, and taking him inside. Enver's lips parted as he looked down at me. I sucked on the shadow double for a moment before pulling away. "I want you to fuck me while I suck him off like this."

Enver's eyes darkened with lust, and he climbed between my legs, grabbing the backs of my thighs to lift my hips up. I wrapped them around his waist again, getting into position, still figuring out the logistics of my plan, but he drove into me without hesitation, wielding enough force to knock the air from my lungs.

"Wait, your other shadows, too," I gasped out.

Enver didn't stop, his fingers digging into my thighs, holding me in place as he rocked into me, pressing in deep and grinding his hips against me. Two more shadows in his visage appeared, though, and I grabbed at the comforter on either side of me.

"Bring them here," I said through a moan.

The shadow doubles knelt beside me, one in each spot. Enver gazed down at me evenly, a contrast to the way he was slamming into me. "What are you planning?"

"I-I told you. I want payback. I want you to feel four times the pleasure as you fuck me," I gasped between thrusts. "So, I'll make use of my mouth and hands at the same time. It might not be six times, but—"

"I can think of a way to make it six," Enver cut me off, coming to a stop, his length throbbing inside me, a physical response to my words.

"What? How?"

His hand slid to my ass. "Here."

He stroked a teasing line down the sensitive space between my cheeks, and I jumped, my face heating. "Woah! Um, no, I don't think I'm ready for that."

His hand retreated. "Hm."

"But even if we, um, used that, what would be the sixth?" I asked hesitantly because now I was curious.

"The human body can accommodate many things. I am sure with proper preparation, both I and one of my shadows could fit in here." He gave a pointed thrust.

I didn't think I could blush deeper, but the fire burning my skin told me otherwise. "You're joking, right?"

He blinked down at me.

He wasn't joking.

"I didn't expect you to be so kinky," I said.

"I do not see the problem," he answered.

"You're not the one who would have to take two of you inside them! Or *three* of you if we had it your way! There's no way that would feel good. I'd die. I think I'd actually die," I responded, my eyes wide in disbelief.

"You would not know until you try."

"You want me to die?" I deadpanned.

He chuckled, leaning down to kiss my nose. "Fine. I am disappointed, but I concede to your wishes."

"You're disappointed?" I repeated, still flustered about what he'd suggested. "Fine. Let me see you do it first."

"Hm?"

"Take two of your shadows and, I don't know, make two versions of me with strap-ons on. Then let them both in your ass at the same time."

Enver pursed his lips down at me. "I do not know what a strap-on is, but I suppose I can infer what it entails. Out of the question."

"Then don't suggest that again."

"I will not." He shrugged. "I will wait for you to suggest it yourself."

I let my head fall back, groaning. "You're impossible."

"No, I am confident in the pleasure I can give you. However, we are getting sidetracked." He gave a hard thrust, and all the heat came rushing back through me again. "Open your mouth."

"I don't think you're the one making demands anymore," I said.

He nearly pulled all the way out of me before snapping forward again in another breath-stealing thrust. "I said open your mouth."

I did, although in a silent cry, and the shadow double in

front of me stepped forward, sliding himself into my mouth again. I lifted my hands, reaching out until my fingers curled around the two remaining shadows' shafts, pumping them in time with Enver's thrusts. The response was instant in Enver. His hips stuttered, and the loudest groan I ever heard from him escaped his throat.

Yes, this was having the desired effect on him. Exactly as I wanted. I stroked the shadows at my sides faster.

I pulled my head away from the shadow double in front of me for a moment. "Don't come until I tell you to."

A muscle in his jaw ticked. "Nell, I have held myself back all night. I am also sensitive," Enver said, pausing his thrusts. "If you keep this up, I will not last long. I can barely restrain myself as is. I will not be able to stop myself, even if you ask."

I didn't answer, attempting to take the shadow double in front of me as far down my throat as possible. My hands continued to move, my thumbs pressing against the tips of the other two shadows, spreading their pre-come around, using what I could as added lubrication.

"Nell," Enver ground out.

My tongue traced along the veins of his shadow's length, and Enver moaned. I dug my heels into his sides, using the leverage to rock myself against him, forcing him to move inside me again.

"I will not last," he warned me again, voice strained.

I pulled back again so I could speak, looking up at him. "Beg me. Beg me to let you come."

His eyes flashed dangerously. "Do you truly believe you are the one in control right now?"

"I am," I said, although my confidence wavered at the intense look he was giving me.

"Is that so?"

His shadow double fisted my hair, yanking my head back down, pressing himself against my lips. I let out a startled breath, and he pushed himself back into my mouth, silencing me. Enver pulled my hips down at the same time, impaling me on him. His body moved over mine, his lips at my ear as he spoke again. "If you are in control, then stop me."

I groaned around the shadow in my mouth and then sucked him hard, my hands gripping the others tightly, not willing to let up. Not willing to let Enver win this one. He swore under his breath, his hips snapping forward in rough, uncontrolled thrusts.

"I do not beg," he ground out. "You want to provoke me? Fine. Then, I will not hold back and take what I want from you."

He bent my legs so my knees touched my chest, and then his pace changed. His thrusts turned brutal, jostling my body, sliding me up on the bed, forcing me to take the shadow double further down my throat. I fought against my gag reflex, saliva pooling in my mouth, making it easier to accept him deeper. My hands twisted around the shadow doubles at my sides, my movements uncoordinated and rushed, trying to keep up with everything.

The shadow double inside my mouth brought his other hand to my neck, squeezing it. "I can feel myself in your throat," he spoke, his voice gravelly. "Do you like that? How deep I am?"

Muffled noises escaped me as Enver pounded into me mercilessly. I tried to look up at him, but the feat was difficult with the way the shadow double held my hair and throat. Enver's breath turned ragged as he watched the space where our bodies connected. "So beautiful," he groaned. "Look at how well you are taking me. Taking us. You look perfect like this. Filled with me. Surrounded by me."

The more he spoke, the rougher his voice became, and the more I could hear his control slipping. It was exactly what I wanted. To see him unravel. He thought I wanted him to beg, but that wasn't true. I wanted to watch him lose his composure like this. The shadow under one of my hands twitched, and Enver moaned again, the sound addicting. I squeezed around him, lifting my head as much as I could, and his eyes met mine, half-lidded and heavy with desire.

"Do that again," he rasped.

I complied, and his jaw tightened, his hips slamming against me.

He grunted. "Yes, just like that. Again. You..." He shuddered, his eyes falling shut. A drop of sweat slid down his neck, and I realized his body was taut with tension, his muscles straining.

"You are going to make me come," he warned in a low moan, his rhythm becoming uneven, his hold on me turning almost painful.

I rolled my hips against him in encouragement. I didn't know how much more I could handle, either. I steadied myself, breathing in through my nose, before attempting to take the shadow double in front of me all the way into my throat. I knew I could do it, and I knew it would set Enver off. I knew it drove him crazy to see me swallow all of him.

"*Nell*." His voice was guttural and raw, an unspoken plea interweaved with my name.

He placed my leg over his shoulder, allowing him to release it and bring his fingers to my clit. I'd thought about denying his orgasm as he'd done to me so many times, but that thought disappeared the moment he touched me. I cried out around the shadow double, and my throat tried to close around his thickness, causing my entire body to spasm. The noise that left Enver's mouth as it did was the dirtiest sound I had ever heard from him. Absolutely debauched and incredibly sexy.

The shadow double in my mouth finished first, a flood of cool liquid coating my tongue as he withdrew, painting my face with the rest of his spend. Moans chorused above me, and the shadow doubles at my sides closed in on me. The way they pulsed under my fingers was the only warning I had before they came, shooting their release all over my breasts.

The shadow double holding my hair yanked my head up, forcing me to face the real Enver. He was a mess. Sweat matted his black hair to his forehead and made his skin glisten under the light of the chandelier. His mouth was parted as he panted, needy moans spilling out every few seconds. The sight was so unbelievably erotic I unconsciously clamped around him again.

"*Fuck*," he swore, his hand leaving my clit to curl around my neck as he buried himself deep inside me one last time.

I moaned as he came, feeling him pulse and spill inside me. "Enver, please," I begged. "Touch me."

He shoved my other leg over his other shoulder, now freeing his other hand, continuing to choke me as he expertly worked the spot between my thighs over again. It didn't take much to send me spiraling into oblivion. After so many denied releases, I came apart quickly, falling silent as my orgasm tore through me, hard and fast. I shook uncontrollably, arching up against Enver as I clawed at the sheets. The pleasure was blinding, my vision going white as the world fell down around us.

Enver let go of my throat, working me through the aftershocks of my climax, drawing everything out until I couldn't take anymore and whimpered a protest. He dropped forward, his hands on either side of my head as he kissed me, not caring that his shadow's come covered my lips and chin. He ran a tongue under my lip, gathering his release, and feeding it to me as he slipped his tongue back into my mouth. My legs slipped from his shoulders, and I brought my arms around his neck to keep him close.

"Should I make you come again?" he breathed.

I stilled. Right. He'd never let me come only once. Swallowing, I shook my head. "No, Enver. I'm too sensitive. I really don't think I—"

"Then I will not," he assured me, kissing me instead. "I wanted to give you the option."

After a long moment, he shifted his weight, pulling out of me to lie down next to me. I curled up against him immediately, and he smiled, not put off by the stickiness covering my torso. "You are a mess."

"You did say that's what you wanted," I mumbled, still attempting to catch my breath.

"It is a good look on you."

"Your come?"

He hummed, kissing my forehead. "No. Your flushed cheeks and disheveled state. How you look so thoroughly satisfied. I will have to use my shadows more often."

I smiled back at him before tucking my face into the crook of his neck. Silence settled between us as he skated his fingertips along the line of my spine.

"Are you all right?" he asked after a little while. "I know all this must have been a lot for you to handle."

I knew he didn't just mean the sex. I tried to move even closer to him, my gaze falling on the new—now fully healed—wound on his chest. "I am. Physically, at least."

"What is on your mind?"

Deciding not to dig up my confusing feelings about finishing the labyrinth, I shifted to the next thought that popped into my mind. "I feel like I failed Isla. Like it's my fault she lost her challenge."

"Why do you believe that?"

"I think I've been put in everyone's challenges to help guide them onto the right paths. Or that's what I *thought*, at least. Everyone I met before Isla completed their labyrinths. I must have met them for a reason, right? Yet Isla..." I trailed off, my chest tightening. I would never forget the sight of her eyes becoming unfocused and her expression turning blank as she transformed into one of Enver's many mindless servants. "I know she tried to kill you, but even you don't know why she hates you so much. Why she was desperate enough to go that far. I wonder if she did have a valid reason for doing what she did. I'm also worried that by failing her, I have failed my challenge."

Enver hummed, petting my hair. "I can at least assure you Isla has not caused you to fail your labyrinth."

I turned my chin up so I could see him. "Are you sure?"

"Yes. Your last challenge awaits."

"Oh." Once again, I faced the reality I was one challenge away from being separated from Enver forever. I snuggled into him, needing to feel him as close as possible. "Why do you think she waited to attack you until you were in the throne room?"

"It is the only part of my castle with no windows," he said. "She must have known she could not defeat my shadows."

"She also said she'd been looking for something. Some kind of key."

"I am not sure what she searched so hard for. I only know she never found it, even after all this time."

And now she never would.

My heart sank, and I changed the subject. "Why is your throne room so secluded, anyway?"

His motions stopped, his hand resting at the base of my neck. "I cannot remember why it was designed that way."

"Are you ever scared to remember your past?"

"I could not feel fear until today," he reminded me.

"Oh, that's true." I rested my chin against his collarbone, gazing up at him. "I'm afraid of your past."

"Why is that?"

"I'm scared you could be the murderer Isla thinks you are."

He gazed down at me, his expression unreadable. "Is that so?"

"I'm not scared because you could be a murderer, though," I

admitted, reaching my hand up to his face to smooth out the crease that appeared on his forehead. "And I still don't believe you actually killed anyone before." I hesitated before speaking again. "I'm scared because I don't think I'll care either way. Even if you killed someone before, even if you did horrible things, none of it matters to me. I don't care about who you were, Enver, because I know who you are now. And this version of you is the only one that matters to me. Nothing you might have done in your past could stop me from caring about you."

His face softened at my words. "My little lover," he murmured. "For over a century, I have existed in shadows and loneliness, unable to recall my past or the reason for my cursed existence. Never caring nor fearing, unable to die no matter what I tried. Nothing ever mattered to me before. Yet, everything is different now. I still do not fear my past, and I still do not fear the cause of my curse. But now..." He cupped my cheek, his thumb stroking my skin affectionately. "I fear losing you."

My breath caught, and Enver rolled me onto my back so he could climb over me again, his powerful arms bracketing me beneath him. "Enver."

"Losing you..." His lips brushed against mine. "Your smile, your kindness, your heart. *That* is something I cannot bear. You are what matters most to me now. If I lose you, then I lose everything. I would rather have my heart, my memories, and my emotions torn from me again than be without you. I have known darkness for so long I thought I would never know anything else again, yet the time I have spent with you has been the brightest and warmest of my existence."

I blinked away the sudden moisture in my eyes, wrapping my arms around him, and lifting myself to kiss him. He eased me back down into the mattress, kissing me back tenderly, our bodies melding together. I wanted him. I couldn't stop wanting him. Not when he kissed me like I was the only person in his entire world. Not when he held me like I was the most precious thing he had. Not when he told me he needed me the same way I needed him.

My thighs parted, and he brought a hand down to my backside, squeezing it before hoisting my leg around his waist. I sighed into his mouth as he entered me again. This time, it was slower. The desperation from earlier had dissipated, leaving us with a simple longing to be with each other. He took his time, moving unhurriedly and drawing out his strokes. We held each other close, our kisses never-ending.

"I don't want to say goodbye," I breathed against him.

"Then we will not say it yet," he responded, trailing adoring kisses down my neck.

I clutched at him, my heart aching. He didn't understand. I didn't want to let him go. Not now. Not later. Not ever. "Enver, I—"

"Hush, my little lover," he crooned. "We have not said goodbye. Do not let go of me just yet. Stay with me. Remain in my arms and fill the hollowness of my heart. Just for a while longer."

"I wish you could love me," I whispered, the confession slipping out before I could stop it, my words laced with a vulnerability that only made the ache in my chest more painful.

He didn't answer right away, dragging himself out of me and languidly pressing back in. I moaned, and his lips moved back up my jaw, peppering me with kisses until he reached my ear. "I wish I could love you, too," he murmured back, his deep voice filled with a longing that matched my own.

And that was truly the cruelest part of him.

That, despite how much I wanted him to—despite how much he wanted to—he could never love me.

I opened my mouth to speak, but his lips found mine again, silencing anything I could have said in response.

25

Lying in his bed together, Enver spent the night fulfilling his promise to kiss every inch of my body. With soft, unhurried kisses that made me sigh. With long, heated kisses that made me ache for him anew. With deep, passionate kisses that made me tremble under his touch until he decided to relieve my torment, his lips and tongue taking an intermission in their exploration to move between my thighs and leave me gasping and clutching at his hair.

I tried counting the kisses but lost track around two hundred and sixteen.

"Say you are mine," Enver murmured as he kissed the side of my calf.

"I'm yours," I told him as his lips moved a centimeter to the left, dropping another kiss down.

"Until when?" he questioned, his breath hot on my skin as he pressed his lips down again.

"Until..." I trailed off, my chest growing tight. I couldn't bring myself to say what he wanted to hear. Not when the inevitable was approaching.

I would have lied if only just to have that moment with him. But I couldn't force the words out. Because I didn't know if it would be a lie, and it scared me.

Enver didn't ask me to finish. He continued to trail kisses down the inside of my calf, and I tried to pretend his worship would last forever. When he placed his last kiss on my foot, he crawled up over me and started all over again, his light caresses eventually lulling me to sleep despite how hard I fought to stay awake, not wanting to give up any remaining time with him.

I awoke much later, finding myself tucked against him, one of his arms laid over my waist, the other under me, cushioning my head. He was still asleep, his bare chest falling and rising rhythmically. His expression was peaceful, his long lashes resting against his pale cheekbones. I took my time studying his face, wanting to memorize every line, every curve, every angle. The sharpness of his jaw, the slope of his nose. Everything. I wanted to burn the image of him into my mind. I reached up to trace the shape of his lips with my fingertips before leaning in to kiss him. I kissed his chin next, then his neck, moving myself lower in the bed so I could kiss the scars over his chest. The ones Isla left on him had already faded, now white and smooth, blending in with the others.

Enver stirred then, and I looked up to see his eyes flutter open. His obsidian irises focused on me, and his lips curved up into a lazy, content smile. "Good morning, my little lover."

"Good morning," I responded softly.

He looped an arm around my waist, hauling me up the bed until our faces were only centimeters apart. He captured my lips in a long, lingering kiss. I melted into him, and he sighed into my mouth in response. Neither of us spoke, although a hollow feeling grew in my chest—an invisible force pressing against my lungs, making it harder and harder to breathe.

I knew why. I refused to think about it.

When Enver broke away, I spoke first, unable to meet his gaze. "Can we take a bath together?" I asked, my pulse quickening as my voice wavered.

"Of course," he responded.

A knot formed in my throat as Enver lifted me out of the bed, carrying me to his washroom. I tried to focus on his warmth, how his body felt against mine. How his scent clung to me, amber, geranium, and vanilla. I needed to remember that. So that when I returned home...

I pushed the thought from my mind, the hollow feeling threatening to consume me entirely. I couldn't think about it. I wouldn't. I didn't let Enver go as we settled into the tub, clinging to him. He didn't say anything about my behavior. Only washed me with gentle touches, his lips never far from my skin.

I don't want to leave him.

My mind betrayed me again, the thought slamming into me with such force it left me shaking in Enver's hold. I fought against it. I tried to ignore it. But it kept coming back. Over and over, even as we left the bath. I stayed quiet until I caught sight of the dress he brought for me to wear. The dress I wore the night I met him at the club.

It sent a flurry of panic through me. I knew why he'd chosen it. "I don't want to wear that."

His lips curved down. "Nell—"

"It's too short," I said quickly, wrapping my arms around myself. "I want something longer."

He hesitated a moment, and I thought he would deny me, but then his expression softened, and he nodded. I watched him retrieve one of the dresses I used to dislike. Now, though, I wanted to wear something of his, no matter the history behind it. I wanted to bask in the redolence of him. I wanted to be surrounded by him, to drown in him.

I stepped into the dress—a pure white, flowing gown that draped low over my breasts and fell to my ankles—and Enver laced up the back, his knuckles skimming along the exposed skin of my spine. I passed off the continuously growing tightness in my torso as a result of the dress being tied too tightly, but as Enver stepped away from me, the sensation only increased. It hurt to breathe.

"What if I give you back love?" I burst out, the lump in my throat making it almost impossible to speak. "What if you can love me when I complete your labyrinth?"

"Nell."

"You have been getting so many emotions back. It's not that crazy of a thought," I pressed on, desperate for any excuse. Desperate for any reason to stay. "Maybe love is what I have to give you in the end. Then I can stay, and we can work together to help you break your curse—"

"Eleanora," he said, and my voice died in my throat. "You are traveling down a dangerous path. You are giving in to false hope. There is no guarantee that I will remember love should you finish your challenge. There is a vast multitude of other emotions that have yet to return to me. There is also a chance love might not return at all."

His words left me numb. Because I knew he was right. Because I knew he was trying to protect me. To not let me lose myself in my desperation again.

I didn't resist as he turned me to face him, his palms cupping the sides of my neck. "You must return home, Nell. Your life is there, not here. I could not ask you to stay with me, knowing the price you would have to pay. I cannot be the one to take your freedom away from you again. You cannot live in darkness as I do. The stars I once promised you are out of my reach within this castle."

I stared at him, my lips trembling. "Why...?"

He didn't say anything, waiting for me to continue, and I could see the determined resolve in his gaze.

"Why are you doing this to me?" I cried, feeling tears burn

in my eyes, blurring my vision. "You brought me here, you asked me to stay, and now you're telling me I can't? That I can never have any of what you promised me? Why does it have to end like this? Why are you so willing to give me up after saying you couldn't bear to lose me? You said you wanted me!"

The tears fell, hot and fast, and I broke free from his grasp, stumbling back and scrubbing the back of my hand over my cheeks. I put my back to him, wanting to hide my tears, even though I knew he'd seen them already. He said nothing as I fought to breathe through the tightness in my throat, and his silence only made the pain worse.

After a moment, his slow, cautious footsteps approached me. "Nell."

I shook my head, refusing to look at him. He exhaled, moving in front of me and taking hold of my jaw. He tilted my head up and bent down, kissing my tears away. The action was so familiar it only made more form in my eyes. He was patient, continuing to kiss away each and every one until they finally dried. When he straightened out, he brushed the remaining wetness away with his thumb. I leaned into his touch, fearing the time when I would never feel it again. "I wish there was another way," I whispered.

"I am truly sorry," he apologized quietly. "For giving you hope and then being the one to take it away. You must know I would give you the world if I could. Yet, I cannot. I can only make this decision easier for you. I would not forgive myself if I kept you here. You have given me so much—I cannot take any more from you."

Another lump formed in my throat, and I closed my eyes, not trusting myself enough to speak. More tears escaped. He wiped them away again, his warm and comforting hands lingering against my skin. "Please don't make me do this," I said, my voice cracking.

"Nell," he said, and this time, his voice sounded equally torn.

"I thought it would be fine. I thought I could be strong and leave you and all this behind. I convinced myself I could do it. But I can't. *I can't.*"

"You can," Enver insisted. "You do not belong here. If you remain here, all that waits for you is darkness. This place is a prison for me, not a home. It would become a prison for you, too. You may think you want this now, but in the end, you would regret your decision. You would regret choosing me."

"No," I argued. "I wouldn't."

"You would," he said softly. "And I do not want to see you live with that regret. I cannot be the chains that bind you here. I refuse to become your curse. You must remain free. You must forget me."

"I won't be able to forget you," I said, my fingers curling into his shirt. "I won't be able to live a normal life again. Not when I know there is a world out there beyond my own, that you exist, and that we will never be together again. I will never be able to find someone like you, Enver."

"Stop," Enver commanded. "You can find happiness again. You will not always be stuck in this memory with me. You will move on. You will find love."

Panic lacerated me, creating physical pain. "I don't want to! I want to stay here. I want to be with *you*. I want to love *you*—"

"No," Enver cut me off, his voice growing rougher, his composure cracking. "This is not what you wanted, Eleanora. This is what I manipulated you into believing you wanted. Remember that and return home."

"No," I sobbed. "Enver, please..."

"Eleanora—"

"Stop calling me that!" I choked out through my sobs. "You're trying to put distance between us by calling me that! Stop it! I don't want to be without you, Enver!"

"*Nell.* If you keep on like this, you will only destroy us both," he whispered, his voice filled with thinly veiled agony.

It broke my heart. It told me I wasn't the only one hurting. That this was just as hard for him as it was for me. That he was suffering as much as I was. I threw myself at him, hugging him to me. "I can't leave you here alone. It's not fair."

"I have been fine by myself for over a century," he reminded me, his arms falling around my waist, holding me just as tight. "I will remain so. Only now, I will have a fond memory to turn to when the darkness and loneliness become too much. The memory of you."

My heart cracked further. "Can't I just come back? Even if I finish the labyrinth?"

"No," Enver said firmly. "When you complete the labyrinth, you will have what you yearned for. That will not be me. You will have no reason to come back."

"If I'm desperate enough to see you, won't you come to me again?" I asked, my throat scratchy.

"No," he murmured. "I will not come to you. So, do not try."

Tears streamed down my cheeks. "You're being cruel again."

"Then remember me as cruel. Let it lessen your sorrow."

"Enver, please."

"You will never be free if your heart beats for mine," he said. "You must move on. Find the one who will love you the way you deserve to be loved. Do not let yourself be tethered to darkness and stained by shadows. You have to let go of the impossible." His fingers trembled as he drew me in closer, his hold on me tightening briefly as if he were afraid I would heed his words and vanish. "You have to let go of me."

He then pried himself away from me, letting me go. His eyes burned into mine, waiting for me to say something. But I had nothing to say. Not anymore. Not when I finally understood. Not when I could hear the pain in every one of his words. The unshakeable resolution in them that matched his gaze. He wouldn't let me stay. He wanted what was best for me, even if I struggled to agree.

"Do not keep pushing," he said, tucking my hair behind my ear. "Because I will shatter. I cannot resist it all—I am not strong enough. I will drag you into my endless torment if you stay by my side. And I would rather suffer alone in the darkness for the rest of my existence than subject you to such despair, my precious, precious little lover."

My lips quivered as I nodded, reaching up to cradle his face in my hands, needing to touch him. "I understand," I whispered. "I won't push anymore. I won't fight it. Just... just don't act like it's over yet. Please. Just pretend I'm going to my next challenge, and you will be waiting for me when I finish."

He leaned into my touch, his soft breath feathering across my skin. "I have already been doing that, Nell. I have been doing that since the moment I met you. Pretending I could have you. Pretending that a monster like me deserved you."

"Then continue to do that," I begged, my voice shaking. "Let's pretend a little longer, okay? Until I finish my last challenge. Just until then."

"Okay," he agreed.

Not expecting him to accept so easily, I hesitated, but then he stepped back, waving his arm. A shadow portal materialized, and my heart dropped into my stomach. "No, not yet," I said, my heart thumping painfully in my chest. Shadowy tendrils crept up from the floor, encircling my wrists and ankles. I tried to fight against them, dread swelling up in me. "No, Enver, no, please! I'm not ready! Just a little longer!"

He stood still, his expression guarded, resembling how he'd been the first time we met, back when he was cold, distant, and unfeeling. But now he couldn't hide the emotions in his eyes. The agony. The fear. He was fighting against himself, breaking himself apart to make this easier for me.

"You have six hours," he said. "Finish, and return home."

"Enver, please," I begged, my breath coming short and fast. "Not like this! Let me fight for you—"

"Fight for yourself, Eleanora. Do not fight for me." He turned his back on me. "I am not worth the battle."

The shadows dragged me backward toward the portal, and I struggled against them, stretching my hand out toward Enver, trying to reach him. He ignored me, unmoving. Even as my cries filled the air, his name catching in my throat again and again as I fought between trying to breathe and calling for him, my voice ringing out until I could no longer see him. Until the darkness Enver would remain in forever swallowed me up and he was gone.

The shadows spit me out a moment later, and even through my tears, I could see I was still inside the castle. As soon as they released me, I twisted on my heel, rushing down the hall, searching for any door that could lead me back to him. He said the castle would always lead me back to him. I would go back to him and convince him to let me stay. That we could find a way to be together.

I rounded a corner and crashed into someone so hard it sent me sprawling to the ground.

I immediately looked up, expecting Enver, only to feel my heart drop in disappointment when my eyes fell upon one of the castle servants. But then, as I took in her features, my skin crawled.

I recognized this woman.

She was the one immortalized in Enver's castle gardens. I was sure of it, despite the differences in her appearance here compared to the statue's portrayal. Instead of porcelain, she was now made of flesh. Of golden skin and short black hair instead of the long locks the statue depicted. She wore the servant's attire instead of the flowing dress, though it did little to diminish her elegance. Her dark brown eyes were vacant as she offered me her hand, her movements robotic and unnatural. My pulse skyrocketed, but I held my hand out to her before realizing what I was doing.

Then, when our hands touched, the pendant around my neck burned fiercely. Worse than ever before. I gasped, ripping my hand away from her and falling back. But instead of landing on the hallway carpet again, shadows pooled under me and I fell through the floor into darkness once more.

26

Sheeting rain pelted down on me when I came out of the darkness, and I rolled onto my side to avoid it falling into my face. I wiped my eyes, ridding them of both raindrops and tears. My mind was reeling, the pendant still burning against my skin as I pushed myself to a kneeling position, glancing around me. It was dark, and the heavy rain made it nearly impossible to see anything until a lightning bolt lit up the sky, revealing a stone gazebo only a few paces from me. Thunder cracked, and I scrambled to my feet, deciding it would be good enough shelter as I got my bearings. Another streak of lightning flashed, and I made my move, nearly slipping on the damp and slick steps leading into the gazebo.

Soaked and shivering, I pushed my hair out of my face, waiting for lightning to illuminate my surroundings. Each flash gave me two seconds. One revealed a shadowy castle outline in the distance, and another lit up a stone path leading through what seemed to be a garden. Shrubbery wet with rain swayed in the storm's wind, petals from flowers littering the grass and path.

I didn't recognize any of it. My chest tightened as I accepted

I'd entered my final challenge. Been *forced* into it. "Bring me back," I whispered into the darkness. "Please. I don't want to leave him alone."

No shadows answered my request this time.

My lip trembled, and I bit it hard, clenching my fists as I fought back the lump in my throat. "I'll fail on purpose."

Thunder crashed so hard in response that it made me jump. I glanced over my shoulder as lightning once again provided vision, catching the sight of two men hurrying toward the gazebo. My heart lurched, and I slipped out the other side, keeping against its frame, my back pressed against a column as I hid.

"What nonsense do you plan to claim now?" a harsh, hushed voice asked as I heard the pair's heavy footfalls climb up the gazebo's steps. "You have wasted enough of my time. Must you do this during my daughter's celebration, too?"

"You have to listen to me," the other man responded, voice rising as he spoke. "He is up to no good. Your daughter is in danger with him!"

"They are to be married," the first man snapped. "I cannot interfere with my daughter's wedding on your baseless claims, Kayn."

"They are not baseless," the second one, Kayn, gritted out. "You are blind if you do not see the danger lurking in the shadows."

"I have investigated your every claim, and there has never been one shred of evidence for your allegations."

Kayn made a sound of frustration. "You are making a mistake. How can you marry your daughter off to someone who has a questionable background?"

"Did you forget you also have a questionable background?" the first man challenged. "Have you forgotten what your father did to this kingdom?"

"I..." Kayn fell silent for a moment. "I don't trust him."

"I will not lie and say I trust him completely either," the first man admitted. "But Evangeline trusts him. That is enough for me. He has done nothing to incur any of our distrust, either."

"Yet. He hasn't done anything *yet*. Your blind trust will get both you and Evie killed one day, Solomon—"

"Enough, Kayn. Speak further, and you will be no longer welcome in my home," Solomon interjected sharply, before his tone lightened as he spoke again. "I know you worry about Evangeline. I know you have protected her all this time. But she is an adult. She can make her own choices."

"I understand," Kayn muttered. "At least be cautious of him. Please. For both your sakes."

"I will. I truly appreciate your concern. You have done more for our family than most would. But Verofer has shown nothing but loyalty and adoration for Evangeline. If they love each other, I will not be the one to stand between them."

"Right," Kayn responded stiffly.

"Rest assured, though, should your claims have proof, I will not hesitate to banish him from this kingdom." A heavy sigh came. "Take your time in returning," Solomon said, and then I heard one pair of footsteps walking away. "Evangeline will know something is wrong with you. I do not want to bother her with your accusations during such a joyful time."

Silence fell, and I didn't move, rain dripping down my face in rivulets. An itch in my nose was the only warning before I sneezed. I tried to stifle it, but it was too late. I froze, my eyes squeezing shut as I held my breath, hoping the rain covered the noise.

But when I opened my eyes again and looked up as a streak of lightning crossed the sky, a man leaning out of the gazebo came into sight.

He looked down at me, and I barely made out his hazel eyes and damp red hair before the night hid him again. I scrambled up from the ground, prepared to run, when a hand closed around my arm, hauling me back into the gazebo.

"Sorry!" I spluttered, stumbling after him. "I didn't mean to listen in!"

He released me, and light filled the gazebo. I stared at the ball of white magic he held out in his hand for a moment, surprised. So, there was magic in this world, too. The man's wet hair fell onto his face, sticking to his forehead. The top layer of it was pulled back into a small topknot while the rest fell to just above his shoulders. "Who are you? What are you doing here?"

My gaze shifted back to his face, and I gasped as my eyes roamed over his white skin, up to pointed ears. "Are those real?"

His brow furrowed, then his gaze went to my ears. "A human? Here? How?"

I hesitated a moment. The past times, I'd been brought straight to the one doing the labyrinth, but for some reason, it didn't feel right this time. As if Kayn was not the one I was here for.

Or maybe that was because I didn't want to be here.

I understood why Enver forced me to leave. I knew this was for my own good, but it didn't mean it hurt any less. Didn't stop the longing from making it feel like someone had ripped my own heart out. I understood Enver more now than ever before, which only added to my ache for him.

"Do you desire something so much you would do anything to have it?" I asked, forcing myself to speak.

He tensed, eyes narrowing in suspicion. "Are you a witch?"

"No!" I said quickly, the accusation distracting me from my sorrow for a moment. "I'm just a normal human! Here to help someone. I just don't know if it's you or someone else. Are you challenging the labyrinth?"

He pursed his lips, taking in my soaked form. "The only thing you're helping at this moment is yourself catching a cold.

Here. Come with me. You're obviously not from around here. I should be able to find something dry for you to wear."

I nodded, shivering, following him out of the gazebo, the ball of light in his hand lighting up a path for us. I wouldn't turn down dry clothing. I didn't know how long I'd be stuck here. "Is what you want so desperately, Evangeline?"

Kayn glanced back at me, his expression guarded. "You know of Evie?"

I shook my head. "No. I overheard you."

He faced forward again, and I had to hurry to keep up with his long strides. "Yes. She is the woman I desperately crave. It might sound pathetic to you—"

"It doesn't," I said immediately. "I know what it's like to want someone so badly it hurts." My throat tightened. "Knowing you can't ever have them. It's not pathetic. It's terrible and cruel."

Kayn slowed his pace as if noticing I struggled to keep up, but didn't respond. We veered off to the left, the stone path turning into dirt. I looked up at the castle in the distance as we approached a secondary, much smaller structure. Although not as grand as the neighboring stronghold, it was quaint and well-kept. We approached an oak door, and Kayn opened it, gesturing for me to go first.

I did, and warm air and the scent of cedar surrounded me. A fireplace in the room's corner roared to life with no one around to kindle it. Startled a bit, I stopped, but Kayn brushed past me. "I'm aware my place isn't as resplendent as the main castle, but my circumstances aren't as noble, either. I am fortunate I was given a place to stay, to begin with." Curious, I turned to him, but he crossed the room, heading up a wooden staircase. "I'll return with clothing for you."

"Thanks," I said, looking around the room. It was mostly bare, with the furniture added as if on a second thought. I moved into the next room, peeking into what I assumed to be his bedroom and finding it in a similar state.

I heard Kayn coming back down the stairs and I backed out of his bedroom, blushing a bit at being caught. He frowned at me. "This is all I have, but it should fit," he said, handing me a bundled up dress and a towel. "And here, use this to dry off your hair."

I smiled wryly. I was sick of wearing someone else's dresses. "Thank you," I said as I took them, looking for somewhere private.

"You can change in my bedroom. I'll wait out here."

Nodding, I did as he said, closing the door behind me and peeling off my soaked dress. I used the towel to dry myself off as much as possible before unraveling the new dress. It was beautiful. Pure black and floor-length with long sleeves made of scalloped lace. The bodice was a corset with a built-in bra and boning, also made of lace, but embroidered with black beads in swirling patterns. I almost didn't want to put it on. It looked expensive. But I also didn't want to stand around in a strange man's home nearly naked, so I stepped into it. Strangely, it fit me perfectly. It clung to me like a second skin, not the slightest bit too big or too small.

I tried to comb through my hair with my fingers, but gave up, picking up my shoes and returning to the adjoining room.

Kayn was shirtless now, drying his hair with a towel, muscles rippling as he moved. His head tilted toward me as he heard me approach, his eyes raking over my body. A hint of a smile crossed his face. "Perfect fit."

I tried not to feel self-conscious. "Is this dress yours?"

"It was a gift for Evangeline," he said, tossing his towel onto a small table, picking up a dry shirt, and pulling it over his head. "It's fine, though. I can buy her something else. That looks like it was made for you, anyway."

"Is she your ex-lover or something?"

Kayn frowned. "We have never been in a relationship, although I have admired her since we were teenagers."

"Has she ever had feelings for you?" I asked, feeling awkward. I didn't know how I was supposed to help someone with an unrequited love.

"Yes," he said, his jaw flexing. "Until he came along."

"Who's he?"

"Verofer. The one she is supposed to marry. But I plan to stop it. No matter what."

Any doubt that Kayn was not a participant in the labyrinth disappeared. I recognized the pattern now. Wanting something so desperately but going about it the wrong way. I needed to guide him on the right path for him to succeed.

Unless...

My pulse quickened, remembering my earlier threat to the shadows. If I sabotaged this challenge, would I return to Enver? Although Isla's failure hadn't caused me to fail, her challenge hadn't been my final one. Kayn's *was*.

Which meant there was a chance I would return to Enver if I ruined this.

"How can I help?" I asked.

Kayn folded his arms over his chest, regarding me with a suspicious expression. "Who are you to want to help me?"

"It's what I'm here to do," I told him.

"What do you get out of it?"

My heart skipped a beat. "What I want."

It was what I wanted. Enver was what I wanted. I was sure of it. He believed I would regret it if I stayed with him, but I knew I wouldn't. I would regret not trying to get back to him. I would regret not being by his side. Not being his.

But... failing also meant dooming Kayn to an eternity of being Enver's servant. Could I do that to him? Condemn him to something I was so afraid of? Just so I could be with Enver?

"For some reason, I believe you," Kayn said, relaxing his

posture, unaware I was plotting his demise. "Fine. There is something you can do for me."

I pushed away any guilt that tried to settle into me. "What is it?"

"I need your help in getting Evie away from under her father's watch," he said. "The wedding is supposed to be in a few days. A ball is being held tonight to celebrate the *auspicious* couple." He spat out the word auspicious like an insult and began pacing the wooden floor. "It will be crowded and the perfect chance for me to try to convince her not to marry Verofer one last time."

"And if she still insists on getting married?"

A flicker of anger crossed his expression, but he quickly schooled it. "Then there is nothing more I can do. I will fall back and stay silent. All I want is Evie's happiness. I have to try to protect it."

Sympathy flooded me, and the self-reproach I felt at what I planned to do grew heavier. He seemed to really care about Evangeline. Enough to give her up if it meant she would be happy. I swallowed, thinking of Enver. Was that how he felt about me? Was that why he pushed me to complete the labyrinth and escape? Did he truly believe my leaving would lead me to happiness?

Tension laced the slope of Kayn's shoulders, making his movements stiff. I reached out and touched his hand softly. "I'll help you. Don't give up. She might see reason yet."

Kayn went still, his gaze shooting to where we touched and then to my face, the intensity in his eyes causing me to draw my hand back. Before I could open my mouth to apologize, he gave me a curt nod. "Thank you. Then we must fix your hair. I believe I have some makeup around, too, if you want it. Evie tends to leave her belongings wherever she flits about."

"You want me to go to the ball?"

"Yes. You will attend as my guest."

I blinked. "What if that gives Evangeline the wrong idea about us?"

"Perhaps a little jealousy will help move things along," Kayn said with a smirk. "Besides, this is a good way for you to get close to her without arousing suspicion. She'll be curious who my guest is."

"Okay," I agreed, grimacing inwardly. Aki's ball hadn't left the greatest taste in my mouth about them.

And Enver's...

I didn't think anything could compare to his.

"Come," Kayn ordered, crooking a finger at me. "You will already stand out with that odd hair color, but let's make sure you don't stand out because you still look half-drowned."

"Right..."

I followed Kayn back into his room, allowing him to sit me in front of a desk with a mirror. I stared at my reflection and had to agree I looked drowned. My eyes were still red-rimmed from crying, my hair was lifeless and damp, and my skin was devoid of color. Kayn dug through a dresser drawer before pulling out a comb and ribbon.

I stayed silent as he manipulated my hair into a bun, pulling out some strands to frame my face, and then tied it in place with a ribbon. "How did you do that so easily?" I asked, surprised.

He pointed to his own hair. "Experience. And Evangeline used to make me do her hair all the time when we were younger."

I smiled. "Her own personal stylist."

Kayn chuckled. "You could call it that. I'd say more like her manservant. Now, I believe I have some rouge. It should add a little color to your face. One moment."

I had no idea what that was, so I nodded as he disappeared and returned with a small pot. I sat still as he applied a red shade to my lips and then applied some to my cheeks with a lighter hand. "Did you also do her makeup?" I asked when he finished, admiring how the makeup *did* bring back some color to my face. I looked way more put together. More than I had since the night at the club.

The thought made me a little mortified. Enver had basically only ever seen me at my worst—no makeup on, messy hair barely combed through with my fingers, dark circles under my eyes, dry skin...

Yet he still thought I was beautiful? Was he blind?

"I did anything and everything she asked for," Kayn said, interrupting my spiraling thoughts. "I still would. I can never say no to her."

The amount of devotion in his voice struck me. "You really love her," I said quietly.

"I do," he confirmed. "I love her."

My throat grew tight. To have someone say so confidently that they loved her... Evangeline was lucky. She had what I could only yearn for.

Kayn checked the time on a pocket watch, and then helped me stand up. "It's about time we head out. Do you remember where I found you? The gazebo in the gardens? That's where I want you to bring Evie. I'll show you which door to take that will lead to it once we're in the ballroom. It will lead you right to it."

"What if she doesn't want to come with me?" I asked, suddenly nervous.

Kayn walked over to his wardrobe, shrugged on a black vest, and donned a black suit jacket. "She'll go with you. Trust me. Just tell her I want to talk to her. And don't tell anyone else. I don't want the chance that her father will overhear. Let the ball get into full swing before you attempt to get her outside. She'll have lots of attention on her in the beginning."

"Okay," I responded.

"Shall we go, then?"

I nodded, and he led the way. The rain had stopped, and the clouds had parted, allowing the moon to light up the way to the castle. We entered through a side entrance, and I could immediately hear the murmurs of voices, faint laughter, and the muffled sound of an orchestra playing. Kayn offered me his arm, and I slipped mine through his as we climbed up a stairwell and entered a hallway where a handful of people were chatting, all dressed elegantly.

They all turned to look at Kayn as we passed by, their reactions all differing, but all overwhelmingly negative. Some scowled, some moved back as if to keep as much space between us and them as possible, others shot dirty looks, and one even openly scoffed and turned his head away, muttering something I couldn't quite catch, but sounded like *traitor*.

I frowned, glancing back, but Kayn shook his head. His lips pressed into a thin line, but he said nothing. The music got louder as we approached a set of double doors. Two guards stood on either side, and they opened the doors for us as we approached.

A rush of voices and violins filled the air, and the sight of dozens of people greeted us. My eyes widened in awe at the elegance and size of the ballroom. Large stained-glass windows lined the walls, crystal chandeliers hung from the ceiling, and gold filigree decorated every inch of space between. One side held an expanse of delicious looking food, and the other sat a string quartet, playing a cheerful waltz.

A hush fell over the guests closest to us, their gazes darting between Kayn and myself. Kayn stared straight ahead as he strode past them, his grip on me tightening as whispers erupted around us. My stomach twisted as the guests parted for us as we walked, with one woman almost tripping over herself to get out of the way.

"There's Evie," Kayn said, nodding toward a raised dais.

My heart skipped a beat as my gaze landed on Evangeline—

the same woman I'd crashed into in Enver's castle. Except now, she had long hair and wore an elegant ballgown, exactly as the statue in Enver's garden depicted. Now, there was no doubt. Why was she here, though? What connection did she have with Enver's castle?

Evangeline was laughing at something someone said, her melodic voice cutting through the noise of the crowd. Long black hair fell halfway down her back, contrasting against the white dress she wore. She had a golden complexion, her cheekbones high, her lips full, curved up into a beautiful smile.

Next to her, a man sat on a throne on the dais. His eyes narrowed as he stared into the crowd, a tight frown on his lips. He shared the same skin tone as Evangeline, although his black hair was cut short and haphazardly styled up and out of his face.

A muscle jumped into Kayn's jaw as he glowered at the man. I didn't need to ask to know it was Verofer—Evangeline's betrothed.

I didn't want to make assumptions based on first glances, but I could see where Kayn was concerned. Not once did Verofer look at Evangeline as she chatted animatedly to the crowd around them. Even when she tapped him on the shoulder, as if asking him to partake in conversation, he simply brushed her off, turning his head.

"She's beautiful," I said, when I found my voice again.

"She is much more than that," Kayn murmured. "Much more."

As if hearing Kayn speak, Evangeline's attention turned toward us. Confusion clouded her expression as she took in our entwined arms, her body going still. He pulled me closer in response, his arm sliding around my waist.

Evangeline's eyes widened and then met mine. I forced my lips into a flustered smile, which she returned with a tight one after a moment. She nodded toward me in greeting before returning to the discussion around her, though her smile faded completely.

I immediately felt like an asshole. I pulled my arm free from Kayn. "Maybe this isn't a good idea. She already seems hurt—"

"No," Kayn interjected firmly, taking my hand and pulling me away from the crowd. "We continue with my plan. This is my last chance."

"But—"

"Did you not say you also get something out of helping me?" Kayn asked, his expression darkening as his hand slid up to grip my biceps. "Does that not matter anymore?"

I hesitated, lowering my head. Kayn's life wasn't the only life I would ruin if I went through with this. If I trapped Kayn in Enver's labyrinth, he and Evangeline would lose each other forever. Maybe Evangeline was trapped in Enver's castle right now because Kayn hadn't completed his labyrinth yet. Maybe their challenges were tied together like Rielle's and Silas's. I would be taking away their chance at love for my own selfish reasons.

I'd been brought to the labyrinth because I desperately wanted to be loved. Could I really destroy someone else's chance at it? When it was within reach for them? When it could never be in reach for me? And even if I succeeded in my plan of failing my challenge, could I live with the knowledge of what I'd done to Kayn and Evangeline? Watching Kayn and Evangeline roam around Enver's castle mindless and empty for the rest of eternity? What would Enver think? After realizing what I had done to be with him? He'd wanted me to leave. To be happy. To have a chance at the love I wanted so badly. Would this be a betrayal to him, too?

I knew the answers to my questions, even if I refused to admit them. I wouldn't sacrifice another person's happiness for my own. I couldn't do it, not even for Enver. Even if it meant losing him.

I didn't realize a tear had spilled down my cheek until Kayn brought up a hand to wipe it away. "I'm sorry. I let my emotions get the best of me just now. I shouldn't have snapped at you," he said.

"It's okay," I said, taking a shaky breath. "I'll still help you. The plan is still the same, right?"

He nodded. "Yes. Approach her in about an hour. Take that door to the side there, and it will lead out to the gardens."

"Okay," I replied, looking at the door he pointed at.

"I need to prepare some things, so I will meet you out there."

"You're leaving me?" I asked, my eyes widening. I grabbed his wrist as he turned to walk away. "Wait!"

He raised an eyebrow. "You can handle yourself for an hour, can't you?"

"I... I guess."

"I am sure there will be many suitors to keep you occupied," he said, giving me a brief smirk. "You're quite eye-catching. Especially since you arrived with me."

I let him go but felt no more confident. "Okay."

"Thank you, by the way," he said. "There would have been no one else I could trust for this task. You have made this so much easier."

I frowned after him as he disappeared back into the crowd that still scattered around him. I wasn't sure he'd be thanking me if he knew what I'd initially planned to do to him.

My heart clenched.

I didn't want to think about that now. I needed to focus on ensuring that Kayn and Evangeline got their happily ever after.

I pushed all thoughts from my head, focusing on people watching. Contrary to Kayn's prediction, no one came up to me. People stared—they definitely stared. And whispered. I felt self-conscious and fought the urge to hide behind something.

Every so often, I glanced back at Evangeline, finding her

and Verofer still on the dais. The people around them changed intermittently until only a few remained. Verofer barely interacted with anyone the entire time, ignoring Evangeline, and appearing more annoyed by each passing minute. I eventually had to turn away from them, irritation making me grit my teeth. How could someone ignore their fiancée like that? Why did her father defend a man like that? Did he not see how much he seemed to be annoyed by her presence?

I wasn't sure how much time passed, but I was starting to get antsy when a soft hand landed on my shoulder. I jumped, startled, turning to find Evangeline. Up close, I realized she was a bit taller than me, her skin flawless and dewy. She smiled at me. "Hello. You are Kayn's guest, right?"

"Um, yes," I said, stepping back and holding my hand out. "I'm Nell."

"Evangeline," she responded, ignoring my hand and curtseying.

Oh. Right. I awkwardly curtseyed back. "It's nice to meet you."

"You as well," she said, her smile faltering. "I'd actually like to discuss something with you if you don't mind."

I stared at her, wondering if she would ask about Kayn and me. He hadn't told me what to tell her if she did. "Oh, sure," I said, trying to think of a lie.

"I'd like to go somewhere more private. Let us step outside."

"How about the gazebo in the gardens?" I suggested, realizing this could make my job of getting her outside easier.

She considered it, then nodded. "Yes, that'll do well. Come on, before I get dragged into more soul-leeching conversation."

I followed her to the door that led out to the gazebo, and she glanced around to ensure no one was looking before slipping through it. Her pace was quick as we made our way through the castle halls to an open-air walkway that spilled us out into the garden. Clouds had covered the moon again, but she held out her hand, conjuring a small ball of light, just as Kayn had done earlier.

"Don't tell anyone," she said, giving me a half-smile. "My father would have me imprisoned."

"For magic?" I asked, assuming that was what the light was.

She gave me a quizzical look. "Yes?"

I held my tongue. Was it banned here or something? "What did you want to ask me about?" I asked, trying to change the subject.

Her expression turned uneasy. "About Kayn. I've never seen you before, and I've known Kayn for almost my entire life. How did you two meet?"

"We met just recently," I lied, as we grew closer to the gazebo. "At the, uh, tailor." They had tailors here, right? I hoped so.

"You're not from around here, are you?" Evangeline asked, coming to a stop. Her eyes widened, concern filling them. "You don't know..."

I also froze, staring back at her. How had she caught on so quickly? "Don't know what?"

"You have to leave this place," she said, her voice dropping into a hushed whisper as she grabbed my hand. "Leave now. Don't come back. I don't know what he wants with you, but you need to go."

Her reaction caused my heart to race in my chest. She pulled me toward the gazebo, and my stomach sank. Something wasn't right. "Wait—"

A shape moved in the darkness, and then Kayn appeared in front of us. Evangeline pulled up short, a gasp escaping her. She fell back, nearly bumping into me. "Kayn? What are you doing out here? You should be inside."

Kayn didn't move, his face impassive. "You have left me no choice, Evie."

Evangeline held onto me tighter, her hand trembling. "What are you talking about?"

"I cannot allow you to marry Verofer. I won't let him take you away from me. If you won't believe he's a danger to you, then I have to do something to protect you from him."

"He's not a danger," Evangeline said, her voice rising. "If anyone is a danger to me, it's you!"

Fury filled Kayn's face, and he shot forward. I quickly put myself between him and Evangeline, my heart in my throat. "Kayn, wait, what are you doing?" I demanded. "This was your plan? To intimidate her?"

"You've played your part. Now step aside," he snapped.

I tried not to flinch. "No, listen to me, whatever you're thinking isn't the right way to—"

Kayn's hand darted out, grabbing my arm and jerking me forward before shoving me roughly to the side. I hit the wet stones of the path, barely catching myself on my palms and narrowly avoiding a head injury, momentarily shocked by his violent reaction.

"Kayn, leave her out of this," Evangeline said as he stalked toward her, holding her ground despite her quaking voice. "This is between us."

"Is your decision final?" Kayn asked her. "Are you really going to marry him?"

"Yes. I am. I love him," Evangeline whispered back, turning her head away from Kayn. "You have to accept that."

Kayn shook his head. "No. I don't. I won't."

I pushed myself back up to my feet, the split skin on my palms burning. Kayn turned toward me, his face hard. Without warning, he lunged. But not at Evangeline. At me. He grabbed my arm again and bent it painfully behind my back, immobilizing me as he moved behind me. The feeling of a cool blade against my neck for the second time in my life made me freeze.

"Kayn, what are you doing?" Evangeline asked, her hand shooting over her mouth.

"Anything I have to," he answered, his voice tight. "I know you, Evie. You won't let me hurt her. Even though she's the one who led you out here."

"Kayn, please. Stop this."

"Take this," he ordered, holding his free hand to her. A small vial of liquid sat in his palm. "Drink it."

Evangeline didn't move, her eyes trained on the vial. I winced as Kayn pushed the dagger deeper into my skin. "Don't," I told her, trying to stay calm. "Kayn, you can't do this. You won't get what you want this way."

Kayn scoffed. "No, I will get *everything* I want this way. Trust me. I've had this planned for a while now. And I won't let you stop me. Take it, Evie. Drink it."

"What is it?" she asked, and the ball of magic in her hand flickered.

"Something to prevent you from running away. It's only temporary, and it won't hurt you."

Evangeline looked between me and the vial. "I..."

"Don't," I repeated, hissing in pain as he dug the dagger far enough into my skin to spill blood.

Evangeline lurched forward, taking the vial from Kayn. "Fine," she said. "I'll drink it. But let her go."

"I will. After you swallow every drop," Kayn promised, and then his tone softened. "It won't have any lasting effects. I promise. Nothing that happens to you tonight will. I don't want to hurt you."

Evangeline's eyes blazed with anger as she ripped out the cork and poured the liquid down her throat. Ice flooded my veins as she finished, then held the empty vial back out to Kayn. "There," she said, glaring at him. "Now release her."

The dagger disappeared from my throat, along with his hold on me. "Good," Kayn praised, moving closer to take the empty vial from her, only to throw it to the ground, letting the glass shatter by her feet. "Now continue to be compliant for me. He should be here any moment."

She stared at him, and the clouds parted enough to let the moonlight through, allowing me to see the fear blossoming on her face and the tears in her eyes. "No—" Her protest was cut off as she coughed, swaying on her feet, reaching out to Kayn for support. "You said you wouldn't hurt anyone," she rasped.

"I said I wouldn't hurt *her*," he responded, holding Evangeline steady. "You'll never love me as long as Verofer is around. I have to get rid of him."

Blood rushed through my ears as Evangeline gasped for breath, her body crumpling into Kayn's arms. I had to do something. I had to stop this.

But if I don't, I'll fail.

For a second, all I could hear was my heartbeat. If I failed, I could be with Enver.

All I had to do was not intervene.

"No," Evangeline whimpered, clinging weakly to Kayn. "Don't, Kayn, please. Leave him alone. Please. I'll come with you. Don't hurt Verofer."

"It's too late for that," Kayn said. "You should have listened to me a long time ago. Then I wouldn't have been driven to this."

"Please," Evangeline whispered, and her desperation struck me.

No. I couldn't fail. I couldn't stand here and let this happen.

Before I could do anything, though, Kayn brought up the dagger and plunged it into Evangeline's chest. She jerked in his grasp, a low moan escaping her lips as I stood there, stunned. Blood poured out from the wound, and the sight of crimson finally launched me into action. I shot forward, intent on stopping him, but I'd barely taken three steps when the light in Evangeline's palm went out, and darkness blanketed us again.

I looked again. No. It didn't go out. Something smothered it. Extinguished the light from the moon, too. A thick, physical presence. One with a chill that I recognized.

"Let her go."

The familiar voice made my heart stop. Made the world seem slow as the darkness parted again and the source of the shadows appeared, materializing out of the night itself.

Enver.

His eyes were sharp, filled with fury, his expression deadly.

I opened my mouth to call for him, relief flooding through me, when Evangeline's weak voice rang out first. "Verofer."

27

Dizzying apprehension washed over me at Evangeline's words. *Verofer?*

"I will not tell you again," Enver spoke, his voice laced with malice, his shadows rising around him. "Release Evangeline. Now."

My hands shook, my stomach twisting at the revelation. *No.* Enver couldn't be Verofer. Verofer had been the man sitting on the dais, hadn't he? Did Enver have a twin that he couldn't remember? It had to be that. This couldn't be Enver... but then why did he look and sound exactly like him? How could he control shadows like Enver did? Why, despite trying to convince myself it wasn't him, did I instinctively know it was?

I had to be in Enver's past. Isla had mentioned that nobody knew Enver's real name and that he never introduced himself to any of the labyrinth participants by it. I thought she'd meant he simply never revealed his name to anyone. Not that no one knew him by the name of *Enver*.

It hit me then. The statue of Evangeline in his garden. The unexplained warmth he felt around it. The dresses that filled his wardrobe. The way they fit me perfectly—like the one I wore now, despite it being bought for her.

The world seemed to tilt under my feet.

I once wondered how Enver had become such a skilled lover. Suspected that he must have had a partner before. Now I knew that person was Evangeline. She was the one he'd forgotten when he'd lost his emotions and memories. But she was more than just his lover—Kayn had said Evangeline was set to marry Verofer.

Evangeline was Enver's *fiancée*.

The thought had me taking in a shaky breath, my body trembling as a deep cold settled into my veins. The familiarity he'd said he felt with me that he couldn't explain, the way he believed he instinctively belonged to me and I to him, and the warmth he said I gave him...

They were echoes of what he must have felt for Evangeline.

He didn't belong to me. He belonged to her.

"*Shadowspawn*?" Kayn said, his tone caught between disbelief and anger, causing me to pull myself from my thoughts. His eyes narrowed at the shadows writhing in the air as he held Evangeline's limp body against his chest. "I knew you were hiding something. How is this possible? Your kind was destroyed."

"You will find out firsthand what it means to be destroyed, if you do not release her," Enver threatened, his shadows growing.

"Does she know what you are, monster?" Kayn asked, a sneer on his lips. "Does she know about the darkness that fills your veins? Does she know what will happen if you lose control of it?"

Enver's silence caused Kayn to bark out a bitter laugh.

"She doesn't know," he concluded. "What do you think would happen if she found out? Do you think she would love you? Do you think Solomon would still accept you? No. He would kill you within a heartbeat. You are nothing more than an abomination. A monster that has no place in our kingdom. You should be dead."

Enver took a step forward, his gaze turning murderous. "You know so much about me yet still dare to provoke me? You seem to have a death wish. One I will happily grant for you. Release her or die."

"You want her? Be my guest," Kayn said, shoving Evangeline toward Enver roughly.

Enver caught her as she pitched forward, his arms circling her waist, holding her tightly to him. He lowered himself onto one knee, keeping Evangeline in his hold, moving with gentle caution as he checked her over. "Evangeline," he said softly, as if afraid his voice would wound her further.

Seeing him hold her so tenderly made my heart stop and something inside me splinter. He delicately brushed strands of hair away from her face, his fingertips tracing her cheek, the curve of her jaw. His gaze was gentle and full of something I'd never seen from him before.

Love.

It was full of love.

Evangeline stirred in his arms, moaning softly as her eyes fluttered open. "Verofer," she whispered, her voice barely audible as she tried to raise a shaking hand to his face. His lips parted as he leaned into her touch. "You need to... get out of... here."

He shook his head. "No, Evangeline—"

"Please, I..." she broke into a harsh coughing fit, her hand falling to her side as she went limp in his arms again.

Enver swore under his breath, readjusting her in his arms, keeping her head supported with his hand. "What have you done to her?" Enver asked, his anger barely restrained.

"I would be more worried about yourself if I were you,"

Kayn said. "I wonder what Solomon will do to you when he realizes you're Shadowspawn. Although it will probably pale in comparison to what he'll do to you for killing his daughter."

Enver's gaze narrowed, the muscles in his jaw clenching. "Killing?" He glanced down at Evangeline again, his free hand quickly moving to her neck, checking her pulse. His body tensed, and he picked up her wrist, checking there as well. "Evangeline? Evangeline!" He turned back to Kayn, his face contorting into a snarl. "*What did you do to her*?"

Suddenly, the shadows surged again, exploding outward. I flinched as they slammed into Kayn, sending him crashing against the gazebo. The force caused one of the stone pillars to crack. "I take it she's dead already?" Kayn asked as he grinned over at Enver, his breathing labored. "That was fast."

Dead? He'd killed her? That wasn't possible. Evangeline was at Enver's castle, one of the labyrinth's many servants. She couldn't be dead. Kayn had to be lying.

Wind rushed by me as shadows struck Kayn again, slamming him into the ground. He groaned, his bottom lip splitting, blood pouring out as he pushed himself up. "You know, it's your fault it had to be like this," he spat at Enver. "I told you to leave her. You refused to listen. I warned you."

I turned back to Enver, opening my mouth to tell him Kayn was lying, but my voice died in my throat. He still held Evangeline in his arms, his entire body shaking, his face twisting with agony as he cupped her face. "No. *No.* Evangeline. Wake up," he urged.

The sight of him cradling her lifeless body tore at my heart, the desperation in his expression shredding it apart further. But before I could do anything, Kayn shifted, drawing my attention back to him. He brought back the dagger he'd used to stab Evangeline, aiming it at Enver. "Enver!" I cried out in warning.

Enver's head snapped toward me at the sound of his name, and as our eyes locked together for the first time, he inhaled sharply. His dark gaze bore into mine, the familiar intensity of it searing through me, causing a painful longing to rise in my chest. His brow creased, a myriad of emotions flickering through his expression. Confusion. Shock. Realization. Anger. But there was something else there, too, something that made my heart race even faster—recognition.

Every instinct inside me urged me to go to him, but as I stepped toward him, he held onto Evangeline tighter, his knuckles turning white. He searched my face, the unease in his expression morphing into something stricken, his voice strained as he spoke. "You—"

Kayn launched the dagger at Enver, making me jolt forward, my body moving before my mind, instinctively moving to protect him. Enver's gaze never left mine as his hand shot out and caught the dagger effortlessly, rotating it to reposition it better in his hand, gripping the hilt firmly.

"Who are you?" he demanded, curling Evangeline into him with his other arm as if protecting her from me, too.

The question and his actions made me stop in my tracks, my throat tight.

I was wrong. He didn't recognize me.

"Do you have time to get distracted?" Kayn asked Enver casually. "The poison will kill her unless I give her the antidote. We don't have much time to heal her wounds, either."

Enver dragged his attention from me, glaring at Kayn as he rose to his feet. He lifted Evangeline with him, his hold on her still delicate. His shadows pulsed in the air, his rage palpable. "You poisoned her?"

"Yes, so make your next decisions wisely."

"What is it you want?"

"I want you gone," Kayn said simply. "Solomon will arrive soon. You will admit to attempting to murder Evie. Then you will rot in prison. Once that is done, I will feed her the antidote and tend to her wounds. I won't even mention the fact you're Shadowspawn."

Enver's nostrils flared. "She trusted you. She cared for you. And you harmed her to this extent? Just to rid her of me?"

"You left me with no choice," Kayn reminded him harshly. "I told you to leave her. You chose not to listen to me. I won't let a monster be with Evie."

"I will kill you," Enver said, his voice dropping dangerously. "I promise you that. I will end your miserable existence for daring to harm her."

"Ah, I don't think so. I have the antidote, remember? It's not on me, either, nor would you find it in time if you tried. If you kill me, then Evie will die as well."

Pure hatred laced Enver's features at Kayn's threat. "This will not make her love you."

"It will be enough for me to know she will never be with you," Kayn replied. "But since you seem interested, who knows what will happen in our future? Perhaps Solomon will grant me her hand in marriage in return for protecting her from you. A monster like you could never deserve Evie."

I turned toward Kayn, anger coursing through me, my fingers curling into fists. I tried to reel it in, knowing I only had a limited amount of time to get him to change his mind. I couldn't afford to antagonize him. "Kayn, this isn't going to get you what you want," I said, gaining his attention.

He spared me a glance. "This again? I already told you it is."

"No, it's not," I said. "What did you want from the labyrinth? Evangeline? Doing this will only make you fail! It won't make her love you. You'll lose her forever if you go through with this."

Kayn rounded on me, and I faltered back a step as he strode toward me. "What do you know? I suggest you keep your mouth shut before I decide to silence you myself. You have nothing to do with this."

Shadows rose between us, preventing him from getting any closer to me. "Stay away from her," Enver warned.

Kayn scowled. "Why are you protecting her? She lured Evie out here for me. You'd protect her even though she's the reason your fiancée is dying in your arms?"

My heart dropped. "No, I—"

"She's been helping me all this time," Kayn continued.

I didn't dare look at Enver for fear of what I'd see on his face. "Kayn, stop this," I tried again. "Listen to me. You will fail if you go through with this. You'll be trapped in the labyrinth—"

"What are you talking about?" Kayn snapped, and the shadows lurched toward him threateningly. "You keep mentioning a labyrinth. What does that have to do with me?"

I stared at him, unable to find my voice for a moment. "What? You're doing the labyrinth, aren't you?"

"Take a look around you," he said, throwing out his arm. "Do you see a labyrinth anywhere? Have you lost your mind?"

"No, that's..." I trailed off, my eyes widening. If it wasn't Kayn doing the labyrinth, then who was?

The sound of shouting voices and approaching footsteps filled the air. I turned toward the source of the noise and saw a group of people moving toward us, torches in some of their hands, flames billowing in the wind. My stomach lurched, and I turned back to Enver, who was still glowering at Kayn.

Kayn smirked, giving Enver a self-satisfied look. "Here they come. Remember, choose wisely. Admit to your crimes, and I'll give her the antidote. Don't, and Evangeline dies. And as for you?" Kayn shrugged at me. "Sorry, but you're of no more use to me. I sincerely hope you led a fulfilling life up to this point. I don't think Solomon will let you go."

"Enver, don't do this," I said, ignoring Kayn, my mind scrambling to come up with a solution as I turned toward Enver. "There has to be another way—"

Our gazes met again, and for a moment, his expression softened, causing my breath to hitch. He was looking at me like he did in the future. Not as a stranger, but as someone more profound. As a lover. His eyes were full of warmth and longing and...

"I am sorry," he whispered.

"Enver—" I started, but his shadows shot toward me without warning. Not expecting it, I plunged backward, tumbling into the garden hedge. The shadows twisted around me, holding me still and sliding over my mouth to prevent me from crying out or speaking.

"Even after knowing the truth, you still protect her," Kayn mused. "How noble. Well, it doesn't matter to me. Nothing she could say would save you."

I struggled against the shadows but found I couldn't move, couldn't make a sound. As the gathering of people grew closer, one figure broke out and rushed ahead, dark hair flying out behind her. "Evangeline!" she screamed, and the familiarity in her voice made my heart sink.

Isla.

It was Isla running at Enver and a lifeless Evangeline.

He took the heart of someone he should have never touched in the first place.

Do you know what happened to his first love? He killed her!

I went completely still, terror dawning. It all made sense now. It was never a physical heart she'd been referring to.

And I knew exactly what was going to happen now. Why she would come to believe Enver had killed Evangeline.

But Enver didn't.

I screamed into the shadows, fighting against them with all my strength, desperate to get them to release me. I needed to stop this. I needed to save Enver. If I could, then he wouldn't be cursed. He wouldn't lose his memories or emotions. He wouldn't be trapped. He wouldn't be alone anymore.

He wouldn't be with you, my mind whispered.

A lump rose in my throat, but I pushed it back. I didn't care. I didn't want his love at the cost of his suffering.

"What have you done?" Isla cried shrilly, running up to them, coming to a dead stop as she noticed the blood staining Enver's clothing and dripping to the ground. "Oh, gods—Evangeline! Let go of her, you monster!"

Enver stood stiffly, not reacting to Isla, turning Evangeline away as Isla tried to touch her.

The shadows muffled my cries as I tried to call out, my muscles burning as I fought against the bindings that kept me hidden and silent.

The rest of the group arrived, and Kayn put on a show, dropping onto the ground on one knee, coughing hard. "Solomon, hurry, please. There's something wrong with Evie!"

An older man stepped up to Enver. Tall and intimidating, his dark hair was streaked with grey, and a silver crown sat on his head. His eyes widened at the sight of Evangeline, and he rushed forward, closing the distance between them. "Evangeline!"

Enver still didn't say anything, remaining silent and motionless, clutching Evangeline to his chest.

"What have you done to my daughter?" Solomon seethed, reaching for Evangeline, but Enver didn't budge, refusing to hand her over. Solomon reacted immediately. He struck his hand out, striking Enver across the face. "Release her, *now!*"

Finally, Enver relented, allowing another man who moved forward to remove Evangeline from his grasp. But his hands remained in the same position, as though he were still holding her, his gaze fixed on her limp body. The man who took Evangeline knelt on the ground, laying her on a patch of grass, and two others dropped beside her to check on her.

"I attempted to end her life," Enver said, his expression

devoid of emotion, his voice detached. "She asked to call off our marriage, and I retaliated."

No! I tried to scream, tears welling up in my eyes, my throat aching.

Solomon recoiled, but before he could say anything, Isla screamed, drawing my attention to her. She knelt beside Evangeline, her hand on her wrist, her eyes wild. "She has no pulse! Solomon!"

A smirk flashed across Kayn's face, and I realized he'd planned this, too—for someone to notice that she didn't have a pulse. He didn't want Solomon to believe Enver had attempted to kill his daughter. He wanted Solomon to believe Enver *had* killed his daughter.

And Enver wasn't going to correct him.

He was going to sacrifice himself for Evangeline.

Solomon brushed past Enver, crouching beside Evangeline, shoving the other people surrounding her away, checking her pulse for himself. Kayn staggered toward them, the blood and bruises on his face adding to his performance. "Evie, no, she can't be," Kayn gasped, falling to his knees beside them and touching Evangeline's face. "Evie, no." His voice cracked, and he turned toward Solomon with tears in his eyes. "He has magic, Solomon. Shadows. He killed her..."

"Evangeline," Solomon said, his voice hoarse. "This can't be."

"Solomon, he is Shadowspawn!" Kayn cried. "He used shadows to kill her. I saw it happen. I couldn't stop him."

Solomon went deathly still for a moment, but within the blink of an eye, he was on his feet again in front of Enver, gripping Enver's shirt tightly. "Is this true?"

"Yes," Enver said, still staring at Evangeline.

Tears streamed down my cheeks, my chest hurting so much I struggled to breathe. I kept fighting against the shadows, but I already knew it was too late. It'd been too late from the second

Kayn threatened Enver with Evangeline's life. There was nothing I could do.

Rage swept across Solomon's face at Enver's admission. "Did you believe you would get away with this, that you could get away with murdering my daughter, you vile creature? I trusted you to care for her and protect her, and you betrayed her in the worst way. You deserve a fate worse than death."

Enver didn't react. Didn't try to defend himself. Didn't try to stop what was about to happen. Only looked at Evangeline.

I thrashed against the shadows, my tears blurring my vision. *No. No!*

"You took everything from her," Solomon said, his voice raw with pain and anger, raising his hand, a light forming in his palm. "You took her happiness. Her future. Her past."

Enver's hands clenched into fists.

"You stole her heart."

My breath hitched, and I tried to get myself to close my eyes, to not have to witness what would happen next, but I couldn't. I stared, going still, watching as Solomon's magic grew brighter.

"I will take everything from you," Solomon vowed, his expression darkening.

Suddenly, Enver's gaze lifted, finding mine through the darkness. The light from Solomon's hand revealed the pain etched into his face and the wetness in his eyes.

His lips moved, barely noticeable.

Save her.

Then Solomon thrust his hand into Enver's chest.

Enver jolted, a blinding flash of light filling the air, making me snap my eyes shut. The shadows disappeared and I collapsed into the dirt, blinking the lingering white spots away. I looked back at Enver and Solomon, seeing Solomon pull his hand free of Enver's chest, a dark, shadowy object in his grasp.

It pulsed in his hold, tendrils creeping out of it and curling around Solomon's wrist.

Enver's heart.

"I will make sure you never speak her name again," Solomon said. "Never remember the warmth of her love. Never recall the light she brought to your life. Never feel anything ever again—the same fate you have condemned her to."

Enver collapsed to his knees, his hand going to the gaping hole in his chest. Blood coated his torso and hand, flowing in torrents to the ground.

"I will not let you die," Solomon continued, using his free hand to fist it in Enver's hair and turn Enver's head up toward him. "You will suffer for all of eternity in a prison of my creation. Alone. Until you lose all sense of time and self. Until you beg for a death that will not come."

It took everything in me to remain still and not run to Enver. If I did, him protecting me would have been in vain. I needed to stay hidden and silent.

A trickle of blood spilled from the corner of Enver's mouth.

"You will never harm anyone again, Shadowspawn," Solomon snarled, his hand going from Enver's hair to his throat, squeezing it. "I should have turned you away the moment Evangeline brought you into our lives. I should have never considered you my family. I will regret that until the day I die. She deserved so much more than this. Than you. A monster wearing the skin of a fae. You will suffer your fate where your kind suffered their own demise."

Enver said nothing, staring blankly ahead. When Solomon released him, he slumped forward, collapsing into the crimson-stained grass. Our gazes met, but his eyes were now vacant and devoid of life. As they closed, a single tear fell from his lashes.

My body moved before I could stop it, and I surged to my feet, but another flash of light blinded. I froze, blinking rapidly, my eyes readjusting to the night, only to find Enver gone, just a pool of his blood remaining.

Solomon's figure slumped to the ground beside Evangeline, sobs breaking the silence of the night. Isla wrapped her arms around him, crying as she repeated Evangeline's name over and over.

"My daughter, my Evangeline. My light," Solomon whispered, his hand cupping Evangeline's cheek.

Evangeline's body glowed faintly, and Isla gasped as Solomon brought the shadow heart to her chest. "What are you doing?" Isla demanded, whipping her head toward him.

"I'm hiding this somewhere he will never find it," Solomon responded as Enver's heart seemed to disappear into her chest, the light fading along with it.

"His heart doesn't deserve to be near her," Isla hissed, her shoulders shaking. "I will make him pay. I will kill him for taking her away from us. From me."

"There is no need for you to sully your hands, Isla. The curse has been placed. He will pay for what he has done for all of eternity."

Isla shook her head. "No. That's not enough."

I held my breath, waiting. Waiting for Kayn to give Evangeline the antidote. To save her. But he didn't. Instead, he stood above Solomon and Isla, a pleased expression growing on his face, letting them grieve over Evangeline's body. As if sensing my gaze, he looked directly at me, his lips curling into a triumphant smirk. He pressed a finger to them, warning me to stay silent.

My stomach churned. He wasn't planning on saving her. Not in front of them. Then what happened to Evangeline after this? How did she end up in the labyrinth? Kayn must have saved her at some point. Had he stolen her away from them under the guise that she'd been killed? Let Solomon believe his daughter was dead? Be the reason why Isla believed Enver had killed Evangeline?

No. I wouldn't let that happen. I could stop this, at the very least.

I launched myself out of the brush, and Kayn's eyes widened. Solomon turned toward me first, straightening out in alarm.

"He poisoned her—" I began, my voice a shrill cry, but shadows rose from the ground, slamming into my chest, cutting me off. I gasped, trying to push through them, but the world tilted as the shadows enveloped me, and I recognized the feeling of being transported as I fell backward.

28

Once on the other side of the portal, I hit the ground hard enough to knock the air from my lungs and make my ears ring. It took me a second to recover, the ringing gradually giving way to the faint sound of water trickling. My eyes shot open, seeing the night sky, now clear and decorated with stars instead of heavy clouds.

A sharp intake of breath came from my left, then the rustle of fabric, followed by a pained, guttural whisper.

"*No.*"

Enver.

"Nell, no," he breathed, the words choked and desperate.

I turned toward him as he staggered toward me. The heartbreak and despair in his voice was mirrored in his expression as he dropped to his knees beside me. His hands found my face, cupping my cheeks. They shook, as did the rest of his body. His touch was light, careful, as if he was afraid he would break me.

Like how he'd been with Evangeline.

I couldn't tear my gaze away from him. The memory of his heart being ripped out played over and over in my mind. The image of him lying in a puddle of his blood. His silence. His acceptance. Tears filled my eyes again as I reached my hands up and put them over his. "I'm sorry," I whispered.

Not for failing the labyrinth. But for the cruel fate he'd endured. The one I couldn't spare him from.

Our shadow rings eddied and tangled together, their tendrils twisting around our fingers as if trying to keep us close.

Enver's face crumpled, his forehead coming to mine, his breath shuddering. His fingers tightened around my face, his lips finding mine, pressing hard, his kiss tasting like my tears. I closed my eyes as his lips brushed over my cheeks, eyelids, and forehead, kissing away my tears and pain.

I let him, despite the ache in my chest, the knowledge I wasn't the one he longed for. It would be the last time. I would be selfish just for a moment longer. I would pretend he was mine, and I was his, and that we could have our happily ever after. That there was no curse, no labyrinth. Just us.

His lips left my skin, and I opened my eyes, not ready to let him go yet. He stared down at me, his thumbs tracing my cheeks as his jaw set. "I will not let this happen. I will not let you be trapped here with me. The labyrinth will not claim you."

"How long do we have?" I asked. "Before the labyrinth takes me?"

"Mere moments," he told me, "but do not worry. Our oath—"

"Let me have oblivion."

My request was composed. Soft.

His reaction was not.

He recoiled, his entire body stiffening. His lips parted, and his eyes flashed, hurt, denial, then anger swirling in their dark grey depths. "No," he said.

"Please," I whispered, knowing I was being selfish, but I didn't know if I could handle it—knowing that everything he felt toward me was mistaken. That what he felt drawn to was the reminder of Evangeline, not me. They loved each other, even if they could not remember.

"I said *no*."

He released my face, hands sliding behind my back and knees as he stood, lifting me with him. I swallowed, struggling to get out of his grasp. "Enver—"

"Do not ask this of me," he cut in, his voice hard. "I refuse to be the one who damns you to this fate."

"It's already too late!"

"We made an oath," he snapped, his voice rising with fury. But as our gazes met again, the anger flickered out, replaced by a haunted look that swept across his face. "You swore to become mine."

I shook my head, my chest tightening. "I'm not yours. I won't ever be yours. You—"

"Have I not suffered enough?" he asked, strained. "Have I not endured enough torment? I will not survive, Nell. I will not survive if I have to spend eternity with you within my reach yet forever out of my grasp."

"Enver, please."

"You will haunt me. Every second of every minute. Every hour of every day. Your warmth. Your scent. Your voice. The softness of your skin. The taste of your lips. The memories of you will drive me insane. And then when I inevitably break, I will come to you for comfort, only to be reminded of what I can never have again," he told me, his voice rough and anguished. "I will gaze upon your lifeless eyes and see them stripped of the warmth and light that once defined you. I will know your soul, once so radiant and beautiful, has faded into an unbearable nothingness. And I will forever be burdened with the suffocating weight of knowing it was all my fault. It will be agony beyond measure."

"Enver," I tried again.

"It will never end," he promised in a whisper. "I will have no reprieve. I will live my greatest fear every day for the rest of my existence. You may choose to forget me, but I will never forget you, my little lover."

My eyes grew wet again as he spoke the nickname he'd given me. It wasn't teasing this time. No, there was a deep, agonized sadness to it—a plea. Tears spilled down my cheeks, and Enver leaned down, once again kissing them away.

"Do not do this to me," he pleaded. "Do not let me fall further than I have. You can call me cruel. You can call me heartless. You can call me a monster. But do not ask this of me. You are my only solace, and you are asking me to ruin it. To ruin you. And I will not. I cannot."

My throat felt too tight to speak.

"I know I do not deserve this, but... *please*," Enver begged, and it was a ragged sound, tearing free of him. "Do not leave me. Please, stay here. Stay with me. I am begging you, Eleanora. I cannot lose you."

"Enver—"

"I have lost everything. You are all I have now—all I want. I will give you the stars I promised you, even if I have to destroy entire constellations to do so," he rasped, clutching me to his chest. "So, please. Stay with me."

I couldn't do this. I knew it would hurt. I knew I would suffer. But the thought of Enver suffering, of him blaming himself for my fate when none of this was his fault to begin with, was even more unbearable. What he feared happening with me was already happening with Evangeline. She was trapped here with him, but neither of them recognized each other—*could* recognize each other.

I refused to cause Enver any more pain than he'd endured already. If I was destined for ruin, then I'd rather have him be the one to ruin me.

And... I was already used to being a stand-in for someone else. I was used to being unloved. This would be no different from my life before. Maybe I was never meant for anything more than that. Maybe I was never meant to be loved. Never meant to have a happy ending. Maybe this was all I was meant for.

I would have no future. Enver had no past. At least together, we could have the present. At least we could take comfort in each other.

I buried my face into his neck, his black hair tickling my forehead. "I'll be yours," I breathed into his skin.

A shudder went through his body and his hold on me tightened briefly before he let go, settling me onto my feet. His arms wrapped around my waist, keeping me close. I couldn't bring myself to look at him, but he reached out and tilted my chin up, forcing me to meet his gaze.

There was no hint of satisfaction. No pleasure in my surrender. Only a quiet, deep-rooted relief, and an even greater tenderness.

Before, it would have made my heart soar, and would have me convincing myself he would end up loving me one day, but now it only hurt. He didn't love me. He never would. Even if one day someone completed his labyrinth and gave him love back, the feeling wouldn't be for me.

"Say it again," he requested.

"I'm yours," I whispered.

"The oath will be sealed soon."

I nodded, not knowing what to say, feeling anxiety building in my chest. *It will be fine*, I told myself. *I'll be with Enver*.

Enver pulled me to his chest, his arms wrapping around me. His chin rested against the top of my head, and my heart pounded against my ribs, waiting for the inevitable. Moments passed, and I clung to Enver, squeezing my eyes shut.

Nothing happened. Nothing changed.

Eventually, Enver pulled back, his brows drawn together. I

looked at him, waiting, watching as a frown flitted across his face. "This is strange."

"What?"

"I do not feel the pull of the oath, nor of the labyrinth," he said.

"What does that mean?"

He slowly shook his head. "I do not know."

Behind him, his castle loomed, catching my attention. "You said I had to make it to the top of the clock tower to complete my labyrinth. Yet, I appeared here. Where I started."

"Perhaps because I was out here when you returned?" Enver suggested.

I glanced behind me, taking in the statue of Evangeline again. "No. I don't think it's that. Maybe... maybe my last challenge isn't over," I said, my breath catching.

The pendant.

I reached for it, finding it incomplete. One ruby shard was still missing.

Enver tensed, and his hand shot out, grasping my wrist tightly. "No. It is over. You are here with me. You have failed."

My mind raced. Why would I return here if the challenge wasn't complete yet? Did it mean Kayn was here somewhere? But hadn't he gotten what he wanted? Why wasn't his labyrinth completed, then?

The moonlight caught the water flowing down the statue of Evangeline, drawing my eyes to her illuminated features and displaying her serene expression.

Evangeline. She was here. She had been here all along. I'd assumed it was Kayn's challenge to which I was linked. But what if...

"Enver, can you summon a servant here?"

"For what reason?"

I turned to him, my mouth dry. "Call for Evangeline."

He hesitated, his muscles tensing, but after a moment, a

shadow portal appeared. I pulled my wrist free of his hold, a lump forming in my throat.

Evangeline stepped through a moment later. Her black hair was cut just above her shoulders, her face impassive, and her hands folded together in front of her as she bowed her head to Enver. "My lord."

I studied Enver's expression closely as he regarded Evangeline. There was no hint of recognition. No inkling of the love that had filled his face when he'd gazed at her before. Nothing. He looked at her as if she were a stranger. As if she were just another one of his many servants.

I opened my mouth to speak, but the words were stuck. It hit me then. If I was right—if this really was Evangeline's labyrinth and I helped her complete it—she would be free of its grasp. She would remember Enver. Her fiancé. Her lover. What would happen then? Would she refuse to leave him? Would she try to get him to remember her? To remember everything they had together?

Would Enver feel the same warmth he found in me in her again? Would he realize it belonged to her in the first place?

If I saved her, would I be the one losing everything?

Enver's touch on my face startled me, and he cupped my cheek, guiding me to face him. "What is wrong?" he asked gently.

I stared into his eyes, their obsidian depths pulling me in, the concern I found there making me ache stronger for a love that wasn't mine. His hand on my cheek only reminded me of how tenderly he'd held Evangeline. How he'd cradled her against him. The way he looked at her then was not the same as he looked at me now. It never would be.

I would never have the love he had for her.

"Enver..." I began, my voice trembling. I would not get between them. I would not stop Enver from having the love he deserved.

"Yes, my little lover?"

A lump formed in my throat, and I raised my hand to his, the shadow ring on my finger brushing over his. "Can you do what you did before? Back with Agatha and Oliver? Can you pull Evangeline from oblivion?"

He glanced at Evangeline, frowning. "Why?"

"Please."

Enver didn't make a move to pull away from me. "Tell me why you are asking me to do this."

"Just do it," I whispered, afraid of losing my resolve.

His fingers flexed against my cheek, his eyes darkening. "No."

Tears threatened again. "I need you to bring her to me."

"Why do I feel as though I will lose you forever if I do as you ask?" he murmured, his thumb tracing over my cheek. "I feel your pain. Did you forget? You are hurting. Deeply. What does this woman have to do with it?"

"Enver, please," I pleaded, my voice catching as my hand tightened around his. "I need to do this."

A muscle feathered in his jaw, but he finally turned to Evangeline, pulling his hand away from my face. I could hardly breathe as Enver stepped closer to Evangeline, his fingers brushing against her forehead.

At his touch, Evangeline closed her eyes, but then they snapped back open, wide and frantic. A gasp left her lips as she gazed up at him, tears filling her eyes immediately as she reached for him. "*Verofer.*"

Enver's shoulders stiffened, and he fell back a step, creating a space between him and Evangeline. "That name..."

"Verofer," Evangeline repeated, and the tears in her eyes spilled over, streaking down her cheeks. "I'm so sorry. I didn't know. I didn't know what Kayn planned to do to you. I should have tried harder to keep him away from us."

"Why do you speak to me as if you know me?" Enver asked,

but his head turned to me, his eyes piercing into mine, demanding an answer.

I took a shaky breath, forcing myself to ignore him, looking past him. To Evangeline, who turned toward me, following Enver's line of sight. Our gazes locked together, and her face paled. "It's you. You were with Kayn that night." Suddenly, anger blazed across her features. "Were you in on everything?"

"No," I said, but she made to move toward me, her hands curling into fists, a faint glow beginning to emit from them.

Enver intercepted her, placing himself between us, his voice rough as he held out his arm. "Stay away from her."

Evangeline stopped, her lips parting, her gaze going back to him. "Verofer..."

I forced myself forward, swallowing the lump in my throat. "It's okay, Enver," I said, coming to stand in front of Evangeline. "Evangeline, I'm also doing the labyrinth."

"You are?" she asked, her eyes darting between Enver and me, confusion written across her face. "But..."

"I have been helping people during their challenges," I explained, feeling Enver's gaze weighing down on me. I couldn't look at him. I would lose my resolve. "I thought I was supposed to be helping Kayn back then, but I was wrong. I think I was supposed to be helping you."

"That can't be," she said. "I wasn't doing the labyrinth back then. It didn't exist."

"What happened after Kayn gave you the antidote?" I asked.

"He kidnapped me and kept me locked up," she said, her voice wavering. "He told me Verofer was dead, but I didn't believe him. I was desperate to escape and find Verofer, but Kayn made it impossible. Then Verofer showed up. I thought to save me, but..." She turned to Enver again, taking a shaky breath. "But he was already like this. He'd forgotten me. I don't know what happened to him."

"Your father cursed him," I told her. "That night, Kayn

deceived everyone. Your father believed you died, and that Enver is the one who killed you. In retaliation, he cursed Enver. He..." I swallowed, the memory coming back to me again, making nausea rise in me. "He ripped Enver's heart out, stole his memories and emotions, and banished him to this castle. Forced him to become the labyrinth's ruler."

"No, why would my father...?" Evangeline's voice cracked, a sob lodging in her throat, and her knees buckled, sending her toward the ground. "No..."

Enver caught her before I had the chance to react. His arm went around her waist, supporting her weight as her fingers curled into the fabric of his shirt, refusing to let him go, even when he steadied her.

"My father forbids magic from being used in the kingdom, yet used it to curse you?" Evangeline asked, and she tugged on his shirt, exposing the scar on his chest. "How could he...?"

Enver didn't move to stop her.

"This is all my fault," Evangeline whispered, pressing her face against Enver's scarred skin. "Forgive me, Verofer. What has my father done to you? Have you been suffering like this since then? Cursed and alone?"

"What is the meaning of this?" Enver asked, his question directed at me again, the tension in his tone almost palpable. "Nell. Look at me."

I couldn't. It already hurt too much. His arm was still around her, and the sight of her clinging to him was like a dagger to my chest. "Enver," I started, hating how hard it was to get his name out, how breathless it sounded. "You know her."

"I do not," he replied, his voice clipped. "Stop avoiding my gaze. Look at me, Eleanora. Who is this woman?"

"Look behind you," I whispered, forcing the words out.

Enver remained still for a long moment before he shifted, his head turning toward the fountain behind him. He never released Evangeline, keeping his arm around her as he faced the statue. My pulse thundered in my ears as heartbeat after heartbeat passed. Enver's head turned up, then back down, his entire body stiffening.

"Who are you?" Enver asked Evangeline, his words so quiet I almost didn't hear them. "What did you mean to me?"

Evangeline lifted her head, her cheeks glistening with tears. "Verofer—"

He suddenly rose, forcing Evangeline to release him, and he backed away, putting space between them. "No. It does not matter. Leave us."

"Verofer," she started, scrambling to her feet. "No, please. You have to remember. It's me, Evangeline. Your fiancée. You have to remember—"

"I do not," Enver interrupted her, his expression hard. Cold. "Do not call me by that name. You have mistaken me for someone else."

Evangeline shook her head, her lips trembling as she stumbled closer to Enver. "I would recognize you anywhere, Verofer. No matter how much time has passed. Don't you remember when you had this statue commissioned? Don't you remember how much time we spent together in this garden?"

"*Enough*," he snarled, and lifted his hand, prepared to send her back into oblivion.

"Enver!" I cried, and his head snapped toward me. "Stop! It's true. She's your lover."

His expression darkened, shadows beginning to seep up through the ground. "No. You are my only lover."

Evangeline drew in a harsh breath of air, and I ignored it, focusing on Enver, my chin trembling. "I'm not. It's been her. All this time."

He glared at me, frustration and fury rolling off him. "Stop. She is no one to me. It has always been you—"

"No—"

"*Yes,* you are my—"

Evangeline threw herself at him, cutting him off as she wrapped her arms around him, holding him tight. "I will make you remember, Verofer. I will not let you continue to suffer. You will not bear the blame for what Kayn has done any longer."

"Release me," Enver demanded roughly. "I am not suffering, I have Eleanora—"

"I only hope I'm strong enough," Evangeline said, drawing back to place a hand against the spot his heart should have beat. "I will undo your curse."

Enver grabbed her wrist, wrenching it back from his scar. "No. Leave us—"

"Nell, tell me, what did my father do to Enver's heart?" Evangeline asked frantically, her head turning toward me.

My throat burned, and my chest constricted. This was it. This was my last chance to stop this, to keep things as they were. To keep Enver.

"Nell," Enver said, and the desperation in his voice stunned me. The panic. The fear. What scared him, though? The thought of remembering everything?

Or the thought of losing me?

Even if he feared it now, it would only be fleeting. Once he remembered everything—once he remembered Evangeline—he would feel the way he used to. The way he was *supposed* to. He would remember who he was meant to love.

Yet, even though this was the right thing to do, the ache inside me spread, becoming so painful I thought I would suffocate from it.

"You have his heart," I told Evangeline, the words ripping free, leaving a gaping wound in their wake. "Your father left it with you. You're the only one who can save him."

"With me?" she repeated. Her expression softened as she looked at Enver again. "Then my father did not destroy it. I will return it and make you whole once more, Verofer. You will never be alone again. I promise."

Enver's shadows suddenly surged. "*No*," he rasped, his hand shooting to her forehead, his fingers centimeters from brushing against her, sending her back to oblivion.

"Remember," Evangeline urged, and a burst of light emitted from her hand, enveloping them, causing Enver's shadows to recede, dissipating into the air as a groan escaped him.

Enver's shoulders curled inward as he staggered, falling to one knee, his hand moving to clutch Evangeline's. She kept it pressed against his chest, her shoulders rising and falling as her breathing grew rough, her brows furrowing as the light grew brighter, more intense.

A sharp pain erupted in my chest, and I gasped, jerking back.

"Something's wrong," Evangeline said, the pitch of her voice rising with alarm. "I don't feel his heart!" Her eyes were wide when she whipped her head toward me. "You said—"

The pain grew worse, and I realized it wasn't in my chest. It was *on* my chest. My gaze dropped to my breasts, and I tore at the front of my dress, seeing the heart pendant glowing brightly, its edges searing my skin.

It pulsed, each throb more intense than the last, as though something inside was trying to break out.

"What? That's my—" Evangeline began, but choked as Enver's hand shot to her throat, curling around it.

My gaze snapped to him, my heart lurching. His shadows crept along his body, dark and sinister, bleeding into his eyes, turning them solid black. A strained whimper came from Evangeline as Enver rose to his feet, dragging her up with him.

I watched, horrified, as Evangeline struggled against his hold. The light from her hand faded, and she clawed at his arm, fighting for breath.

"Enver, no!" I cried, recognizing the darkness that had overcome him. It was exactly the same as the time Isla tried to kill me—when he'd thought Isla was going to take me from him.

The pendant burned hotter as I forced myself forward, closing the distance between us. His shadows writhed and twisted around him, growing more aggressive as he squeezed Evangeline's neck tighter, causing her eyes to roll back.

Panic welled in me, and I launched myself at him, grabbing his wrist and trying to pry his hand off her with all my might. But it was no use. He wouldn't budge. His shadows coiled around me, trapping me against him, crushing my chest to his. The pendant flared so hot between us that I thought it would burn right through me.

"Enver," I said again, my hands moving to his face, cupping his cheeks as I'd done so many times before.

At my touch, his darkened eyes shot down to me. The sight of him consumed by his own shadows made me tremble. My hands slid down to his jaw, tendrils of shadow snaking up my arms, wrapping around my wrists.

"I'll stay with you," I whispered. "Even if your curse is broken and you are free of this labyrinth, I will stay by your side."

He didn't react. The noises Evangeline made grew fainter, her struggles becoming less frantic. It was clear she was fading fast.

"Let her go," I begged. "Let her go, and you will have my heart. My everything. You will be enough for me—you *are* enough for me, Enver. I will give myself to you entirely. Every single piece. I will be yours. I *am* yours."

His voice came out distorted as he spoke—too deep and resonant. "Until when?"

"Until forever," I promised. "Until the world falls down."

I stood on my tiptoes, kissing him. At first, his lips were stiff and unmoving, but they gradually softened, molding to mine in the way only his could.

His grip on Evangeline loosened.

Her fingers curled around the pendant, yanking it off my

neck. I broke away from Enver, catching a brief glimpse of it before she closed her fist around it completely.

The ruby was now complete, glowing brightly and beautifully, alive and full of magic.

The air seemed to pulse, and then light violently exploded around us. Enver recoiled, and I gasped as the heart pendant shattered, sending a wave of heat and light outward, knocking us all backward. I crashed into the ground hard, stars bursting behind my eyes.

I pushed myself to my knees shakily, my heart beating wildly, turning my attention back to Enver. My mouth opened to call for him, but the words died on my lips as Evangeline approached his crumpled form, her hand outstretched. Her body radiated with light, and her harsh breathing cut through the air, causing her shoulders to heave. A familiar shadowy object sat in her palm, pulsating, shadows swirling around it, the pulsing growing stronger and wilder the closer she moved to Enver.

His heart.

Her light wove around his shadows as she stopped in front of him. He knelt in the grass, looking up at her through hooded eyes, the darkness receding until only his obsidian irises remained. His body relaxed as Evangeline's light bathed over him.

"You have suffered too long, Verofer," she murmured. "But no more."

With a subtle shift, his eyes found mine, and time seemed to stop. The hard lines of his face melted away, replacing his usual stoicism with a pained softness.

I stared back, unable to move, to speak.

His lips parted, but before he could say anything, Evangeline placed his heart against his chest. The shadows around it seemed to writhe and recoil at first, as if resisting the light emanating from Evangeline, but when they contacted his scarred skin they calmed, curling around his heart like a protective embrace.

"Please!" Evangeline cried as she pushed against his heart.

Enver's back arched as a brilliant flash of white lit up the night. His heart sank into his chest, the shadows seeping into his skin, turning the pale, smooth lines of his scar black before both the shadows and his heart disappeared into him. His head bowed, his black hair curtaining his face, obscuring his features.

The silence that followed was deafening.

Hours seemed to pass, though it was mere seconds. My stomach knotted, and my chest tightened, waiting for Enver to move, to speak. Anything. Anything to show that he was okay. That the curse was broken.

Evangeline moved first.

She swayed on her feet, her hand clutching at her throat, and then she collapsed, her body crumpling into the grass.

My eyes widened. "Eva—"

"Evangeline?"

My heart stopped. Enver's gaze settled on Evangeline, his brows drawn together, and then he groaned, his hand shooting to his chest.

"What is...?" he started, then stopped, inhaling sharply. "Evangeline," he repeated, this time his voice full of urgency. He launched forward, his hand sliding along her neck, lifting her head up. "Evangeline!"

I had to help. I had to make sure Evangeline was okay. But I couldn't move. I couldn't do anything but watch. Watch as Enver remembered his true love. Watch as I lost him.

"Evangeline, wake up," Enver said roughly, but kept his touch gentle. "Open your eyes."

She stirred, her lashes fluttering. "Verofer."

"Yes, I am here," he murmured.

"You remember."

His hand brushed her hair away from her face. "I remember."

She smiled at him, and I swallowed, forcing myself to look away as Enver helped her to her feet, holding onto her arm to keep her steady. I couldn't handle it. Not the affection in his touch. Not the fondness of her gaze.

My heart couldn't take it.

Something rustled beside me, and then the recognizable chill of shadows crept over me. They started at my feet, curling around my legs, then traveled upward, winding around my waist and torso, leisurely and affectionately. They caressed my skin, cool and soothing.

I knew what they were doing. A tear rolled down my cheek as I remained motionless in the grass, letting the shadows cover me.

I didn't know if I was making the right choice. I had no one to help me with my own labyrinth challenge. No one to lead me on the right path or offer advice. I only had myself and my heart. And my heart told me Enver deserved to be loved. Deserved to never be alone again. Deserved the entire world for how much he had suffered. And if that love was meant to be shared with Evangeline, I would not stand in his way.

I would let him go.

Even if it meant breaking my own heart in the process.

I looked at Enver, trying to blink away the wetness in my eyes. I needed to memorize every part of him. To make sure I didn't forget anything. His touch, his voice, his warmth, his darkness. His eyes, his smile, his laugh, his everything. I wanted it all burned into my memory, even if it hurt, even if it would inevitably break me. I would gladly let it haunt me.

I wanted to remember him.

I wanted to remember us.

The shadows reached my neck, tendrils brushing along my throat like a lover's touch. This was it. I would never see Enver again. Never feel him again. Never be his. Never have our forever.

I couldn't stop the broken sob that tore through me as the shadows reached my chin.

Don't look at me, I begged Enver in my mind. *Don't look.* I didn't want to see what his expression would be. Didn't want to see how I now meant nothing to him.

Enver's head snapped in my direction. His gaze swept over the shadows swallowing me, and realization flashed in his eyes. He released Evangeline, then tore toward me, his movements a blur of determination and urgency. "Nell—"

"Enver," I whispered, before the shadows blanketed my lips.

"*No,*" he rasped, his voice raw and frantic. "*No!*"

His hand stretched toward me, his fingers brushing against the shadows as they closed over my eyes. The last thing I saw was his beautiful face, his lips forming my name, his eyes filled with fierce desperation.

And then I was gone.

29

Whispers of words I couldn't quite catch danced at the back of my mind, turning into shouts soon after. They were muffled and jumbled together, but familiar and grating.

"Nell. Nell! *Eleanora!*"

The sound of my full name pulled me into consciousness, my brow furrowing, two different voices overlapping each other as they pierced my ears. Hands shook my shoulders, and I opened my eyes, immediately wrenching them shut again as the setting sun blinded me.

"Nell," came my name again, and now I recognized the voice as Julian's. His hands tightened on my shoulders, rough and painful. "Are you okay? Say something!"

His body blocked out the sun as I opened my eyes again, staring up into his hazel eyes. His shadow cast over me, the shape inanimate and lifeless. I willed it to wrap around me, to give me the comfort and familiarity of its cool touch, but it remained still and impalpable.

"Nell," another voice said, and then Veronica's face

appeared over me, her skin pale. "What happened? Should I call an ambulance?"

"Where have you been?" Julian pressed. "What's going on?"

Tears brimmed, stinging my eyes, and then trailing down my cheeks.

I was back. This wasn't Morgan tricking me again. I was home.

I'd completed the labyrinth.

And Enver was gone.

I brought my hands to my face and broke down, choking on my tears as Veronica and Julian continued talking at me, demanding answers, growing louder as their concern rose. The sound of Enver calling my name echoed through my mind, drowning out their voices. The image of him reaching for me imprinted into my vision, no matter how tightly I closed my eyes.

Enver was *gone*. There was no going back. It was over. I'd never see him again. Never touch him again. Never see his smile.

"For fuck's sake, Nell!" Julian shouted, grabbing my arm and wrenching me up off the ground.

Startled, my eyes flew open as his fingernails dug into my skin. My surroundings came into focus, and I realized I was outside my house, in front of my rose bushes. Julian knelt in the grass next to me, his other hand going to my jaw, forcing me to look at him.

"You have been missing for an entire *week!*" he snapped, his eyes narrowed. "Where the hell have you been? Don't you know how worried we were? You can't just sit here and cry and say nothing!"

A week?

"Julian," Veronica warned, standing behind him so closely her thighs brushed his shoulders.

She was wearing my clothes. Clothes I knew I had just washed. Clothes I had left folded on top of my dryer. My gaze followed her hand as she tucked her hair behind her ear, revealing a fresh hickey on her neck. Then she dropped her hand down to Julian's shoulder, and a sparkle drew my attention. The engagement ring. Still on her finger.

It brought me back to when all this started. When they'd told me of their affair. When I'd let them place the blame on me. When I'd believed it was my fault. When I'd allow their betrayal to break me. When I'd become desperate.

When Enver had come to me.

Would things have been different if I'd reacted differently then? If I had been stronger? If I had seen my worth? If I'd not blamed myself? Would I not have met Enver? Would I have saved myself from this pain?

Why did Julian and Veronica still have each other when I'd lost everything?

Anger boiled up in me. At them, at what they did to me, at what I'd done to myself.

I owed myself more than this.

"Leave," I said, my voice hoarse and quiet.

Julian's grip on me tightened. "What?"

"I said leave," I repeated, pulling my head free of his grasp and shoving him away from me, climbing shakily to my feet.

Julian also stood up, his lips curling into a scowl, reaching for me again. "Nell, I know you're not brushing me off after I spent the last week searching for you—"

"While you weren't busy fucking my sister?" I cried, slapping his hand away. "Don't touch me! Were you two living in my house while I was missing? Is that why you're wearing my clothing, Veronica? You were so worried about me that you helped yourself to all my belongings?"

Veronica pulled her hand back from Julian's shoulders. Her

startled eyes were the only evidence I needed to know it was true.

"W-we thought you just needed space," she said.

"You are so desperate to have anything that is mine, aren't you?" I asked icily, my body trembling in rage.

"Don't speak to her that way," Julian snapped, reaching out to take Veronica's hand in his. She immediately latched onto it, her fingers threading through his.

I stared at their entwined hands. How had I ever fallen for Morgan's illusion? Julian would never apologize to me. Julian would never choose me over Veronica. Julian would never love me.

And now...

Now, I didn't want him to. I didn't want anything to do with him. Him or Veronica. I didn't need anyone who treated me like this in my life.

"Get your shit out of my house," I said. "Give me back my credit card and get the fuck out of my life."

"Nell—"

"I would ask for everything I ever got you, but I doubt that would even leave you with the clothes on your back."

Julian's face turned red, his jaw clenching. "You're going to throw that in my face again? You're the one who offered it all! You're the one who wanted to buy my love! You're desperate. Desperate to be loved by me."

"No," I said, my voice steady because now I knew what I was about to say was true. "It could have been anyone. You were right before. I *was* desperate enough to give myself to anyone who gave me the slightest bit of attention. It just happened to be you back then."

His eyes narrowed.

I held his gaze, not backing down. "But I'm not desperate anymore. I won't beg for scraps of affection that weren't even there to begin with."

"Bullshit," he replied. "I know you, Nell. You would stay with me if I asked. You would forgive me if I asked. Because that's who you are."

"No," I said evenly. "That's who I was."

The person I was before—the one who would put up with anything, the one who would stay no matter what, the one who would love no matter how little she was loved back.

That version of me didn't exist anymore.

"I deserve someone who will love me the way I deserve to be loved," I told him, my heart clenching at the words. "And you don't deserve me. You never deserved me."

He scoffed. "And who do you think will ever love you, Nell? Do you think anyone else could put up with you for as long as I did?"

His words should have stung, but they didn't. "Me," I said softly, looking him in the eye. "I will love myself. I will learn how I should love someone and how I should be loved back. And that's something that would never be possible with a partner like you. I should have walked away a long time ago."

"So why didn't you?"

"Because I thought I was in love. I thought I loved you. But you were right," I told him. "I don't think I ever loved you. You were just there."

Veronica gazed at me, her face pale, her expression uncertain. "Where have you been, Nell?" she asked again, this time hesitantly.

"With someone who showed me what I deserved," I said, a lump rising in my throat. "With people who showed me what love is supposed to be like. I didn't have the courage to walk away before. I didn't have the confidence to admit that I deserved more. But I do now."

"So, you ran away to be with some other guy?" Julian accused, his tone bitter.

It was almost funny—how he said that while holding Veronica's hand. *Almost.*

Mainly, though, it just pissed me off.

"Yeah, I did," I said, my words cutting. "And he fucked me harder and better than you ever could, Julian. He made me come more times in one night than you did in our entire relationship. I didn't know someone could reach so deep inside me. My legs are still shaking from how big he was. I should thank you for being a good practice dildo. Really helped prepare me for him."

Julian flushed, his lips morphing into a scowl. "You—"

"Now get the fuck out of my life," I said.

"You think—"

"Now," I interjected. "Before I call the cops and report you two for trespassing."

"Our stuff is still inside," Veronica said quickly.

I glanced at her, smiling patronizingly. "Then you're welcome to have someone else come pick it up, as long as you explain why your shit is at my house and why you're not allowed to come get it."

"Nell, please—"

"I want you out of my life, Veronica," I said, ignoring the way she flinched at my words.

"I'm your sister," she protested.

"I don't consider you my sister anymore. You lost that the moment you chose to fuck my boyfriend. Family is supposed to be there for each other, but you betrayed me. Take your fiancé and leave. Hopefully, our mother is more accepting of Julian as your partner than I am."

"I only did it because you have everything!" Veronica cried. "You have a good career, an expensive car, a nice house, and a man who wanted to love you! Yet you never appreciate any of it! You take it all for granted! Meanwhile, everyone always asks me why I'm not like you. Why I'm not as successful. Why I'm not as smart. Why I can't land a good boyfriend."

I blinked, unable to believe what I was hearing. "Did you forget why I had to fight to be successful? I had to support myself after our mother kicked me out—"

"You were eighteen!"

"And you're twenty-eight, yet you still live with her."

"It's because Mom said you remind her of Dad!" Veronica blurted. "That's why she can't be around you. That's why she kicked you out."

Not expecting that, I fell silent. I knew our mom blamed me for our dad leaving, but this was a new revelation.

"Yet she still compares us to this day," Veronica continued. "She doesn't want me to be like our father but wants me to be like you. Find a high-paying job and make money, but don't be like Eleanora. It doesn't make sense! And you never noticed the pressure she always put on me. The only reason she even started talking to you again is because I told her how much money you make."

I tried not to react outwardly. I didn't want to believe it, but Veronica's words made sense. The text message history with my mom would prove it if I searched through it. She never asked to see me. Only asked for money.

"If I am just like Dad, then you are just like Mom," I said slowly. "You both used me for my money like Mom used Dad for money. You both betrayed me like she did to him."

Veronica's face paled. "I'm not like Mom."

"Then why were you content spending my income while sleeping with my boyfriend?"

"That was your fault!" she cried. "You drove him to me. He wasn't happy, and you were too busy to notice or care. He needed me. I was there for him when you weren't. You took him for granted, so I took him from you."

"Is this seriously your excuse?" I asked.

"You didn't deserve him!" she responded. "Not when you had everything else, too."

"You're right. I don't deserve him," I said, smiling at her. "I don't deserve a cheating piece of shit like him. And I don't deserve a selfish, jealous sister like you. You both deserve each other. I refuse to take the blame for what you two did. If Julian was that unhappy, he should have broken up with me. Not cheated on me. If you were so jealous of me, you should have focused on improving yourself instead of trying to steal what I had. And while I regret I made you feel unloved when I thought I was giving you all the love I had, what you two did to me is unforgivable. So, this is the last time I'm going to say this —get the fuck out of my life. I don't want or need you two in it."

I looked between them, seeing Julian's shoulders tense and Veronica's cheeks flush. She opened her mouth, but Julian gave her a stern look, shaking his head. He took out his wallet, plucking out the credit card I gave him, and threw it at my feet. "Let's go," he muttered, tugging her away.

"Wait," I said.

They paused, and Veronica turned back to me.

I pointed at her hand. "The ring. Give it to me."

Her eyes went wide. "What? It's mine."

"Julian bought it with my credit card. Or do you want to be reminded of how your fiancé had to steal money from your *successful* sister to purchase your engagement ring every time you look at it?"

Veronica took off the ring with shaking hands and threw it to the ground. "Fine. Take it."

"I thought so."

"I hope you're happy, Nell," Julian spat at me.

"I will be," I promised myself.

As they walked away from me, I waited to feel satisfied about sticking up for myself. To feel a sense of vindication. But as a familiar car rolled up and my mom climbed out of it, her hair a freshly dyed platinum blonde, I only felt anger.

I forced myself forward, approaching her as Julian got into the car, and Veronica hesitated by the passenger door. My mom looked surprised to see me, her dark eyes taking me in. "Eleanora, you're back. Perfect timing. I think my car needs new tires—"

"Mom," I interrupted her, trying to ignore the pain in my chest that formed as she asked me for money even now. Trying to ignore that my wealth was the only reason she ever tried to be part of my life again. "I want to remind you of Dad one last time."

Her brow furrowed, glancing at Veronica for a split second. "What?"

"I'm leaving you," I told her. "This time it's my decision. This is me cutting you off and out of my life. And like Dad, I won't be coming back. You will never use me again."

"Excuse me? You're my *daughter*—"

"No," I cut her off, shaking my head. "You stopped being my mother the moment you threw me out. When you found out about Veronica and Julian and didn't tell me. I don't have any family anymore."

Veronica let go of the passenger door handle, turning back to me, her eyes filled with tears. "Nell, wait—"

I glared at her, causing her voice to falter. "Don't. It's over. I made my decision. I'm choosing me."

My mom didn't respond. Her expression didn't even change as she returned to the driver's side and climbed in.

"Nell, you'll be alone," Veronica pleaded.

"I already have been for a long time," I replied. "I just never realized it."

Her tears spilled over as she opened the door and entered the car. I didn't know why she was crying. I didn't care why, either.

I watched them drive away, expecting to be relieved.

But instead, I felt pathetic as I staggered back toward my house.

For taking this long to stand up for myself, for being so desperate for love from a person like Julian, and for being so willing to ignore my self-worth for the sake of having someone by my side. To place so much of me in someone else's hands. Enver was right—it was dangerous. But now everything was back in my hands, and I refused to give it away ever again.

I knelt down to the ground, picking up the engagement ring Veronica had tossed. It glinted in the sun as I slid it onto my ring finger.

It stopped at the first knuckle, too small to go further.

I took it off, staring at it, seeing nothing but a reminder of what I had settled for, what I had put up with, and what I had allowed.

What I would never allow again.

I brought my hand back, ready to chuck it as far away from me as possible, but stopped at the last second, closing my fist around it. I didn't know how much Julian had paid for it. I'd already lost enough of my money to him. I needed to return it if I could. My eyes scanned the grass for my credit card that undoubtedly paid for it, and when I found it, I slipped it into my pocket.

Standing, I turned toward my house. My feet felt heavy as I walked up the front steps and through the open door. My stomach churned at the sight of the dirty dishes piled in the sink and how the chairs at the kitchen table were pushed out as if recently vacated. An empty pizza box and a dozen empty beer cans were left on the counter next to a burning candle, too close for my comfort.

The heaviness crept up my legs as I blew out the candle and forced myself into the living room. Blankets covered the couch, and a show that I'd recommended to Veronica—which Julian always refused to watch with me—was playing on the TV.

The weight spread through my arms as I found my way to my bedroom, my eyes trained on my unmade bed. The sheets were crumpled and stained, and a used condom lay on the floor next to the wastebasket.

At least they used condoms, I thought distantly.

I turned, my gaze catching my appearance in my full-length mirror. There were grass stains on my dress. No. Not my dress.

Evangeline's dress.

The heaviness lodged itself in my throat. It took over my body, crushing me from the inside out, and I staggered, reaching out to steady myself on my dresser. My hand knocked against a framed photo of Julian and me, sending it careening to the floor where it shattered. The pain grew worse, making my chest ache and stealing my breath.

I gasped for air as my vision blurred, my lungs feeling like they would collapse.

Why me?

I couldn't stop my thoughts as hot tears rolled down my cheeks.

Why me?

Why was I the one who had to lose everything?

"You promised," I choked out, trembling again. "You promised the labyrinth would give me what I wanted if I completed it. So why—why am I alone? Why did everyone else get what they wanted but me?"

I shook my head, catching my reflection again. I ripped at the dress, tearing it off my body. "I don't get a playful, deep love like Paloma and Neima have. I don't get familiar love like Dio and Luliana. I don't get an enduring love like Aki and Cas. I don't get a desirous love like Morgan and Karim. I don't get an obsessive love like Silas or a self-affirming love like Rielle. I don't get a platonic love like Isla..."

I wrapped my arms around myself, letting out a shuddered breath as I stood vulnerable in my room.

"I don't get your love like Evangeline does," I whispered, the words hurting worse than anything else had.

My tears came harder, faster, blurring my reflection.

"It's not fair. Why, out of all these kinds of love, do I not even get *one*?"

I fell back a step, nearly slipping, glancing down to find a silky piece of lingerie under my foot.

My first instinct was to run. To get far away from this place. To ignore reality and convince myself it was okay.

You deserve to be surrounded by those who cherish you, not those who take you for granted.

Enver's words rang through my mind, and a choked sob came out of my mouth. He was right. I deserved more than this. But I couldn't just let Enver tell me I deserved better. I had to believe it myself, too. I had to want it for myself.

And I did. I wanted it desperately.

Which meant I couldn't run anymore. If I wanted to start over, I had to face heartbreak head-on.

Tears still streamed down my face as I took a deep breath and a shaky step forward and began to clean up. I found a trash bag and threw out all the evidence of Julian's cheating, threw out every gift I'd gotten him, threw out every photo and every memory. It hurt. Hurt to breathe, hurt to relive every memory as I sorted through our belongings. But I kept going. The heavier the trash bag grew, the lighter my heart did.

By the time I finished, night had fallen, and my outside trash barrel was full. My tears had dried, and my hands no longer shook, but the hollow ache in my chest remained. I wasn't sure it would ever disappear. But I knew Julian didn't cause it. No, that part of me belonged to Enver. And it would never heal because I would never see Enver again.

I stared down at the garbage's overflowing contents for a

moment before slamming the lid shut, locking the pain and the past away.

Once back inside, I went straight to my laptop. I opened my e-mails to find over fifty waiting for me from the design company I worked for, each one getting progressively angrier than the last. I didn't bother reading them. I was getting rid of everything that reminded me of the person I was.

Including this shitty job.

I sent off my resignation e-mail and then signed out of everything company related. I had enough money saved up to get through as long as I needed until I figured out what I wanted to do next. Especially now that I wasn't funding Julian, Veronica, or my mom.

A weightless feeling washed over me. For once in my life, I had no responsibilities, no obligations. No one depended on me, and I wouldn't depend on anyone else again. And even though my heart was shattered and my soul was heavy, I felt...

Not quite happy, but like I could get there.

I stood in the kitchen, absentmindedly reorganizing some of the decor, when my gaze passed over my fruit bowl.

Peaches.

A pang shot through me, and I turned away, my hands trembling.

Don't, I warned myself. *He's with Evangeline. He will have his happily ever after with her. He deserves it.*

And I deserved...

A knock at my front door tore me from my thoughts. My heart raced as I approached it. Was it Julian? My mother? What did they want?

I cautiously opened it, blinking in surprise at the sight of Liana standing on my doorstep. "Liana?"

"Nell!" she said and smiled widely, the relief in her voice evident. "Thank goodness. I was worried about you."

My grip on the doorknob tightened.

Her mouth fell open, her hand shooting over it. "Oh, I'm so sorry. I looked up your address in our system. I didn't mean to intrude on your privacy, but I was worried something was wrong. You always come to the library three times a week, so when you missed this entire week without warning, I got concerned. I just wanted to make sure you were okay."

A lump formed in my throat. "I'm okay."

Her gaze softened, a frown crossing her face. "Are you?"

"Yes," I said, choking on my words, tears falling down my cheeks again.

"Sweetie, what's wrong?" she asked, not hesitating to wrap her arms around me. "It's okay."

I shook my head, trying to get the tears to stop, but it was useless. "My boyfriend and I broke up," I told her, knowing no one would believe anything I said about the labyrinth.

"Oh, honey, I'm so sorry," she murmured, holding me closer. "You must be devastated. If you want to talk about it, I'm here for you."

I didn't say anything, standing in her embrace, basking in her comfort. I didn't know I needed it until she offered it. She rubbed my back until my tears dried, then pulled back and smoothed my hair. "Sorry," I apologized, my voice scratchy.

"Don't apologize. We all need someone to comfort us sometimes."

"Thank you for worrying about me," I said, my voice catching again. "It means more than you know."

She smiled at me, warm and caring, and then her face lit up. She opened her side bag, digging around until she pulled out a book and handed it to me. "Here. I saw this at the bookstore and thought you'd like it."

I took the book, a wobbly smile taking over my face. I couldn't remember the last time someone had bought me something. "Thank you."

"I heard it's really romantic."

"I might hold off on reading romance for a bit," I replied honestly, clutching the book to my chest. "I'm having a hard time believing in happily ever after right now."

Liana placed her hand on my arm. "Happy endings are not always about love, dear."

"I know, but..."

"Have you ever heard the saying, the sun is still shining even when clouds hide it from sight? Your happily ever after is still out there, Nell, even if you can't see it right now. It will reappear. Don't give up hope. I truly believe you will have the happy ending you desire."

I swallowed hard. "What if I gave up my happily ever after instead of losing it?"

"Then that would be a tragedy, dear," she said softly, "because your happily ever after is something worth fighting for."

"It's too late," I whispered.

"Is it?" she asked. "Your story isn't over, Nell. You've spent so much time putting others first. Now it's time to prioritize yourself. Have courage."

Have courage.

My hand went to my neck, where Dio's faded bite mark lay imprinted in my skin. Dio had found courage. I could, too.

Liana squeezed my arm gently before letting go, smiling at me again. "I should go. If you ever want to talk or just want some company, you know where to find me."

"Liana, wait," I called as she began to walk off, my heart pounding in my chest. "I might not be at the library for a while."

Her smile grew. "I'll see you when I see you, then. Go get your happily ever after, Nell."

I needed to get back to the club.

I rushed back into my house, searching for my purse and phone, and it hit me belatedly that they were both left and lost in Enver's castle. My keys, too. I groaned. *Shit.* My car. It was still at the club—if it hadn't been towed yet.

I found my spare key and hurried out the door, not wanting to waste any more time. Who knew how much time had already passed in Enver's world? The thought had my pace quickening until I was half-running back to the club. When I arrived, I sighed in relief, finding my car still parked there. A handful of brightly colored tickets were tucked under the windshield wiper, but that beat paying an impound fee. I stashed my key under the wheel well before turning to the club's entrance and walking up to it.

To where I'd first met Enver.

My steps faltered, my throat closing up. What if I was setting myself up for more heartbreak? What if I was too late?

Shaking my head, I swallowed my fears and forced myself forward. I hadn't given Enver a chance to see if he would choose me. I'd run, like I'd always done, even if it was with good intentions this time. I hadn't fought for him—I'd let him go.

That was something the old Nell would do. I wasn't going to give up so easily. I wanted to at least try to fight for my happily ever after.

My pulse quickened as I entered the club. It was nearly empty, too early in the night for a crowd, and no one paid any attention to me as I walked around, unsure of what to do. I tried calling for Enver under my breath, standing about where I thought I stood before, but nothing happened.

Maybe he couldn't sense me yet. I settled into a booth, waiting.

And waiting.

The minutes ticked by, and I started to fidget. Enver had found me through the labyrinth's curse last time. What if he couldn't now because the curse had been lifted?

My heart sunk further with every passing hour, and as

eleven o'clock hit, the club started to fill up. Couples came together on the packed dance floor, the speakers playing a slow, sensual beat. I watched, trying to ignore that hollow ache within me, pushing aside the whispering voice in my head.

He's not coming.

He won't ever come.

I shook my head, trying to disperse the cruel voice.

He's gone.

"No," I said out loud.

Gone.

Forever.

I didn't know when I started crying again. All I knew was that it hurt. It hurt to know he was gone. To know he wasn't coming back no matter how much I waited, no matter how much I cried.

I remained in the booth even as the club emptied. I barely heard the bartender's words when he came to escort me out. I declined his help when he asked if I needed any. Said no to a ride home. Ignored him when he asked if there was anyone he could call.

It just made me cry harder.

I walked away from the bartender, not caring where I was going. My feet brought me to the alleyway Enver had led me to before. To the door that didn't exist anymore. Only a brick wall remained now. I placed my hand against it, the rough texture scraping against my palm. My lips trembled as I let out a harsh breath. There was no evidence Enver even existed. No way back to him.

Only my memories and the dress on my bedroom floor that belonged to his lover remained.

I put my back to the brick, feeling it dig into my back as I sunk down to the pavement, the tears still flowing.

I knew what I was doing made me more pathetic. I knew

this wasn't the person I wanted to be anymore. That I didn't want to be desperate anymore.

But I was. I was desperate and lonely and hurting and pathetic.

Just for now, I told myself, leaning my head back against the brick, my eyes falling shut as I tilted my head up toward the night sky.

I would allow myself to fall apart just for now.

Then, I would do as Enver told me to do. I would put myself back together and move on. I would forget him. I would try to be happy without him. I would wait for the clouds to part and the sun to shine.

But for now, I would miss him.

I would miss him entirely. Endlessly.

Desperately.

"Enver," I sobbed. His name was the only part of him I had left, and I clung to it, repeating it over and over as the tears fell faster. "Enver..."

A gentle caress on my cheek made my heart aching harder. The wind resembled his touch, how he dried my tears. It brushed against my other cheek and I leaned into the invisible sensation, allowing myself to imagine it was him, that he was here with me now, soothing me.

Fingertips stroked my skin, and then a phantom caress of lips followed, tracing the path of my tears, kissing away the wetness.

My breath caught.

A hand cradled my cheek, a thumb skimming it gently.

"I told you not to give into your desperation again," he murmured.

I trembled, unable to gather the courage to open my eyes. Too afraid I was imagining it all. Not wanting to lose the illusion yet. "You said you wouldn't come even if I did."

"I lied, my little lover," he said, his confession tickling my lips. "I lied because I knew I would be too weak to stay away from you if you called for me again."

His answer encouraged me to open my eyes, needing to see him, risking the illusion for the chance that he was truly there. His black, tousled hair that curled at the nape of his neck met my gaze first. Then the sharp curve of his jawline, the contrasting softness of his lips, the slope of his nose, the thickness of his dark lashes...

Then, as if he could not wait any longer for our eyes to meet, he tilted my chin up, forcing me to gaze into his obsidian ones.

"Enver," I whispered, my voice cracking.

He was here.

I wanted to kiss him. To touch him. But as my head moved toward his, and his eyes fluttered shut, I stopped myself, pulling back.

He wasn't mine anymore.

His body tensed, like I'd made him uncomfortable, and shame filled me. I had almost kissed an engaged man. I wanted to break away from his touch, but he held onto me, refusing to let go. He looked exhausted as he looked down at me, dark circles under his eyes, his skin paler than usual. Unable to keep eye contact, my eyes trailed down to his chest, finding his scar, and suddenly my throat was closing in alarm. If Enver was here, then...

"You're still cursed?" I asked, stricken, meeting his gaze again, my heart hurting for a different reason now. "No! That can't be. You have your heart back. Why are you here? Why did the labyrinth lead you to me again? You can't still be trapped, Enver, that's not fair—"

"I am not," he cut in, his voice gentle and soothing as he took my hand in his own and placed it against his chest. "Evangeline undid the curse. I am free of the labyrinth."

I went still, feeling his heart's steady, comforting beat under my palm. It really was back.

He was free.

"How...?" I started, overwhelmed with awe and confusion.

"I do not have long," he told me, his grip on my hand tightening. "This magic will not allow me to remain here for more than a few moments."

So, I'll lose you again? The thought burst into my mind, the pain returning, but worse than before. One goodbye had been hard enough. How would I survive two?

His gaze softened, and in a heart-stopping moment, I recognized the expression on his face—the affection in his eyes, the tenderness, and the longing. It was the same look he'd given Evangeline when Kayn had poisoned her, and she lay limp in his arms, now directed at me. One that could mend shattered hearts and make broken dreams come true. One not meant for me.

Why are you looking at me like that? I wanted to ask, but the words clogged in my throat, the intensity of his expression taking my breath away.

"Come with me, Nell," Enver murmured, his request quiet and sincere.

Come with him? As in...

His warm breath washed across my lips as he moved closer, his hand crushing mine to his chest, forcing me to feel how his heartbeat quickened.

"I cannot stay here," he told me, "but I cannot leave without you. My heart may have been returned to me, but my chest still feels hollow. A part of me remains within you. I have told you before—I will not be whole without you. I need you. Come with me. Please."

My heart stuttered in response to his words, its pace matching his own heart's rapid tempo. "But you're engaged," was all I could say.

"No," he said quietly. "Verofer was engaged. I am not that man anymore. I will never be that man again."

"What? But Evangeline—"

"She understands what you are to me. Even before I was cursed, I realized—" Enver cut himself off suddenly, distracted by shadows that began to dance along his skin. He glanced down at them, then our entwined hands, and then back at my face, a grave look crossing his face. "The magic is fading. Do not worry about Evangeline. You have to make a decision. Quickly. I will answer all your questions later."

My heart pounded. This wasn't an easy decision. I had so many questions, not enough answers, and not enough time. He was asking me to leave my world behind. To leave my life behind. Everything. For him.

It hit me then—I barely knew Enver. Even more so now that he had his heart and memories back. If I thought about it, the majority of our relationship had been based on lust. Yet, even so, I'd been so ready to stay in the labyrinth with him. I'd felt the same draw he said he'd felt toward me. The same sense of knowing. Of need.

"Will I ever be able to come back here if I go with you?" I asked, my mouth going dry.

"When Evangeline recovers, it should be possible," he responded, a slight edge to his tone as if displeased by my question. "You will not have to leave your world forever, but I cannot guarantee when she will be able to transport you back here again. She needs to regain her strength first. Breaking the curse has exhausted her magic."

I considered it. If I said yes, it wouldn't be forever. I could come back eventually and settle things I would need to settle. If I said no, I would lose Enver forever.

"I want it to be your decision this time," Enver said, his hand tightening around mine. "I have chosen you, but I will not force you to choose me."

I already knew my answer. I already had thought I lost him once. I wouldn't lose him again.

"Say yes. Come with me, my little lover," Enver coaxed, the shadows growing thicker, the seconds slipping through our entwined fingers. He was so close to me I could taste his breath as he spoke and feel his pulse thrumming rapidly under my palm, betraying his calm exterior. "I have chosen you, so choose me. Let me be selfish and steal you away. Let me love you the way I could not before. The way I wanted to before."

A rush of air left my lungs, his words filling the hollowness I carried, lifting the weight that bore me down. That was right. Enver *could* love me now. No longer would it be an empty promise—it was a vow. He would be mine, and I would be his.

"What if I can't love you properly?" I asked, the last of my worries slipping through my lips. "Would you still want me?"

"There will never be a time I do not want you, my little lover," Enver responded, his gaze steady, his voice firm. "Heart or not. Love or not. I will always want you. I will always be yours."

"Until when?" I whispered.

"Until the world falls down," he promised.

And I gave in to him, as I always did.

Willingly and without hesitation.

But this time, he was giving himself to me, too.

Enver sensed my answer before I even opened my mouth. His lips descended on mine, my breathless *yes* swallowed by his kiss. It was hungry, greedy, and claiming. And as his arms and shadows wrapped around me, dragging me into him, the world fell away around us, replaced by the overwhelming sensation of being complete—the one only Enver could provide me with.

"Yes, I'll come with you," I told him between kisses, and he drew me closer, holding me like something precious.

"My favorite word," he breathed, then rose, gathering me against his chest.

I wrapped my arms around his neck, and the shadows responded to our embrace, weaving around us, binding us together as we kissed once more.

"We will both learn how to love each other," Enver promised softly against my lips as the darkness swirled and deepened around us. "Together."

"Together," I echoed as the shadows finally engulfed us entirely, ready to spirit us away.

To begin our happily ever after.

I smiled in the dark, realizing the labyrinth had given me what I wanted in the end.

Enver.

EPILOGUE

Nell's sweet voice flooded my veins.

"*Enver.*"

The sound of her needy, whispered plea made my chest expand with an emotion I'd forgotten and caused the darkness that always lingered at the back of my mind to thin. The warmth of her body underneath mine seeped into me, a balm against the chill that never truly went away, even with my heart back in my chest.

Her fingertips ran down my back, leaving searing trails of pleasure in their wake, and a groan rose in the back of my throat.

The darkness dispersed even more.

She had been in my world for a little over a week, in my home that had once been my prison. After the curse broke, my castle had returned to its former state. No longer tied to my mental state, the walls were free of ruin and despair, the tapestries and rugs were no longer torn and faded, the gardens outside were flourishing once more.

But I could not say the same for myself.

A phantom pain stabbed through my chest, and I

gritted my teeth against it. The darkness started to encroach again, a coldness seeping back into my bones. After a century of not feeling, the return of my emotions was overwhelming, the extremes nearly driving me mad. I was either euphoric or wrathful, disconsolate or exultant. The smallest of things could trigger a shift in my temperament.

Yet what I felt strongest was cold fury. It stirred within me, a bone-deep hate taking over every waking thought if I let my mind drift. Toward the curse. Toward the one who had cast it. Toward the one who had been the cause of it.

The taste of vengeance lingered on the tip of my tongue, and an ever-present urge to enact it inundated my body, causing my muscles to flex and my blood to boil.

Nell shifted beneath me, calling out my name again, this time breathless. My gaze drifted down, a spark of possessiveness igniting in me at the sight of her writhing under my hand encased too tightly around her throat. Her pretty blue eyes burned into mine, her perfect lips parting to form my name again.

My grip slackened, but she only tilted her head back, baring her smooth neck to me further.

The darkness retreated again.

I leaned down and kissed her, drinking her in, allowing her to calm the cold fury inside of me, replacing it with a fire and heat only she could kindle.

I knew she was worried about Evangeline. I knew she felt guilty. She believed she'd stolen me from Evangeline. I saw it in the way she tensed before I kissed her, the way she would fall silent after I touched her.

It only made me want to kiss her more. Touch her more. Remind her I belonged to her—only her—and that would never change.

It would be easier when I could explain everything to her,

but now was not the time for that. Nell needed to adjust to my world before I told her of its intricacies.

Of how I would reclaim everything that had been stolen from me and destroy all who had wronged me. I would return the century of suffering I had endured tenfold.

For now, though, I would leave Nell ignorant of the darkness inside me.

For now, I would indulge myself.

Indulge in her.

I took one of her wrists in my hand and pinned it above her head, my lips leaving hers to trail a path down her neck, biting down over the now almost-faded puncture wounds Dio had left on her neck, causing her to moan sweetly. I would leave a mark over them every day until they disappeared entirely. Until nothing remained of her encounter with him. Until there was no trace of him on her. No trace of anyone but me.

"Enver," she said again, and I knew I would never tire of it. It had been too long since someone called my real name, too long living under a false guise.

I would never go back to being Verofer. He was as dead as the ones who ruined him were soon to be.

Nell's legs wrapped around my waist, drawing her lower half up and into mine, grinding herself against my hard length. The scent of her arousal surrounded me, something I had not been able to appreciate as much before. The curse had taken more from me than my memories and my emotions. It had stripped me of my innate abilities and instincts. It had boiled me down to almost human—*if* humans could survive for over a century and control shadows.

And as Nell had said once, humans could not do that.

The memory had a faint smile crossing my face.

Nell's free hand wandered over my shoulders, up my neck, and to my newly pointed ear. Desire rushed through me as she thumbed over the tip. Once she had gotten over the initial surprise of their shape, she quickly figured out they were a sensitive spot.

And she was merciless in her torture.

A low rumbling came from my chest as I fought the urge to bury myself deep in her and show her how merciless *I* could be.

Instead, I tore her hand away, placing it with her other above her head, conjuring my shadows to keep them bound. They curled around her, anchoring her arms in place, and she arched further into me, a sigh leaving her lips.

"Do not move your hands my little lover, or I will have my shadows do more to you than hold you down," I warned her.

She swallowed, and I traced the movement with my fingers, her skin soft under my touch. After hiding my shadows for so long, the fact I did not have to around her filled me with an immeasurable sense of satisfaction and freedom. She did not truly understand the weight of my shadows, but she embraced them and took pleasure in them.

It made me wonder if my kind would have still been destroyed had they used their shadows for pleasure instead of power.

Then again, I planned to exert both kinds of power. One for control over others. One for control over Nell.

"I want you inside me," she panted.

"Is that how we ask for things, pet?"

She flushed at my word choice, and my blood ignited again with lust. My hand slipped between us, then under the hem of her bunched up night dress, my fingers teasing her skin as I moved closer and closer toward the heat radiating from the apex of her thighs.

"Please," she tried.

I ignored her, my fingers slipping into her underwear, the back of my hand brushing against the soaked fabric as I dipped two fingers inside her without warning. Her hips jerked in response, a cry filling the air, and I bit down hard on a nipple poking through her dress, making her cry choke into a whimper. Her walls clenched around my finger, and all I could think about was how she would feel around me when I was inside her.

But not yet.

I released her nipple and slid my fingers out of her, making her look at me with desperate, pleading eyes.

"Your desperation is calling out to me again," I told her, though the connection between us the labyrinth had allowed me to feel had disappeared. "You already have me, my little lover. What more could you yearn for?"

"It's never enough," she said breathlessly. "I want more and more of you. I will always be desperate for you."

Satisfaction rippled through me, and I lost the little restraint I had. My fingers curled into the delicate fabric of her dress, and I tore it down the center. The sound of the silk ripping and her soft gasp sent another surge of desire through me. The tattered dress lay on either side of her as I moved down her body, spreading her thighs, taking one long lick through the drenched fabric of her undergarments before ripping them away with a jerk of my hand.

Nell took in a sharp breath, looking down at me. "Y-you could have just taken them off! You didn't have to ruin them!"

"Consider it a preview."

"Of what?"

"Of how I will ruin you, my little lover."

Her eyes widened, and I took a moment to appreciate the sight of her spread and splayed before me.

I pressed a kiss to her inner thigh, soft and teasing, and smirked as she trembled. Agonizingly slow, I trailed kisses higher and higher until my mouth was hovering over her heat, purposely letting my breath wash over her. I waited, listening to her shallow breaths quicken again until her hips began to rock up, trying to press against my mouth.

Her scent drove me wild, and her eager movements only increased my hunger for her. I had wanted to take it slow and tease her, but now all I wanted was to taste her, to drown in her.

And I would not deny myself.

I would not deny myself anything anymore.

My hands gripped her thighs, fingers digging into flesh as I parted them wider, holding her open and at my mercy. I descended on her and groaned as her taste exploded on my tongue, the sound mingling with her own moan. My mouth closed over her, lapping up her arousal, licking and sucking with no rhythm, no patience, no focus on what I knew drove her wild—only on sating my craving.

Her scent, her taste, her sounds... They all sent the darkness retreating further. The fury replaced by need. The hollowness filled with her, her, *her*.

Her back arched off the bed as I finally circled her clit, settling into a pattern as I increased my pressure and pace, flicking my tongue over it before sucking.

"Oh, God," she moaned, her body writhing against my hold. "Please—"

"God? Not quite. I am more monster than deity, my little lover," I murmured, my lips brushing against her tantalizing warmth as I spoke, causing her to shudder. "I will not give you divine pleasure. I will devour you instead."

Her hands pulled at the shadows restraining her. "Enver—"

I nipped at her, cutting her off, making her body jerk, and then I soothed it with a slow circle of my tongue, savoring her taste, her pleasure, her moans.

"You're not a monster," she gasped out.

I lifted my gaze to her face, seeing her staring back down at me. Her pupils were blown wide with desire, but her expression was a mix of affection and determination.

The phantom pain stabbed through my heart again. I released one of her thighs to thrust two fingers into her in response. Her head fell back, and I returned my attention to her clit, sucking, licking, and circling, all while pumping my fingers in and out of her, the wet sounds of her arousal almost drowning out the sound of my name spilling from her lips.

She wanted me to believe her. She thought I had said I was a monster because of the words she once used against me.

But I had not.

I was not a monster for what had been done.

I was a monster for what I would do.

The darkness crept forward again.

"Enver!"

This time, her whimper was of pain, not pleasure. I released her thigh, glancing at the deep indents my nails had left in them and noticing my shadows had woven around her legs, constricting and crushing. My gaze shot to her face. She wrenched her eyes shut, her teeth biting into her lip as if trying not to cry out again. The shadows around her wrists had also tightened, the skin underneath the black coils already reddening.

They loosened, then withdrew as I reined them in, my jaw clenching. My shadows were harder to control with the loss of my relic—another victim of the labyrinth.

Nell's eyes opened as I freed her wrists, but instead of pushing me away, she reached for me. I did not stop her as her hands tangled in my hair, urging me up toward her. I braced myself on my elbows above her, taking in the shy, affectionate smile on her lips. Smiling as if I had not just hurt her. As if she did not know my shadows could have easily broken her.

As if she did not realize that the monster in me could easily ruin her.

She pulled my head down, and I kissed her, allowing her to distract me from my thoughts. Her hips rolled against mine, and she sighed into my mouth as one of her hands drifted down my chest and stomach and into the loose fabric of my pants, wrapping around my length. Our kiss turned fierce and hungry as she stroked me, her grip tightening as I ground myself into her palm.

When I could not take anymore, I sat back to rid myself of my clothing, tossing it to the floor before positioning myself between her thighs again. Her gaze swept across my body, resting on the scar on my chest. The way her eyes softened made the hollow ache return. Her lips parted as if to speak, but before she could, my hand slid into her hair, tugging her head back as I drove into her.

The heat and slickness of her core engulfed me, making us both groan. Her walls fluttered around me as I bottomed out, her body going still, fingers digging into my shoulders as she adjusted to my thickness.

I hid a smirk against her neck. I thought she would get used to it, but I also took pleasure in the fact that she had not.

Withdrawing, I pulled out completely, then drove back into her, the force of it jolting her body. My teeth scraped the column of her throat, and she choked out a cry when I repeated the motion, feeling the vibration of her voice under my lips as I pressed a soothing kiss against the spot. She tightened around me, and I could not stop a low groan from escaping me.

In response, she rocked her hips up, thighs wrapping around my waist, one of her hands tangling in my hair. "More," she pleaded.

I released her hair to hook my arm under her knee, pushing it toward her chest, angling my hips to plunge in harder, deeper, faster. "As my little lover desires," I murmured.

Her head fell back into the pillows, her eyes fluttering shut, her lips parting in soundless gasps. With every thrust, her breasts bounced, and the sight enthralled me, the feel of her around me enticing me to sink deeper and deeper.

It was not enough.

A shadow formed, sliding over her stomach, splitting to curl around her breasts, their tendrils sweeping against her nipples, making her back arch, her body roll against mine.

It would never be enough.

Her eyes flew open as another shadow moved between us to tease her clit. "Enver!"

"Mm, I do love the way you say my name when you are falling apart," I said, holding her against me as I sheathed myself inside her, remaining there for a moment, grinding against her. "Such a sweet cry. Call for me again, Nell. Tell me who you belong to. Who you are begging for."

"You," she breathed, squeezing around me as my shadows teased her, coaxing another rumble from my throat. "I'm begging for you, Enver. Only you. Desperate only for you."

Her words hit their mark, possessiveness and desire burning through me, and I resumed thrusting into her, swallowing her gasp with a bruising kiss. The bed shook, the headboard colliding into the wall as I slammed into her, my shadows continuing to work her over as her thighs trembled, her breathing growing more and more ragged.

I tore away from her lips, watching her unravel beneath me. Her eyes locked onto mine, her fingers threading into my hair, keeping me facing her as her walls constricted around me, quivering, ready to snap.

As if I would look away.

As if there was anything worthier of my gaze.

"You are beautiful," I told her, my voice rough, and she moaned.

I commanded a shadow to slide inside her heat next to my shaft, stretching her further. The effect was immediate. Her back bowed off the bed, her orgasm ripping through her, causing her to clamp down on me, creating an exquisite sort of torture as I continued to drive into her, the tightness and friction making it harder and harder to restrain myself.

She released my hair in favor of gripping the bedsheets, her head rolling from side to side as I did not relent. "Enver," she said, half a moan, half a whine.

"Again," I demanded.

She shuddered but did not resist. Did not try to escape my hold or shadows.

I smiled at her obedience.

More shadows materialized, wrapping around limbs like ribbons, dragging her hands higher above her head until her arms were fully stretched out. Their darkness contrasted against her white skin, the sight causing a satisfied hum to vibrate from my chest. I let her shaking leg down, placing it back around my waist, admiring how my shadows twisted and twined around her.

She looked up at me, cheeks flushed, lips swollen, eyes glazed over. Her fingers twitched in their bindings, breath coming sharp and short.

My hand moved to her throat.

She tensed, her breath catching, but I only softly stroked my fingers along her skin, coaxing her to relax. My shadows paused their ministrations at my will, giving her a momentary respite. I knew it was hard for her to calm down—that she was sensitive from her first orgasm, and everything must have felt more intense, but my touch won out.

Her muscles relaxed, her lashes fluttering.

And then I tightened my grip, pressing my thumb against the hollow of her throat, my shadows resuming their teasing. She let out a small sound, her walls clenching around me as I started thrusting again, driving myself impossibly deep. Her hips rose to meet me, and it was my turn to moan, my hand around her throat flexing before increasing the pressure on it.

She let out a choked noise that set my blood on fire. Her

body shook, her legs slipping from my thighs. I used my free hand to grip her thigh, bringing it back, holding it there as my pace increased. I could feel the pressure rise in me, pleasure shooting through me with each thrust, with each breathless sound from her. My muscles tensed, and I gritted my teeth, trying to stave off my release, wanting her to come again first.

She was close. I could tell by the way she fell silent, her body straining against mine, teetering on the edge.

I knew what she needed to send her over.

Dipping my head down, I brushed my lips against her ear before I spoke. My voice was low and dark, my words serving as both a promise and a warning. "You are mine."

Her pulse beat frantically under my fingertips as she whimpered her response, and then her body seized, her core convulsing around me as she came once more. The sensation wrested my own release from me, and with a groan, I buried myself into her. My body spasmed as wave after wave of ecstasy tore through me, hot spurts of my release filling her, each one followed by a jerk of my hips.

The phantom pain in my chest subsided, and the void filled once more, even if only temporarily.

I released her throat but did not pull out, intent on staying like this as long as possible. Inside her. Feeling whole at last. She only managed to take in one deep inhale of air before I stole her breath once more with a kiss. The shadows melted away, and she wrapped her arms around my neck as she kissed me back, not caring about her lack of oxygen.

"My little lover," I murmured against her lips.

I would never let her go.

The darkness inside me stirred as if it agreed.

BOOK TWO

Nell and Enver's story will continue in 2025.

ACKNOWLEDGMENTS

To my readers, know that without you, there is no me. Thank you, thank you!

To my family, I really hope you didn't read this... just kidding. My mom has been telling me to write sex scenes for a decade now. Thanks, Mom. Thank you to everyone in my family for believing in me. And to everyone who didn't—it's not too late to start!

To my partner for life and death, Tyler, who helped me write this book in more ways than one—I love you, Moore! You're my real-life book boyfriend and even better than fiction. To my cats, Ven, Nellie, Poe, Aki, and Sebastian, I do this for you. May my books provide you with the life you deserve. And to my turtle, Buddy!

To Jessica Cunsolo, author and friend extraordinaire, who spent countless hours with me in Discord helping me make every sentence "look pretty," and then talked me off the edge when I thought everything was terrible—thank you for your patience, all your feedback, and for hyping me the entire way! To SJ Moquin, Lauren Jackson, and Kenadee Bryant, you're the best group of friends an author could ask for. Thank you!

To Mason, Rodney, Van, Ava, Grace, Jane, Noda, Leigh, Deb, Cayleigh, and Ami, thank you for all the sprints and support! You're all the best!

To Zara, thanks for never putting me in "horny jail" on Discord despite the things we discuss, and for being an awesome friend!

ana Godoy, Rachel Meinke, Ali Novak, Flynn Novak, (Lizzie) Seibert, Katarina E. Tonks, Alex Evansley, y Anne Blount, thank you for being such a huge part of my writing journey! I am inspired by you all daily! May the Cohenist Cohenas stay together forever.

To Isabelle Ronin, who is always there for me and so kind and firm in her belief in me—thank you!

To Brooke, who encouraged me, hyped me up, and let me vent on our calls when we were supposed to be talking about work-related things. Thank you!

To Sean, Jimmy, Brandon, Jeremy, Alyssa, Tim, Rob, Nate, Jake, Josh, Hank, Kyle, Jerry, and Brandon too—thank you for putting up with my yapping, offering me encouragement, and playing games with me! (And special thanks to Sean and Jimmy for liking my every TikTok, lol!)

To V, you are my best friend, and your support and excitement have been vital. Thank you! NYC when?

To Tommy, Shareef, Avarie, Bri, Pat, Casey, Andrew, Becca, Kyle, Matt, Anna, Koga, Sam, Jenna, and Julia—sorry for always referring to you as my "IRL friends," and thank you for believing in me!

To Deborah, Sol, Ezra C, Ezra P, Kyndel, Vidya, Tristen, Meghan, Megan, Cyn, and Jenn—thank you for putting up with me making the café my second home and for your endless kindness, friendship, and amazing drinks!

To all the amazing artists out there who have drawn my characters—thank you! Please find my social media to see their incredible art!

And finally, to my alpha and beta readers, Leigh, Angela, Sarah, Erin, Amy, Brittany, Amani, Emma, and Ashley—your input was PRICELESS and helped make this book the best it could be. Thank you!

ABOUT THE AUTHOR

Jordan Lynde is an author, creator, and freelance writer living in Western Massachusetts. When she's not busy being a hopeless romantic and writing about romance at the local coffee shop, you can find her being the homebody she is, playing video games in her favorite chair or cuddled up watching k-dramas with her three cats and turtle.

Find her at **@JordanLynde_** on Instagram.